HOW TO FIND YOUR WAY IN THE DARK

ALSO BY DEREK B. MILLER

Norwegian by Night

The Girl in Green

American by Day

Radio Life

Quiet Time (an Audible Original novel)

HOW TO FIND YOUR WAY IN THE DARK

DEREK B. MILLER

Houghton Mifflin Harcourt
Boston   New York   2021

For information about permission to reproduce selections from this book, write
to trade.permissions@hmhco.com or to Permissions, Houghton Mifflin Harcourt
Publishing Company, 3 Park Avenue, 19th Floor, New York, New York 10016.

hmhbooks.com

Library of Congress Cataloging-in-Publication Data
Names: Miller, Derek B., 1970– author.
Title: How to find your way in the dark / Derek B Miller.
Description: Boston : Houghton Mifflin Harcourt, 2021. | Series: A Sheldon Horowitz novel
Identifiers: LCCN 2020057651 (print) | LCCN 2020057652 (ebook) |
ISBN 9780358269601 (hardcover) | ISBN 9780358450337 |
ISBN 9780358450498 | ISBN 9780358270096 (ebook)
Classification: LCC PS3613.I5337 H69 2021 (print) | LCC PS3613.I5337 (ebook) |
DDC 813/.6 — dc23
LC record available at https://lccn.loc.gov/2020057651
LC ebook record available at https://lccn.loc.gov/2020057652

Book design by Emily Snyder

Printed in the United States of America
1 2021
4500827558

For Camilla, Julian, and Clara.
You are my light.

CONTENTS

twi′light cri′mes, *law.* **a.** crimes of a lesser degree **b.** crimes of a question-able moral nature **c.** crimes of possible moral virtue *(controversial)*

PART I

TRAGEDY

GOD'S PROMISE

I T WAS ONE YEAR and one day since the Palace Theatre fire in Hartford where his mother burned to death, and now twelve-year-old Sheldon Horowitz and his father were on their way back from the headstone unveiling in the battered Ford truck they had inadvisably borrowed from the Krupinski brothers to make the journey. Joseph glanced at his son to see whether he'd fallen asleep but he hadn't; instead, he was a chorus of unspoken words.

There had been a brief event at the synagogue, and then they left Joseph's brother and his two children behind. They had their own loss to contend with. Sheldon's head was flopped back on the seat. He was tired and moody after their visit, and Joseph knew that the long drive back was taking its toll on his beloved son.

The question of whether to get him talking or not was a delicate one.

Long silences between them over the past year were nothing new, and in Joseph's view, they were mostly his own fault as he had been the one to abandon words first—although, when he was feeling more gracious with himself, he sometimes thought the words had abandoned him. It made no practical difference: Sheldon's withdrawal from verbiage was a response to Lila's death itself. It was one more thing Joseph could blame himself for, and it wasn't the worst one.

"There was a fire" was all Joseph had been able to say after pulling Sheldon out of class and onto the schoolhouse steps last year. It was a Monday. She was expected that morning. Instead, he received an official call. The next two words were going to be "your mother," but he didn't get that far.

"Your mother," he is now grateful he didn't have to say, "burned to death with your aunt Lucy in a movie theater in Hartford. She was there because of me."

If he could have gone on? At the time, nothing. Sheldon was eleven. Joseph knew enough not to burden a boy with a man's sorrows.

Sheldon—perceptive, emotional, and connected to Joseph like a magnet to iron ever since he was a baby—had understood immediately what the fire had done even if his father couldn't say it. On the schoolhouse steps, he had reached out to comfort his father rather than the other way around.

Since then, silences have appeared in their lives; they arrive as unpredictably, and are accepted as easily, as an evening rain.

On most occasions, Joseph left Sheldon to his peace, both for the boy's benefit and his own. Sheldon Unleashed, Sheldon Provoked: These were formidable characters that Joseph avoided. It wasn't only the intensity of Sheldon's emotions, it was also the range of his mental gymnastics and argumentative tactics. The kid was a young Sherman on the intellectual battlefield, and Joseph lacked his agility.

Tonight, Joseph knew, was not the time to raise Cain. Not in an unfamiliar moving vehicle in the dark with weather coming in. Not after hours of a journey. Not after seeing his mother's name carved into a stone on the ground and tragedy itself seemed to be testing the boy's will.

It was going to be slick soon too. Joseph could feel it in his fingers on the wooden steering wheel. New England can teach a man more than he'd ever want to know about weather, and Joseph had long since taken those lessons to heart.

Sheldon shifted in his seat and Joseph realized the Beast was going to wake itself.

"What's on your mind, Donny?" Joseph said, calling him what the toddlers used to call him back in kindergarten when they couldn't pronounce his name. He was the only one who still did and Sheldon seemed to tolerate it.

Sheldon flopped his head over and looked at his father.

"Well?" Joseph prompted. "Who else you going to tell?"

"The Krupinski brothers," Sheldon said, which is not what Joseph had been expecting.

Outside, the white birches slipped past them like specters. The sleek black of the road became as something living when the rain started to fall —slowly for a moment and then a downpour. The asphalt river slithered beneath their thin wheels as the truck began to rattle in the winds. The darkness encroached on them because the sky was as black as the forest and the headlights were too weak to illuminate any future.

Joseph gripped the large wheel tightly and leaned into it as if he were driving a tractor.

"What about them?" Joseph asked, trying to drive and talk.

"I don't think we should have borrowed their truck."

"Why not?"

"I don't think we should owe them anything."

"We don't. When we dropped off the pelts in Springfield, we were doing Old Krupinski a favor. So, we're even."

"We're not even," said Sheldon flatly. "Lenny and I think they're selling your pelts down in Hartford for more than they're telling you and we're not getting our fair share. We do all the hunting and trapping and preparing the pelts and they only sell them. They're thieves and they think we're suckers who haven't got the balls to call them out."

"We?" asked Joseph with a smile.

"I help."

"You do," Joseph said, glad that Sheldon was coming around.

Lenny Bernstein was Sheldon's best friend and the only other Jewish kid around for a thousand miles as far as either of them knew. He was a year older, but the boys were in the same grade because Sheldon was reading more and faster. They often took off after school on their bicycles, and Joseph was glad that Sheldon had someone to confide in and bond with, though he wished their conspiracy theories about the Krupinskis' nefarious ways would end —even if the boys weren't entirely wrong.

"What are you proposing?" Joseph asked.

"I think that when we get back home, without overthinking it or anything, we should run them over and call it an accident."

Joseph smiled and squinted past the wipers that were no match for the storm.

"Running over two people is pretty tough," he said, as though consider-ing it. "They've got to be lined up like bowling pins and be just as blind."

"Maybe we could tie them up first. Then run 'em over," Sheldon sug-gested, relaxing into the kind of banter they both always enjoyed.

Joseph saw a flaw in the plan. "Accidentally run over two people? As an alibi, it's a tough sell."

"We could say Ronny and Theo jumped out in front of the truck as a practical joke and it all went horribly, horribly right. Everyone would be-lieve it. They're idiots."

"I wonder if that imagination is going to get you into trouble some-day."

"Or out of it," Sheldon countered.

"Probably both, I suspect."

They drove on silently for half a mile. Joseph concentrated. The road had no curb and no lights, and the rain played tricks with the headlights. After a time, Joseph addressed Sheldon's accusation. "I'm sure they are skimming a bit. But the arrangement's a stable one, and it keeps away people I don't want near us. The garment business, the fur trade, the factories, the retail — there's a lot of money in that sector and there are dirty hands greasing those wheels. I'm on the quiet end of it out here. There's no need to be greedy, and I think me and you and . . . well . . . I think we live OK. And besides, Old Krupinski served in the Great War too. He and I have an understanding. We have everything we need."

"We don't have everything we need," Sheldon said.

Joseph didn't want to push further, but for the moment, Sheldon was talking without exploding, and it was better to have him come clean when he was in this state of mind. So, Joseph said, "Come on. Out with the rest. We're all we've got left."

"Uncle Nate acted like he was in charge of everything," said Sheldon. "And we went along with it. The stupid clothes, the stupid prayers. Stand-ing around like a couple of dolts pretending it all means something when we all know Mom and Aunt Lucy weren't even there."

Joseph had been wearing his only suit, which was black because he had only one need for a suit. Sheldon's funeral jacket had been bought in Springfield on their way down to Connecticut. They'd found a secondhand clothing store that smelled like mothballs and wood polish. For fifty cents, it fit him well enough. Using scissors, Joseph had dutifully ripped the lapel in line with Jewish custom to show that vanity was not distracting them from thinking about those they had lost.

At the cemetery, the Massachusetts men looked like country versions of Mutt and Jeff compared to Nate's three-piece suit from G. Fox & Co. Sheldon's older cousin Abe was in a tailored hand-me-down, and Mirabelle— sixteen already and looking like a lady—was wearing one of Lucy's gowns.

Joseph knew Sheldon wasn't wrong about Nate's domination of the proceedings, but it wasn't the most interesting thing Sheldon had said.

"When you say they weren't there, what do you mean? You mean their spirits?" Joseph asked.

"I mean their bodies."

There had been nothing but ash. The film reels were made of nitrate. Nitrate, when burned, creates its own oxygen. A nitrate fire is a hell machine. It burned in Hartford for two days; water only made it burn hotter. When the ground was cool enough, the firemen sifted through the ash. All the gold had melted, but they found Lila's diamond pendant in what had been the aisle; proof to Joseph she'd been trampled on the way out.

The rabbi collected some of the ash and buried it, calling it "Lila Horowitz" like it had once been a person or maybe still was. Joseph brought the diamond home and put it in her jewelry box. Ever since the funeral a year ago, he would occasionally glimpse Sheldon touching it. He never interfered.

"We talked about this, didn't we?" Joseph asked.

"Yeah," Sheldon said. "I wanted to bring her ashes back to the woods and scatter them there. Uncle Nate said, 'No,' mumbled something about expectations, and you accepted that. Now we've borrowed the Krupinski truck to see a rock placed over a cup of ash."

Sheldon's voice was calm, and this pained Joseph even more.

"I wanted that too," he confessed.

Sheldon turned fully and placed a leg up on the bench seat. "So why didn't we?" he asked.

"I'm sorry" was all Joseph could say. More than that and he wouldn't have been able to see the road.

"I know you are," Sheldon said. "That's why I haven't said anything."

After nearly a minute, Sheldon added, "I'm sorry too."

Joseph had been encouraging Lila's trips. She came back refreshed and energetic and more affectionate. Hartford may not have been as sophisticated or glamorous as Boston, but it was the *big city life* that Lila was missing and Joseph didn't want her to miss anything. He thought he was a good husband and father, but he also knew that he was reclusive. That he was still shaken from his experiences in France. That the round and full life his wife deserved was beyond his capacity to provide. All he could do to honor that reality was try to be permissive.

The newspapers later said that the projectionist was a man named Arnold Krevich. He was a heavy smoker and often puffed away as the films played. Krevich had seen bad things during the Great War and everyone knew his nerves and temper were frayed, which is why he had taken a job sitting alone in a dark room with nothing but the rhythmic whirr of the reels for company. He wasn't supposed to smoke, but management feared telling him to stop.

In reading the accounts, Joseph was sympathetic to Krevich's condition because he understood that aversion to noise; the endless, pounding, arrhythmic, explosive noise that went on day after day after day until it fell silent long enough for a whistle to blow, sending men over the top of the trench to be cut down as machine guns rattled.

Krevich escaped the fire, having seen it first. In the hospital—being treated for smoke inhalation—he said an errant ash, still too hot on the way down, ignited the film that burst immediately into flames, lighting up the other reels he'd never bothered returning to the studios because he was a half-assed man.

The fire spread to the white canopy on the ceiling that was soaked in a flammable material to keep it pristine.

Burning tar from the roof ignited the skirts of fleeing women, turning them into human lanterns.

"There isn't even a body," Joseph had tried to tell Sheldon but didn't.

"Smoke. Your mother has become smoke. Your mother is part of the sky now."

In Hebrew the word for sky is *sh'myim*. Broken into two words, it means "there is water." Hidden, there in code, is God's promise of life in the heavens.

Joseph had wanted to explain what he and Sheldon had really needed to Nate and the rabbi last year when it was time to make decisions; he had wanted to do what Sheldon had wanted and take the ashes home, but the fashionable brother and the learned man were both adamant that it was wrong and disrespectful.

He should have told them he didn't care and made a separate peace for Lila and himself and Sheldon, safe in the certainty that his actions would have been countenanced by a forgiving God, and if not, it was no God he needed.

He'd seen hundreds of men gassed to death on a battlefield that was nothing but a killing floor. Dismissing God's concerns was no challenge.

Not Sheldon's, though. His concerns were at the center of Joseph's attention. He knew he had failed—from the boy's perspective—and given in to both Nate's wishes and the rabbi's instructions. He'd presented the decision with platitudes rather than truth. He had said how funerals are for the living, not the dead, and if burying them brings comfort to others, it is a mitzvah—a blessing—as it is our job to ease the burden of others as best we can.

It was all true and it was all bullshit also. The truth of his *motives* was that a refusal to bury the women side by side would have ruptured the family, and something inside Joseph told him not to do this. Some instinct told him that Sheldon would be better served with his remaining family intact. Joseph would have to find a way of keeping Lila present and close to their home in Whately. He had tried to cook the foods she made, and he brought her up in conversation when he and Sheldon spoke. But it was forced and they both knew it. Her distance—the distance of the ash—was always on their minds.

"Maybe an hour more," Joseph said, as the rain splattered off the curved hood of the Ford. Sheldon said nothing and Joseph answered what Sheldon didn't ask: "If it gets much worse, I'll pull over. We can wait it out like we do when we're hunting."

Sheldon looked over at his father's hands holding the wheel. When Sheldon watched bus drivers, their hands barely seemed to touch the wood, but his father's hands—scarred from barbed wire, snares, and a youth cutting and hauling ice on Fresh Pond in Cambridge and Breeds Pond in Lynn—held the wheel like it was a rope and the two of them were dangling from a mountain.

When Joseph was a teenager, he worked the tail end of the ice trade—cutting, stacking, hauling the ice for transport back to Boston where it was shipped down to New York for drinks before Prohibition or peddled door-to-door locally in the Back Bay. Summers he went to Maine, where he'd cut the trees for the sawdust that would line the ship hulls where the ice was stored below the waterline.

He told Sheldon that he liked to stand on the pier and watch them depart for Europe and the Caribbean. "I wanted to be a pirate. Not a lot of Jewish pirates, though." He'd placed his hands in his pockets and stuck out his chest and called himself "Errol Flynnowitz!" They both had laughed until Joseph had said, "It's funny, it is. But you know why? Because the world can't abide a Jewish hero, that's why. And once you understand that, it takes the fun out of the funny."

"You're a hero, Dad," Sheldon had said to him.

Sheldon knew only the contours of his father's service as Joseph wasn't much for discussing it. He had served in the 26th Infantry, the Yankee Division. In April of 1918, he was in Apremont-la-Forêt in France nearby the fighting in Saint-Mihiel. When that conflict had started in mid-September, American forces fired a million rounds of artillery in the first four hours. When the shelling stopped, Joseph was assigned to be a wire cutter. His job was to crawl headfirst into no-man's-land on his belly and clip the barbed

wire so later troops could storm across the earth to the German positions
—storm through a hail of defensive machine-gun fire into a smoke as thick
as prayer. Sheldon thought the medal given to the entire company—not to
Joseph personally—made him a hero.

Joseph had tried to dispel Sheldon of all these ideas because he thought
they were dangerous and might lead him into the next war—a war he was
sure was coming, sometime, someplace—so he tried to deter him. And if
that didn't work, he'd already taken some other precautions.

Headlights came up behind their truck.

"Looks like someone's in a hurry," Joseph said, looking back. "I say we
let him pass, huh?"

He applied the brakes, and the car behind them came alongside.

It wasn't a car but a truck. Sheldon looked across his father's arm at the
driver. He had a thick mustache and wore a black suit, white shirt, and
black tie. His hair was raven-black and matted down hard on his head like
a helmet; his face was rounded and thuggish. He looked at Sheldon and
Sheldon looked back at him. Each regarded the other.

Sheldon watched the man as he first looked down at his lap then turned
upward to examine Joseph, who was wearing his British wool trench cap.
The driver removed a cigarette from his lips and threw it out the window.
He then placed both hands on the wheel.

"Dad?" Sheldon said.

"What is it?"

"Something's wrong."

That was when the trucks slammed together.

Joseph was not an experienced driver. The craving that some men enjoyed—for speed, wind, and the thrill of reckless possibility—was not part
of his spirit. He was a man who had raised himself from the trenches of
France to the gentle hills and woods of New England with such a lightness
of touch that even the animals paid him no heed when he passed. This had
been enough for him. The company of his wife. His son. The vista. The
dawn.

The inexperience cost him. Rather than correcting their course, he braced himself on the wheel like it was something firm and stable and trustworthy. As his body jerked right, his hands spun the wheel. With a dark left-hand turn coming up and slick roads below, Joseph entered the turn too fast and panicked.

As he whipped the wheel hard to the left in a last-ditch effort at control, the full weight of the truck pressed down on the front-right tire and the pressure was too much — it blew out in protest. The Ford lurched and started to go over.

"Daddy!" yelled Sheldon, and he lunged for his father as the truck keeled over onto his side and skidded into the trees by the shoulder.

The front smashed into an oak, and when it did, the engine forced the steering column into Joseph's chest and jammed the sharp edge of the floorboard into his leg.

Sheldon's head would have slammed into the window and the earth had it not been cradled by Joseph's two strong arms that had wrapped themselves reflexively around him at the moment of impact.

When all stopped and all was still, Joseph's arms went slack. Sheldon fell down to the ground on his side of the cabin. His father was pinned between the steering wheel and the seat; his chest compressed, his voice wheezing: "Donny."

"Daddy," Sheldon said again, planting his feet and reaching up to try to free him.

Joseph knew wounds. He had seen hundreds, and though he was no medic, he knew on sight which ones caused a man to bleed out and which ones didn't. He hung above Sheldon, his blood dripping down on his only son, and he knew this was the end.

He didn't have much time.

"Take it," he said to Sheldon, reaching out his hands to him.

It looked to him like Sheldon had suffered only a few scratches, and he took it as a blessing that he had lived long enough to know that his son would be all right. It is all, in the end, that a father can hope for and all he really wants.

"What?" asked Sheldon. He didn't understand.

"Take it," his father whispered, his lucidity fading.

There was nothing there. Nothing in his hands.

"Take it, Sheldon. Take it all."

"What, Daddy?"

"The love. Take it. Take it all."

Hands clasped together, Joseph Horowitz bled out and died.

HOME

SHELDON WAS LONG GONE when an early-morning newspaper delivery van discovered the accident and Larry Evans, the young driver, found Joseph's body. Larry had never seen an overturned truck before. Its failing headlights cast a candle-yellow light across the face of the beech tree forest. He approached the wreck fearing the worst. Inside, he found Joseph; his body was limp and hanging like a forgotten rag doll, still pinned by the steering column. Raised in the city and unaccustomed to death, Larry left Joseph there and sped off. A few miles later, calmer with the distance, he felt guilty and ashamed, and drove to the local police station to share what he knew. The cops took note and headed down unhurriedly, an ambulance in their wake, to collect the body. It was brought to the quiet hospital in Northampton. The night nurse found a cracked leather wallet in Joseph's pocket containing an expired military ID and photographs of a very beautiful woman and a little boy. Calls the next day to the Veterans' Bureau eventually led from Joseph Horowitz to his brother, Nathaniel, down in Hartford. The search for family was hindered because Nathaniel Horowitz had changed his family name to Corbin for business reasons.

When Larry found Joseph, Sheldon was walking. He walked through the rain that washed off the blood and trailed it behind him. He walked because he had to get home. If he could be at home, the feeling of his parents would return to him and it would be light there, and warm, and the smell of them would be on the sheets and in the scent of the kitchen and the aging of the wood.

The villages did not have big electricity yet. The main lines were installed but many families like his own — still pinched from the Depression or unable to make the transition to modern ways — were opting to wait. Three hours later, cold and shivering, he slowed his walking when the rain stopped. Ahead, candlelight flickered from the darkened windows of the predawn houses where working men were waking and women were preparing their breakfasts to send them off to fields and factories. With the lights to guide him, Sheldon crossed into familiar land where he often bicycled with Lenny Bernstein after school along Mill River.

Sheldon had the impossible feeling that his parents were up ahead, behind the beech trees, waiting for him.

His mother would be finishing a dress from a design she had copied from the Sears catalogue with fabric bought in Springfield and his father would be washed and cleaned, his black hair nicely combed and his shirttails tucked in, his fingernails scrubbed back to white with a brush that Sheldon had once tried using but had found too painful. Clean and ready for the day but not prim, not delicate like Uncle Nate with his soft hands and weak lips. His father's shoulders were nine miles wide.

They had been fine-looking parents when they were preparing for town, and Sheldon had been proud of them. He was not alone in thinking his mother looked like Hedy Lamarr — her eyebrows more natural, though; her lips less severe; her eyes less moody.

Lenny tried to get Sheldon interested in pictures of Lamarr in the same way he tried to get him interested in pictures of naked French girls, but it never took for the obvious reason. Lenny had spent almost every day since birth with Sheldon and should have known better. And yet, he didn't.

"The movie is called *Ecstasy*, Sheldon. You're not even trying," Lenny had said to him one day down by the river where they often met to chuck stones and compare notes.

"I'm saying she looks like my mom," Sheldon said. "What do you want me to do? Not notice?"

"Your mom's a knockout, Sheldon, but she's not Hedy Lamarr," Lenny said.

"Try to imagine my mom in black-and-white."

Lenny looked at the picture anew and relented. The bad news was that he started to look at Hedy Lamarr differently. The good news was that he started looking at Sheldon's mom differently too. Sheldon, however, was not amused.

Still walking—fifteen, twenty miles from the crash—Sheldon tried to picture what his father had handed to him as though it were an object. The best he could imagine was a glowing blue ball. What kept Sheldon warm, though, was imagining the many ways he wanted to kill the man with the mustache.

The sun was rising over the rooftops of Whately when Sheldon finally arrived at the edge of town. The pastel sky was clear and the light was more promise than relief. Autumn was coming, but the dawn reminded him of last spring. In April, still silent with grief, Sheldon had been stunned by the depth and richness of the sunrises and sunsets. He and his father would sit out and watch them. They blazed most unnaturally and haunted his dreams.

Sheldon had dried off and his clothes, like his muscles, were stiffening. He approached his own house with the gait of an old man. In his head, he knew the house was empty and that he was an orphan now. But the idea—like fine sand in still water—had not settled into his soul. The notion that he would never see his parents again . . . ever . . . was too outlandish to grasp. He was abandoned but didn't feel abandoned. He felt they were only separated by a divide he couldn't see or name.

One day, after a class on astronomy, Sheldon and Lenny Bernstein had plopped themselves down on the grass by Mill River and decided to try to imagine the entirety of the universe.

Sheldon had said it couldn't be done because even in your mind you'd have to keep spinning your head around to take it all in. "Like a camera," Sheldon had said. "You can only see what's in front of you. And since you're in it . . . you can't see it all."

Lenny had had the bold idea of moving the stars. "Just stick all the stars in the front. You know?" Lenny had said. "Group them all together. It's your imagination. You can do that."

"Then what's left in the back?" Sheldon had asked.

"Nothing. Nothing's in the back. You just moved it all to the front. The stars and rocks and moons and stuff. So now you can see it all," Lenny had said, feeling creative. "You can put stuff wherever you want."

Sheldon hadn't been convinced. "Just because you moved the furniture, doesn't take the room away," he said. "You're still trying to look at the whole room while you're standing in the room. But the rest of the room is still behind you. Doesn't matter where you stacked the furniture."

Lenny had thought this was a good point. They had agreed finally that it was impossible to imagine the entire universe because there was no place to stand to take it all in.

Now, at the door of his home, Sheldon tried to imagine the entire universe gone. Jewish learning taught that every human being is a universe and that the death of a person is the destruction of a universe. If picturing it all was impossible, so too was picturing it all gone.

What was strange, though, was how it seemed *more* impossible.

And so Sheldon wondered: If two things are impossible, can one be more impossible?

Yes. Yes, it can.

His mother dying was impossible. His father dying was also impossible. Each alone was impossible. And both of them? Reduced to ash and carbon? Infinitely more impossible, an impossibility built from the collision of two impossibilities—a sort of antiuniverse imploding ever inward into a smaller and smaller space that is infinitely deep because how could loss be anything but?

As Sheldon reached the door of the cottage, it was past eight o'clock in the morning. Instead of opening the door, though, he collapsed in front of it because he didn't want to go inside where nothing was waiting for him.

He fell asleep there on the porch until long past noon when an orange sun woke him with a light that was nothing like warmth.

No one came for Sheldon that first day. For most of it, he stayed in the kitchen and waited, though he wasn't certain for what. His father's clock was one of his few relics from the Great War. The others were his brass lighter, his Mauser rifle, and his trench cap, which was still with him on the road. It was the clock, though, that possessed all the magic. It was an eight-day clock and it hung on the kitchen wall looking properly foreign, elaborate, expensive, and incongruous but still elegant and welcome.

"Much like your mom," Joseph once joked.

She heard. Didn't laugh.

The clock was still running. It was Joseph, as always, who had wound the still-beating heart of the house, but Sheldon didn't know when. As he sat there and listened to one second following the next, he felt a compulsion to keep listening as if he were obeying an ordinance from an authority he couldn't name or understand. He needed to hear time passing. He needed to hear each tick of the clock his father had wound because these were his last words, and when the clock fell silent, so would his voice.

In time, as the sun settled on Sheldon's first day alone, the feeling of stillness and even anticipation—surely his parents would be home any minute—began to pass. By ten o'clock at night, the ticking of the old clock stopped. Alone for the first time, Sheldon remembered that he was supposed to be sitting shiva for his father.

No. It was more than that. Sheldon had not been to Hebrew school or regularly attended synagogue. His Jewish learning had come from conversations in the woods. There was something else he was supposed to be doing.

He pictured Joseph there, his lifeless body in the truck.

Sheldon had left his father's body alone. He had left the dead unattended. Wasn't that against Jewish law? Wasn't someone always to stand guard over the body? Had he failed already in his first duty as a man?

• • •

"You can never do wrong in my eyes," Joseph had once told him.

Lila, who had been listening, wasn't so magnanimous.

"Really?" she'd said. "So, when Sheldon and Lenny snuck into the high school last Christmas and replaced the baby Jesus with a stuffed monkey named Scopes, you were only pretending to be mad at him?"

Unwilling to think any more about having abandoned his father in the truck, Sheldon stood and wound the clock again. When it started, he placed his finger on the black edge of the smaller steel hand and started turning the hours backward.

Shortly after dawn of the third day, a knock at the door woke Sheldon. Groggy and weak from not eating, Sheldon was disoriented when he rose from the kitchen floor rather than a bed. His shoulder hurt and he realized —standing to look in the mirror—that he was bruised from the accident. There was a purple welt on his forehead and some scrapes on his cheek. His hair was matted, and his neck was smudged with grease.

He hadn't changed his clothes since the wreck, and the presence of someone else made him aware of it. As his mother would have expected, he buttoned the top button of his bloody shirt before answering the door.

It was Lenny Bernstein. Lenny barely glanced at Sheldon as he burst inside looking for something to eat. Lenny's own mother was a notoriously bad cook. She boiled the life out of everything and served what was left as soup.

"Why haven't you been in school? You were supposed to be back from Connecticut two days ago," said Lenny.

There was nothing interesting in the icebox. Lenny found some dried beef and started chewing on that. The fact that he didn't complain was telling.

Satisfied now, Lenny finally took a good look at Sheldon, and said, "Jesus Christ. You get in a fight? What the hell happened to you?"

As Sheldon opened his mouth to explain, Lenny interrupted. "You need a bath. You got to get out of those clothes."

Lenny stepped over to Sheldon and tried to pull his shirt off. It stuck to Sheldon's chest and Lenny peeled it off him as if he were skinning a fish. "Were you cut? Is this your blood? This isn't even your blood. You're bruised up," Lenny said, looking at the black and blue marks on Sheldon's shoulder and abdomen. "But there isn't a scratch on ya. Did you cut somebody else? Damn, that's one tough synagogue.

"Come on. Strip. Down to the bone," Lenny instructed. "I'll warm up some water on the stove and get it in the tub. You can take a shallow bath. I'll fetch you some clothes. Miss Simmons knows you were down at the funeral home, so you can lie about it and say there was some family emergency. What's she gonna say?"

Lenny warmed the water on the gas stove and carried the heavy pot to the bathtub, where he poured it in, mixing it with some colder water to increase the volume. Sheldon stepped into it naked and turned the water to blood as he ran the washcloth over himself with a bar of white soap. Lenny forced Sheldon to drain it and sit there shivering as he warmed another pot and poured it in. They repeated this until Sheldon was clean and Lenny satisfied.

From the bedroom drawers, Lenny pulled out a pair of dungarees that buttoned up at the chest and a white work shirt with three buttons and no collar. These weren't school clothes, but they were clean and a number of farm kids came to class looking far worse.

"You've barely said a word. You in one of those no-talking moods?"

"I'm talking," Sheldon said.

"You want to explain what's what to me?" Lenny asked.

"I can't."

"Suit yourself."

Their walk to school was light and airy on that Friday morning. They turned off the main road for Mill River, which was running shallow from the drought. Hands in their pockets, the boys stepped lightly from rounded stone to rounded stone, Lenny leading the way and Sheldon matching Lenny's steps, glad not to be talking.

Sheldon halted where the river crossed beneath the road through a wide culvert. Someone had tossed a paper from the road above and it was still dry.

"*Boston Daily Globe*?" Lenny asked.

Sheldon shook his head. "*Sentinel.*"

Lenny didn't rate the *Fitchburg Sentinel.* He was a *Boston Daily Globe* guy and never explained the reason, but Sheldon slowed to a halt and opened it up. He wanted to see whether the accident was mentioned as Lenny passed through to the other side.

Newspapers had always been a comfort to him. His father often read the evening editions aloud over dinner and brought up topics that he and his mother would discuss. Along with the new radio and the old phonograph (and school), newspapers were Sheldon's gateway to the world. Joseph liked to say that newspapers didn't tell people what to think, but they did tell them what to think about, and it was helpful for people to share questions because it was the only way to arrive at a common answer. Their family needed to follow along too, he had said. "We don't want to be left out, do we?"

Sheldon flipped past the big news and looked for a picture of the Krupinski truck, but there was nothing.

He landed on page four, which had a strange photograph of a dozen hands all clapping under a headline that read, THE UNSEEN HAND . . .

It was an advertisement for motion pictures and provided the show listings at the bottom.

Sheldon had not been to a theater since his mother died and was certain he'd never go to another movie for the rest of his life. The advertisement read:

```
Send an expedition to Africa to film this glorious
novel in its authentic locale! Locate a little Eng-
lish boy to depict the heart-stirring story of a be-
loved Dickens character! Search the world for the one
man who knows better than all the others how people
lived in Elizabethan days! It is for your entertain-
ment that an army of the world's greatest talents is
ever on the march, forging ahead to open new vistas
```

for your delight. Spare nothing, says Hollywood, to
make the motion picture theatre the happy haven it
is, the place to which millions may confidently come
for the freedom from boredom and care . . . for romance that warms the heart . . . for hearty laughter
and eye-filling beauty. The unseen hands applaud—and
we who make the motion pictures hear the echo. It
guides us, inspires us, challenges us to fresh en-
deavors to make the movies better and better.

"Sheldon," Lenny yelled back at him. "We're already late!"

Sheldon didn't hurry up, though. Balancing on two rocks as the river babbled under his legs, Sheldon lowered the paper and stood there looking through the culvert at Lenny.

This wasn't the first time Sheldon had become sidetracked on their way to school, but they really were late and Lenny was sick of getting into trouble. He shouted: "Miss Simmons's father is the sheriff. He's going to kill us. Can we go?"

"I don't know what I'm supposed to do," Sheldon said.

"Left foot, right foot, repeat," Lenny said, his voice amplified through the culvert. He was framed by the black circle as though it were an enormous scope on a rifle.

"You think things can just go on like before?" Sheldon asked.

"You mean because of your mom?"

Sheldon didn't answer.

"No," Lenny said. "I guess not. What does your dad think?"

"I don't know."

"You should ask him."

Miss Simmons was sitting on the school steps in her long thick woolen skirt watching the children play at recess when Lenny and Sheldon came strolling up. Lenny's left foot was soaked from having slipped in the river. It was 10:30 in the morning and two hours after school began. For these two reasons, she'd have normally turned the two boys around like little soldiers and marched them right back home with an assignment to explain to their parents why they'd been removed from school today, but Carol Simmons saw that Sheldon Horowitz was trailing in Lenny's wake and her heart went out to him. He had once been a vivacious, talkative, highly motivated student and then his mother had died in that horrible fire, and he'd turned inward and quiet and withdrawn. He was still an excellent student and she thanked heaven for the boy's father, who — though no educator himself — was dogged about Sheldon's progress and was a stable force in his life. She knew this well because she'd lost her own mother when she was young.

Miss Simmons stood as they approached.

Sheldon looked clean and cared for; his bushy black hair was washed and combed, and aside from some boyhood scrapes on his cheek and an odd bruise on his forehead she chose to ignore, he looked neat if a bit thin. She was glad for that. He was hard to manage and more of a personality than she might have preferred, but Carol Simmons had a soft spot for him. Such beautiful blue eyes shining out from under that mop.

"Sheldon? Are you doing OK?" She knew he'd been to Hartford and she knew why.

Sheldon didn't know how to answer that. Compared to everyone else in his family, he was doing pretty well. "I don't really know how I'm supposed to be doing, ma'am," he said.

"No," she said, brushing down her pleats and checking her hair. "Of course not."

Sheldon sat out the day at his desk watching Miss Simmons. The blue skies were calling the wind back and the trees were starting to blow and dance again outside the classroom window. Sheldon, though, wasn't interested in the leaves; he was watching the pleats on Miss Simmons skirt move back and forth. They weren't affecting him like they did last week, though. Before his father died, Sheldon had been watching her legs. Now it was the fabric itself that commanded his attention. It was a tweed pattern of some kind. Mostly gray with tiny threads of red and blue woven in. It looked heavy, clothing for winter but open underneath. What a thing, Sheldon thought: to walk around all exposed like that all the time.

After school, Lenny had baseball practice, so Sheldon walked home alone. Though mid-September, it wasn't sweater weather yet. There were faster ways to get home than retracing his footsteps along the river, but he didn't want to take them. As best he could, he returned on the same stones and tried to revisit the same thoughts along the way.

Sheldon stopped when the cottage came into view. There on the doorstep were the Krupinski brothers—Ronny and Theo—both wearing suspenders that held up stained work pants. They wore matching engineer boots of the same size. He wondered whether they could keep the pairs straight.

Ronny was older and thicker with a barrel chest, and was close to twenty years old. He had the brain of a newt and the body of a boxer. His eyes were too close together for even Bible thumpers to dismiss the monkey theory of evolution. Theo was more slender and taller and two years younger. If he was any smarter, Sheldon didn't know it. What he did know was that the brothers barely tolerated him and his family because—for reasons he didn't understand—being Polish was better than being Jewish. The standoff between them was on account of Old Bruno and Joseph having both served in the war. And maybe Bruno knew in his heart that Joseph was strong and clear-eyed whereas he was now a folding drunk.

Ronny the oaf saw Sheldon first. "Where's our truck, Little Shit?"

The truck? Sheldon hadn't given any thought to the truck since leaving the accident. It hadn't crossed his mind that he'd left the truck behind with his father. Not that he could have done anything about it.

"There was an accident," Sheldon whispered.

"What was that, Little Shit?"

"There was an accident," Sheldon said, raising his voice with his indignation.

More than that, Sheldon didn't want to say. The knowledge of what happened was sacred to him somehow, as though holding on to the secret of his father made the truth his alone. If he'd been inclined to tell anyone, it would have been Lenny, and after him, Miss Simmons. He wasn't about to hand that over to Ronny and Theo Krupinski.

"What kind of accident?" said the hissing, slithering Theo.

"A bad one," said Sheldon.

Ronny took a step in his direction and Sheldon took a step back. Either one of the brothers could snap Sheldon in two and everyone knew it.

"Where's the fucking truck!" shouted Theo.

"South of Leeds. Sylvester Road. Check the bushes."

Theo took another step toward Sheldon, but Ronny stopped him.

"Where's your daddy?"

"None of your business," said Sheldon, trying to sound tough and brave but achieving neither. There was nothing he could do to his voice to make it intimidating. He hated that. He hated that about being young. At best, he could hold his ground. He decided not to step back again.

"So, he's not home, then," said Theo, the smarter one.

Theo tried the cottage's doorknob and found it open. Sheldon had never thought to lock it. Did it even have a lock? The town was too small and isolated for wandering thieves, anyone local who robbed them would be caught, and what was inside anyway?

Theo walked in and pulled Ronny in after him.

Watching the Krupinski brothers invade his house was worse than being punched. Standing outside his home, he felt like the brothers were desecrating a grave.

"Get out of there," Sheldon said under his breath.

The world did not yield.

"Get out of my house," he said louder but not loud enough, not loud enough to fill the Krupinski brothers with the dread to wake them from their actions and change their minds, not loud enough to reach any ears but his own.

Sheldon stood there shaking with rage. Minutes passed but Sheldon couldn't move his feet. When they emerged, the brothers were not empty-handed. Ronny, the larger of the two, was carrying Joseph's clock in his arms with the care he would give to a sack of potatoes. Theo was carrying Sheldon's mother's monogrammed suitcase that Sheldon knew instantly was filled with all her best clothes and the few pieces of jewelry she hadn't been wearing the night of the fire.

Frozen in place as he watched this, Sheldon didn't scream. The air in his lungs felt like a solid mass that couldn't be pushed out; the muscles were too tensed around them to even move. Fists clenched, he tottered as Ronny walked up the road.

"Collateral for the truck. We'll be back for the rest. We know you've got more hidden away someplace. You fuckin' Jews always have more hidden away. But we'll find it. Don't you worry."

BURN

SHELDON WAITED OUTSIDE his house until darkness trying to think of what to do. He could have gone inside, but he didn't want to. The house wasn't only vacant now. It was also violated and gutted. He knew what a carcass looked like after it had been cleaned and the guts removed. It's not really the animal anymore, only a hollow shell of one. Sheldon never got entirely used to seeing animals in traps or suddenly dead after a clean shot, but the sight of them cleaned and hanging never bothered him. The soul was long gone. That's what the house looked like now.

It was an Indian summer night and the dry air was smooth and soft on his skin. It was quiet too. There were few houses here to the west of town out by the forest. Not a car passed him that evening, only one horse and buggy that Sheldon took to be Mr. O'Neill, who dealt in scrap metal and spent the rest of his time restoring furniture he'd collect at people's houses and lug back to his garage in a cart pulled by Mickey—a horse that wasn't getting any younger or prettier.

Neither Mr. O'Neill nor Mickey saw Sheldon in the shadows as they passed. He listened to the footfalls of the horse and the crunching sound of the wheels as they faded off into the distance and left only the silent breeze behind.

Someone would find him eventually. This was the understanding that came to Sheldon in the silence after the horse and owner had gone. Maybe not tonight as he stood there, but sooner or later.

Sooner or later they would wise up to his situation.

Sooner or later they'd tear him away from here and send him to Hartford and Uncle Nate and Abe and Mirabelle. He was sure of it. He was too young to live on his own and the town was too small to not see it happening.

Sheldon pictured that. He and Mirabelle in the same house. The smell of shampoo in the hallways.

There was no going back to the house now. There was no living there anymore. The house wasn't a home or a refuge now. It was a place. A place without life.

But he wanted the clock back. And the suitcase and the clothes and the jewelry.

And Sheldon Horowitz wanted them now.

That's when Sheldon thought about his father's lighter.

He used to play with it all the time. It was a solid brass piece. Not like those fancy new Zippos he'd seen around. This was a trench lighter. It was made from an old bullet casing that was wrapped in a second casing that he could move up and down along a ridge with his thumb, which displaced the cap. There was an iron wheel near the top, and when the cap was off and the windscreen was up, a single flick would shoot sparks onto the soaked cotton wick. It was a beautiful thing, a relic from the war, a keepsake.

It was the thought of the lighter that made Sheldon walk back into the house.

An oil lamp burned on the kitchen table, and beyond its reach, the house was dark. Each doorway was a shadow hiding something unseeable. There was no fire in the fireplace, and his mother wasn't here to brighten the night with the candles she'd place on the windowsills. Summer or winter, the dark was always pushed back by her one way or another.

Taking the oil lamp with him, Sheldon walked up the stairs in his dirty shoes, leaving prints behind him. In his father's closet he found his ruck-sack, a green canvas number with leather straps and brass fittings. It was a little big for Sheldon, but it would do for his plans.

Back in his room, he found two pairs of trousers, some underwear and socks, three shirts he liked, and a winter parka.

In his parents' room, Sheldon's worst suspicions were confirmed. The

Krupinski brothers had cleaned out his mother's closet and taken his father's army medal. The drawers were all overturned. Her jewelry box was gone. From the opened dresser drawer, Sheldon removed his father's infantry patch and a sheathed bayonet, neither of them worth a damn to the brothers. When he left the room where he used to snuggle between his parents on winter nights, he didn't look back.

Downstairs in the kitchen drawer, he located Joseph's brass trench lighter.

He slid up the shield and smelled the wick. It smelled sharp and caustic like gasoline.

Sheldon took a last look around. Nothing that he cared about was here anymore. Not the people, not the things, not the future. The past he loved so much had been gutted from this place. Whatever was left was inside his head or in the possession of the Krupinski brothers.

And what was inside his head wasn't nearly enough. He wanted his stuff back.

He lit the tablecloth on fire.

The edge caught, gently at first, until the fire started to widen along the frayed edges. Before it began to spread, the fire had only been an idea —one he could put out with his fingers the way he'd once seen his cousin Abe do to a wick. This fire, though, was now more than an idea. The thin blue edge crept higher up the fabric, and soon Sheldon smelled the smoke that was rising up to the ceiling and spreading outward, a cloud inside his own house.

In a moment, it was beyond all control. What had started as an impulse had become a fact that lived outside of him—a creation larger than the creator, a creation bent on consumption and destruction.

Sheldon stepped back in fear and awe at what he had made. And yet, as the flames reached the ceiling, he wasn't sure whether he even wanted them to stop. As he watched everything he ever knew begin to burn—as he thought of his mother and the movie theater and all the people who must have been rushing to get out but who were trapped by the smoke and the dark—a part of him was thankful that the stillness had ended, that a decision had been made by someone, and whether the world would soon be better or worse, it would at least be blessedly different.

He backed out of the kitchen and tripped over the threshold on the way out, landing on his backside.

As he pushed himself backward, the first waves of scorching heat blasted his face. The shock of it against his skin jarred him, and for the first time since the car accident, he started to cry.

Sheldon's crying was silenced under the cracks and groans of the burning house and the sound of the wind being sucked into the fire. Sheldon crawled away, and at the front steps, he raised himself to his feet and distanced himself from the fire with his rucksack in tow.

As the flames arrived at the windows upstairs and fed themselves on his parents' bed and curtains and wooden furniture, Sheldon made for the shed where his father kept the garden tools and the hunting gear that wasn't out in the forest shack. He climbed inside with the rucksack and his last worldly items and, closing the door behind him, slumped down to the floor, bent his face into his knees, and finished his crying as the fire outside engulfed the rest of the house and collapsed it to the ground.

Sheldon wasn't aware that he had fallen asleep until he was woken by an adult hand on his arm.

"Sheldon?" asked the man, as he pulled him out of the shed.

Mr. Simmons was the town sheriff and the father of Sheldon and Lenny's teacher. Sheldon had never met him personally, but his father had often wished him a good morning in town. Mr. Simmons had a close-cut gray beard and thinning hair. He was a soft-spoken man. There was a revolver on his belt.

"Yes, sir."

"You're in my daughter's class, right?"

"Yes, sir."

"Was there anyone inside?"

"No, sir."

"Well, thank God for that. Stand up now." The sheriff took Sheldon under his arm and lifted him up. The fire was still burning hot, but the top floor had long since fallen in and Sheriff Simmons wasn't moving like a man in a rush. He removed a handkerchief from his pocket and cleared ash from Sheldon's face. He grimaced at his own handiwork: "That didn't help much."

Sheldon didn't reply.

"You OK?" he asked Sheldon.

"I guess so."

"Where's your dad?"

"There was an accident," Sheldon said.

"What kind of accident?"

"We were driving back from Hartford and the truck turned over."

"Well," said the sheriff, removing his hat on account of the heat. "Where is he?"

"He's . . . he . . ." The words caught in his throat, but Sheldon forced them out. "Dead."

"He died? And you're telling me you're here all by yourself?"

"Yes, sir."

"What happened?" asked Mr. Simmons. "You knock over the lamp or something?"

"The truck belonged to the Krupinski brothers. They did it. They stole my parents' things and then burned down my house."

Simmons was confused. He should have received a call about an accident, especially if the boy was here alone. "Why would they do that?" he asked.

"They came and took our stuff because of the broken truck. Payback, they said. And they knocked over the lamp on their way out. But my dad didn't wreck their truck. Someone drove us off the road. Slammed right into us on purpose. A man with a mustache in a suit."

"Ronny and Theo," said Mr. Simmons in a way that told Sheldon it was not an inconceivable notion to him. He ignored the part about the man and the suit. "What did they take?"

"My dad's clock and my mother's jewelry box. The one with the diamond in it and the little green stone. Her clothes too. Took it all away in her suitcase with her initials on it."

"Lila," said Mr. Simmons, his voice dropping off slightly.

"Sir?"

Sheriff Simmons surveyed the catastrophe around him with his hands on his hips. The fire smoldered.

"You got anything you can bring with you? Clothes and such? You can't stay here."

"I got my bag in the shed," said Sheldon. "Grabbed what I could."

"Get it and come with me," said the sheriff.

The Krupinski brothers lived with their father west of Whately. Their white house was set far back from the road at the end of a dirt path that split left to the house and right to the sagging barn. The brothers, Sheldon knew, spent most of their time in the barn. Light streamed from the cracks and edges of old planks. The house across the way was dark.

Sheriff Simmons pulled the car up to the barn and stopped thirty feet out.

"You wait here."

The sheriff strode purposefully to the door of the barn. Without a pause, he knocked. When the door creaked open, Ronny Krupinski stuck his head out and Mr. Simmons took that as an invitation to walk in.

Sheldon sat in the car and waited. The only sound was the wind, and he could smell the smoke on the breeze.

Not more than two minutes went by before the sheriff had both young men walking out the door in handcuffs. Simmons had his revolver out as he marched them to the space between the barn and the house where the headlights from the patrol car lit up the grass in a golden stain.

Old Bruno was nowhere to be seen.

Sheldon watched as the sheriff's gun motioned for the brothers to sit. "We didn't do nothin'," said Ronny.

"That kid's a fucking liar," shouted Theo. "He burned his own place down. You can't trust them dirty Jews." Simmons wasn't interested. He vanished back into the barn and came out with his gun in one hand and Sheldon's mother's suitcase in the other.

At the car window, he stopped and leaned in. "It's got L. H. engraved on the top. Lila Horowitz, I'm reckoning." Sheldon nodded. "I'll go back for the clock. You check to see if everything's in here. I took a peek. That little diamond you mentioned. Three rings, four pairs of earrings, a few silver necklaces, and a silver broach with a green rock set in the middle."

"An aventurine stone. It's from India," Lila had once told Sheldon. "The Orient. Someday you'll go there, Sheldon," she said. "You'll see the whole world."

"That's my mother's," Sheldon said.

The sheriff nodded and picked up the new two-way radio they'd installed back in January after the new budget was passed. Radios were still rare and Simmons liked to use it whenever he had the thinnest of excuses. This time, the need wasn't so thin.

"Alice? I need you to send Timmy out to the Krupinski place. They robbed the Horowitz family and then burned the place down. I got the boy in the back seat here. I can't have them all in the same car. Have him hurry it up," he said, and then was quiet for a moment. "Yeah," he continued, "there's more. Joseph Horowitz is dead—what?—no, they didn't do it. An accident on the road. Let's start calling around and see if we can't find him. I'm gonna take the kid home with me and have Carol look after him until we track down some family. I remember something about the brother being in Connecticut."

Outside, the Krupinski boys were popping up and down with indignation and threatening Sheldon, which wasn't helping their case with the sheriff, who walked over to Theo and kicked him in the ribs as though he'd been thinking about it since first seeing his face. Timmy showed up twenty minutes later. Little older than Ronny, he pulled them both up and hauled them back to his car.

Stone-faced, Sheldon watched them with eyes fixed like a hawk. Ronny ran his finger across his throat and Sheldon looked on, impassive, as they disappeared into the shadowy depths of Timmy's police car.

HARTFORD

SHELDON NEVER WONDERED where Miss Simmons lived. Or how she lived. Like all adults he wasn't related to, she seemed to magically pop into existence whenever he was around and vanish when he was gone. Aside from wondering what her legs looked like, Sheldon hadn't given Miss Simmons's private life any thought until he walked through the front door of her house.

Carol Simmons lived with her father. When Sheldon stepped inside, a floral scent hit him that was almost as powerful as the cigar smoke it was trying to mask. He didn't understand it as the smell of intergenerational warfare, both combatants locked in an uneasy battle for supremacy inside a house neither could leave.

Miss Simmons greeted him at the door like a long-lost relative, not a teacher. She buried his face between her breasts and held it there as she hugged him, lamenting his suffering and pain, all of which was momentarily abstracted amid the smell of her and the feeling of her skin against his right cheek.

"Are you hungry?" she asked.

"Of course he's hungry," said Mr. Simmons. "Give him the leftover pot roast."

Sheldon ate like an animal. He placed his napkin on his lap first, like his mother had shown him, and he used a fork and knife rather than his hands, but those were the only concessions he made to civilization because after those preliminaries his primal needs took over. He hadn't had a hot meal since Hartford. He drank three glasses of milk in the course of the meal, and when he was done, Miss Simmons took him by the arm as if he were a drunk and walked him upstairs to a guest room that smelled like laundry detergent. It was the best smell Sheldon could remember; it smelled like order, which was the exact opposite of death.

Sheldon tumbled onto the bed like a felled tree while downstairs Sheriff Simmons placed a series of calls that ended with Joseph's brother, Nate Corbin.

The next day, Sheldon met Lenny at their favorite spot by the river. Word about his father had spread across town by lunchtime, and that meant Lenny would know and want to talk to him, assuming that he wasn't angry for not being told.

They arrived at the river at almost the same moment in the midafternoon.

Lenny was magnanimous when they met, and he hugged Sheldon and then placed a hand on his shoulder after they had sat down.

"Why didn't you say anything, Sheldon?" Lenny asked him.

Mill River was as wide as a stone's throw. Today it flowed strong, and each piece of grass or bark or twig floating on it was a boat that twisted and turned on its way southward to the Atlantic.

"I don't want to go crying in front of people."

"I know but . . . this isn't a skinned knee."

Sheldon didn't reply.

"You want to come live with us? My parents love you. Or the parts they know about, anyway."

"My uncle Nate is coming to pick me up today. I've got to go live with my cousins."

"In Hartford?"

"Yeah."

"That's hours away."

"I know."

"So, like . . . a whole different school and friends and stuff?"

"We can write," Sheldon said.

Lenny didn't look convinced. Lenny had never written a letter. He wrote some jokes and tried to write a radio skit once but never a letter. Soldiers wrote letters. And grandmothers. But normal people?

"You think you're gonna come back?" he asked.

"Someone killed my dad, Lenny. Someone drove us off the road on purpose. And something's telling me, they didn't think it was my father who was driving."

"What do you mean?"

"You know that army hat my dad wears? The one from the war? Old Krupinski's got one too. We were driving his truck. And they were skimming from my dad and I'm thinking . . . who else were they skimming from? Somebody, that's for sure. Why only fleece us when they could do it to other guys too? I think one of their dupes decided to teach the Krupinskis a lesson. So . . . I'm gonna find out who did it and get them."

"The Krupinskis?"

"No. I already got them. I want the driver."

Sheldon told Lenny the truth about the house fire. How he set it. How he blamed it on Ronny and Theo. How easy it had been to tell the lie and how good it had felt after what they said and did to him. How simple it had been to make things right with only a little courage and few well-placed words.

Lenny barely blinked as Sheldon told the story. At the end, he was duly impressed but worried.

"I'm not saying they didn't have it coming," said Lenny. "But . . . you burned down your house, Sheldon. I'm just thinking that . . . we're not supposed to bear false witness against our neighbors and all that."

"They weren't very neighborly."

Lenny nodded but not in agreement. His head always bobbed up and down when he was thinking, a strategy that bought him time.

"That guy ran us off the road on purpose, Lenny," Sheldon said. "Even if they did plan on getting Old Krupinski and not my dad, the guy with the mustache saw me. I mean . . . we locked eyes. And he did it anyway. So, fuck 'em, Lenny. I'm going to get him. Because we're also supposed to honor our mothers and fathers too."

"You're not supposed to avenge 'em," said Lenny. His voice was low.

They didn't often talk about serious matters. Then again, until last year, serious matters had never come up.

"So, I'm supposed to sit back and take it? I don't think so," Sheldon said.

"How're you gonna find him?" Lenny asked.

"The guy had a suit and a fancy haircut and a mustache. He's got to be from a city. Springfield or Hartford, I think."

"Could be New York or Boston or Miami for all we know."

"The Krupinskis don't go that far with that truck. Whoever it was knew the truck. They go to Springfield and Hartford. Maybe Boston and New York, but we were coming north, so that rules out Boston, which is east. I think I can find him."

"How?"

"It's like those books and radio shows, you know? Like with Dashiell Hammett and Rex Stout? Nero Wolfe and Archie Goodwin? You know. It's just detective work. My dad used to read them to me all the time. Mom thought they were too grown-up for me, but my dad read them at bedtime when I was eight. When I was ten, he started making me do the reading and then even Mom would come in. We'd all take turns. I told you about that. You made fun of me for reading with my parents, and I pushed you in the river. You don't remember?"

"Yeah, but . . . I wouldn't have put those things together."

"Think about it. How would Nero Wolfe put it all together? He'd think it through. Somebody tried to run us off the road. Who? Someone the Krupinskis fucked over. Who had they fucked over that ends up with a guy in a fancy suit driving us off the road on the way back between Springfield and Northampton? I'm thinking it had to be someone with money and power and muscle and stuff. Someone big who decided to go Al Capone on them. Not some farmer. Not some craftsman. A business type. If I can find out who the brothers were doing business with, and which of them might be up for dirty work, I might be able to get them."

"Get them?" Lenny was growing incredulous. "Track them down and find the guy, Sheldon? Find the muscle who works for money and power? What are you gonna do if that works? You haven't even had your bar mitzvah yet."

"What the hell has my bar mitzvah got to do with anything?"

"You know. Being a man and stuff. And . . . you know. We're Jewish."

"What of it?"

"There aren't any Jewish detectives, Sheldon. Come on. You think the Shadow is Jewish? Sherlock Holmes? Nero Wolfe? Jews don't get to do that kind of stuff."

"My father defended France, but he couldn't have asked questions wearing a hat and smokin' a cigarette?"

"It's not the same thing."

"Why not?"

"Because . . . I don't know," said Lenny.

"I do," said Sheldon. "Errol Flynnowitz, that's the reason."

"You making jokes now?"

"No. I'm understanding one."

Lenny wasn't following this part of Sheldon's thinking, but one thing was clear to him. "OK, try this one: You're twelve," said Lenny, opening his palms to release the crazy back into the cosmos.

"Come off it, Lenny."

Lenny Bernstein looked at Sheldon. He'd never seen him like this. He'd never seen him ramped up. Not like this. Not even after his mother died.

"You gonna shoot the mobster?" Lenny asked.

"I got rifles in the shed. I know how to use them. I'm pretty good, actually."

"You gonna put a rifle in your rucksack?"

"I got things to work out!" Sheldon said.

"I'll say."

An hour later Sheldon sat alone on the curb of the tiny brick police station with his shaggy hair, wall clock, rucksack, and a woman's suitcase filled with frocks and jewelry. The day was spent, and dusk was rising to a wind. The sun was orange and its light sharpened the edges of the trees across the street.

Out of a bush came a raccoon.

Sheldon knew them as night creatures, but it wasn't so unusual to see one about in the daytime from time to time, especially when garbage was piling up in the cans. This one found a stale crust of bread and — seeing Sheldon on the other side of the street — decided to sit there and watch him as she ate.

"I'm not the funny-looking one," he said to her. "You are."

He named her Sally. Sally was not convinced by anything Sheldon had to say.

"I mean, look at yourself. Sitting there on your fat ass stuffing your face with your feet out. Thieves have masks like yours when they're gonna rob a bank or something. Did they get that from you, or did you get it from them? I'll bet they got it from you, you little thief."

Sally stopped eating. Sheldon thought he'd touched a nerve.

"My uncle Nate's coming to get me and we're going to drive back on the same road where my dad died, you know that? And then we're going to drive right past the movie theater in Hartford where my mother died." Sheldon looked out to the woods. "I could make a run for it, you know. Make for the forest. I can hunt and trap and stuff. I could live out there. Fresh water in the stream, meat in my belly." If there was more to the thought, Sheldon didn't share it with Sally.

Uncle Nate emerged from a black Ford wearing a dark suit, tie, and fedora. He tilted it back and placed a cigarette between his lips as he walked to the side of the car where Sheldon was sitting. Wordlessly, he flicked his lighter half a dozen times before giving up.

"I don't suppose you have a light?" said Uncle Nate.

Sheldon handed the brass house burner to his uncle, who lit up and — if not feeling better for it — at least he was able to step into the only conversation available.

"Well. Hell, Sheldon."

"Yeah."

Nate had already passed through such a range of emotions and so many prepared speeches on the long drive up to Whately that by the time he opened his mouth he was already spent.

"You're gonna live with us now," he said to his nephew.

"Yes, sir."

"I got two kids of my own and now you on top of it. My wife. Your mother. Now my brother. While this is happening, I've got people breathing down my neck at work and I'm in a pinch you'll never understand," he said to Sheldon. "So, don't be thinking you're the only one with problems."

"No, sir."

"What's with the clock?" Nate asked, after letting out a long breath of pure smoke.

"It was my dad's. It goes where I go."

Nate turned and looked at the Ford and considered the space.

"You're bunking up with Abe. If he doesn't want it in the bedroom, you'll have to work it out between you."

"Yes, sir."

Nate folded his arms and looked around at the hillbilly town he had escaped from all those years ago. He still didn't understand why his brother had stayed.

They'd had the talk in 1922. Nate worked at one of the remaining wool mills. He hated everything about it and said so. "I hate the smell. I hate the pay. I don't like the feel of the wool on my hands. I hate the chemicals. And there are no women here, Joe. No women I haven't known since elementary school. That pool's exhausted, you get me? I either don't want to see them naked or I don't want to see them naked again. I want to go to Hartford. It's swinging now with the economy turning around. There are speakeasies. There's dancing and short-hemmed dresses, and they all think I'm Italian. Those are the kinds of girls I need in my life. And they smell good and you can get away with things in cities that you can't in small towns."

"Who do you know in Hartford?"

"Nobody, which is the best thing about it. There's a synagogue there. It's Conservative, but I can play along. I'll see the rabbi and tell him I'm moving to town. I figure he'll hook me up. The Jewish community's big down there. It's connected."

"He's not a pimp, Nate."

"I'll find you one too. You know . . . the kind who can handle your moods and likes a guy with a history."

Joseph said nothing.

"I'll visit," Nate said. "But it would be better if you came to me."

Joseph stayed with the cottage and the woods and the quiet. Nate found Lucy in Hartford and he married her, and then Lucy introduced her friend Lila to Joseph and inexplicably she liked him. It rankled Nate, because Lila was the most beautiful woman he'd ever seen not projected onto a screen, and while Lucy was lovely, Lila was a stunner. He didn't understand how Joe had managed it. But these questions didn't matter anymore. The theater was closed, and the cast was dead.

Sixteen years later, Nate looked at Sheldon. "That's it, then? The clock, the suitcase, and the rucksack?"

"Couple of things are left in the shed," Sheldon said, pushing the clock into the back seat of the car. It made noises. The Krupinski brothers had handled it roughly; it was going to need care. "Some stuff in the hunting shack. But that's all."

"What's your friend's name? The comedian your dad says you pal around with?"

"Lenny."

"Whatever's left, you tell him he can have it. We don't have the space. You write him a letter."

"OK."

"Get in," said Nate, looking around at his own past for what might be the last time.

INMATES

ARTFORD, CONNECTICUT, GLOWED LIKE a magic lantern beneath the low clouds of that autumn night. Sheldon had never approached a big city after dark before. He'd been in Boston a few times. Springfield a few more. But not at night. He half expected to feel the edge of the light when he reached Hartford as though it were a physical barrier he had to penetrate. For all their glimmer and promise, though, the city's lights were cold and he knew the place to be a crematorium.

Sheldon and Nate had not spoken during the car ride. The weight of circumstance overwhelmed any impulse to talk. With all that had happened and was yet to come, there was surprisingly little to say because of how little there was to decide. The path was forewritten. Sheldon was to mourn and go to school, much like last year. Nate was to provide food and shelter and abide by state laws directing the education of children until they were of age and employable and could graduate and move out. Abe had a year to go and would be out in 1939. Mirabelle had two.

In their silence, Nate was considering that the kids would have to pull their weight and make their way in an unfair world. Their predicament was painful and Sheldon's doubly so—Nate was not oblivious to this—but it was not unprecedented, and the world had thrown far more at people with far less. Many of them were in Europe.

"You're going to stay out of trouble, right? Make this easy on me?" Nate said to Sheldon as they entered Hartford.

Sheldon turned and looked at him. He wanted to say yes almost as much as he wanted to push Nate out of the car for asking. Instead, he said nothing and looked out the window at the tall buildings and streetlamps, the black cars and elegant people walking down the streets as though Christmas were around every corner.

The Horowitz-turned-Corbin family lived in a three-bedroom brownstone that nicely blended in with all the other brownstones nearby. It had three floors with a bay window in the front parlor. Sheldon had been here maybe a dozen times over the years, mostly for holidays because they had more space and a formal table.

What Sheldon felt first, on entering the house, was the absence of a woman, of a mother. Though tidy, the house felt unruly. There was no one to define the mood and temper the people inside, and so they were left adrift.

Without a woman, everything felt unpredictable. It was a place of emotion without direction.

Sheldon didn't notice her at first, but once he looked around, he saw Mirabelle leaning against the bannister of the staircase with her arms crossed over her chest and her dirty blonde hair tied up neatly in a bun. She wore a simple black dress with a white collar, but the expression she wore was far less monochrome. There was red in her face and it wasn't makeup. Whether it was anger or grief or sadness, Sheldon couldn't tell. She seemed to be tolerating everything and everyone. Despite it all — or because of it — she was terribly pretty; grace against a storm.

"Hello," she said, resigned to the fact of him.

"Hi," Sheldon replied.

She blinked at him over stiff lips, and though her welcome was harsh, he was grateful she was here. He hadn't lived in a house with a woman for more than a year. She was a little scary, though. Beautiful but definitely scary.

For Mirabelle, it was obvious that Sheldon's invasion was another change in a litany of changes that only added more trouble to the trouble she'd been having. For the moment, she was keeping everything to herself.

Abe sat halfway up the staircase on the red runner wearing a black suit, a white shirt, a black tie, and a fedora. To Sheldon, he looked halfway between a Hasidic Jew and a gangster. With the fedora tipped forward and his elbows on his knees, Abe looked more like the latter. Despite being a teenager, Abe folded beneath the weight of life like a grown man. There was a sadness in his face that robbed him of a youthful humor.

"Welcome to hell," said Abe.

"It's not my first visit," said Sheldon.

Abe nodded his head. "They say bad news happens in threes. Uncle Joe makes it three. Guess we're all in the clear now."

"Yeah, smooth sailing," said Sheldon.

"That all you got?" Abe nodded at the rucksack, the clock, and the woman's suitcase.

"That's all there is."

"I heard about the house."

Sheldon didn't reply to that.

"You planning to put that thing in my room?" Abe asked, looking at the clock. "'Cuz I'm not thrilled about sharing a room. Jerking off in peace was the only good thing around here."

Sheldon looked at Mirabelle, who was not shocked by this nor, it seemed, insulted by it.

"Can I please?" Sheldon asked.

"Jesus Christ," said Abe, tilting his hat up and rubbing his face. "Don't go all soft on me. Come on," he said, standing up.

Sheldon walked up the stairs one step at a time and then hauled his history up behind him at what seemed like a slower pace. At the top, with a sigh, Abe led him to their room.

Twin beds were pressed against separate walls with one window in between that looked out on the street, the brownstones across the way that were a mirror of the Corbins', and the passing black cars and wood-paneled trucks. There was a dresser at the foot of each bed, and Abe's woolen blanket was folded to military perfection on the one to the left. The other bed on the right was unmade. A folded pile of sheets and a gray blanket awaited Sheldon.

"That's you," Abe said, pointing.

There were two trophies on Abe's dresser. Sheldon didn't inspect the inscriptions. Otherwise, there were no pictures, no photos, and little else that was personal aside from a stack of books, a stack of newspapers, and a typewriter.

"It's like an insane asylum in here," Sheldon said.

"What makes you think it isn't?"

"Nothing, I guess."

"Close the door."

Abe flopped down onto his bed while simultaneously tossing his fedora across the room onto the hat rack like Sheldon had seen in the movies, when he used to go to movies. With his back to the wall, Abe crossed his legs and motioned for Sheldon to take a seat opposite him on his own bed after the door clicked shut.

The springs squeaked when he sat on them. Sheldon sat back and crossed his arms, trying to look grown-up even though he knew that the effort showed and the gesture failed.

"Someone ran us off the road," Sheldon said to Abe. "A guy in a fancy suit and a mustache. My dad was murdered. I'm going to find out who did it."

Abe's face didn't change. He nodded toward the window. "There's a car across the street with a wiseguy in it. He's been here for months. Go look. Was it that guy?"

Sheldon didn't like humor like this.

"Fuck you, Abe."

"I'm not kidding around. Go look at the window. Black car across the street. He's been watching us for almost three months now."

"Someone really did kill my dad," Sheldon repeated.

"And I'm saying," said Abe in an eerily calm voice, "go look out the window. Because there's shit going down here in Happyland and I believe you."

Sheldon didn't know Abe very well. He was six years older but the distance between twelve and eighteen was a lifetime. Abe was almost done with high school, and Sheldon wasn't entering it for another few years. Abe had a girlfriend named Marjorie, a driver's license, and he worked part-time after school at the G. Fox & Co. department store downtown selling men's shirts and suits. What Abe might find funny was a mystery.

"If you're messing with me on a day like this, it would make you a grade A asshole."

"I agree with that," Abe said, his voice low and flat.

Sheldon walked to the window and looked out. Like Abe said, there was a black sedan parked on the street. Inside was a man wearing a hat. The car was across the street, and Sheldon saw the driver's elbow sticking out. He couldn't see the man's face, and from his suit and body language, he could have been anyone. Sheldon didn't see any smoke coming out of the exhaust.

"Who is he?"

"Who is he? That's my question. I asked my dad. He said he had no idea and that I should mind my own business. I know he's not a cop. He's never knocked on our door. He's never stepped out and walked into another house. So, that narrows things down a bit. My guess is he's with the Mob and he's watching Dad for some reason. I do think, though, it's got something to do with the missing guns at the armory."

Sheldon looked at the man. He couldn't be sure, but it didn't really look like his guy. The thickness of the guy was off.

"My guy had a mustache."

"He doesn't have one. Then again, men shave."

"It was one of those bushy ones. People with those don't shave them off. They name them."

"You're probably right. Too bad. Would have tied everything off in a nice, neat wrapper and we'd know exactly what to do."

"What's going on, Abe? What missing guns?" Sheldon asked, still looking out the window. The man in the car, sensing that he was being looked at, looked up at Sheldon. Sheldon didn't look away. They stared at each other until the man lost interest in a twelve-year-old boy trying to stare him down.

It wasn't his guy.

"It's got something to do with my dad. You know he works for the Colt Armory, right? He's an accountant?"

"I guess."

"You know what an accountant is?"

"Not exactly."

"Businesses have money coming in, and they have money going out because it costs money to make money, and they need to keep track of how it's all moving around. There are more than ten thousand people employed at

Colt. The place is an industrial-era miracle. That's a lot of moving parts and a lot of moving money. Dad helps keep the numbers straight."

"OK," said Sheldon, informed but uninterested.

"You know what the armory is, right? You and your dad know all about guns?"

"I don't know that much about guns. What I know is how to shoot. And I know animals and the woods and tracking and skinning and stuff like that."

"All useless here," said Abe, reaching up for a newspaper. It was the *Boston Daily Globe*. The massive headline from a few weeks back read, ITALY ORDERS JEWS TO GO. "You see this? They revoked Italian citizenship from foreign Jews. They've got six months to clear out of Italy, Libya, and the Aegean Isles—wherever the hell those are. Says here"—Abe pointed to a spot in the paper—"that they might be headed for Italian East Africa because apparently there's no mention of that place in the edict and because Jewish refugees are being denied entry by all other European countries. The entire continent wants them gone. All of them."

"Where are they supposed to go?"

Abe shrugged.

"What has that got to do with us?" Sheldon said. He went back to the bed and sat across from Abe.

"It means Jews are getting squeezed. You see, my dad got promoted a couple of months ago. To my dad, this is the biggest deal in the world. A Jew getting promoted at Colt? It's the most goyish industry you're likely to find outside a mayonnaise factory. He takes it as proof that we're climbing the big ladder of America. But I smell a rat."

"I don't understand," Sheldon said.

Abe put away the paper and tried to explain. "The Colt Armory makes guns. Lots and lots of guns. They've been here in Hartford since before the Civil War. The guy who runs it is called Samuel M. Stone. One of the men under him is Carl Henkler. He's American but he's German, and he thinks he's entitled to the East Coast itself. He's also a numbers guy and Dad says he's smart. I think he might be too smart. Because, the thing is, guns started going missing from the factory sometime earlier this year. Not a lot of them, but enough to get noticed. Stone put up security at the doors and had bags checked and started having dogs wander around at night, but so far nothing's worked. No one can figure out how they're being smuggled out of the building. A place that big isn't going under because a few hundred guns get swiped, but Stone isn't one to get robbed, so he's on the warpath. Not to mention that if it got out that Colt was being robbed — right when there's a war on the horizon — it might make the big buyers skittish and that could kill any kind of deal. So Henkler hired my dad to start combing the accounts to narrow down where the losses are coming from and, I suppose, make them stop. This came months after the big fire, and Dad took the job because he thought that any change, any chance for something good, was worth taking. Shortly after that, that asshole in the car started showing up. Comes back all the time."

Abe motioned to the window and everything outside it.

"You think this is connected to my dad too?" Sheldon asked.

"Do you?" Abe asked him.

They didn't feel connected. Sheldon was pretty sure his theory about the Krupinskis pissing off the wrong guys was a good one, and it didn't need any complicated connections to Colt. Sure, the Mob might be involved in both cases, but they've got their hands in everything according to the papers.

"Not especially. But who the hell knows?"

Abe removed a Lucky Strike from a half-crumpled pack and packed it with an expert hand against his palm. "'Who the hell knows' is the correct answer to the question. And I believe the answer to *that* question is Carl Henkler."

Sheldon uncrossed his arms and placed his palms on the blue-ticked mattress. The cotton was rough. He looked at the clean folded sheets.

"So, you believe me? About my dad?" Sheldon said.

"Yes. I do. I might not have believed it if that car wasn't there, but it is. So, yeah, I believe you."

Abe put the cigarette at the edge of his mouth, where it stuck like a magnet. He removed a brass Zippo from his pocket and started snapping it open and whacking it shut. Sheldon's feet twitched back and forth off the side of the bed.

"We gonna do something about all this or are we supposed to just sit back and take it?" Sheldon asked.

Abe smiled at him.

"What do you think?"

Dinner was a bean-and-chicken soup with chunks of tomato served with two slices of dark bread. Mirabelle delivered it to the table without an apron or a word. The new family of four sat in the kitchen at a round table, a yellow light illuminating the proceedings from beneath a red glass, which cast the ceiling in the color of warning. The Jack Benny show was playing on the Zenith. On the program, Jack had bought a horse and clearly knew nothing about it.

"So, you've seen this horse, Mary?" Phil was saying.

"Oh, sure."

"What does it look like?"

"Like any minute two men are gonna step out of it!"

The audience laughed, but the Corbin family wasn't really listening.

Nate put down his spoon, wiped his face, and sat back. A wind had picked up outside that was harrying the windows. He looked at them long enough to see whether a tree was going to present itself through the glass, and when he was convinced it wasn't, he turned his attention to Sheldon.

"Tomorrow's September nineteenth. You lost some schooling but not much. Mirabelle can walk you to your school tomorrow, and she'll continue on to the high school. They're going to test you first thing and you need to do as well as you can, otherwise they'll place you back a year and that means you'll be living here a year longer, which isn't something we need. You understand what I'm telling you?"

"Yes, sir," said Sheldon.

"Abe has some old clothes. Somewhere," he added, glancing at his son, who nodded. "He'll find them for you, and you'll comb your hair and make like you belong here. I don't want any missteps or drama from any of you," Nate said, looking squarely at Mirabelle this time. "I've got things on my mind and things I need to sort out. When I get home from work, I expect the three of you to be a help to me. I expect dinner on the table, homework to be done, and the chores completed. This family is going to keep moving its way up, so help me God; I don't care what's being thrown in our way to stop us. You all understand me?"

"What about my dad?" Sheldon said. His hands were clenched in his lap.

Nate didn't look up at him. "We're burying him tomorrow. Next to your mom and near Lucy."

"I'm supposed to go to school?"

"We're burying him after school. You need to take that test. I don't want to hear another word about it."

Mirabelle cleared the plates in silence.

"You're all wrong. He's a fine-looking horse. See, I got a picture right here."

"Golly, look at him. But why's he lying on his back?"

"You got the picture upside down."

"Oh, look at that. He got up."

Sheldon lay in bed after dinner with his arms crossed behind his head as Abe, shirtless and as taut as a Greek statue, crossed his legs and read the paper. Neither spoke. The ceiling above Sheldon's head was white, and the paint was peeling along a single crack that meandered like a new river through an arctic frost. Sheldon and Joseph used to hunt in winter too when the boredom of the cobbler work during the cold season became too much.

"Let's get out of here," his father would say to him. He'd blow out the candle for effect and Sheldon would bounce up like a caged dog shown a new door with a field beyond.

Massachusetts winters could be powerfully harsh, but they were variable too. After ice storms came days of crackling beauty and blue skies. Their L.L.Bean boots would crunch through the frozen top layers into the powdery and loose snow beneath. If Sheldon was careful and lucky, he could leave behind absolutely perfect footprints.

His father would quiz him along the way, as much for education as conversation.

"What are we following?" he would ask Sheldon.

"Snowshoe hare."

"How can you tell the snowshoe from a cottontail or jackrabbit?"

"Snowshoe's got a much wider print. Toes farther apart."

"And the cottontail?"

"Too easy."

A rustling of the newspaper snapped Sheldon back to Hartford. The ceiling lost its magic. The woods vanished.

"Don't you ever sleep?" Sheldon asked Abe, pulling the blanket up to his neck.

"You've shot a gun, right?" Abe asked him, putting the paper down. "You and Uncle Joe?"

"Lots of times. Why?"

"What's it like?"

Sheldon knew that Abe considered his earlier and rural life both exotic and cool; significant somehow. Hunting. Trapping. Camping out. Shooting. His father, though, never did. Nothing to be proud of. Nothing inherently interesting. "Better the world didn't have guns," his father had once said. "But they're here, so you might as well know how they work. There's more to learn about the woods, though. That's where the magic is."

"It's not really like anything else," Sheldon said, snuggling into the bed more deeply. "It's just . . . I don't know."

"Is it hard?" Abe asked.

"No. Anyone can do it. That's the whole point. They're made to be simple."

"Right," said Abe. He folded the newspaper. A giant advertisement for Chesterfields dominated the lower half of the page. A smiling woman was holding a cigarette from behind a globe; beneath it, the caption read CLEAR ACROSS THE MAP THEY SATISFY WITH MORE PLEASURE FOR MILLIONS. At the top of the page, the section heading read FEMININE TOPICS.

"You planning on shooting somebody, Abe?"

"Go to sleep, Sheldon. You got a big day tomorrow."

• • •

But Sheldon couldn't sleep. The strangeness of the house and the constant city noises kept him awake. After Abe had stopped moving, Sheldon slipped off the blanket and stole out of the room. He didn't have a plan or destination in mind, but the cold floor and being vertical made him want to pee again, so he started walking along the bannister to the bathroom at the end of the hall.

As he padded almost silently on the worn rug, he caught sight of Mirabelle in the next room through a crack in the door. She was lying on her bed, back to the wall, reading a book. She wore a short flannel nightgown and her legs were bare. Her right leg was extended and the other—the one closest to Sheldon—was up. The book rested against her thigh.

Sheldon didn't mean to stop and stare at her, but he did. Though only sixteen, Mirabelle looked to Sheldon like a grown woman, and he had never seen a woman's perfect curve from beneath the knee to the panties. The closest he had ever come was with his mother and nothing about this was the same.

He was fixed to the spot. If he moved, she might look up, and if he stayed too long, she absolutely would. There would be no explaining it or apologizing for it. He began to tremble.

Mirabelle's bent knee dropped slowly toward the bed and revealed a strip of pink satin.

When Sheldon looked, Mirabelle raised her eyes from the book and smirked at him.

Sheldon ran down the hall to the bathroom and closed the door too loudly. He turned on the faucet, and the water splashed out onto his pajama top and the waistband of his bottoms. Cursing, he placed a hand towel against the wet spots and tried to dry them, but it only pressed the cold water against his skin, which was probably just as well.

Calming himself down, he used the toilet, washed his hands, and—mustering what courage he could—walked back down the hall to his room, not looking at what was surely a mischievous and superior smile on his older cousin's lips.

THE FACTORY

T HE NEXT MORNING, Nate sat with the three youths at the breakfast table with a cup of coffee and a piece of toast on his plate. Everyone was eating in silence when Nate sighed; looked at Mirabelle, who did not look back; and then made an announcement. "It has been brought to my attention," he said, each word feeling like an admission of usury and fraud and guilt, "that attending school on the day of Joseph's funeral might raise eyebrows. For that reason, all three of you will be dismissed from school today." Nate raised a finger to stave off any words from Sheldon. "And all tests and other matters will be rescheduled. I have placed a call to the school secretary, who has informed the principal, who will inform the teachers. However, I can't have you wandering around the city, and I don't trust you to stay home where you belong. Therefore, you are coming with me to the armory, where you will be put to work doing . . . something. I don't know what. I'm sure Mr. Henkler will have some ideas." Nate picked up his coffee cup. "So, that's that. We leave in half an hour."

They dressed Sheldon in Abe's old clothes. The white shirt was too long, so they doubled the cuffs back and buttoned them, tucking the shirttails deep into his trousers before wedging him into a gray sweater that could have been mistaken for his if no one looked too closely.

None of it mattered. Walking through the angular brick city beside Mirabelle guaranteed that no one would ever look too closely at Sheldon.

Mirabelle wore a wide-brimmed hat and long gloves that reached her elbows. Almost as tall and nearly the same size as her mother, Mirabelle had filled out more than was good for her at age sixteen. There was no going back to denim now. She was a child, but one with the swagger of an adult gone awry. Nate didn't like it, but he needed a woman to explain to her what he didn't like and there were none around.

Nate had wanted to purge all of Lucy's belongings. Not because he was unemotional, but because ridding the house of the stuff would have reduced the risk that any of it might set him off. Tears had always flowed too easily in his family. When they were young, it had been Joseph who led them through the dark days of the Spanish flu after their parents had died. They had both sobbed, but it was Joseph who did so without shame. It was confusing to Nate: A battle-hardened soldier who still had the mud of France between his teeth had the capacity to cry? Had the war made him soft? Either way, Nate was embarrassed by it because gentiles rolled their eyes at the expressed emotions of the Jews.

They kept the clothing after Mirabelle seized the charity bag and gave her father a look as cold and murderous as death.

On the way to the armory, Mirabelle slipped her arm through her father's as they walked. She gave her father a smile.

Sheldon saw it. He didn't understand their relationship or whether every emotion she expressed was honest or calculated. But he was pretty sure they had the day off from school because of her.

Abe wore a suit and walked beside Sheldon through pools of brilliant sunlight and islands of darkened shadows, his face brightening and then hiding away as he strode down the busy Hartford street, his shoulders effortlessly rolling and dipping to avoid contact with the passersby who were on their way to change the world into something more amazing than it already was. He was an animal moving gracefully in his element.

Abe saw that Sheldon was staring at him and didn't understand that he was the subject of Sheldon's awe; he thought it was the energy of the city.

"You know the phrase 'Yankee ingenuity'?" he asked Sheldon.

"I guess."

"It's because of Hartford," Abe said, his hands in his pockets and looking to Sheldon like a man who owned a yacht. "In many ways, it's because of Samuel Colt and his revolver. Colt was born here. Back in the 1860s, during the Civil War, he perfected precision manufacturing processes that allowed for the mass production of the guns. Out of that one industry came a set of skills that helped create a whole host of machine tools that could be used for making other things, tools like turret lathes, drill presses, and milling machines. Once those things started being made around here, all kinds of precision manufacturing came out of it and Hartford boomed. Really, the Colt Armory built this whole place. And then Richard Gatling and John Browning — they made guns too — got in on the game. From those innovations, we got Weed sewing machines, Royal and Underwood typewriters, Columbia bicycles, and even Pope automobiles. By the late 1800s, America had become the world's economic superpower because we were constantly inventing and building and manufacturing the most complex machines. Hartford was the center of gravity for this. Not Boston. Not New York. Right here. People forget that because those places are bigger, but the ideas and the energy came from here."

This is where Abe's optimism and bright mood shifted.

"Dad's job is right at the center of the place where it started," Abe said. "And he thinks it's because some magnanimous German is promoting the local Jew up the lines because he's so good at his job. But everything I see when I look out the window tells me that's not how the world works. We got the Mob watching the house, and we got the German giving my father a fancy job that no Jew has ever come close to having before. And it's not just some accounting job, which isn't here or there. It's this unwinnable assignment to save Colt's reputation. I mean, think about it. A Jew being told to save Colt's reputation? That's nuts. He's being set up. If things work out, Henkler takes the credit. But if things don't work out . . . guess what? It's blame-the-Jew time. I think Henkler's already reckoned he's going to fail, and that's why he hired Dad. So now we've got an Italian outside the window and a German in the office squeezing Nate Corbin. There's no way to win, because winning pisses off the Mob and losing activates Colt to blame Dad. What I'm saying — if all of this is too much for your twelve-year-old brain — is that we're fucked."

Sheldon half listened to Abe and his conspiracy theory about the Axis powers closing in on their family. He wasn't convinced. Did Henkler even know Uncle Nate was Jewish? After all, Nate had changed his name to Corbin. So maybe all of this was imaginary. Sheldon didn't want to ask Abe, though. Abe was too certain to question. And besides, all these ideas were abstract to him compared to the hard facts he'd recently been dealt.

As Sheldon walked among the throngs of people down to the promenade next to the Connecticut River that led to Coltsville, he was taking in the enormity of an East Coast metropolis while scanning the city streets for the man with the mustache.

They arrived close to nine o'clock. Sheldon paused to take it in. The Colt Armory was the largest single building Sheldon had ever seen up close. It wasn't tall, but it was wide. Very, very, very wide. Standing in front of it with the river behind him, Sheldon thought it was a mile wide as he gazed at the building's bright-white turret topped with a blue onion dome trimmed in gold. To Sheldon, this looked like something straight from *The Arabian Nights*, not New England. It had magic and mystery written all over it.

"Inside, kids, I don't want to be late," said Uncle Nate.

Nate walked his children and nephew through the main building, narrating a tour he had given to a thousand dignitaries as the heavy, rhythmic pounding of enormous industrial machinery set the pacing of their steps.

"The motive power for the entire operation is that steam engine. The cylinder is thirty-six inches in diameter. It has a seven-foot stroke, a thirty-foot-in-diameter flywheel, and it weighs in at seven tons. The steam comes from two cylindrical boilers, each twenty-two feet long and seven feet in diameter. The power is carried to the machinery upstairs by a belt working off the flywheel that is one hundred eighteen feet long by twenty-two inches wide and travels at the rate of two thousand five hundred feet per minute. All that power drives machines for chambering cylinders, turning and shaping them, boring barrels, milling lock frames, and drilling mortises and so on.

"This place," said Nate, "is a miracle of engineering and science and innovation. This building alone helped put America on the world map. Welcome to Colt."

Sheldon, Abe, and Mirabelle followed their father up a flight of wide stairs to the machinery floor. As they turned to continue their upward climb, Sheldon looked down a corridor five hundred feet long with a sixteen-foot ceiling and what Abe would later tell him were one hundred and ten windows.

"We've been here before, obviously," Abe said to Sheldon, as they climbed up to the assembling department and then into the offices where Nate was planning to barricade them for the morning. "He's saying all this for your benefit."

Mirabelle was saying good morning to a man in his eighties. Abe said, "That's William Cluff. He started here in 1874 when he was nineteen. He knows everything and everyone. He's been here for sixty-four years, if you can believe it."

✈

UPSTAIRS IN THE OPERATIONS ROOM, Carl Henkler heard a commotion moving toward his office door and — in preparation for the inevitable — removed his reading glasses, folded them, and closed the ledger he'd been studying as Nate Corbin, his tall son, his beautiful daughter, and a boy in badly fitting clothes entered his office. He knew about Nate's brother's death and surmised that the boy was the orphaned nephew. He did not envy a man caring for three children alone. Henkler barely saw his children during the week and he was glad for it, convinced that leaving their rearing to his wife was best for all concerned. A father provides the conditions; the mother provides the service. For Corbin, his hands were now filled with both. It was not a reasonable position to place a man, though no one had chosen this, so Henkler tried to be sympathetic.

"Mr. Henkler," said Nate, too officious for Abe's liking. "You've met my son, Abe, and my daughter, Mirabelle, before. This is Sheldon, my nephew. I mentioned my brother last week."

Carl Henkler stood, and after screwing a cap back onto a fountain pen, he moved to the front of his desk, placed his hands behind his back, and nodded. "Yes, tough times indeed. I'm sorry for your loss, Master Corbin," he said, addressing Sheldon as he'd never been addressed before.

"It's Sheldon Horowitz," Abe said, correcting him because his father had not.

"I see," said Henkler.

Abe tilted his hat forward and flopped down into a wooden swivel chair. It was his father's desk. He picked up a folder containing a list of weapons rejected by the prover after their final inspection.

"Maybe this is your problem right here," said Abe. "The prover pretends to find a few blemishes and these otherwise perfect weapons find their way to the dumpster and then out the door to the Mob, who then uses them to gun down some rivals. I think I solved your case, Mr. Henkler."

"Yes, that's a vivid imagination you have. But every weapon rejected by the prover is accounted for and destroyed."

"Destroyed?"

"We can't be lowering our standards, now can we?"

"Of course not. You only want the best here. Like my father, for instance."

"Exactly right," said Mr. Henkler, placing his hands in front of him and knitting his fingers. "I'm sorry for the loss of your uncle. I hear he was a very interesting man."

"I'm trying to find out who killed him," Sheldon blurted out.

"Are you now?"

Nate started to laugh and nearly tripped over himself getting to Sheldon to shut him up. "No, no. It was a road accident. A terrible, terrible accident, and Sheldon was in the truck at the time. A car was passing them in foul weather. Joseph lost control of the wheel."

"He was run off the road," Sheldon insisted. "By a man in a suit and a mustache. I think he was a hit man for the Mob."

Mirabelle crossed to Sheldon and placed her hands on his shoulders. She looked at Mr. Henkler from beneath her wide-brimmed hat, and said in a low voice, "We're conducting a murder investigation, you see. We might need firearms of our own, actually. I see they now make women's guns small enough to fit into a garter belt."

"OK!" shouted Nate, opening the office door and ushering the children outside. "Thank you, Mr. Henkler, for your time. I'm going to put the boys to work papering the guns in the packaging room. It'll be good for them to get their hands a little dirty and see what perfection looks like. I will continue with my review of comparing the manufactured numbers with the packed numbers to complete my survey of missing units and see if we can't find a pattern. Do they always go missing on certain days of the week, for instance? Who might be working at those times? Good day, Mr. Henkler."

"Mr. Corbin." Henkler nodded as the family moved out the door and closed it behind them.

"With me," said Nate through clenched teeth.

Sheldon followed his uncle and cousins across the vast production floor to a storeroom where racks upon racks of blue-metal pistols and rifles were being collected, wrapped in paper, and then placed into crates as gently as babies are placed into cribs.

Nate pulled the three offenders into a corner where the industrial pounding sheltered their voices from the packers.

"Let me explain something," Nate said. "Mr. Henkler is a great man. Beloved. He hires veterans who have lost limbs in the Great War—people no one else will hire—and has put them to work on the factory floor as respected professionals. He promotes people like me who are often overlooked or passed by because the world is not a perfect or fair place. He has the respect and attention of Samuel M. Stone, who has the respect and attention of the mayor, the governor, and, as far as I can tell, the heads of industry in every major nation on earth. We do not joke with Mr. Henkler. We do not embarrass ourselves in front of Mr. Henkler. We do not put our futures and finances at risk by being anything other than absolutely professional and reliable for Mr. Henkler. You two," said Nate, pointing at the boys, "will remove your jackets, roll up your sleeves, and help Mr. Carmine there in the blue shirt wrap the guns for packing. There is a correct way to handle them so your grubby fingerprints don't end up on the perfectly polished metals. We don't want the first thing a new customer sees is a blemish caused by you. The order from the principal is 'perfection.' Anything less than perfect on the line is removed by the order of Mr. Stone. Spending a morning surrounded by perfection will hopefully have a lasting impression on you.

"Hat off," Nate added.

Abe rubbed his hands together and removed his hat.

Sheldon was sufficiently intimidated and could already feel the wrapping paper and heavy guns in his hands. Abe, however, was not.

"They make close to a hundred thousand items here a year. You said you're losing at most twenty guns a week. How is this a big deal and why don't you just tell the cops?"

Nate looked at Abe—who was already taller than his father—as though he couldn't understand how someone so stupid could have come from his own loins.

"Twenty a week is more than eighty a month or upward of a thousand a year. That's more than one percent of the entire inventory, and at twenty dollars retail on average, that's twenty thousand in lost revenues to a corporation that employs thousands of people. Beyond that, if word leaks out that we tolerate this, we put our reputation in jeopardy. I already explained this to you. Reputation is everything. There are already questions being asked because the *Hartford Courant* has heard unconfirmed rumors of our little problem. I'm going to have to solve it before the story breaks."

"The Corbin Detective Agency," Mirabelle said. "Sorry," she added, turning to Sheldon. "I meant Corbin and Horowitz, Private Detectives. Two cases already. Murder and industrial espionage. That gives your Nero Wolfe one on the jaw, doesn't it?" She winked at Sheldon.

"This family is hanging by a thread!" Nate said, raising his voice. "You think this is a joke? You think my brother's death—his father's death—is a joke? Do you?"

"No," said Mirabelle, her eyes narrowing into hatred, her voice sharp, her enunciation perfect. "I think Uncle Joseph was one of the greatest men I've ever known, and I'll probably never meet another man like him. He was kind, strong, masculine, gentle, uncompromising, and more dedicated to his family than any other man I have ever known. I don't know whether a man with a mustache deliberately ran him off the road and killed him or not. But what is absolutely clear to me is that if his death was as equally meaningless as Mom's I'm going to scream and never stop."

"Nothing happened," Nate whispered.

"Nothing happened to Mom," Abe repeated to Mirabelle, placing an understanding hand on her shoulder. "Nothing happened to Uncle Joe either. Nothing's happening in Germany. Nothing's happening in Italy. Nothing's happening in Czechoslovakia or Austria. Henry Ford isn't trying to turn Americans against the Jews, and Congress isn't keeping Jewish refugees out of America. Everything's fine, Mirabelle. We're overreacting. It's all going to work itself out. You'll see. Take Dad's word for it."

Nate took Mirabelle by her upper arm and pulled her in close. "You will remove your mother's evening party gloves and accompany me to my office, where you will do your homework so that someday you might finish high school and not end up a tramp."

"My homework? You think trigonometry is what's standing between me and moral downfall?"

"You will grow into a lady, like your mother, no matter how far back I have to clip your wings to make it happen. And you," he said to Abe. "You will be respectful of Mr. Carmine here and do what he says until I come back and tell you to stop. And you," Nate said to Sheldon, "will drop this nonsense. I am pained by your father's death. I know you are too. But I will not have you distracting us from our grief by a child's revenge fantasy. Are we all clear on how the rest of the morning will progress before we leave for home, dress for synagogue, and bury my brother beside my sister-in-law and my wife?"

LENNY

LENNY BERNSTEIN HAD NEVER RECEIVED a letter before. He'd heard of them. He'd received cards on the holidays from grandparents — cards you shake and watch cash fall out. But a letter? Who'd write him a letter? Sheldon. Sure. He'd mentioned it. But . . . seriously?

"You sure?" Lenny asked the postman, who stood in the doorway with the flat expression of a grown man being questioned by a thirteen-year-old.

"Am I sure this is a letter?" he said.

"A letter for me?"

The postman recovered the letter from Lenny's hands, held it up so they could both see it, and pointed at the addressee line on the white envelope.

"Is your name Lenny Bernstein?"

"Yes."

"Is this your address?"

"Yes."

He handed the letter back to Lenny and wandered off without drawing the last and final conclusion.

Lenny closed the front door and swung onto the sofa of his parents' small Victorian house. The windows were open, and the day was breezy and bright. There was stained glass at the top edge of their bay window that cast orange, yellow, and blue trapezoids over a thinning carpet.

He tore the envelope open as though it were a provocation.

The letter was typed. And typed *badly*. Lenny didn't know that Sheldon could type, but from the looks of it — eraser marks and cross-outs and accidental capital letters here and there, and missing letters elsewhere — it seemed like he was intent on learning at Lenny's expense.

At the top left was Sheldon's return address, just the way Miss Simmons had taught them at school. Below that was the date—September 19—only four days ago. Under that it read, "Dear Lenny."

Dear Lenny!

Dear Lenny!,

Everything and notHing has happened since I got here. I work pope woke up today planning to go to school. Instead, we went to the BColt Armory and I wrapped guns in paper for &four hours and then I changed into black clothes and buried my dad.

It was like burying my mom only I knew he was in the boX this time and I could see the pale bearers pallbearers straining to carry it.

When we had the service for my mom, my dad stood behind me the whole time with his hands on my shoulders. He kept touching my head. I was mAd at him and stuff for burying my mom here and not spreading her ashes back at home, but I wasn't that mad. This time I was standing next to Abe and Mirabelle. They were there the first time too, I guess, but I can't remember them.

I felt like I was a thousand million miles away watching it through a telescope.

When I was little, my dad came into my room one time after I had a bad dream and he explained that we never have the same bad dream twice. They get use d up and never come back. But this funeral was exactly like going bnack to the same bad dream. I stood in the same place and listened to the same bullshit from the same people. Only this time he was missing.

What else? Hartford's got a lot of girls in it. And cars. And horses. It smells bad after it rains, which is exactly when you think it should smell better. I figure all the manure gets stirred up like a brown soup, and if it's hot the next day, the sun burns off the water and you smell it everywhere. Abe calls them shit storms. Maybe that's the history of the term. If not, it should be. Someday we'll only have cars and no horses. Will we still have shit storms? These R things I wonder about.

Abe's OK. He does a lot of push-ups and sit-ups and exercising and stuff, like he's a boxer or something. He's lean and tall and skinny but he's got muscles. I think he's training for the army or else to take on the Mafia single-handed, but Uncle Nate says America isn't ~~gonna~~ going to fight any more of Europe's wars and we're not going to spill any blood to defend all those European kolonies so they're all going to have to work it out.

Abe's not getting on that bus. He keeps reading the papers about what's happening to the Jews and he gets really, really steamed up. He circles the articles and stacks the papers on our dresser in the bedroom. He's really pissed at the Italians who are kicking out all the Jews, and obviously SHitler and the Germans.

Did I tell you about the Mob guy watching us from a car across the street? I'll have to write another letter about that because I've only got the one more piece of paper. That's a whole other thing!

What else?

Anyway, all this with Abe made him get into a fight last Friday. He said there are these guys who listen to some priest on the radio called Charles Coughlin who says the Jews are to blame for everything and are trying to start the war. There were three of them so obviously Abe got his ass kicked but I think he gave as good as he got. Abe said that he knows one of them

from his high school and that the other two are drop-
outs.

Now Abe's all bruised up and he's looking for some
~~rev~~ payback. Says one of the guYs is Willie MacCullen
and that his dad owns a ~~prawn~~pawn shop on Park and he
wants to rob it. Mirabelle loves the idea and—I don't
know, I guess I'm going too.

You know you have to eat this letter after you read
it, right?

So anyway, we're thinking maybe we'll knock it over
tomorrow night. I don't know when you'll get this letter, so maybe by the time it arrives, we'll already
have done it. I suspect so.

What else?

Living in the city is really something else. I get
the feeling all the time like they're trying to civi-
lize me like they did with Huck Finn. Better clothes,
comb my hair, say this, don't say that. I don't like
it so much, but then I look at Mirabelle and see what
being civilized might be like. I worry a little ~~cuz~~
because it's made her elegant and fancy, but it's made
her angry too because she has to keep her mouth shut,
which isn't really for her. She's one confusing girl,
I'll tell you that. And, yeah, she's as pretty as I
remember. Prettier. It sort of hurts.

I still can't believe I'm really here and my parents
aren't. I keep thinking I'm coming home soon. I know
people die. But I guess I didn't realize they stay
dead. Do you know what I mean?

Write back, OK? I want to know what Bruno Krupinski is doing and what's happening to what's left of
my house. And you should get the rifles and stuff from
the shed and hide them. Maybe under your deck would
be a good idea. Once word gets around that we're gone,
someone's going to break in and ~~snatch~~take the stuff.

```
Fy dad's rifle—the one he brought back—is a good one.
Hold on to it. Oil it. Wrap it up. I'm going to be
needing it.
   Your fuddy buddy,
   Sheldon
```

Lenny folded the letter and placed it back into the envelope. Gripping it tightly in his fist, he walked into the kitchen and wordlessly removed a pack of matches from a small iron box beside the fireplace. He lit it on fire and tossed it into the hearth.

PAWNS

Sheldon Horowitz had never robbed anyone of anything other than their smugness, pride, or superiority until he took away the Krupinski brothers' freedom, but that was an exception. He had never stolen stuff. He wasn't a thief and he didn't much like the idea because he didn't want the label. So, breaking into a pawn shop as an act of vengeance was going to be something new especially when he wasn't even avenging himself but someone else for something he didn't understand. Abe saw slights everywhere and in everything. He said anti-Semitism was the water they were all swimming in, but they couldn't see it or taste it because they were too used to it. But he could. He had the sight.

Was it a legitimate reason to knock over McCullen's pawn shop? Probably not. But Abe was family and that was that.

Crouching behind an early 1930s Buick on Park Street in Frog Hollow with Abe and Mirabelle, Sheldon figured he'd be excited by the heist, but he was surprised to find that he wasn't. It seemed like *something* to do rather than *the thing* to do, and since Abe was in charge, Sheldon felt as though he were going along for the ride.

Mirabelle, on the other hand, was loving it. She was dressed in black slacks and a man's black turtleneck sweater, and somehow the masculine clothes made her look even prettier.

Abe signaled that it was time for them to make their move.

It was nine o'clock at night. Nate was at the office as usual, and Abe said he wouldn't be home until close to eleven. That was their window to make the score — or settle one, in any case.

It was Tuesday night and the office workers in the area had all gone home. A few cars were parked along curbs for couples dining out. Two men in hats and jackets strolled by on the opposite sidewalk discussing Roosevelt. Everything was bathed in the yellow of the electric streetlamps.

"So, it's like this," Abe whispered. "There's an alley to the right of the shop. Halfway down there's a door that leads inside. I'll use this crowbar to pry it open. Once we're in there . . . we take what we want. But we do it all quiet-like. Five minutes. We take our bags, we walk out the way we came in, and then we split up and meet back at home."

"With the loot?" asked Mirabelle.

"With the loot," said Abe.

"And why are we doing this again?" Sheldon asked.

"Revenge, Sheldon. It's your idea too."

"Mine?"

"You asked before if we're supposed to sit back and take it. I said no. So here we are."

Sheldon didn't reply. He did, however, reach into the pocket of his trousers and feel his father's brass trench lighter. If there was a question in his fingertips, the lighter didn't answer it.

"OK, let's do it."

Abe stood up and walked across the street with the short crowbar palmed in his hand and running up the length of his arm.

Mirabelle took Sheldon by the hand, smiled at him as though they were about to take a ride at the carnival, and pulled him up and out into the street.

Mirabelle had held his hand at the funeral too, had gripped it wordlessly as the rabbi intoned in a language none of them spoke, even the dead. Here in Frog Hollow, in the after-hours quiet of the downtown district, Sheldon's hand felt warm and hers felt soft. He would have followed her anywhere.

They caught up to Abe in the alley at the door between two garbage bins that stank of rotten meat and buzzed with flies. Abe's hands shook slightly from nerves, his knuckles still bruised from the fight, as he positioned the edge of the crowbar between the door and its frame next to the doorknob. In a swaying and silent count to three, Abe rocked, rocked again, and then —with all his weight—slammed his hip into the bar, ripping the doorknob and its metal guts out of the old wood and onto the street, where it skidded to a halt and glistened like the golden heart of a slain beast.

"We're outlaws now," Abe said. "There's no going back."

Mirabelle smiled; both validated and bemused. Sheldon, however, felt entirely unchanged.

When Abe opened the door, a tiny bell above it rang, and for a moment, they all stood silently. When nothing happened, they moved inside.

Sheldon had never been inside a pawn shop before. He'd seen the outsides; he'd even stared at this one before when walking past. It was located in the first floor of a three-story building. There were two large display windows on either side of a black door. Above the windows, painted by hand, were WE BUY OLD GOLD SILVER & PLATINUM. DIAMONDS, WATCHES AND JEWELRY APPRAISED. 100,000 USED TOOLS FOR ALL TRADES. EXPERT WATCH AND JEWELRY REPAIR. A COMPLETE STOCK OF SHOTGUNS, RIFLES, AMMUNITION, FISHING RODS & REELS. BOUGHT, SOLD, AND EXCHANGED. The one that had caught Sheldon's eye, though, was the last sign over the guitars in the window. In the black of the corridor inside the shop, this is what he wanted to ask Abe about.

"It says accordion lessons are given here," he whispered.

"What?" said Abe.

"Accordion lessons. You can take accordion lessons here."

"So what?"

"Isn't that weird?"

"I don't know. Is it?"

"I think it's weird that anyone wants to take an accordion lesson at all," said Sheldon, trying to keep his voice down.

"I guess." Abe was leading, Sheldon was in the middle, and Mirabelle was behind them. "This isn't important, Sheldon."

"And if you were going to take accordion lessons," continued Sheldon, undeterred by the lack of interest, "why would you do it at a pawn shop? They're not really set up for that, you know. Who wants to go shopping for a watch or a trumpet and listen to some doofus learning the accordion in the corner?"

They entered into the back office, where Teddy McCullen sat day after day buying stolen items from drunks and junkies, and running book on sporting events. His chair was a high steel one made of red Naugahyde with a crack in the middle and a permanent double dimple. It faced a high counter for talking to people on the other side. There was no glass, no chicken wire. The desk was littered with newspapers and books, staplers and tape, a green banker's lamp (off now), and a snow globe with the Terminal Tower inside. Written across the bottom was I'D RATHER BE IN CLEVELAND.

"Why would anyone rather be in Cleveland?" Sheldon whispered.

Mirabelle had lifted the partition to the main room and was starting to place objects in her laundry bag as quietly as possible. She looked focused, discerning, and happy.

"No one would rather be in Cleveland," Abe said, trying to shut Sheldon up by answering his questions for a change. Abe, though, didn't know his cousin well enough yet to know that answers only helped Sheldon further refine his questions.

Abe checked the register for cash and found none. He squatted down and started running his hands beneath the desk looking for keys.

"It's just weird," Sheldon whispered. "The only place you'd buy a snow globe of Cleveland would be Cleveland, and if you were already in Cleveland . . . you wouldn't buy a snow globe saying you'd rather be in Cleveland. Because . . . you'd already be there."

"They're gifts for out-of-town friends, Sheldon. They're tourist kitsch." Abe found two sets of keys that he hoped would open the cabinets to the jewelry and watches. He palmed them carefully and stood up.

"But if no one would rather be there—"

"OK, you know who'd rather be in Cleveland? Jews in Germany. And Italy. And Poland. And Europe in general. They'd rather be in Cleveland."

Sheldon hadn't thought to go international.

"I really need you to focus on stealing, OK?" Abe said, trying desperately to shut Sheldon up. "The accordion lessons don't matter. The snow globe doesn't matter. And if you even *think* of taking the snow globe, I will make you eat it. Are we clear?"

Sheldon nodded while taking the snow globe and placing it gently into his empty laundry sack.

Mirabelle had jimmied the lock on the watch display and was now snatching them up by the handful and dropping them into her bag. Abe opened a display cabinet filled with shotguns and old pistols. He removed a revolver with wood handles and held it up.

"You're heavy," Abe said to the gun.

"It's a Colt 1917 from the war," Sheldon said, glancing at it. "My dad came home with one. He traded it for some traps we use for bobcats. You should see if it's loaded. You just . . ." Sheldon showed Abe how to pull back on the cylinder release.

"Yeah. It's loaded," said Sheldon. "Be careful, OK? It's a double action so pulling the trigger will make the gun shoot even if the hammer isn't pulled back."

"You really know a lot about these things."

"Your Underwood typewriter is more complicated than a gun, Abe."

Sheldon and Abe both heard footsteps and looked over at Mirabelle to see what she was up to. Alone with her wealth of distractions, she'd wrapped a flapper's purple boa around her shoulders and was holding a nickel-plated trumpet over a black case lined with plush green felt.

That was when they heard the unmistakable pump of a shotgun accompanied by footsteps on creaky stairs at the far end of the office behind a door.

"Where does Mr. McCullen live?" Sheldon asked. "Is it possible that he lives upstairs, which is where he teaches the accordion lessons? Because all of a sudden that would make a lot of sense and prove that my question was—"

The door started to open.

Mirabelle might have looked like she was in her own world, but she was the first to take action. She dropped the trumpet, grabbed her bag, and hurled herself toward the exit with the speed of a ferret.

Sheldon—unlike his clever cousin—was frozen in place as he watched Mirabelle run, but his paralysis ended when Abe squeezed off a round from the Colt that shattered a baroque mirror on the far wall. The crash of the falling glass snapped him back, and Sheldon bolted after Mirabelle into the dark corridor under the bell that dangled like mistletoe and out to the alley where they'd come in.

Behind him, Sheldon heard a shotgun blast followed by the pump-chambering of a second shell, but he didn't have long to wonder whether Abe was all right because that second Abe's hand grasped his collar and yanked him out of the alley.

"Faster!" Abe yelled, as though he could command Sheldon's legs to grow.

Mirabelle's purple boa was lying up ahead, discarded in the gray street like an exotic snake, and she was already fifty yards farther on, running as fast as a track star with her bag clenched to her chest. A shadow, she disappeared into a side street as Abe pulled Sheldon in the opposite direction. They sprinted together along the sidewalk, keeping their heads low in case Mr. McCullen had a mind and a chance to shoot them off.

There was no second shotgun blast, and after five solid minutes of running, the boys turned into a large park and fell hard behind a bush, where they panted and watched for the flashing lights of a thousand police cars that never came.

As their hearts slowed and their breathing returned to normal, it was Sheldon who spoke first.

"You're still holding the gun."

Abe was lying on his back in the damp soil under the bush. He squeezed the handle of the gun. "You're right." He opened his laundry bag and tossed it in with his take. Sheldon propped himself onto an elbow, his heart still again, and asked, "Did you shoot at Mr. McCullen?"

"No. I got nervous and squeezed. I'm sure he's fine. I hit the mirror."

"Did he shoot at us?"

"Don't know. Might have been a warning shot." Abe looked down at his own torso and legs and then over at Sheldon. "We look OK."

"Where's Mirabelle?" Sheldon asked.

Abe didn't know. He didn't seem concerned either. She was the fastest runner of the three of them and clearly had the quickest reflexes too. "Home is my guess," he said, lying back again in the damp soil.

Sheldon and Abe looked for trouble as they approached their town house. The street was empty of cops, thugs, or Mr. McCullen. The only light they could see was the electric bulb burning from Mirabelle's window, which they both took as a good sign. Nate's car wasn't there.

The parlor was dark as they stepped inside. Both boys removed their shoes and made their way up the creaky stairs to the second floor. Mirabelle was already showered and dressed for bed in a long satin slip with lace straps. Her hair was pinned back in a ponytail and her light brown eyes blinked at Sheldon, who was staring at her.

"What?" she finally asked.

"Nothing."

"How did you get back so fast?" Abe asked her. Her appearance made him sniff his own clothes. He'd have to shower too.

"I didn't stop. Where have you been?"

"Under a bush in the park."

Mirabelle rubbed her hands together. "Checked your bags yet?"

Abe and Sheldon were still clutching theirs. They both looked down as though they'd forgotten about them. Mirabelle reached out, took both of them, and said, "Come on!"

Sheldon had never been inside Mirabelle's room before. He'd looked in. He'd seen her on the bed. He'd seen the lamp and the book on the end table and the little silver wind-up clock with the bell on top and the red hands. But he'd never gone so far as to push the door open and step inside.

When he did cross the threshold into her room, it was like stepping into an H. G. Wells or Jules Verne story. He could have been stepping onto another planet or out of a submarine onto the bottom of the sea. He didn't feel prepared as he was only wearing socks.

Mirabelle's laundry bag of stolen items was on her desk. Sheldon had remembered it being black, like any good robber's bag, but now he saw it was a deep purple. Where would she had gotten a purple laundry bag? In the light of her room—with the door now closed behind them—Sheldon saw that his own bag was actually a dark-blue pillowcase and Abe's was the matching one. Without ceremony, Mirabelle dumped her bag onto her quilted bedspread.

Everything sparkled like a pirate's treasure. There were a dozen wristwatches, two dozen rings of a thousand colors, and necklaces and bracelets and earrings. Everything she took was small and looked priceless, though Sheldon knew immediately it couldn't all be precious as they'd robbed a pawn shop, not a jewelry store. Then again, he was no judge. Maybe the jewelry was gold. Maybe it was plated. Maybe it was bronze. For the moment, though, it didn't matter. It glistened.

Mirabelle ran her hands through it all without grasping any one piece. She lifted a handful of loot gently from the bed and let the pieces fall back down. She smiled at them with a look of guilt-free joy. "We're rich!"

"We're thieves," said Abe.

"We're both," she said, smiling. "What did you get?"

Abe dumped out his bag. Twenty-one dollars in cash fell out along with four boxes of bullets, the Colt pistol, a stapler, a dozen silver necklaces, a man's Freemason ring, and a pinkie ring with a skull on it.

"Huh," said Mirabelle. "You stole his stapler?"

"I guess so."

"You get any staples?"

"No."

Mirabelle reached for the pistol, and Sheldon immediately said, "It's loaded."

She pulled back her hand. "Maybe you should take it."

"I don't want it. Why would I want it?"

"I'll keep it," said Abe. "Maybe we can finally tap on the window of the Mafia guy who's usually out there. Find out who he is, what he wants, and then tell him he can't have it."

Mirabelle picked up a silver Hamilton wristwatch with a black face and leather strap, and handed it to Sheldon. "A present."

Sheldon took it and held it as though it were an actual present she'd picked out at a fancy department store or jewelry shop instead of an item she'd recently lifted in a heist. Aside from his father's enormous Austrian wall clock, Sheldon had never owned a watch before. His father had one, and when Sheldon was little, he'd play with it—and chew it, according to his mother—but he'd never worn one. Even holding it made him feel more adult.

"Thanks," he said.

"Did you get me a present too?"

It was a good question, actually. Sheldon lifted up his own pillowcase and dumped the contents on the bed. As he did, he became painfully aware that he had missed the point of the night's activity.

The snow globe—and nothing else—hit the bed, bounced once, and settled.

The snow inside whirled around the Terminal Tower in a frantic and harmless storm.

Mirabelle picked it up and made a cooing noise as though she were lifting a kitten from a basket. Abe closed his eyes in disgust, but Mirabelle's theatrics made him smile and all three started to laugh.

"Cleveland," she said. "How did you know?"

CHER AMI

MIRABELLE WAS A JUNIOR in high school. She had told her father that her best subject was English because she knew that girls were supposed to like English, reading novels about sad people, and correcting grammar so they can become secretaries and perform the general etiquette of ladyhood. It wasn't true, though. She really liked science, and her favorite class was biology. Assigned to the second seat in the third row from the left, Mirabelle would sit with rapt attention as she listened to Mr. Knightly talk about anatomy and procreation and breeding animals and how this taught us a thing or two about evolution. Today, however, was proving especially interesting because Mr. Knightly was talking about one of his great passions: pigeons. It was less a study of birds than of history, but he did have a tendency to speak to his interests, which may have been what made it all interesting.

Pigeons had never remotely interested Mirabelle. They were filthy things that soiled benches and cooed most uncharmingly, but Mr. Knightly was insistent that they were fascinating, and he was going to prove it to them. Before getting into the science of it, he wanted to explain why.

"Come, come. Come forward. Out of the seats; forget the seats," he said. He was a short, slender man. He had a face one couldn't imagine without his glasses. His hair was blond, longer than it should be, and unruly to distraction. He was unmarried and of an indeterminate age. Nothing he said, and no tone in his voice, ever suggested that he wanted to be anywhere or doing anything but teaching his students about the world. "Come closer. Come see with your own eyes.

"What is it?" he asked, pointing at a bird in a cage.

The class giggled.

"Come on. I'll give you a hint. It's not a turtle. OK, your turn."

"It's a pigeon," said a male voice behind Mirabelle. She'd moved to the front and had sat on a desk, which she'd never done. She crossed her ankles and leaned forward as though examining a magical work of art.

The class giggled again. The obviousness of it all, the foolishness.

"Yes, yes," said Mr. Knightly. "But what kind? What makes it special? Anything? Anyone? Anything . . . unusual?"

"There's something on its left leg," said Mirabelle—though she hadn't expected to say anything. His question had seemed to be directed to her in such a way that she'd been unable to remain aloof. She leaned in farther . . . far enough to risk falling off her desk. At first, she thought it was one of those scientific markers with numbers on them, but that wasn't it. It looked like a long bullet attached by rings to the bird's leg.

"Any guesses as to what it is?" asked Mr. Knightly.

The other students leaned in closely too. No one uttered a sound.

"I could tell you," whispered Mr. Knightly. "But why tell you when I can show you?"

The cage opened with a clinking sound, and the pigeon responded by hopping onto Mr. Knightly's extended hand. He then grasped the pigeon gently and extended the pigeon's leg. With his right hand, he unscrewed a tiny cap on top of the cartridge. From it, he pulled out a tiny scroll. Ever so carefully, he unrolled it and handed it to Mirabelle.

The paper was very small but not so small that she couldn't read it. It was typed on a pinkish slip of paper. At the top, it said, "Pigeon Message."

"Go on, read it aloud. It's the start of a very sad story," said Mr. Knightly.

```
We are along the road paralell to 276.4. Our own ar-
tillery is dropping a barrage directly on us. For
heavens sake stop it.
    Whittlesey
    Maj. 308th.
```

The class did not make a sound. They were confused at first. "Is that real?" asked Matty Tomlin.

"Yes," said Mr. Knightly.

"Someone wrote that? That happened?" asked a boy who rarely spoke.

"This pigeon," Mr. Knightly replied, "is a homing pigeon. Sometimes they're called carrier pigeons or messenger pigeons. The one who carried that very real and very specific message was named Cher Ami. Back in October of 1918, Major Charles Whittlesey was in the Argonne Forest in France. His five hundred and fifty men were surrounded by German troops. To make matters worse, the Americans were dropping artillery fire on Whittlesey and his men. The Americans didn't know this, of course, and it wasn't intentional, but it was devastating. Unable to signal their location, Major Whittlesey sent Cher Ami into the air with that desperate message. The bird flew straight into enemy fire, and Whittlesey and his men saw Cher Ami shot down. You can just imagine the horror and the sudden desolation of knowing that your only chance at survival had fallen from the sky in front of your very eyes. Moments later, though, and against all odds, Cher Ami rose again into the air and took flight! Through air riddled with bullets, choking on smoke, and his tiny ears clapped by the thunder of artillery every second, the pigeon flew twenty-five air miles through enemy territory into the Allied sector. When Cher Ami arrived, they inspected him. He'd been shot by the Germans and his right leg was barely attached to his body. He was blind in one eye. The capsule with Major Whittlesey's message, however, was still clamped to his leg. They read it and immediately stopped the shelling. By the time Whittlesey's battalion was rescued, one hundred and seven men had been killed, and one hundred and ninety had been injured. Major Whittlesey was awarded the Medal of Honor whereas poor Cher Ami's leg had to be amputated. In time, the 308th became known as the Lost Battalion. A silent movie was made about them. Cher Ami was awarded the French Croix de Guerre with palm. He died at Fort Monmouth in New Jersey in 1919 from his wounds, and he was taxidermied."

The students were all silent. Mirabelle held the message as though it were the first copy of the Torah. Their reverie was broken when a boy named Michael Ashton ventured, "Mr. Knightly. How do you have the message?"

"I don't. It's a copy. I know, so unfair! You feel cheated! But don't. I took a photograph of the exhibit when I toured Washington, and then I typed it up for dramatic effect and put it on Herman here. Herman, I think we can all admit, isn't a very good name for a war pigeon, to be honest. Can you imagine pointing at the sky and shouting, 'Here comes Herman! We're all saved!' I can't. And I'm the one who just said it! Luckily, there's no war. Herman here has never heard a noise louder than a car horn and has never faced anything more dangerous than limp lettuce and raindrops."

The windows all began to rattle. A wind was picking up outside. Mr. Knightly looked at the windows with some dismay.

"Speaking of which," he said, "it's getting windy out there. We're going to have to hurry in case there's a storm. Because today we're going to release Herman from the loft that I put on the roof and send him to the eleventh grade class at Marblehead High School north of Boston, more than one hundred and twenty miles away from here. I'm including a note that says, 'Looks like a big storm is coming!' Who's with me?"

They thought he was joking. Mirabelle spun her new sapphire ring around and around on her middle finger in nervous excitement, an excitement that had carried over from the thrill of the heist to her mad run through the streets of Hartford to the thrill of Mr. Knightly's lesson — both tragic and soaring.

Mirabelle was feeling good.

James Bianchi must have sensed Mirabelle's mood and misunderstood its source and meaning, because he placed his hand on her thigh as the other students slid off their desks and started to walk outside.

Mirabelle had made the modest mistake of making out with James after the Christmas dance last year. It had started off sweetly enough with his soft lips and closed eyes, his hands resting on her shoulders as if she were a statue of Venus (with arms). But after the tip of her tongue touched his and created a wave of pleasure in them both, his hands filled with lead and dropped immediately away. Mirabelle thought he had shorted out like a cheap lamp bulb, but she was wrong. His hands had gone right to her ass. The squeeze made Mirabelle open her eyes and retract her tongue. When she did, she found that his eyes were already open.

It was like looking into an octopus.

So, she bit his lip.

Hard.

James had yelled and grabbed his face. He started calling her names she didn't deserve, and his eyes became hostile and threatening. Instead of stepping back and recoiling, Mirabelle had shifted her weight forward and closed ranks on him, almost daring him to try something. From her new battle stance, her eyes took in all the light, and her sensations all the details. That was how she felt the drop of his blood drip from her own lip and fall into her outstretched hand. James watched her lick the rest of the blood from her lips and then smile. Mirabelle wondered if she was a vampire because she felt charged and electric and his blood tasted sweet.

"Sorry, Jimmy," she said, not sorry. "You startled me."

James Bianchi turned wordlessly and staggered away down the hallway toward the boys' room. Mirabelle had gone back to the dance and spent her time swinging with Katy Fisher to the school band playing a decent rendition of Benny Goodman's "Swingtime in the Rockies."

Mirabelle looked down at James's hand loitering on her thigh now. What did he think he was doing? It wasn't an apology. It wasn't a sign of affection; he hadn't said a direct word to her since he had stopped bleeding back in December. Was he making a pass at her in the middle of biology class?

People's motivations didn't make a lot of sense to Mirabelle. What she understood best was what she liked and what she didn't like. And this she didn't like.

James looked at her.

She looked at him.

He smiled a smarmy smile, and so Mirabelle smiled back and stuck a pencil in his ear.

James spun off toward the display cabinet filled with animal parts in jars and smashed into it, knocking over a squirrel fetus in formaldehyde as Mirabelle scampered away—free of consequences, of guilt, of history—to catch up with the rest of the class on the roof, where the wind was bashing the door against the concrete wall outside.

The students there were laughing and raising their arms like wings as Mr. Knightly let go of Herman, who soared into the sky with the speed of a soul that had been too long from heaven.

STORM

T HE GUST THAT LIFTED Herman skyward was indeed becoming a storm. Out on the coast far south of the school, boats were blissfully unaware of the weather coming in because the newspapers had been wrong. In the late morning, adventurers had sailed out for leisure or fishing in Long Island Sound. On the Atlantic side, they entered the open waters of the New York Bight.

By two in the afternoon, however, the weather had changed. And by four o'clock on September 21, 1938, New England was facing a hurricane.

Not that Sheldon knew this at first.

He was walking home from school when the first drops of rain came down. Not straight down, though. They whipped at his face like tiny razors.

The last time he had been soaked was when he walked back from the crash, and he wasn't in the mood to do it again. It wasn't the water that bothered him, it was the emotions that overtook him and made him tear up. Pulling his schoolbag closer, Sheldon broke into a jog as the sun failed and the sky became as black as a moonless night. A wind picked up that was violent.

Sheldon was only two blocks from home, but the spectacle of Hartford under the onslaught was so intense that he stopped under a blue and white awning by a grocery store to watch. Three women and two businessmen had already taken shelter there.

"The newspaper said nothing about a storm," said a man in a black suit and wing tips.

"Nope," muttered one of the women.

The rain was now pounding down so hard that cars were pulling over, their drivers unable to see out of the windshields. The shower was turning into a stream, and the stream into a river over the black asphalt of the street as it ripped through the city center as if poured from a bucket.

Rainstorms in New England were not unfamiliar. Usually, in Sheldon's experience, the heavier the storm, the shorter it lasted. But this time was different. The wind was bending the trees across the street at impossible angles until one of them snapped. The adults all gasped, and the three women went inside, away from the windows.

He could have gone inside too, but Sheldon decided to run. Clutching his schoolbag against his chest, he was drenched in an instant; his soggy shoes slapped their way down the street and up the steps to the Corbins' town house.

The hurricane of 1938 had hit.

Dripping wet, Sheldon removed his shoes and walked into the center of the living room, where he stared out the giant bay window at the chaos outside. The giant oak tree that had been blocking the view of the street with its thick leaves had lost one of its main branches. Sheldon stepped backward from the maelstrom and bumped into a dining-room chair, which he sat on; he stared at the storm as though it were a newsreel from the front of a war.

This was supposed to be a day to plan out his investigation, solve the mystery of who killed his father, and then plot his revenge. As Sheldon could best reckon it, Nero Wolfe would have made a list of all the companies that bought pelts in Hartford and then he'd have sent Archie Goodwin out to interview them all and ask whether they bought from the Krupinski brothers. "The blue Ford Model 51," he'd have said to shake up their memories. "Shiny. Not new, but new for them. Had their names stenciled on the side like they were something. You know the one."

Would anyone answer these questions from a kid? How does a twelve-year-old get adults to talk about adult stuff?

It felt hopeless. How does a kid get things done in this world?

Sheldon stood and trailed water across to the kitchen, where he found some cookies in a glass jar and helped himself to three. He returned to the chair and watched the storm while crunching the small nuts in his molars.

And . . . were these pieces of chocolate? He'd heard about these; Lenny had been going on about them. Some woman who ran the Toll House Inn got the idea of putting chocolate in cookies, and it appeared in the papers, and now the country was going wild. Toll House cookies they were calling them. Mirabelle must have heard about this and given it a go.

They were good. Very good.

Sheldon sat there, sopping wet, eating cookies, and watching pieces of wood fly past the window while the rain came down in an epic torrent.

What if?

What if he made a list of shops that sold fur items like coats and gloves and such? He could probably learn that from newspaper advertisements and even the phone book, no need to be a gumshoe. And then, instead of being disappointed that he wasn't a grown-up, he could walk in and say, "Hey, my uncles are the Krupinskis from Massachusetts. I got a message for the man who buys their stuff." If the owner looked confused or said that he didn't know them, Sheldon could move on. On the off chance someone said, "Yeah, what's the message?" he could say, "Yeah, they were arrested for arson and they're going to be in jail for a while, so you might need to buy from someone else." And then he could look carefully into their eyes and see if that was surprising. Maybe one of them would say, "Arrested? Aren't they supposed to be dead? My guy was supposed to run those bastards off the road," and Sheldon would say, "Which guy was that?" And the boss would say, "Oh, that was Reggiano Grana Padano. Yeah, he drives everyone off the road for the right price if I tell him to," and then Sheldon would say, "Where is he? I want to meet the guy." And the boss would say, "Oh, he's down at the Irish bar pretending he's Irish. If you take the gun your cousin stole from McCullen, you can probably pop him right there." All this would be great news, and Sheldon could shoot the guy he was talking to, because he'd been the one who ordered the hit in the first place, and then he could head down to the pub, pop Grana Padano after saying, "Remember me, asshole? I'm back," which would put the whole thing to rest before *The Lone Ranger* went on the radio later tonight. That is, unless all the power lines and radio stations were out by then, because this storm was looking crazy-ass crazy.

Chocolate *in* the cookies. It was genius, really.

Abe and Mirabelle burst into the house as Sheldon was finishing his fourth, which, now that he had company and self-insight, might have been at least two too many.

"Hi," he said to them.

Mirabelle was laughing with her hand pressed against the wall for balance, but Abe looked more serious. He said, "Power lines are down everywhere. I saw three cats in trees, and then I turned around and there were two."

Mirabelle stopped laughing. "Where did the cat go?"

"After your pigeon," said Abe.

Mirabelle shook out her hair like a shaggy dog, kicked off her waterlogged leather shoes, and as she walked toward the stairs, she left behind wet stocking prints on the floor. She went upstairs to change. Abe wiped his face and dried his hair with a kitchen towel. "When did you get back?" he asked Sheldon.

"A few minutes ago."

Abe had a mischievous look to him. He turned to Sheldon. "Want to throw a ball?"

"You mean a baseball?"

"On the sidewalk, away from the power lines. I want to see what'll happen."

For the next ten minutes, they comically tried to throw balls to each other with twenty feet between them while standing in knee-deep rushing water. They never caught a single one. The answer to Abe's question was "you lose baseballs."

Something metal made a crashing and screeching sound down the street and they stopped to look.

One car had skidded into another one that was parallel parked on the opposite side of their street, and was now sideways and stalled. Water and debris were building up on the driver's side of the car, which was serving as a dam to the floodwater, which quickly rose until it covered the driver's window. The man inside opened the passenger's-side door and stepped out. Losing his footing immediately, he was knocked down again and again by the rapids until he finally reached a streetlamp and recovered his footing. Once on the sidewalk and out of the center of the road, he waded knee-deep through the water into the deli across the street and disappeared inside.

Abe, who'd been watching the man, started looking around and noticed something else. "He's not here."

"Who?"

"The thug who's been watching us from across the street. He's not here."

FLOOD

NATE WAS HOME BY SEVEN when the worst of the storm had moved north to Massachusetts. Nate instructed the children to place blankets over their bedroom windows in case the glass blew out. With no view outside, the house became a crypt. That night, Abe, Mirabelle, and Sheldon played poker on the living-room floor by candlelight. Their primary radio ran off the AC electric grid that was down, but Nate still had a battery-operated farm radio, the kind they had in Whately before the town had power.

The radio played as they did.

At 8:00 Sheldon insisted they listen to *The Lone Ranger* on WTHT, which met no objections. At 8:30, they tuned into *Tommy Dorsey* on WTIC, then *Bob Crosby's Orchestra* back on WTHT at 9:00. *George Olson's Orchestra* came on at 9:30, which bored them all, but *The Greatest Man in the World* broadcast at 10:00 on the same station so they left it on. After that, Nate told them to clear out and go to bed.

Schools would be closed the next day; the radio had announced it. Nate opened a liquor cabinet and removed a bottle of Teacher's Highland Cream and poured himself a tall whiskey.

In Sheldon's half of the room, he sat across from Abe, who was stripped down to his tank top and boxer shorts. His knuckles were still scarred, the swelling in his eye was still fresh, and Sheldon could see the purple bruises on his forearms where he'd warded off blows from McCullen's son and the other bastards who'd assaulted him. On his pinkie (now that his father was out of sight), he had slipped on the skeleton ring they'd stolen from the shop. In that getup, Abe looked like a silent killer. It made Sheldon wish he looked big and scary too.

"I'm never going to find him," Sheldon said to Abe.

Mirabelle had given Abe a new watch also, a Zenith with a black face, a black leather strap, and white hands. He held it as if it were a small pet and wound it slowly; it sounded like a safe being cracked by a master thief.

"Mustache man?"

"No one's going to tell a kid anything," Sheldon said. "I thought I knew where to begin. But I don't. Not really."

"Where were you going to begin?"

"Find out who bought stuff from the Krupinskis. Find out who they screwed over. Follow the bread crumbs back to mustache man."

"You think he's here in Hartford?"

"Or Springfield. Lenny said he could be in Miami, though. Or Paris. That it was all in my head."

"He's sort of right. I mean, yeah, mustache man's probably around here, but he could just as well be in Boston or New York as Hartford so that's not a good plan. Your problem is that you're looking through the wrong end of the telescope, Sheldon."

Sheldon's feet twitched. They did this when he grew contemplative.

"Think about it," Abe added. "Who knows the business associates of the Krupinskis?"

"I have no idea."

"It's like your brain is avoiding the answer. Let me ask you an entirely unrelated question. Who knows who all your friends are?"

"I do."

"Who knows all your enemies?"

"I do."

"Let's try again. Who knows everyone the Krupinskis do business with?"

Oh.

"The Krupinskis know."

Abe silently saluted him with two fingers from his bed.

"The brothers are in jail," Sheldon said. "Only Old Krupinski's left and he won't tell me nothing."

"What's his real name?"

"Bruno."

"That's a dog's name."

Sheldon didn't disagree.

Abe placed his watch on his thigh and, reaching up with his right hand, opened the top drawer of his dresser and removed the revolver.

"One of the reasons there are guns," Abe said, "is to even things out between people who are big and strong and wrong, and people who are short and weak and right."

"Is that still loaded?" Sheldon asked. "My dad was really serious about unloading weapons we weren't using."

"I don't know how to unload it."

"It's simple, you just—"

"I don't give a shit. Listen, Sheldon. You take a gun—this one if you want—and you walk right into Old Bruno's house and you ask him who killed your father. You're twelve. You're not scary, I get that. Your balls haven't even dropped yet. But Mr. Colt made this gun scary enough to even things out for you. If Old Bruno knew your dad, then he knows about you and he won't have any doubt that you know how this thing works. You've killed a hundred animals, Sheldon. He's just one more monkey. So, you point it at him and say, 'Tell me who killed my dad and I won't shoot you.' Now, he probably won't believe you, and even dashing off a round might not scare him. So, you need a bigger plan and here's what I think." Abe tapped his temple with the barrel of the gun. "You say you're going to shoot him in the head and then make it look like suicide. To make that believable, you hold up a piece of paper and say it's his suicide note. You already wrote it. So, he has to make a choice."

Abe looked over at his Underwood typewriter, still cooling from Sheldon's marathon letter-writing session to Lenny. "No need to bluff either. You could type up a nice suicide note for him right there. Read it to him. Something like 'Without my precious sons in my meaningless life, I've got nothing. I'm alone and only getting more alone. I have nothing to live for. So long, cruel world.'"

"That's terrible," Sheldon said.

"There's time to work on it. The point is, you show up and demand answers. I can come with you if you want. I got nothing to lose."

"Would you really? You'd come with me?"

"I've always wanted to see where you grew up. My dad's from there and we never go. I'd like to see it."

"Yeah, but I burned the house down. There's nothing to see anymore."

"Dad said the crazy brothers did it."

"No, I did it. I lied to get them locked up."

Sheldon told him the story. Abe listened, expressionless. When Sheldon was finished, Abe said, "They said that? About the fucking Jews and coming back for the piles of gold?"

"I didn't say gold."

"It's what they meant. They think Jews sit on piles of gold like that dragon in *The Hobbit*."

"What's a hobbit?"

"It's like a dwarf but less hairy and with better manners. It's from a new book that just came out. You might like it. Anyway, they said that?"

"Yeah, they said it."

"So, you did what you had to do."

"Maybe I didn't have to."

"Oh, please," said Abe, his admiration turning into total disgust. "Jews wait too long to throw a punch, and we're always second-guessing ourselves. You think the fuckin' Italians are out there second-guessing themselves? You think the Irish are? The Greeks? The Russians? You think people in the Mob are thinking, 'Oh no, should we really have slit this guy's throat from ear to ear? Maybe he wasn't going to say nothing. Maybe we were hasty.'"

Abe chuckled at his own joke. He tossed the revolver back into his underwear drawer and pushed it closed. He picked up the watch again. He turned the crown backward. Slowly. Clicking and clicking again.

Sheldon didn't understand any of this. He didn't know anything about people from those countries. In Whately, the world was made of only Christians and two Jewish families. All the Christians were Protestant and interchangeable; if they had heritage from Europe, it never came up in conversation. Here, according to Abe, the Christians were broken up into groups, and they all had qualities that Abe thought were self-evident.

"You know why, don't you?" Abe said.

"Why what?"

"Why we keep second-guessing ourselves. It's because we're trapped. Don't you see? Henry Ford is blaming us for the Depression. The Nazis are saying we're all communists and degenerates. You know this guy Julius Streicher? After the Berlin Olympics two years ago, he says they're going to need to exterminate all the Jews. That means murder, Sheldon. Fuckin' Roosevelt won't let in the refugees because he says they're a threat to national security. Says that if America lets in the refugees — Jews like us — some are going to be commies and others — well, they won't be fascists, but they'll report back to the Germans because if they don't, the Germans will kill their relatives. It's in all the papers! Mr. Olson waves them around every Thursday."

"Who?"

"Mr. Olson. My social studies teacher. He hates the Nazis something fierce and he shows us this stuff. It's right in the papers! It's not like it's a secret or anything. It's everywhere. I collect them." Abe nodded toward the dresser, but Sheldon already knew this.

Sheldon looked outside at the storm. His father had once told him that glass is actually a liquid. When Joseph was in France, he saw stained-glass windows at a cathedral and the priest showed him how the bottom of each windowpane was thicker than the top. "They're melting," the priest had said. Joseph said it was an amazing thing to consider. Not only the fact of the windows, but to have been discussing something so small in the midst of something so big.

Sheldon thought that Abe was waving around pieces of paper in a world that looked solid but was actually melting. The difference here was that no one was bothering to talk about it.

"Here's why Jews are silent about it all. Two Jews are accused of killing a Christian," Abe said, setting up a joke. "They're facing the firing squad. One of them puffs out his chest and yells, 'What would you do? Would you stand there like cowards and murder two innocent men?' and his friend, tied to the other pole, whispers, 'Don't make trouble.'"

Abe didn't laugh. Neither did Sheldon.

"We're quiet, they come for us. We speak up, they come faster. I'm telling you, Sheldon. We're getting squeezed. And I'm not going to stand around like that guy tied to the pole. Neither one of them. I'm not letting it get that far."

Sheldon woke to Mirabelle's face. She was kneeling over him, and the longest strands of her hair were tickling his nose and cheeks. She was smiling weakly at him. Her eyes, he noticed, were more hazel than brown. There was an explosion of green around the pupil. He didn't want to speak because he didn't want anything to change.

For some reason, his pillow was wet.

"Morning, sleepyhead. There's work to do."

Work?

"I thought school was canceled," Sheldon said, rubbing his left eye.

"It is. Which is why you and Abe are going to help Dad sandbag the Connecticut River with about a thousand men from the WPA."

Sheldon turned his head toward the window. The wind had let up, but the gutter had broken, and now the rainwater was pouring onto the glass and obstructing everything outside.

"It's raining," said Sheldon. "A lot."

"The river is rising six inches an hour. It's going to overflow the dikes. Dad wants you and Abe to help make it stop."

Sheldon had looked at Mirabelle many times, most often when she wasn't looking back. He had never stared so directly into her eyes at such close range.

"That doesn't make any sense," Sheldon said.

"You stack sandbags and they keep the water back."

"No, I mean . . . if they have a thousand people stacking up bags, they don't need me."

"They don't."

"So . . . ?"

"Dad needs you. He wants Mr. Henkler and Mr. Stone to know that the Corbin men were there with their sleeves rolled up helping save the company."

"I'm a Horowitz man."

"Yeah. Well."

"That's nuts," said Sheldon.

"It is. It's also true. Most things are nuts and true."

"If that was true," said Sheldon, framed by her hair that smelled like almonds and chamomile, "that would be nuts."

"Now you're getting it."

Mirabelle stood and Sheldon sat up. He had put himself to sleep thinking about the mystery of who was stealing the guns from the armory. It didn't affect him much, but he liked the puzzle. If guns were being smuggled out, but all the doors had guards who were checking the workers' bags and pockets, how were they getting out?

Nero Wolfe would have made a giant map of the armory and used a red wax pencil to mark all the entrances and exits. Uncle Nate said that most of the windows don't open, but the buildings are enormous so obviously some of them do. If there was a dumpster outside, one of the men could be tossing the guns out and collecting them later. Or some men below the window could stretch out a blanket and a worker inside could throw the weapons out and have them land in the blankets like the people who jump from windows and are caught by firemen in the Buster Keaton movie he once saw before he stopped going to the theater.

The chances of getting caught, though, seemed rather high. Until recently, Sheldon had never tried to get away with much. Maybe it was easier to get away with things if you're of a mind for it. Abe certainly seemed to be. He wanted to get in as much trouble as he could, as though he could bust out of the problems of the world single-handedly like the Phantom or the new Superman guy.

None of this explained why his pillow was wet, though.

Lenny had said he'd seen one of those comic books, but Sheldon was pretty sure he hadn't. The newsstand in Whately didn't have any copies of anything back in June, or July, or August, and where had Lenny been other than Whately since then? Nowhere, that's where. How he got hold of his one-and-only copy of *The Escapist* from Empire Comics, Sheldon still didn't know, but beyond that, Lenny's cache was limited. He must have heard about it in the newspaper or on the radio and tried to embellish. Lenny did that sort of thing. He wasn't a liar; he would never lie to Sheldon. But he liked to add to stories to make them more interesting to people.

Like that time he found some pictures of naked girls and said they were French.

"How the hell do you know they're French?" Sheldon had wanted to know.

Lenny — unlike Sheldon — had finished his bar mitzvah over the summer and was therefore a man according to Jewish law and tradition, which meant little in their rural New England village, but at that point in their conversation, it had meant everything to Lenny.

"Ah, you're still a kid," he said. "What do you know?"

One black-and-white photograph showed a naked woman on her knees facing the camera with a smile. She was in a field with a wooden barn in the distance. Her arms were locked behind her head, and her sloping breasts pointed menacingly at the boys.

"She's not speaking French," said Sheldon. "She's not wrapped in the French flag. I don't see a bicycle with a basket holding any of those French breads. I think you got suckered."

"What difference does it make, Sheldon? It's a real girl, all naked and smiling. When have you seen one of those? Don't touch it, for God's sake," Lenny said, smacking Sheldon's hand away from the photo.

"Why not?"

"I don't want to be thinking that you've touched it."

"Is that the only one or have you got more?"

Lenny had one more he'd been protecting in a newspaper. In this one, a topless woman posed with a lyre. She was sitting without a smile and a sheer skirt was draped around her thighs. Her hair was short, dark, and perfect, as if she were in a silent film. Her eyes were enormous and her look coquettish.

"This one's classy," said Sheldon, taking it out of Lenny's hands and slapping away his attempt to retrieve it. "The first one looks like she's laying an egg. But this one. I'd like to meet her."

"Yeah. You'd know what to do," Lenny had said.

Lenny's discarded newspaper was the *Fitchburg Sentinel* from July 11, 1938. Splashed across the top was the banner headline, HUGHES SPANS AT-LANTIC IN 16 1/2 HOURS, with a side column titled, TEN KILLED IN PAL-ESTINE AMBUSCADE — BOMBINGS, SLAYINGS TERRORIZE DISTRICTS AS ARABS WAGE UNRELENTING WAR ON JEWS.

Lenny folded the front page into a boat.

Sheldon pawed the card with the musical nymph, ignoring Lenny's handiwork.

"I'd know," said Sheldon, after deep consideration. "I already know what goes where, and after that . . . I wouldn't be afraid to ask questions."

Sheldon wished that Lenny had seen that Superman comic and could tell him more about it. It seemed to Sheldon that Abe wanted to be someone like that; someone to correct the wrongs of the world all by himself.

Sheldon still wasn't sure whether Abe's claims about anti-Semitism were real. He couldn't see it, or touch it, or taste it. It wasn't in the laws like it was in Germany, or the way that the Negroes had separate schools. That was all written down. It was law. It was policy. Abe kept saying it was there, but Uncle Nate said it wasn't. Either way, Sheldon was off to sandbag the river and keep it from overpowering the dike that protected Colt.

Mirabelle was still standing over him smelling like she did.

"I don't want to get wet," Sheldon said. "I hate getting wet in the rain. I have my reasons. Also, I can't swim. Not so good, anyway."

"You just need to look busy," Mirabelle said. "No one's expecting you to be very helpful. You're twelve."

"Noah's storm wasn't this bad. It was only longer," said Sheldon, in a last-ditch effort to go absolutely nowhere.

Mirabelle had said the river was rising six inches an hour. Maybe that meant the rain was falling six inches an hour — or close enough — which was the same as . . . one hundred and forty-four inches a day. Divided by twelve, that was twelve feet a day. Twelve feet a day times forty days was . . . almost five hundred feet of water! That would have covered everything. Sheldon didn't know how tall Mount Ararat was but . . . close, right?

"You're exaggerating," Mirabelle said.

"No. I'm really not!"

Sheldon wasn't simply "wet" as he tried to lift the fifty-pound sandbag onto his shoulder like the other men who were building the dike.

Ducks get wet.

Penguins get wet.

Otters get wet.

Those things get wet and then they get dry again. Those things only get wet on the outside. Sheldon was wet on the *inside*. This was a never-going-to-be-dry-again kind of wet.

Every step he took was like lifting a tree trunk rather than a leg. Every move of his arm was like wading through the rapids of a river. Every moment that passed was one step closer to being filled up like a water balloon and then chucked off a high bridge into a wide barge where he'd explode and there'd be nothing left but little scraps of clothing and eyebrows.

Abe was beside him in the storm with a bag on his shoulder the size of a giant dead dog. The river was filling up in front of him. The armory was a hundred yards behind them, where teams of men working like a chain gang were carrying boxes of materials out the front door and — assisted by staff — carting them off to higher ground.

Abe whacked his sandbag into place and turned for another.

"How long have we been here?" Sheldon yelled through the rain and the sounds of the men working and the trucks that were running.

"Nine minutes," Abe shouted.

"It really feels longer."

"Think of how it is for the men who are actually carrying things," Abe shouted.

Everyone around Sheldon was carrying things.

"I weigh a hundred pounds," yelled Sheldon. "The bags weigh fifty."

"So?"

"Fifty when they're dry. They aren't dry anymore. Now they weigh more than I do. I can't lift more than me."

"Stop whining, Sheldon!"

"Where's Mr. Henkler?"

Sheldon didn't like talking because it helped the rain get into his mouth and make him even wetter, if that was possible. Also, everything was loud. The rain made a constant noise so every man on the line yelled to be heard. The river below him was pressing itself into knots as white rapids formed on the surface. Sheldon shaded his eyes with a hand on his forehead because it helped him hear Abe's answer somehow.

"He's inside."

"Inside?"

"Yes!" said Abe, as his sack thunked down on the others. Sheldon followed him to the truck where the others were stacked.

"Where's Uncle Nate?"

"I don't know."

"So why are we doing this if no one's around to care?"

"For God's sake, Sheldon. You do it because it needs to be done!"

That wasn't good enough for Sheldon. He couldn't lift a bag from the truck, let alone carry it twenty feet and slam it down on a pile that was now up to his waist.

"I need to pee," he yelled.

Two men nearby smiled and shook their heads. Sheldon didn't care and neither did his bladder. If all went well, he could probably unscrew his leg and empty that out too.

When Sheldon turned toward the armory, it looked foreboding and alien in the gray and the wet, but he didn't care. The giant Aladdin dome with the stars was sopping wet, which you wouldn't expect of an Arabian artifact but there it was. Beneath the blue dome was a door and inside the door was a flight of stairs leading up to the landing with Mr. Henkler's office where — very nearby — was a toilet.

Inside the antechamber of an enormous hall, the worker bees were collecting crates and carrying them out. Crates of equipment, of machined parts, of complete weapons — a depot of armaments that could have supplied the Union against the Confederates. The floor was an inch deep in water, and a large man with strong arms tried to hand Sheldon a box half his size, but Sheldon put up his hand to signal he wasn't interested. "I'm going to the bathroom," he announced, and he walked on with an air of propriety that quelled any questions.

The stairs were also wet. He couldn't imagine why one of the worker bees downstairs from the WPA or Colt would have come up to the executive offices, but he followed the footprints until they ended at Mr. Henkler's door. Sheldon, on an impulse to satisfy his curiosity and solve this minor mystery, peeked through the office windows, and standing right across from Mr. Henkler were two men dressed exactly like the man with the mustache.

UNDERWOOD

A T NIGHTFALL, as the rains continued, Sheldon and Abe and Mirabelle sat together at the kitchen table picking at the chicken, carrots, and potatoes that Mirabelle had half-heartedly roasted for them. But the food had dried out by the time she'd removed it from the oven. Nate was not home. Abe had decided to light a fire to dry out the house even though it wasn't especially cold. The dining-room fixture above them was the only one lit downstairs. The radio was off and the house felt forlorn.

As Abe finished off his meal, Sheldon told them about the men he'd seen and insisted they were gangsters.

"Pinstripes, hats, the whole nine yards," Sheldon said.

Throughout the day, Sheldon had kept the news to himself, rolling the fact of it over and over in his mind and trying to make sense of it. Mr. Henkler had promoted Uncle Nate specifically to find out who was smuggling the guns out of the armory. That meant he wanted the smuggling to stop. Abe said that the black car had shown up shortly afterward to intimidate them into not solving the mystery because they wanted the gunrunning to continue. That car was filled, Abe believed, with a mobster who wanted Nate scared. That's how the vise worked: Nate had to solve and not solve the problem at the same time.

If he didn't solve it, he'd be fired. If he did solve it, something even worse could happen. So why in the world would the people who wanted it to continue be in the office of the person who wanted it to stop?

"I think they showed up to threaten Mr. Henkler directly," Sheldon said. "And maybe some of those workers carrying the crates were taking them to higher ground, if you catch my meaning." He ate a carrot. It was limp. "No one would have noticed in a hurricane. Personally, I think they should have shown up wearing undershirts and jeans like the rest of us, and no one would have given them a second thought, but for reasons I can't figure out, they decided to come in their gangster suits. Maybe they don't have any other clothes. Anyway, I don't think anyone noticed they were there."

"You did," said Abe.

"I peed for twenty-eight minutes," Sheldon said. Maybe it was an answer. Maybe it wasn't.

"It doesn't make any sense," Mirabelle said, making two of the limp carrots dance like Charlie Chaplin did with the dinner rolls in *The Gold Rush*. "Unless," she added, without a smile, "the gangsters gave up trying to intimidate Dad and decided to go right over his head and intimidate his boss instead. So maybe this is good news because Dad won't stress about the problem anymore."

"Unless Mr. Henkler caves to the threats and fires Uncle Nate," Sheldon said.

Mirabelle danced the carrots offstage.

"That's not what's happening," said Abe quietly. Having worked hard during the day, he'd eaten more than half the chicken and potatoes. Neither his father nor Mr. Henkler had seen him work, but the other men had. They'd watched the strong young Corbin kid body-slam the bags, and they'd seen his sweat mix with the rain like theirs had. That was worth the pain in his shoulders and back.

"What is happening?" Sheldon asked.

"I'll tell you in a minute. Where were you today, anyway?" Abe asked Mirabelle.

Mirabelle had been with her friends. And some of those friends had been boys. Boys Abe would not have approved of; non-Jewish boys who watched Mirabelle like she was a baked Alaska spinning around the cake display at the diner. Boys who made her feel alive and desirable and not at all an outsider. Like a *Jewess*.

"I was with Alice. I went to her house and we put on sad faces and watched the rain."

"Sure you were."

"Where do you think I was?"

"One step closer to being tied up in a basement in Sicily, I imagine."

"Do you think we should tell Uncle Nate what we saw?" Sheldon asked, not understanding the implications of the conversation.

"He won't believe you," said Abe. He put his utensils down and folded his arms across his chest. "He'll say you made a mistake."

"I didn't. I know what I saw. I'm totally, totally positive."

"We believe you, Donny," Mirabelle said. Abe blinked slowly in confirmation.

"Stop calling me Donny!"

"Why? Uncle Joseph used to call you that."

Sheldon drew in his lips and looked at her sternly without saying anything.

"Because Uncle Joseph called you that, that's why. And you miss him," said Mirabelle.

"What do you know," Sheldon said. It wasn't a question.

"I know you were crying in your sleep last night. I woke you out of it. Why do you think I was there? To tell you about the sandbags?"

"I was not!"

"Were too."

"Was not!"

"Sheldon," said Abe, more calmly than Mirabelle. "Your mother died a year ago. Your father less than two weeks ago. You're twelve years old and you've barely said a word about it. Of course you were crying in your sleep. You've got nothing to be embarrassed about. You should be glad you did. It means you aren't so broken that you can't."

"You two never talk about Aunt Lucy," Sheldon answered as quickly as possible, trying to change the subject by drowning them in it. He knew it was a bitter thing to say. That's why he said it.

"No, we don't," Mirabelle admitted.

"Why not?" Sheldon said. "Aunt Lucy was nice."

"Yes, she was," said Mirabelle. "She was very nice."

"Because," said Abe, "your uncle Nate is banging some whore every Tuesday and Thursday night to make himself feel better while leaving us all alone to feel miserable, and we like to stay away from the topic so our food stays in our stomachs. Now you know."

"There's more," Mirabelle said quietly.

"No, there isn't," Abe said, and gave her a look that Sheldon had never seen. For the first time ever, Sheldon saw Mirabelle take a hint.

After dinner, Mirabelle and Sheldon listened to the radio downstairs while a fire burned in the fireplace. Abe didn't join them, though, because he wasn't in the mood.

Upstairs in his bedroom, he pulled his wooden office chair up to his desk and sat in front of the Underwood typewriter. It had been his mother's. He'd moved it into his bedroom after she died. She liked to write poems and often typed letters to her friends rather than handwriting them. He had asked her why one time, and she'd said it was fun, that maybe she'd get a job as a secretary. "I'm a good typist, actually. My spelling is superb. I was always good at school," she'd added distantly.

Abe was still angry at Mirabelle for what she had been about to tell Sheldon. Being a tough rebel was one thing, but there was a line, and she needed to learn not to cross it.

She ought to know better too. When Lucy died, Mirabelle sobbed into her pillow. Abe had to go into her room and lie down with her until she became too exhausted to cry. Once in a while, she did the same for him. They didn't talk about it, but something had become clear to both of them: They were both cutting their father out of the equation entirely. Without him for support, they only had each other. And now Sheldon.

Neither Abe nor Mirabelle knew if Nate had been unfaithful before the fire. What Abe did know was that it definitely started happening a month afterward. Nate may have been weak or already in love or needy, but none of that mattered to Abe or his sister. They hated him for his betrayal and his abandonment of them even though they weren't kids anymore, even though they knew people died sometimes, even though their family had weathered the Depression better than most largely on account of Nate and his willingness to do whatever was needed to keep food on the table.

His father was blind now. Abe could see it. Nate had fallen into the trap of thinking that the world that hated him for what he was had accepted him for who he was, and that this was going to change things for everyone else in the long run. It was the same trap that had him believing he had healed the wounds of the family by keeping them busy and fed, and that he had secured their future among well-meaning and benevolent gentile benefactors, and that he was beyond the pain of losing his wife and his brother because he'd found some arms and legs to hide in. All of this, for Abe, was a failure of imagination, a condition that invites disaster.

All around him Abe saw these failures. A failure to see what was beyond the horizon or immediate sight.

The failure to see effect follow cause.

A failure to anticipate the consequences of one's own actions.

His father had fostered an inability to look into the future and imagine the *probability* of civilization being ripped away with the same careless regard that this hurricane was taking of New England, this hurricane that still battered his windows and that the newspapers were already calling the worst natural disaster in American history. More than six hundred people were dead from the storm and the numbers were rising. Two billion trees had fallen. More than nine thousand homes had been flattened. Hartford's own Katharine Hepburn — Mirabelle's model of feminine perfection — had lost her beach house, washed away like a stain.

Imagination was necessary, but it wasn't enough to survive. Jews had imagination aplenty but that didn't always help. Abe needed to *know*. He needed to know for sure what Henkler was up to because he wasn't going to get hoodwinked by being too timid to face the facts; he needed to know who that man was who'd been watching their house; and he wanted to know with certainty what this all had to do with his family. Because his father was in a dream, and Abe knew he'd never wake up.

Sheldon had burned down his own house to avenge his father, recover what was his, and neutralize a threat. The kid was only twelve years old. And now he was out there gunning for the man who drove them off the road. Impossible. But he was trying. How could a man on the edge of eighteen like himself do any less than his kid cousin?

Knocking over a pawn shop out of anger wasn't enough. That was child's play. He needed to crack this and there was only one way to do it.

Abe reached into a dresser drawer and removed the pistol and placed it next to the typewriter for inspiration. He put a cigarette at the edge of his lips, rolled a sheet of paper into the Underwood, and began to type. He was going to show up at the armory, put the gun against Henkler's temple, and get the answers. At that point, things could go only one of two ways. Abe was prepared for both.

He was finished with both letters by the time Sheldon came up to bed. Maybe he'd heard Abe typing away and decided to leave him alone or else he and Mirabelle had occupied themselves downstairs with chess or the radio or books. It didn't matter. Abe had had the time he'd needed. Sheldon wasn't chatty when he climbed into bed in his blue-striped pajamas. He turned away from Abe after uttering "good night" to which Abe said the same. He was a good kid. A soft kid in some ways — soft at heart and sentimental — but tough and capable too.

He was still young, though. He didn't know what forces were out there working against him every day from the shadows — though these forces were increasingly now in the light. He'd learn in time. For now, though, Abe had to save the family all by himself.

It was 10:30 at night by the time Sheldon was fast asleep and Abe was able to slip out of the house with the gun and the two letters in a brown lunch bag. It was raining but it was more of a steady and normal rain now, the back end of the storm that was now in Maine or Canada as far as he knew. Nate was still out with his diversion — a blonde who worked at a sales desk at G. Fox & Co. who couldn't have been more than twenty-five — and Mirabelle was presumably sleeping too. Abe's walk through the city streets felt like the night they'd hit the pawn shop, when they crept from shadow to shadow and every streetlamp was an enemy sentry. But tonight, it was easier to navigate. The power grid was down. Millions were in the dark, with a few candles or gas lamps burning. Trees rested on cars as Abe walked through knee-deep water in the street on his way to the armory.

Henkler was still in his office when Abraham Corbin walked in and closed the door behind him. The rest of the staff was long gone as the sandbagging had ground to a halt around nine. The sheer scale of the future cleanup was inconceivable for the moment. The estimates Mr. Henkler had heard on the radio were only estimates; a full audit of damage was going to be needed; discussions with insurance companies and banks were going to be interminable; and even returning the factory to full production levels was going to be time-consuming. The business, after all, depended on a constant flow of raw materials followed by the distribution of product, more or less like any other production. With the roads blocked, the electricity down, vehicles unable to come or go, and the workers in a state over whatever matters they had to attend to . . . it was going to be a juggling act. That Mr. Henkler knew. But this—Corbin's kid showing up in the middle of the night—he didn't expect.

"Your father isn't here," Mr. Henkler said, rubbing his eyes.

"No," said Abe. "I didn't come to see him."

"I beg your pardon?"

Abe had seen no one outside. No one on the floors on his way up. No other offices lit. This lonely office was a glowing fishbowl at the far end of the solar system.

"I came to see you," Abe said.

Abe unwrapped his paper bag and placed his hand inside it but did not remove the Colt 1917. Sheldon had called it a double action and said that pulling the trigger would send the hammer back and release it into the bullet. This was different from the old guns of the Wild West where the cowboys had to pull the hammer back first. "That's why they did that fanning thing," Sheldon had said. "My dad said it was all for show, though. You couldn't hit a barn that way."

Mr. Henkler removed his oval reading glasses. Abe couldn't decide if that made him look more German or less.

"Why would you come to see me close to midnight? You should be home. When your father hears about this, it is not going to bode well for either of you. Leave my office, please."

"I want to know who those two mobsters were. The ones here in your office this morning. I want to know what your business is with them and how my father is related to it. I want to know who the guy is outside my house watching us. I want to know if you're setting up my father to take the fall for the missing guns that you're stealing from Colt to sell to the Mob as a sideline. I want to know if you're setting up the one guy everyone will naturally pin it on. And when I say that I want to know, I mean you're going to tell me. And you're going to do it now."

Mr. Henkler stood up. His face was going red with anger. He was not used to being talked to like this, especially from a child. Especially from . . .

"Sit the fuck down," Abe said, pulling out the gun. "And leave your hands on the desk."

"You just got your father fired and you just went to jail," said Mr. Henkler. He was admirably calm on the outside. Abe had to give him that.

"You're going to tell me the truth. And if you don't—"

"If I don't . . . what? You're going to shoot me? Please."

"If you don't, I'm going to create a new truth. A truth that works for me."

"I have no idea what—"

Abe looked at the gun and thought again of Sheldon burning his own house down. Now that he was here, holding the thing in his hand, having crossed the proverbial Rubicon, he suddenly felt a surge of respect for his little cousin. The balls on that kid to do what he did. The will. The notion filled him with pride. Uncle Joseph had been a war hero. His cousin was a slayer of dragons. If he got out of this and made it to eighteen, Abe decided that he was changing his name back to Horowitz.

"The one with the mustache," said Abe, playing a hunch. "He wasn't here today with the other two guys. But the other times. Thick bushy mustache. Mobster. Tell me his name and I'll leave."

Mr. Henkler sat there clutching his desk. He ran a gun factory. He was surrounded by an inventory of no fewer than a thousand guns on the floor this very minute, not counting the Colt .45 automatic that was chambered and in his top desk drawer. Mr. Henkler had no doubt he could reach in and get it and put a round in the boy's chest. Who was this boy anyway? Nothing. A nobody. He came from a race of weak and pale people who were little more than Negroes. At least the Negroes had some virtues. At least they won some medals in Berlin back in 1936. What do these people do?

They can *count*.

Not this one, though. This one was bad at math and couldn't run the odds.

Still.

Shooting a seventeen-year-old local Hartford boy in the middle of the chest wouldn't look good. And the Jews were gaining quite a foothold in the city. Sure, the doors were still closed to them at proper institutions like the Protestant Hartford Hospital and the Catholic Saint Francis Hospital. Harvard, of course. And Yale. And Princeton. Other places had set quotas to keep them out. Still, they were gaining ground like vermin whose natural predators had been killed off. So, where did a snot-nosed brat from a tribe like that find the gumption to pull a Colt-made weapon on a proper American man like himself? One of proper heritage at that. It boggled the mind. It really did.

Mr. Henkler told Abe the man's name. He was obviously the man the boy was referring to. He was the muscle in the area and Mr. Henkler had been threatened by him in the past. A brute with a single name. Not that he'd been at Colt more than once or twice. Mr. Henkler had no loyalty to that man. Passing his name on might move this all along, and it was certainly better than having to shoot a child in his own office. Besides, what could the boy do with the information?

"Business is a complicated game that you wouldn't understand," Mr. Henkler said. "Your father doesn't understand it either. Not really. It's not the paperwork, you see. It's the relationships. You do business with people in power and together you prop each other up. Not everyone is a fine, upstanding citizen. People like the men who came in here—and others of their . . . ilk—are relied on, from time to time, to grease the complicated machinery that powers the world. It is a machine in its own way. Now, put that gun on my desk and get out. I will decide in the morning what to do with you."

Abe stood up, but he did not put the gun on the desk. He pointed it at Mr. Henkler's head and walked around to his side of the desk.

"What the hell are you doing now, you ingrate?"

Abe placed the barrel of the pistol against Mr. Henkler's temple. His hand shook. His whole body tensed. The muscles in his legs, his abdomen, his forearms. It was like diving into water that's too cold—the muscles constrict and use up all the oxygen and leave the lungs gasping for more. His whole machinery trembled; an engine overtaxed.

Mr. Henkler knew the name of the man who had killed his uncle Joseph, who had killed Sheldon's father. Mr. Henkler said he was doing business with the mobsters who were threatening his family. Mr. Henkler had promoted his father into a job where he was going to be a scapegoat for his boss's own financial or political ends. Abe shook with rage and fear and the certainty that everyone he knew was in danger and that there was no way out.

Mr. Henkler reached up to take the pistol away from his head. When he did, his brains splattered all over the far end of the office.

Looking down at his hand and the smoking revolver, Abe wasn't sure he had even made the decision to pull the trigger. The dead body in front of him was flopped over; blood was seeping out of its skull onto the floor like a punctured bag of syrup.

Abe's hands trembled. He looked up and around. There was no one there. No new sounds. No sirens or boots rushing up the steps. No echoes or reverberations. No hand of God smiting him. Only a new kind of silence.

Everything that happened next was an emotionless dream. He performed the actions he'd imagined back in his bedroom in front of the typewriter; he was able to perform them only because he had already done them over and over and over again in his mind. Abe prepared the crime scene as a sequence of gestures that were as scripted as religious ritual.

Untucking his shirt, he wiped any fingerprints from the gun. Using a pen from Mr. Henkler's desk, he carried the gun by the trigger guard and placed it in Mr. Henkler's right hand. Abe then gently pressed Mr. Henkler's hand around it. Then he dropped it to the floor.

Abe opened the desk drawer to return the pen, and when he did, he saw the .45 automatic. Abe took the gun and left the pen behind.

There were papers on the desk. Work papers that showed Mr. Henkler had been busy. Would a man be working and then suddenly stop in midtask to put a bullet in his brain?

Using the edges of his hands, Abe collected them all, rolled them up, and shoved them into his pants so he could throw them out later. Maybe burn them. The whole city was awash in paper and debris. He could hide them anywhere.

There was water on the floor from his dripping clothing, but water was the surface of the world now. It too was everywhere. It was a clue to nothing.

Abe walked out of the room and closed the door behind him. Samuel Stone's office was down the hall on the right. He covered the distance quickly and then crouched down and slid Mr. Henkler's suicide note under the door.

A fire-escape door led to an alleyway behind the armory that was filled with broken crates and boxes. Abe burst through the door, faster than was wise, and walked north through puddles up to his ankles. He was sheltered from view on either side by towering brick walls that could have been waves; Abe was a fleeing Moses at the bottom of the Red Sea escaping punishment for smiting the slave master.

Five blocks away, he found a garbage can filled to the top with rainwater. He removed the papers from his pants and shoved them in with the rest of the detritus. They soaked in the water, the ink and blood ran, and they became a part of whatever had been there before.

Thirty minutes later and back in bed in dry boxer shorts, Abe lay with his hands under his head staring at a ceiling that was so dark it might have been a clouded night sky or a premonition. Across from him, Sheldon's right foot stuck out from his blanket, and after fifteen minutes had passed and Sheldon didn't move, Abe rose from the bed, pushed his cousin's foot back onto the mattress, covered it up, and then returned to his bed and tried to quiet his mind.

"Don't make trouble," said the cowardly Jew facing the firing squad. If he was going to be shot anyway, wouldn't it have been better to die for one's actions rather than inactions?

Yes, thought Abe. It was an imperfect code to live by, but was still better.

✈

THE NEXT DAY there was nothing in the papers about what he had done and nothing on the radio. Just like the pawn shop heist, which he was certain would come back to them but never did. The hurricane was the news and the damage the topic. With the weather finally breaking and blue skies appearing, the devastation outside looked like the end of a nightmare or a war. People emerged from their city homes in a daze. The roads were still flowing but were no longer filling. A few buses were returning with the refugees who'd fled the city and gone to relatives farther inland or westward.

The coast was almost fifty miles to the south, but salt was in the air. The newspapers were running pictures of tankers on their sides, washed up against the shore like toppled skyscrapers. The headlines were no longer about the crisis in Czechoslovakia and were all focused on the leveling of New England.

All offices, however, were closed. Abe's father was told not to come in "by order of management" and didn't know why. He was unable to reach Mr. Henkler by phone for more news and he didn't dare call Mr. Stone or anyone else. With the unexpected day off, Nate forced the kids to attend synagogue for the Sabbath that evening. Sheldon listened. Mirabelle stared out the window and Abe was utterly silent.

When they returned home that evening, the entire family dispersed. Sheldon didn't retire to the bedroom because Abe's presence took up far more than his half of the room. Instead, he sat down on an oversize blue velvet sofa in the parlor and randomly pulled down a book by Mark Twain. *A Connecticut Yankee in King Arthur's Court.*

Sheldon had read *Tom Sawyer* in school back in Whately, and of the authors on the shelf, Twain was the only one Sheldon recognized. After a few minutes of reading, he came on the first sentence of a section called "The Stranger's History."

```
I am an American. I was born and reared in Hartford,
in the State of Connecticut—anyway, just over the
river, in the country. So I am a Yankee of the Yankees
—and practical; yes, and nearly barren of sentiment,
I suppose—or poetry, in other words. My father was
a blacksmith, my uncle was a horse doctor, and I was
both, along at first. Then I went over to the great
arms factory and learned my real trade; learned all
there was to it; learned to make everything: guns,
revolvers, cannon, boilers, engines, all sorts of
labor-saving machinery. Why, I could make anything
a body wanted—anything in the world, it didn't make
any difference what; and if there wasn't any quick
new-fangled way to make a thing, I could invent one
—and do it as easy as rolling off a log. I became
head superintendent; had a couple of thousand men
under me.
```

Sheldon looked up. The great arms factory in Hartford? Was he writing about the Colt Armory? Sheldon had never read anything in a book about anything he had actually seen, anything that he didn't have to imagine but could remember instead. In that moment, he felt something new and astonishing: the sense of being at the center of the world. Twain gave Sheldon a feeling that the world was watching him, that an eye in the sky knew where he was on the map and that the things he saw or experienced or learned or said might matter somehow. That he might be part of something larger than himself. Forgetting his family and their moods and traumas, Sheldon continued to read until the phone rang and Uncle Nate walked into the living room to answer it.

The expression on Uncle Nate's face caught Sheldon's attention. It was an expression of absolute shock. Sheldon inadvertently glanced at the stairs, which helped him to remember that Mirabelle and Abe were both safely home and that—for now—whatever news was coming through the telephone would not be catastrophic to him.

He wondered if Uncle Nate had looked the same when he had heard the news of Aunt Lucy and Sheldon's mother. Or his brother. Uncle Nate must have been standing in the same spot.

Nate placed the phone back in the cradle and immediately walked to the kitchen and poured himself a tall glass of bourbon, which he did not typically do. Sheldon watched, unable to concoct a scenario that would have prompted this.

He suddenly felt a terrible need to be close to Mirabelle.

He raced upstairs, and without knocking or thinking at all, he burst into Mirabelle's room.

"Hey? What gives? You have to knock, you little—"

Sheldon walked right up to her and placed his hand on her head. She looked at him and didn't object. The feeling of her hair, of the warmth of her scalp, was enough for the moment. He left the room with Mirabelle watching him—perplexed—and he sought out his oldest cousin.

Abe was sitting on his bed with a copy of *Popular Mechanics.* On the cover was a water-skier being pulled by a dirigible. It was an old copy. Sheldon had seen it before.

"What's up?" muttered Abe without much interest.

"Nothing," said Sheldon, clearly lying.

Abe looked at him and saw that he was vibrating like a guitar string.

"You been eating catnip?"

"No."

"So, what then?"

"Uncle Nate got a phone call."

"That's not interesting yet," Abe said, flipping a page.

"He's drinking a big glass of bourbon."

Abe folded the magazine.

"You know what's going on?" Sheldon asked.

"I'm sure he'll tell us," Abe said.

• • •

Nate didn't tell them until the next day, when it appeared on the front page of the newspaper. Carl Henkler, it said, had committed suicide.

Maybe.

A janitor had found him, and Samuel Stone had cut short a business trip in New York to find a note under his door that he submitted immediately to the police. Somehow the newspapers had gotten hold of it and printed it in full.

Dear Mr. S. M. Stone,

It is with regret, shame, and humiliation that I have reached the only ending for the path on which I put myself. Within the past year, I have made closer business ties to a crime family in an effort to better serve the company and ensure our free flow of merchandise that their operations were going to threaten. At the time, I thought it was a pragmatic business decision. However, that changed. They started requesting several hundred weapons a year that could be acquired without their needing to pass through a traditional point of sale. Why this was important to them, I didn't ask.

When you became aware of the missing inventory and asked me to solve it, I knew at once I could not. I therefore hired Mr. Nathaniel Corbin as a proxy. I instructed Mr. Corbin to solve the mystery while I simultaneously withheld key documents he would need to do so. My plan was to run him in circles long enough to find a solution. Unfortunately for me, Mr. Corbin proved dedicated and unrelenting in his service to the company and was coming close to solving the matter just as news reached me that various newspapers had heard rumors of the missing inventory. This would have shattered Colt's reputation at a moment when war looms in Europe.

The walls were closing in and it was only a matter
of time until my actions would be exposed.

During the stock market crash, I heard stories of
men jumping to their deaths. At the time, this struck
me as absurd. Now I understand why.

To my family: I am sorry. Please forgive me.

Carl Henkler

Nate read them the letter at the kitchen table to the sound of chain saws and axes as the WPA workers chopped apart the storm-felled trees.

Nate shook his head when he finished. "It just doesn't make any sense."

"What doesn't?" Abe asked.

"All of it. He was the most rooted and steadfast man I've ever known. All business. No emotion. I suppose it's not impossible that he decided to do business with the criminals. The world is held together by a delicate balance. I understand that," Nate said very quietly—almost to himself. "But suicide? He's not the type. He's a dealmaker and a numbers man. He would have found a solution. He didn't need a way out. Not like this."

"You really think you can know a man just from working with him?" Abe asked. "He might have needed the money. You don't know."

"The paper has questions too," Nate said, flipping to a related article. "The wife said she'd never seen the gun he used. It was an old model that he didn't prefer and she insisted that she knew guns. She said he kept an automatic in his drawer. She was quite insistent, it says here, that anyone with even a passing knowledge of guns could tell a revolver from an automatic. The article says that revolvers like the one used are known to be even more reliable than .45s, so perhaps that was on his mind. He was German, after all. But no automatic was recovered from his desk and his wife is insisting it wasn't suicide. And for another thing"—Nate skimmed over the paragraphs to find the relevant bit—"it says here that the revolver he used had two empty shells in it, not one. The police are looking to take fingerprints from them. They said that a man as familiar with guns as Mr. Henkler would have filled the cylinder with six new rounds. When would he have discharged a single round before firing this one? If he'd been at a range, he would have spent the rounds and replaced them. All of them, not just one. They searched the office for a second bullet hole but didn't find one."

"How many bullets were in his head?" Mirabelle asked.

"That's not funny," Nate said.

Sheldon looked at Abe. Abe wasn't talking.

Mirabelle crossed her arms over her chest and leaned back. She'd finished one piece of toast and an egg, and had been sipping tea, but she wasn't thinking about the suicide now. She was thinking about other parts of the letter.

"He said nice things about you," Mirabelle said.

"Yes," Nate said. "Assuming he wrote the letter."

"If it was murder," Mirabelle said, apparently unbothered by the subject, "why would a mobster include nice comments about you?"

"I can't imagine a reason," Nate said. "That's why Mr. Stone believes it was suicide, which brings me to my second piece of news." Nate took a gulp of his coffee as though it were a stiff drink at a bar, and then said, "Mr. Stone called me. He wants to see me on Monday. I'm pretty sure he's going to give me Henkler's job. I think he's promoting me. If so, this is going to turn our fortunes around. All of ours. It's going to make all kinds of things possible. Summer vacations in the Catskills. Maybe a trip to Europe."

"We don't want to go to Europe," Abe said.

"Sure we do! Paris, Rome, Berlin. Here I come!" said Mirabelle.

"Trust me," Abe said. "Forget Europe."

"Speak for yourself," Mirabelle said. "Actually, now that I think about it, maybe you killed him, Dad. I mean . . . it makes sense."

"That isn't funny either."

She tilted her head and opened her hands. "You write a nice suicide note that makes you look good, you kill him, you get his job. I'm not even angry."

"A man is dead, Mirabelle. Can you not feel that?"

"So now what?" said Abe.

"We will all go to the funeral. Show our respects. Let the widow see that we came. Let the community know that if I'm stepping into his shoes it's with the greatest humility. Because . . ." Nate shook his head.

All of Nate's thoughts and emotions were spinning too fast. His wife had died a year ago. And then a promotion. His brother only recently. And now another promotion? If he wasn't sitting, he'd have to brace himself.

"When your grandparents died in the flu," he said to all of them, "Joseph — Uncle Joe — was back from the war and he wanted to stay in Whately. I wanted him to come to Hartford with me. I told him that this is the land of opportunity. That everything's possible in the city now. We'll have to fight through some unfairness and some bigotry, but so does everyone else. And if we persevere and focus on what's important and work hard — and be seen to work hard and fit in — we can get there. We can go from that wooden cabin in the Berkshires to a brownstone and from being cobblers to running a department at Colt." Nate looked at Abe. "We can get past being Jews."

"Why do we have to get past being Jews?" Abe asked. "Are we doing something wrong? We're model citizens. We're the stars of the show. Milton Berle, Peter Lorre, the Marx Brothers, Chaplin, Jack Benny, George Burns —"

"All right, Abe."

"Eddie Cantor, Al Jolson . . . Hedy Lamarr, for God's sake! And what about the fact that for three thousand years we've applied our heads and our hearts to the deepest questions of human existence and created a legacy of moral learning that has informed and defined —"

"Enough, Abe! We live in the real world," Nate said. "We need to fit in, and it's worth it. You could try asking everyone you just listed but none of those people exist; they're all stage names and you know why. Milton Berle is Mendel Berlinger. George Burns is Nathan Birnbaum. And your Hedy Lamarr? Hedwig Eva Maria Kiesler. None of that was going to work. And they knew it!"

"Is that really what you think?" Abe asked Nate. His voice was little more than a whisper.

"That's exactly what I think. And you're looking at the proof. Everyone came over here as immigrants — us, the Irish, the Italians, the Polish, the Chinese, for heaven's sake, and we got labeled and we had to shed some baggage and learn how things are done."

"By assimilating. Cowering. Begging."

"Adapting," Nate said. "Isn't that what they're teaching in your biology class, Mirabelle? Adaptation? You adapt. You're wonderful at it. You're going places, and I see it."

Mirabelle said nothing.

Nate was still upbeat and wanted to share the feeling. "I think we should all take a trip after I get the job. Rent a car. I read that the Boston Symphony Orchestra has started playing a new concert hall called Tanglewood. It's not far from where Uncle Joe and I grew up. Maybe we can drive up there and listen."

"Classical music?" Mirabelle asked, with a hint of alarm.

"It's culture, Mirabelle. We're moving up. Don't you see? Adaptation. And half the musicians are probably Jews," Nate added for Abe's benefit. "What do you say, Sheldon? Would that be OK? To go so soon?"

Sheldon didn't answer. Instead, he asked if he could be excused from the table.

Nate frowned. "Why? What's wrong?"

"I don't feel good." It was partly true. Sheldon was starting to sweat.

Nate thought he understood. "Maybe we can go someplace else. Also, you don't have to go to Mr. Henkler's funeral, Sheldon. People won't notice your absence, and we were just at a cemetery with your father. It's only natural you'd feel this way."

"Thanks, Uncle Nate."

"Yes, you're excused."

Sheldon picked up his breakfast plate and glass, and dropped them off by the sink for Mirabelle to clean. He didn't turn around to look at anyone as he made for his bedroom.

The Underwood No. 5 typewriter was a skeletal machine where all the gears and levers and parts were exposed to the elements. Above the letters, in steel, was a quarter-moon of hammers packed together and arranged like the hull of a tiny ship. Press the key and a hammer rose on an arm that for a moment looked impossibly long before the ribbon rose to meet it, and then the hammer smacked through the ink and left behind an imprint on the white page; a scar in the form of a letter—letters that became words, words that begot sentences, each one a whisper that might have left an echo. This is what Sheldon wanted to find out.

He sat there. There was no paper on the rubber scroll now. Leaning forward, Sheldon looked at it and squinted. Could he make out even a single word there that was the same as the words in the newspaper? Did Abe write that letter in this very room and slide it under Mr. Stone's door? If he did, did that necessarily mean he killed Mr. Henkler? Maybe he found Mr. Henkler and, thinking fast, swapped out the real letter for this one that helped Uncle Nate.

Which was crazy and didn't solve the mystery of the missing .45 automatic. But was it crazier than Abe *murdering* Mr. Henkler?

The rubber cylinder didn't give away any secrets so Sheldon looked in the garbage bin for drafts but there were none. He then looked at the ribbon and wondered if the ribbon had a memory of the letters pressed into it, but he saw it was made of cloth or fabric and was black through and through. The hammers had made an impression but left no mark: a perfect crime.

Sheldon stood up and paced around the room.

The stacks of newspapers on the dresser. The fights on the street. The pawn shop. All that talk about Jews and gangs and Europe. Being rude to Mr. Henkler when they went to visit him. Had it been leading up to this?

Sheldon wanted to know the truth and he also didn't want to know.

He sat on the edge of his bed for more than a minute before he stood and walked over to Abe's dresser.

He opened the drawer below the newspapers.

The revolver was missing.

GRADUATION

ABE GRADUATED FROM HIGH SCHOOL eight months later in June on a day so clear and blue that Sheldon felt as though a slate were being wiped clean; and even Uncle Nate felt that a new beginning had arrived.

Mirabelle wore a bright-yellow shirtwaist summer dress with white polka dots and crepe-soled saddle shoes of white and black. Seventeen on December 8, she looked like an adult and a movie star. Her mother's clothing strengthened the illusion. Her face was a matronly calm.

Sheldon sat in the bleachers looking down on the green football field filled with graduating seniors wearing red caps and gowns. Nate was on his left and Mirabelle on his right. It was a Wednesday, and Nate had taken the day off. He wore a chalk-stripe blue suit and solid tie but had forgone a hat. With a smile on his face, he bit the end of his pipe and looked down at the field.

"Before they're handed the diploma," Nate said to Sheldon, "the tassel on the mortarboard is on the right side. Once they're handed their diplomas, they move it to the left to show they're high school graduates." He was smiling constantly.

For Nate, the past was now behind them. His son had pulled through a difficult year of moodiness and inexplicable silences, and yet he had focused intensely on his studies, and now he was on his way into the adult world and the workforce. Three children, raised on his own for the better part of a year. Yes, it had become easier after hiring a housekeeper once he was promoted into Mr. Henkler's job. That had relieved the pressure on him and Mirabelle, who had had to take on the woman's role. But it still hadn't been easy; children have their needs and their trials, and their outbursts, and without Lucy there to take the burden or calm him down, it had all required a superhuman effort on his part.

The marching band was taking to the field behind the seniors. They struck up a Glenn Miller tune.

"Oh, there he is!" Nate said. Sheldon followed Nate's finger and tried to tell one red gown from the next.

As nice as the weather was, Sheldon suspected that sitting there was boring for Mirabelle. He asked her if she wished she was graduating too, but she said no.

"What are you thinking about, then?" he asked.

"This. All of this."

"All of what?"

"I didn't think he'd make it," she said quietly.

"What do you mean?"

"Abe. Graduation. I didn't think he'd make it."

"Why not?"

Mirabelle looked from Sheldon to her father, but he was paying them no attention. He was lighting his pipe for a second time and crossing his legs comfortably as he watched the band.

"You know what I mean," Mirabelle whispered.

They had never discussed it. Never intimated or suggested what might have happened. But after the storm passed and Mr. Henkler was buried, their previous and coordinated agenda to wreak havoc on Hartford had been wordlessly shelved; they all shared a sense that it had already gone too far. Mirabelle didn't press for any more heists; the search for Joseph's killer was quietly ended; and Sheldon's private dream of growing up to become an international jewel thief—one who cracked safes and scaled buildings in a black suit and then unfolded black velvet cloths full of sapphires and emeralds and rubies that caught the light of the moon and turned everything into chance and possibility through alchemy—evaporated as effortlessly as a late-morning dream. Abe started disappearing at night and not telling them where he was. When he returned, he conscientiously completed his homework, read the newspapers cover to cover, listened to one of the bands on the radio, and then went to sleep. Sheldon and Mirabelle both knew something under the earth had shifted. Nate, however, evidently considered the children as being on their best behavior and happily attributed this to his guidance and care. He too spent the evenings out. In time, so did Mirabelle.

Sheldon turned to the books downstairs and the velvet sofa beside the fireplace that no one used. Mark Twain and Dashiell Hammett and Rex Stout and J. R. R. Tolkien took Sheldon far away from Hartford, his memories, and all his suspicions.

The only person Sheldon had told about any of this was Lenny. And he'd told Lenny only by letter. He knew perfectly well that if one of his letters fell into enemy hands the world would immediately explode, but Sheldon had already scoped out the typewriter and knew it told no tales on its own. The only two rules he needed were:

1. Never leave an unfinished letter in the typewriter
2. Never throw away a letter with spelling or typing mistakes because someone might find it

He could have handwritten them. Something about typing the letters, though, made him feel more adult. Like he was working at a newspaper or spy bureau and he was drafting communiques that were sent off over the wire to change the course of the war. Lenny Bernstein was his man behind enemy lines. The letters would be attached to the pigeons Mirabelle had described to him — like the one her biology teacher had sent up to Boston before the storm and had, by some miracle, arrived there *before* the hurricane, which had given the teacher on the other end time to talk to the principal about the "bad storm coming" note he'd received — and who then made a few calls south for confirmation — at which point they moved all the kids into the gymnasium away from the windows that, only two hours later, shattered. No one was harmed. Herman the pigeon was declared a hero.

Herman didn't know why, but he ate very well that night.

Sheldon was a very bad typist and made a lot of mistakes. And while — yes — each letter was a world-saving missive from headquarters, that didn't mean he wanted to bother correcting each error by hand with a pencil. After all, it was only Lenny, and he had been instructed to burn or eat Sheldon's missives.

Lenny didn't know what to make of Sheldon's letters at first. They contained stories about a pawn shop burglary and Mirabelle's panties, shotgun blasts and murders, gangsters and politicians. With this kind of subject matter and all the misspellings and smudges and crossed-out words, Lenny had to wonder if Sheldon was OK in the head.

In his first letter back to Sheldon — not long after the storm — Lenny had asked if maybe Sheldon had fallen down or possibly taken up boxing.

I mean, up until now, you've been telling me how great Abe is and how he looks out for you other than getting you shot at and things like that, and how if he wasn't around and it was only your uncle and Mirabelle how weird things would be. Now you're writing to me and telling me that you think he shot some guy, wrote a suicide letter for him, got your uncle promoted, and rather than going straight to jail or hell or whatever, he's just hanging around finishing up his senior year by doubling down on math. It just keeps getting kinda nuts to me, that's all. Then again, I can't really imagine you boxing either. Can you even box at 12? I know you're gonna be 13 in September, but that wouldn't account for the brain damage now, would it?

Around here, I think Mickey the horse died. Mr. O'Neill has a new Buick, or at least it's new for him, and I haven't seen that horse anywhere so either he's retired or dead or food.

I did what you asked. I broke into your shack out in the forest and got those two rifles. I wrapped them up in a blanket and brought them home the back way, the one that goes over the old stone wall that you said was made by the Romans but now I know you're full of shit because Miss Simmons told me the Romans were never out here. She said it was probably the early settlers who made walls to divide up their lands and such things like that. Anyway, who cares.

I don't know what I'm supposed to do with two guns in a blanket. The hard part has been trying to explain to my mom where the blanket is. How does a blanket go missing, she wants to know. And I'm thinking—she's got a point. How does a blanket go missing? Now, as it happens, I know the answer but it's not one I want to share, is it?

You ever heard of the Catskills? Some mountains and hotels and things in New York. Not too far from here. You can bus it. My dad came back from Springfield and said a lot of the Jews from New York are going there in the summers now and they got everything. They got swimming pools and golf and tennis and fishing and all this stuff, and now people who have it hard down in the city are starting to go up there to beat the heat and eat themselves silly at these buffets. He said that the Jews who came over in the 1900s and 1920s came with nothing and they don't get food like that, so to them it's like the American dream or something and they get drunk on it. He says maybe we can go there next summer. The high rollers pay fifty-five bucks for a week and that's for the room and three meals a day and all the shows. He says this is pretty damn expensive compared to the other places, but it's supposed to be one of the best hotels on earth, so that's why.

This winter he wants me and my sister to dress up like elves when we sell the Christmas trees and we're none too pleased about it because it'll feel stupid. He says it'll add to the festive spirit and everyone loves kids dressed like elves. I asked if this wasn't a little weird, us being Jewish and all. He said Mary was Jewish, Joseph was Jewish, Jesus was Jewish, and

all twelve apostles were Jewish. He said what's weird
is the gentiles buying evergreens to celebrate a Jew
born in a desert. You think they had trees like this
in the Holy Land? he says to me. Whoever thought of
selling evergreens to gentiles was a fuckin' genius,
he says. I said you're selling them, and that made him
smile. So . . . I'm gonna be an elf.

I don't think I've ever written this much in my
life. I'm gonna go rest my hand.

OK, I'm back. It's tomorrow now. Well, I guess it's
today again technically, but it's yesterday's tomorrow, which is good enough. My hand isn't all cramped
up, that's the key to the thing.

Wouldn't it be great if you could come to the
Catskills with us sometime? I think it would be great.
My dad says they have these comedians up there. Like
Jack Benny and George Burns and Danny Kaye and these
guys. He says they'll make your sides split open. He
makes that sound good so we'll see. If it's any good,
I'll tell you. Maybe there's something in it for us.
I can tell a joke. Maybe that's how I break into the
big time.

Lenny

The graduation ceremony ended with the mortarboards flying high.

Nate urged Mirabelle and Sheldon to follow him down the bleachers,
where they met up with Abe. Nate grabbed his son's arm, pumping it up
and down as though Abe had just solved the Riddle of the Sphinx. Abe
accepted this with grace, but he didn't look elated like the other graduates
around him.

"I'm so proud of you, Abe," Nate said. "After everything that happened
in the last few years. I wasn't sure . . . but you really came out on top."

An hour later, the sky an even deeper shade of blue, the Corbin family
with Sheldon in tow passed through the open doors of the Brubeck Club.

Hats were taken, a jacket provided to Sheldon with the sleeves rolled up, and a black man with white hair and a slight stoop led them into a dining hall where Roy Fowler—another department head at Colt—met Nate and welcomed him.

Behind Fowler was a banquet hall full of the kind of people Nate admired and wanted to be like. They were wealthy and stylish. They moved with a grace that came from belonging, a pride of ownership over a world of their inheritance and making. The men's suits were tailored, and the women wore the latest fashions bought off the racks at G. Fox & Co. or else copied from the daily pattern in the *Hartford Courant.*

"Welcome, Nate. It's good you made it," Mr. Fowler said, as he held out a thick paw for Nate to grasp.

Sheldon looked around him and smelled the unfamiliar foods. The colors were fantastic. His mother would have loved it here. This was high society; this was the kind of place where photographers wandered around taking pictures of people who would end up in the Society and Personal News section that Abe always threw in the garbage.

His father, Sheldon knew, would have stood with his hands in his pockets watching the patrons as if they were so many beasts around a carcass. He would have considered it all a cheap drama. Sheldon didn't have Joseph's knowingness, but he did think that the people here looked more like peacocks than rulers of the universe.

All that was philosophy. The earthly truth was that the food smelled really, really good and Sheldon wanted to sit down and stuff his face. Unfortunately, Mr. Fowler wanted to have words with him first, which slowed Sheldon down.

"And who are you, young man?" Mr. Fowler asked.

"Sheldon Horowitz."

"And how did you come to be here today?"

Sheldon turned and looked back at the door as the obvious answer, but that didn't seem to be it; the guy was looking for something else. "Abe's my cousin. I was invited."

"Of course you are. Bet you've never been to a club like this before."

"No, sir."

"Of course not. Come in, come in."

Mirabelle walked with Nate to a large round table near tall windows framed by yellow curtains. Abe and Sheldon followed. Abe was sullen and Sheldon didn't know why. The food was going to be great and he had just graduated. It didn't make any sense. At the table, Sheldon sat between his cousins and across from a girl Abe's age named Dorothy, who had also graduated. She must have been a year older than Mirabelle, but she looked shy and her head hung, which made her look younger and smaller. Sheldon thought she looked nice. Mirabelle sat with her back straight and hands folded on her lap. She turned to Sheldon and whispered, "What do you think?"

"About what?"

"All the fancy. All the people who have blue blood."

"People don't have blue blood. They have red blood."

"Nope. It's blue."

"Red," said Sheldon.

"You'll see."

"When?"

"When the blood starts flowing."

"What does that mean?"

"It means Abe is a fox, and this is a henhouse filled with hens who think they're foxes."

"That makes no sense at all," Sheldon whispered.

"And the hens have blue blood," she added, nodding.

"You're weird."

"Put your napkin on your lap."

Mirabelle was on his right, and next to her was Nate and then Dorothy Fowler, Roy Fowler, and his wife, Mary. Between Mary and Abe—on his left—was an empty seat that Sheldon assumed was for Elijah.

During the appetizer, the men spoke about the fine weather for the day, the virtues of a good education, the pleasure of spending the day with friends and colleagues, and the state of the cleanup after the hurricane. They spoke about Katharine Hepburn's home on the coast being washed away, and Mr. Fowler joked, "I hope she had the sense to toss a match in there. They were probably insured for fire but not for the storm," and everyone laughed and laughed. Everyone but Abe.

The appetizer was a salad with lobster tail. Sheldon's experience with lobsters was limited to his trips to the coast with his parents, where they'd sat on picnic benches above the beach at Revere and eaten them with crackers, small tubs of melted butter, and a lot of french fries. His father called them bugs of the sea and had winked before pretending the lobster was attacking him with a claw. He wrestled it off and — to show who won — snapped the claw off and scooped out the meat with a tiny fork. Lila was not amused until, like a dam breaking, she was.

It was clear to Sheldon that the people here took lobsters far too seriously. He gobbled his up like the bug it was.

A group of four black musicians and two white ones struck up some quiet jazz as the main course was served: steak, string beans, and gratinated potatoes. It was served by men in white gloves who miraculously didn't stick their thumbs into the sauce.

The steak was OK but not great. Joseph used to bring home large pieces of meat from the butcher, and he'd carve them himself. He had explained that doing the work himself made the meat cheaper, and with a little know-how and a willingness to get his hands dirty, they all ate better. "You can always wash your hands, Donny. So, roll your sleeves up and get in there." They'd dry the meat, season it, wait, and then grill it. What Sheldon grew up eating was a lot thicker and tastier than this cardboard he was being served, but the people all around him were eating it as though they were French kings at high court.

He didn't get it.

"How's the steak, young man?" asked Mr. Fowler. "Ever tasted anything like it?"

"Not quite," said Sheldon.

"Of course not. You're moving up in the world!"

Sheldon wasn't sure how those two sentences were related, and he concluded that he and Mr. Fowler were not participating in the same conversation. He smiled back to make Mr. Fowler move on.

Abe, however, coughed.

"You OK?" Nate asked.

"I don't know," Abe said.

Over dessert, the conversation turned to the latest gossip from the office.

Mr. Fowler said that after Mr. Henkler had killed himself the police solved the mystery of the missing weapons. It turned out that the one-legged veterans Henkler had hired were smuggling guns out of the workshop in their hollow prosthetics. "He set the whole racket up from the beginning!" Mr. Fowler said. "I remember when we used to call him a saint for hiring those guys. Now we have egg on our faces. Crooks, all of them."

"It might have been the only work they could get, and he forced their hand," Abe said in almost a whisper.

"We're not running a charity, and a crook is a crook."

"Maybe people start off one way and become something unexpected along the way when their options start to close off."

"Only people with weak wills," said Mr. Fowler, slicing his meat.

Abe tried once more. "These guys faced enemy fire in a world war, lost limbs, and then went back to work on their feet ten hours a day in the only job anyone would give them. They don't sound weak-willed to me."

"It's nice that you care about the little people, Abe. It is. But you're on your way to the top, and once you see how many people are down below, you'll be glad you were crafty enough to move your way up. Your father knows. He gets it."

The conversation then turned to politics, and Abe was unable to control himself—much as Mirabelle had predicted. Roy Fowler tossed his napkin onto the table in victory over his baked Alaska and shook his head, addressing Nate. "I'm not thrilled about Roosevelt's stance on Europe at the moment. I'm afraid he's not steadfast enough about our neutrality. They might solve it with Hitler if they give him what he wants over there, but the Germans have themselves so wound up over their treatment at Versailles that they really need something to get their self-esteem up again. If we can settle this Sudetenland problem, let those of German background be ruled by Germans, maybe we can stop all this nonsense. I'm not sure of it, but it's sensible to try."

"Yes," said Nate. "Another war is not good for anyone."

Dorothy, who had said absolutely nothing until now, leaned across Nate just enough to capture Mirabelle's attention, and whispered, "I love your dress."

"It was my mother's," Mirabelle answered.

"Where is she?" Dorothy asked, looking toward the empty seat between Abe and her mother.

Mirabelle whispered: "She burned to death in a fire last year watching *Topper,* with Cary Grant and Constance Bennett. Which I hear wasn't even that good."

Dorothy sat back, her eyes as wide as dinner plates.

"Do you really think we should stay out of a war against Hitler? Against Mussolini?" Abe asked.

"Of course," said Mr. Fowler. He waved over the waiter and asked for a refill of his coffee. Sheldon noticed that Mr. Fowler's wife had not said a word all afternoon other than a few pleasantries. She made no intervention now.

"The arguments are indisputable," said Mr. Fowler, sitting farther back and crossing his legs. Nate sat more formally; he was a guest here, not a lord. "Take a look at this issue of Danzig in Poland that they're all clamoring about. Most of those people are German or come from the German race. I see that Poland has economic concerns, but the racial claims supersede the economic ones. And after Germany's treatment at Versailles at the end of the Great War . . . well . . . it's no wonder they wanted a strong leader to restore their sense of dignity and pride in themselves. They were routed and treated unfairly. Sure, I disagree with their domestic policies. But it's not America's business. Cooler heads must prevail. After all, we're partly to blame for the rise of the dictators, aren't we? Our constant disapproval of their internal policies only weakens the voices of those calling for moderation and peace. We ought to keep our mouths shut, stay out of it, and remain neutral to the end. If there's a war, heaven forbid, America can mediate the results and restore the values of Western civilization."

"The values of Western civilization," said Abe, repeating the phrase.

"Quite right," said Mr. Fowler.

"Does that include the burning of books throughout Germany? The declaration that there is only one legal party? The decree that the Aryan race is superior to all others and that a non-Aryan is anyone descended from non-Aryans, especially Jews? The creation of the Gestapo, the establishment of concentration camps back in 1936, the claims on land belonging to other nations, the constant belligerent threats? America should remain . . . neutral to all this?"

"I think it's very sad what's happening there. But it's of no geopolitical significance, and it's not America's role to step in and defend British and French colonies. We don't have a horse in such a race."

Nate tried to catch Abe's attention and turn the conversation away from the topic of Jews; away from the conversations that he knew Abe was having at Zionist meetings in Hartford at night, where he was learning about the latest oppressions in Europe; away from the latest setbacks in Palestine, where the British had severely limited Jewish immigration with their Passfield White Paper; away from the expulsion of the Jews from Italy and the refusal of any European country to take them in; and away from the tightening of immigration laws in the United States.

But Nate was two seats away. His arm couldn't stretch over both Mirabelle and Sheldon to squeeze Abe's leg.

"In December," Abe said very quietly to Mr. Fowler, "German Foreign Minister Ribbentrop said that Eastern Europe is now Germany's exclusive sphere of influence and that all French security commitments are now off limits. In March, Germany destroyed Czechoslovakia and seized land from Lithuania. Last month, Nazi Germany and fascist Italy signed the Pact of Steel. Western civilization is now on the brink of a civil war of ideas—of destiny—among communists, fascists, and democracies, and you're telling me that we don't have a horse in this race? That the United States of America should remain neutral in a battle for the soul of our civilization?"

Nate knew what was happening in Mr. Fowler's mind. He didn't know the man well, but he knew the type, and he had seen him in action for several years as he presided over a small empire in his worsted-wool suits. Mr. Fowler was thinking that a Jew finally gets invited to the Brubeck Club—makes his first step into society—and his upstart and uncontrollable teenage son decides to grandstand, decides to try to make an established man of Hartford—one almost thirty years his superior—look small in front of his guests and his wife and his daughter on the day of her graduation. A boy who is eating food off his own table is deciding to pick it up and throw it at his host. Nate had never felt so ashamed.

But Fowler only smiled.

"You have a burning sense of justice," Mr. Fowler said to Abe. He then turned to Nate. "That's wonderful. That's wonderful in a boy his age. The young should yearn for justice. Has he been considering law? It's the next obvious step for your family. Isn't that right?"

"Of course. University and law school. No doubt about it."

"Justice," said Abe, more to himself than to Mr. Fowler.

"That's what's happening in Europe right now," Mr. Fowler said, turning back to Abe. "A balancing of the power. Germany wants its pound of flesh, and we understand that. An eye for an eye. Once the balance is achieved, all of this will die down. That's the Old Testament right there. Right, Nate?"

"Absolutely," said Nate.

"No, it's not. That's not what it means," said Abe, even more angry at his father for being weak than at Fowler for being wrong.

The band struck up a slow-tempo version of "I Can't Give You Anything but Love, Baby," and — inexplicably at first — this invited Dorothy back into the conversation. "Have you seen *Bringing Up Baby*?" she said to Sheldon, who until then had been waiting for blue blood to start flowing, hoping it would explain something. "This song was in it," Dorothy explained. "Katharine Hepburn plays Susan Vance, and she's in possession of a tame leopard named Baby. This causes all sorts of problems with Cary Grant, who is starting to fall in love with her but finds her crazy. The leopard is calmed whenever he hears the song. It was so funny, did you see it?"

"Alas, no," said Mirabelle on Sheldon's behalf. "His mother burned to death in the same fire as mine. And during a Cary Grant movie. So — no, we're not seeing movies in dark enclosed rooms doused in flammable material with tiny little exits right now. You see the awkwardness of it, I'm sure."

Dorothy did see the awkwardness of it and felt it too. She seemed to make a private vow to never speak again and fell into a silence that approached a winter stillness after a frost.

Sheldon was starting to get that gentiles were different. He couldn't even fathom a way to keep a Jewish woman from talking.

Cake, maybe. If you gave her cake.

"Not what it means?" said Mr. Fowler. He was a lawyer. Was there anyone better at understanding the meaning of a text than a lawyer? "It's there in black-and-white, young man." His chuckle wasn't as hearty as the earlier ones.

"The words are," said Abe, still very quiet but looking up now. "But the meaning is not. It's a Christian interpretation imposed on a Jewish text to validate the need for Jesus to come and fix the unfixable problems of a seemingly incomplete and petty Jewish theology. Which is pretty much the source of anti-Semitism right there. If Jews took it literally, there'd be a lot more jokes about one-eyed pirates looking for dentists."

Mr. Fowler forced a chuckle and was about to ask a question, but Abe was not having a conversation anymore and he had made his last joke. "The Talmud says we can't take it literally," Abe explained, "because 'no two eyes are the same.' That's why justice can never be mechanical and God needs us to engage and restore it every day. When we lie down, and when we rise up. This is why justice will never come from finding a balance with the forces of evil. It will come by defeating them."

Abe stood. He thanked Mr. and Mrs. Fowler for their hospitality and said he wasn't feeling well and needed to leave. Nate stood too, intent on following him out, but Abe put up his hand and said it wasn't necessary. He'd find his way home. There was no point in ruining a fine afternoon.

On his way out, Abe stepped between Sheldon and Mirabelle, and placed his hands on their shoulders. For the first time in Sheldon's presence, Abe bent down and kissed his sister on the cheek. He couldn't be sure, but Sheldon thought he heard Abe say, "Goodbye."

The rest of the meal passed without incident. Mirabelle was out for the rest of the afternoon with her friends, and Sheldon — having no one to speak to on account of Abe's continued absence — took *Brave New World* by Aldous Huxley to the river close to the armory and read about a world asleep from a drug called Soma. It made Sheldon look up and watch the light twinkle off the river like he and Lenny did in Whately. He wondered if Europe had colors too.

• • •

When Sheldon didn't find Abe at home on his return at dusk and didn't see him when he was getting ready for bed, he decided to walk down the hall in his pajamas to Mirabelle's room and knock.

"Yeah?"

Sheldon opened the door.

"What's up?" Mirabelle was in a softer mood, the way Sheldon liked her best. She was under the covers in her light-blue nightgown. With her makeup removed, she looked much younger than usual. The wall between them — the one she placed between herself and everyone and everything else — was momentarily down like a drawbridge.

"Abe's not here," Sheldon said. "His favorite jacket is gone and a bunch of his clothes. The newspapers are all stacked up perfectly. They're never stacked like that."

Mirabelle was holding a fashion magazine and placed it on the blanket that covered her outstretched legs. She made a thinking face.

"Did he say anything to you?" Sheldon asked her.

"No. The last time I saw him was at the lunch. You?"

"Nothing."

"He must be out with his friends or something. It's graduation night. There must be parties all over the place."

Sheldon stood there unconvinced.

Mirabelle didn't believe it either. If she did, she would have started reading the magazine again and shooed him away.

"Where do you think he went?" she asked.

"I think he went away."

"No. No, he can't. He can't just leave us. Not like this."

As though hearing the truth was all it took to admit it, Mirabelle started to cry.

Sheldon had never seen her cry before. He had never seen her act like anything but a warrior. Now she looked like she needed her mother very, very badly. Even more than Sheldon needed his own.

Sheldon usually backed away from Mirabelle when she became emotional. This time, though, he stepped forward and stood next to her. Her crying was unprotected and open. She looked up at him and then reached for him. He sat on the edge of her bed, placed his arms around her, and hugged her. She began to sob, and as she did, Sheldon realized that, in her own way and like he had, she had now lost it all.

✈

ON HIS OWN BED, his pajama top wet with his cousin's tears, Sheldon sat in silence looking at the empty space where Abe should have been. Had he done it? Had he killed Mr. Henkler? Is that why he left them?

After the first reports came in about the gun having been fired twice and Mr. Henkler's wife saying that he never would have killed himself, there was a wide-ranging investigation that was reported in the papers that Sheldon and Abe had read voraciously. Once it was revealed, though, that Mr. Henkler had had financial troubles connected to gambling, had been behind the missing guns, and did have relationships with certain crime elements in town, the police decided to let the matter lie. Eventually, even Mrs. Henkler stopped agitating for the truth. Abe had been the one to explain why: "Colt paid her to stop."

If he had done it, Abe would be safe now. The investigation was over. Would he have left them anyway? Or was it about more than that? All that stuff he was talking about to Mr. Fowler?

It was a gentle and breezy night, and Sheldon opened the window to let in some life and sound. He missed the smells of the forest and the sounds of the crickets, and wished he was home. The movement of the city air, though, was just enough to calm him.

Ready to try to sleep, he lay back on the pillow and pulled up the blanket. Something, though, was under the pillow.

Sitting up, he moved it aside and saw two items: a Colt .45 automatic and a piece of paper with a single sentence.

THE MAN YOU'RE LOOKING FOR IS CALLED LORENZO.

PART II

COMEDY

TWO YEARS LATER

SLICED BREAD

L ENNY BERNSTEIN HAD IT all figured out. Like everyone else who had it all figured out, he announced it with the customary phrase: "Look. All we gotta do . . ."

Lenny's hands were back behind his head, his feet were stretched out in the grass in front of his house, and he was looking at a cloud that—given another moment—was promising to look like a burlesque dancer's ass. He was prepared to wait it out.

It was summer. Sheldon was sitting beside Lenny and using a long piece of dried grass to nudge a tiny stick in front of some marching ants. They were moving house from one hole in the ground to another (who makes these decisions and on what basis Sheldon had no idea) and Sheldon decided that adversity would breed character in the ants so annoying them was actually a way to help.

One ant—hereby christened Jeff—had stopped to consider his options. It was now a competition to see whether Jeff or Lenny was going to be more interesting.

Lenny continued: ". . . is get ourselves out to the Catskills to one of those fancy hotels where all the acts go in the summer. And get in on it."

"Get in on what?"

"The act!"

"The act."

"I said that. Twice. Aren't you paying attention?"

"To what?"

It was the summer of 1941 and Sheldon was almost fifteen and Lenny already sixteen. The war in Europe had been raging for close to two years and America was not involved. The Bernsteins had invited Sheldon to spend the summer with them in Massachusetts and Nate—having nothing for Sheldon to do—had agreed and put him on a bus. Mirabelle had turned nineteen, was a high school graduate with a job at Underwood, and was dating an Italian who was threatening to propose to her. Sheldon couldn't watch anymore. Getting away seemed like a good idea. Now he was flanked by the likes of Lenny and Jeff.

"To my plan to break into show business and take over the world!"

"The whole world's at war," said Sheldon, watching Jeff navigate the stick while gripping a leaf he insisted on carrying. "Everyone's trying to take it over. We're gonna have some stiff competition."

"All right, fine, just America then. We're not at war. I'm telling you, Sheldon"—Lenny breathed out a sigh of gratitude to God as a perfect ass formed in the sky above him—"that if we get ourselves out there we can get jobs as busboys or bellhops or whatever, and then, you know, one night we do our act. I've heard stories about this happening."

"You've heard stories."

"On the radio. In the papers. Hoboes. Vagabonds. Gypsies. You know. The ways stories get around."

"I really don't," said Sheldon. Jeff had achieved victory. He had gone *around* the stick. All the other ants followed Jeff. Sheldon lost interest and turned to Lenny. "You're not a comedian."

"Miss Simmons says I am."

"No," said Sheldon, putting up a finger. "What she often said was 'What are you, a comedian?' That didn't make you a comedian. That made you a pain in the ass."

"It's a hop, skip, and a jump from one to the other. Most professional comedians started off as amateur pains in the asses."

"Your parents are gonna let us go?" Sheldon asked.

"My dad says he has a friend in Springfield named Jackie Lowenthal. Mr. Lowenthal's got a bad heart because he's been running this bakery for like twenty years and he's been eating half the inventory. He goes to this guy called Dr. Green, who my dad met at a bat mitzvah for Selma Berkowitz.

You remember her? The ginger with the freckles who used to keep putting her ponytail under her nose so it looked like a mustache?"

"No."

"She lived in Northampton? We met her at temple when we were about eight?"

"Is there an end to this story? Or even a beginning?"

"Dr. Green's at Grossinger's in the Catskills. It's the King Kong of hotels, and there are . . . I don't even know . . . hundreds of hotels. So, if things don't work out there, we can walk down the street and we'll bump into another place. Also, if I come up with ten minutes' worth of jokes, I can do the same schtick ten times a day running from hotel to hotel."

"Or you could join a track team."

"I'm thinking you could be a lifeguard at one of the pools."

"Lenny, I can barely swim."

"When was the last time you saw a lifeguard swim?"

"That's a good point," said Sheldon. "But in a pinch . . ."

"How about tomorrow?"

Sheldon and Lenny didn't have the same feelings about being in Whately. For Sheldon, this was a visit home. Walking the long quiet streets gave him a sense of tranquility he hadn't felt since his parents left him unwillingly. He still liked it here. Home had failed him, but it remained home.

For Lenny, this was a place to wave at in a rearview mirror through a cloud of dust on his way toward a better and brighter future.

"I like it here," Sheldon confessed. "I like being back. Hartford's been . . . hectic."

"We'll be back after we're gone. It's not like anything's gonna change here."

"That's why I like it."

"Your life has been an adventure so far, Sheldon. Your letters are better than comic books. Batman's life is boring compared to yours. Mine's not like that. All I've had is your letters and I had to burn those. Dr. Green said we can call on him if we're in any trouble. I don't see us calling on the guy, but it satisfies my parents. We're going. Now you know. It's been nice talking to you."

The prospect of getting a bus tomorrow to go from Whately to Springfield to Albany to somewhere near Liberty, New York—with Lenny talking a mile a minute all the way—gave Sheldon a sense of what his mother used to mean when she used the word "weary."

"You really think," Sheldon said, "that we're going to get to the Catskills, find jobs, and before we know it, you're a world-class comedian?"

"You know how they say, 'It's better than sliced bread' when they mean something's better than the best thing ever?" asked Lenny.

"Yeah."

"I read that it took the Wonder Bread company years to convince people to buy sliced bread."

"How does that help your case?"

"I think," said Lenny, "that things aren't inevitable. I think you make them inevitable and then they only look inevitable on the back end. If it's true for Wonder Bread, it's got to be true across the board, right? I think the first step to success is for you to stop giving me lip and then getting on the damn bus."

The morning of their departure, Lenny was a font of optimism that would have been infectious had Sheldon not been inoculated against the emotion. His eyes still closed, a touch of drool on the left corner of his mouth, Sheldon tried to shut out the happy noises as Lenny bounced around their bedroom like a soldier about to get laid.

"You were right yesterday," Lenny said. "I'm going to need an act. The question is whose. Because knowing what to steal from is a real skill. But at some point, I'm going to have to think of something funny. You don't happen to know anything, do you?"

"Nothing comes to mind."

"It doesn't matter. We got time on the bus."

"The bus," Sheldon repeated, as if it were the name of his new cellblock.

"My mom's making us pancakes before we go. We got some of that grade B maple syrup—you remember, right? Darker, thicker, puts hair on your chest? I think I can smell the butter now. Are you packed yet? They got a lot of sports there. You heard about that? You ever golf? Powerful men all golf. I can't figure out why. They walk around in Scottish clothes in the hot sun sweating for three hours. It doesn't make sense. When we get there, do you want to try it?"

"No."

"I like the idea of it. The gentiles won't let us golf, so now we've got our own golf courses. How about them apples, huh?"

They packed and showered, dressed and ate. Outside, the day was hot and still. The sun beat down on them with a permanence that stopped time. The cicadas were back this year and starting their racket in the sun. Nothing beyond Lenny's front yard suggested that anything was in motion anyplace else or that escape was even possible. Everything driving them forward came from inside Lenny.

The townsfolk knew Sheldon was back because he'd been to visit other old school friends, had lunches and dinners at classmates' homes, and with his fortune from the pawn shop—Abe had left him money from his own take, and Mirabelle had too, on account of his own poor showing—he treated everyone to ice cream and became the pied piper of Whately, if only for a week.

Though he'd been there long enough to catch everyone's attention, it wasn't until they were sitting at the bus stop waiting for the Greyhound that the police cruiser pulled up and Sheriff Simmons stepped out to have a few words.

"Well, well. The man himself. Young Sheldon Horowitz."

"Hi, Sheriff," said Sheldon.

"Carol said you were back in town. Word is you've been doing OK down in Connecticut."

"It's OK, sir."

"I'm glad to see you're standing tall."

Sheldon didn't reply.

"Listen, Sheldon," the sheriff said, taking his hat from his head. "There's been something on my mind and it's something I've been debating whether to tell you, but now that I see how much you've grown, I sort of think it's only fair. Can I have a word in private for a minute?"

Sheldon looked around. There was no one else on the bench aside from Lenny and not another person as far as the eye could see.

"Whatever you tell me, I'm just gonna tell him," Sheldon said, indicating Lenny.

"Sure. OK," the sheriff said, looking slightly embarrassed by the moment. "Here it goes. When your dad died, you tried to tell me something about the accident. At the time, I didn't believe you. What with the house burning down and the Krupinskis stealing your stuff and your father gone and Lila before that—anyway, it was a world on the shoulders of a twelve-year-old boy and I didn't think you had your head all together then. You told me someone ran you off the road during that rainstorm. I didn't believe you. Well—now I do."

Sheldon and Lenny both stared at him.

"In the last three years, it's happened at least twice more that we know of. My brother is in Springfield, and he's a cop too. We share war stories and that gives us a kind of bird's-eye view of what's happening around here; otherwise, there'd be no way to know. As it happens, there have been a couple of car accidents that haven't made a lot of sense, not until we started to see a pattern. For one, when the wrecked cars were examined afterward, there was paint from another car found on the driver's side, which suggests they were bumped before they went off the road. Second, when we looked into the people who were driving—or in your dad's case, the owner of the truck—it turned out that the victims had some shady dealings with some people of a . . . criminal orientation. And third, they all happened at night on small roads not too far from here. So, the point is, it's now our suspicion that some kind of Mob enforcer is doing hit-and-runs to get rid of people. Anyway, all of this is to say—I'm sorry. And I believe you, and people are working on this. We want to catch him too. I don't want you thinking that no one knows or cares. That's a burden I can take off your shoulders."

"Who did it?" Sheldon asked.

"Oh, we don't know that, Sheldon. I'm sorry. We've got people looking into it, though. Efforts are being made."

Lorenzo, Sheldon thought. He couldn't get himself to say it, though.

"OK," Sheldon said. "Thanks, Sheriff. I appreciate that."

"That's something you don't see every day," said Lenny, watching the sheriff return to the squad car and pull away. "I never doubted you but . . . wow, huh?"

Sheldon, though, wasn't listening to Lenny. He was checking his watch. They were forty-five minutes early for the bus. Lenny had talked him into it despite the bus stop being only ten minutes at most from his house. Sheldon did some quick math in his head.

Ten minutes to the house, a few minutes to get one of the rifles Lenny had hidden, maybe eight minutes at a trot to his destination, and he could be back here with time to spare before the bus arrived. Then he'd be gone for more than a month to let things cool off.

"I got something I got to do," Sheldon said, taking off his rucksack to lighten his burden. "Something I should have done a long time ago. Wait for me and watch the stuff."

"Where you going?"

"Abe was right, and I didn't follow it up because I was young and scared, but I'm not scared anymore. And, you know what, Lenny? You're right. Things are only inevitable in retrospect." Sheldon was already off and running as Lenny sat there alone trying to remember what "retrospect" means.

Sheldon had almost forgotten the rifles were there. Lenny had mentioned that he'd wrapped them up in a blanket in his letter and Sheldon was pretty sure he knew where he'd hidden them.

Keeping his head low so as not to bump it or brush a rusty nail, Sheldon crawled under Lenny's back porch on his belly through a gap in the planks and pushed away the dirt underneath until he found the giant blanket he was looking for. Heaving it out of its shallow grave, he reached in the opening and unfolded the blanket just enough to grip the barrel of the Gewehr 98—the Mauser—that his father had brought home from the front.

"It was my enemy's and now it's mine," his father had once said. "It seemed fitting and it's a good gun."

Sheldon yanked, but the bolt handle was caught on the blanket and this was costing him time. He yanked harder, which made things worse. Sucking the smell of cat poo into his nose, he calmed himself down and unfolded the blanket slowly, gently nudged the Winchester aside, then removed the

Mauser. He left everything open and ready for him because he planned to be back soon.

Sheldon shimmied out backward from the hole under the porch. Back in the hot sun, he saw that he was filthy and stunk of kitty excrement.

He cussed.

The Krupinski house was less than a mile away. It was oppressively hot, but time was limited, so he had to jog there. If anyone had been looking out their window, they would have seen a black shadow in the midday sun hauling ass across the yellow land with a German rifle, but Sheldon didn't care. The dirt was masking his features and he felt somehow invisible. Powerful. Certain of himself. He wondered if Abe had felt this way when he confronted Mr. Henkler. Only Mr. Henkler hadn't done anything. Or had he? Sheldon still didn't know. It wasn't clear, even now, whether Henkler had set up Uncle Nate to take the fall for the missing guns—knowing the consequences with the Mob if he didn't—or whether it had only been Abe's theory.

The barn on the Krupinski property was still there, but the house was even more in disrepair than Sheldon remembered; it sagged under the weight of its age and insignificance. The paint was peeling off like leprous skin. The front door was a faded gray and had a brass knob.

He turned the knob and the door opened.

It was dark inside. Sheldon's eyes were accustomed to the brightness of a summer day so the darkness was more complete and more sinister for him than it was for the demon of a man who lived inside. No matter. Sheldon was on a quest and couldn't be bothered with blindness. A few months ago, Timely Comics had introduced a new superhero called Captain America, and on the cover of the first issue, the captain was punching Hitler right in the jaw. Sheldon had seen a copy back in Hartford at Sundial News and Comics, but he hadn't gotten the chance to read it because they'd sold out before he could buy a copy, but the image on the cover had stuck with him. No one was bad-mouthing the Nazis—even now, after the Brits had been at war for a year and a half—and it was about time someone did.

But he didn't feel like Captain America in the foyer of Old Krupinski's house; he felt like Abe.

Sheldon wanted to know the men Krupinski was doing business with. He wanted names and addresses, and he wanted to know what scam had pissed off which party and had led to his father's death. He wanted to know if the brothers had set up his father deliberately that night or whether it was old-fashioned bad luck that the man with the mustache chose that night to run the Krupinski truck off the road.

Or maybe it had been the old man's plan all along. Was *he* the mastermind? Sitting there in the dark in an easy chair with a pipe while directing his evil minions to do his bidding like a small-town Mussolini? The Polish Al Capone of the Berkshires?

What was Sheldon's plan? He'd berated Lenny for not having a plan only yesterday, but he'd been wrong. Lenny did have a plan. He was going to show up at Grossinger's hotel and, step by step, lie and connive and convince and con his way right to the top of show business "like everyone else."

The only plan that came to mind in that moment, though, was Abe's plan: Make it look like a suicide. Leave a note that cleared it all up and moved all the pieces on the chessboard into better positions. It was genius. It was wrong too. Maybe it was both. Abe had made a bold move just like he'd said he would. He'd said that he wasn't going to stand silently in front of the firing squad and wait to die. He was going to go down swinging, just as he'd done in the alley when he was beat up by McCullen's kid and when he faced off against Mr. Henkler and Mr. Fowler.

Sheldon heard a noise coming from the room that had once been a dining room and was now a cave.

When Sheldon walked into the room, he saw the world through the eyes of a fourteen-year-old boy who was confronting the demon of the Berkshires. But Bruno Krupinski was looking out from eyes that were jaded by misery and superstition. They were the eyes of a drunk and a man too lonely for speech. So, when a figure covered in filth and carrying a German rifle walked into his dining room where he was sitting on a wingback chair with a bottle of bourbon, Bruno Krupinski did not see a boy or the shine of a boy's eyes. He saw the ghost of Joseph Horowitz, a veteran of the Great War who had come—finally—to collect his due in the form of Bruno's withered soul.

"Do you know who I am?" said the voice of the ghost.

"Yes. I know who you are."

"Do you know why I'm here?" The ghost's eyes glowed with the brightness of eternal youth.

"You're here for me," Bruno said.

"Yes. You're going to tell me what really happened. You're going to tell me why we were driven off the road."

"I didn't mean for it to end like that."

"Start talking before I send you to hell."

Old Bruno Krupinski took the ghost of the dead Jew at his word. The rifle in his hands was only a prop; the Grim Reaper took your soul without having to use a gun. The ghost of Joseph Horowitz would extend his hand and Bruno would be whisked away to eternal damnation and this was his only chance to confess and repent and lighten his burden before death came, the death that part of him had wanted ever since his wife left him with two boys and said that they were all no good.

She went west to freedom like they all do.

A part of Bruno—the last good part—was still a Catholic whose grandparents talked of the old country. That part of him believed in ghosts and damnation.

Christ was a Jew. Why wouldn't the Grim Reaper be one too?

Of course he would appear as the man Bruno had killed. Who else?

"We were skimming," Bruno said, pouring himself another drink and punching it back. "We were buying your pelts and selling them down in Hartford per our agreement. But we were selling them down there for more than we told you. So that was the first part."

"I always knew you were cheating us," said the ghost with the rifle. "But you didn't run us off the road because you had a good thing going."

"Yeah, well," said Bruno, scraping his fingernails against the fabric of the armchair like an excited cat. "The people in Hartford weren't the nicest types. This was all off the books. No taxes. No paperwork. At one point in 1937, we wanted to raise our prices because the Depression was wrapping up and costs were increasing. But the Mob didn't want to pay more, and they were the kind of people you don't ask twice. So, we came up with the idea of stopping off in Springfield on the way down to Hartford. We sold off about twenty percent of your stock for about thirty percent more. You got paid the same either way, so you didn't ask questions, and the Hartford crew had no idea how many you'd given us, so they didn't know we'd off-loaded merchandise before it got there and made that extra cut. Smooth as silk."

"But you got caught."

"People in Springfield talked to people in Hartford. We didn't think of that. You see, there are a lot of guys with connections out there. And they stay in the game by watching out for one another's deals. We didn't know how tightly that web was wound. I guess we found out."

Bruno nodded in recognition of the full weight of his own greed, stupidity, and arrogance.

"Springfield stopped buying, of course, but we had made some friends and one guy we knew tipped us off that Hartford was coming for violent payback. When you said you needed to borrow the truck" — Bruno took another drink, not as a reward but as preparation for the endgame — "the boys said it was providence. Like God wanted it to happen that way. If we just let it all play itself out, we'd be as snug as bugs and could start over again. Maybe go east to Boston and make a fresh start."

"You knew. Say it."

"We knew."

Sheldon slid back the bolt and chambered a round dramatically. "Who was driving the truck, old man?"

"Oh, I don't know that. Our Hartford guy was Ernie Caruso. He's the one we shorted and the one who wanted blood. Ernie runs a team for Ray Patriarca. They're the biggest Mafia in New England."

"Who's Lorenzo?"

"I don't know any Lorenzo."

"Lorenzo was the driver."

"If you say so. There are a lot of people in this game, but there isn't that much muscle. Only half a dozen guys are out there slitting throats and making widows in this region. There are a whole lot of kneecappers, you see, but not a lot of baby killers. It's not just the killing, you see. It's the not talking. They don't spread that kind of work around too much or someone'll talk. It's inevitable. Maybe this Lorenzo is one of those half dozen. Makes sense, but I don't know."

Bruno had come clean. He was ready for death. There was just one more thing he had to say. "You're shorter than I remember you."

Sheldon didn't understand this. "How the hell could I be shorter three years *later*?"

"I don't know. I don't know how things work on your side."

"My side of what?"

Sheldon looked around. He believed everything Old Krupinski had said despite his being insane. The information was burned into his mind like a brand now, the names, the logic. There was nothing else he needed. The brothers were still in prison, and this guy was living in one of his own making. Time would take care of him soon enough. Killing him would be both murder and a mercy, and Sheldon didn't like the combination.

He looked at his watch. "Oh shit. I'm late. I got to go."

"You're late?" muttered Krupinski. "You can be late?"

"Stay miserable, Krupinski. You deserve it," said Sheldon, turning for the door.

"You're not going to kill me?"

"Take a look in the mirror, old man. You're already dead."

Sheldon ran. The sun had baked the dirt into his skin, but now the sweat from the fear and heat was starting to soften it again. Busting out of Bruno's front door, he knew he had to hoof it if he wanted to get the rifle back into its bag and make the bus stop so Lenny's hopes and dreams wouldn't be dashed.

Except for a few minutes ago, Sheldon hadn't run with a rifle. Hunters don't run. Trappers don't either. If anything, they creep. He'd never really considered how heavy these guns were until now. They were heavier when you were running, that was for sure. He was so lost in his own thoughts that he didn't see Betsy Durkin until he was almost next to her in the middle of Mr. Abernathy's fallow field, which was the quickest way to Lenny's house from the Krupinski house.

"Hey, Sheldon," said Betsy, with sweetness and a bouncy beat.

Betsy was in Sheldon's class. They'd known each other since first grade. She was a little on the butterflies-and-rainbows side of life for his taste, but he liked her well enough and she'd always been nice to him.

"Oh. Hey, Betsy."

"Why are you dressed like a bush?"

"What do you mean?"

She made a motion as though she were washing her face. "You've got leaves and stuff in your hair. It's kind of all over you, actually."

"Oh, right," said Sheldon. "Well . . . I had to crawl under a deck to get some stuff I'd left here. It was . . . well . . . it looked like this and now I do."

"Oh. Why do you have a gun?"

Sheldon remembered he was holding a German army rifle.

"This was my dad's. I'm putting it back where it belongs. Don't need it in Hartford. Obviously."

"Right."

"And . . . how are you?" he asked, knowing that every second was being chipped away by this discussion, but he didn't want to be mean to Betsy and didn't want her talking about this when he was gone.

"Good. You gonna be around?" she asked.

"Ah . . . not really. Me and Lenny are going to the Catskills. Try to get some jobs for the summer. He wants to be a comedian."

"You too?"

"Not so much, no. Maybe a lifeguard."

"Can you swim now?"

"No."

"Hmm," muttered Betsy.

"There are kinks to work out. Look, Betsy . . . it's been swell seeing you, but I really got to get moving if I'm going to make the bus. If I don't, Lenny's gonna be mad. OK? No hard feelings?"

Then he bolted.

After Sheldon had packed the Mauser away, he emerged from under Lenny's deck with twice as much mud, which was now nice and gooey.

Outside, in the blazing light, Sheldon dashed down the road at full tilt, the mud caking on his face. By the time he caught up with Lenny, the bus was emerging from the shimmering distance like a hippo slipping out of an African lake. Lenny's hands were on his hips. "I was about to have a heart attack!"

"I'm here."

"Oh my God. Look at you."

"I know, I know. I'm a little dirty."

"What is that smell?" Lenny asked, as the bus sighed to a halt beside them.

Sheldon put his rucksack on his back, picked the larger branches from his hair, and rummaged in his pocket for his bus fare. Before boarding, he stopped for a moment to catch his breath and his bearings.

"You know, Lenny," he said. "Some days really are stranger than others."

"I'm not so sure, Sheldon. I'm beginning to think you make them yourself."

THE SWEET SPOT

AT SPRINGFIELD THEY CHANGED buses for Albany, and while they were there, Sheldon stripped naked in the men's room, threw away his clothes, and changed into something fresh. Under a flickering fluorescent light with sunlight busting through the cracks in the old door behind him, he washed himself and rinsed his hair three times with hand soap. He dried off with paper towels. At the end of the ordeal, he combed his hair and strutted out like a new man.

Lenny was on a wooden bench inside the main hall, which was as busy as any major train station. His legs were crossed, and he was reading a copy of the *Boston Daily Globe*. He dropped the paper's corner and sized up Sheldon.

"Your boots are a disgrace."

"They were like that before."

"How do you smell now?"

"Better."

"Better than what?"

"How much time have we got?" Sheldon asked.

"None. I got sandwiches and a couple of Cokes. Bus leaves in five. In two hours, we're in Albany, and from there, we go up to Liberty and Grossinger's."

Sheldon sat down next to Lenny. The benches had been polished recently, and at least three brands of aftershave were competing for his attention. As bus stations went, this wasn't bad. Still, Sheldon wasn't thrilled about this Grossinger's plan and he said so.

"Why are we attacking the enemy at the strongest point?" Sheldon asked.

"I admit I don't know as much about this as you do, but I hear that Grossinger's is kind of the top of the top. That and the Concord. You said there were hundreds of places. Why not try someplace else? Make life a little easier?"

"I'd rather work my way down from the top than up from the bottom, wouldn't you?"

"I guess."

"Tips are better if the guests are richer."

People began boarding the bus, and the boys took their seats on the scorching-hot vinyl. They pulled out of the city onto a black ribbon of road, picking up and dropping off travelers along the way. As the bus chugged along at forty miles an hour with the windows down, the wind blew hot against the boys' faces and the sun turned their faces a beautiful bronze.

Lenny ate a ham and cheese and Sheldon a roast beef with mustard. As he had threatened to, Lenny worked on his act. He stared into his notebook and talked to himself nonstop in a hushed voice for more than half the journey, chuckling on occasion when he heard his own joke for the first time.

As Sheldon watched Lenny scratch out longer words and write in shorter ones and break long sentences into punchier ones, he sat back and thought to himself how nice it was to have a friend again.

Bored, Sheldon leafed through the 1940 vacation guide for resorts in Ulster, Sullivan, Delaware, and Orange Counties in New York. There was — out there somewhere — a 1941 edition of this same guide, but neither Lenny nor Sheldon had the high-level contacts required to score such a thing.

The guide was produced by the New York Ontario and Western Railway to encourage New Yorkers to take the rains and get out of town. It was more than 150 pages long and contained pictures as nice as postcards. The introduction began:

Your vacation this year, either during the spring, summer, fall or winter, will be one continuous round of healthful pleasure if spent in the counties of

Orange, Ulster, Sullivan or Delaware, known as "The Playground of the Empire State."

The book promised the "bracing air of the mountains" and said that the various resorts "welcome you to happy and health-giving recreation."

"It sounds nice," Sheldon said.

Lenny wasn't paying attention to Sheldon's reading material. He was working on his act. He erased something and started over, asking, "'Nazi' is spelled with one *z*, right?"

"Yeah."

"'Cuz I hear some people say 'nazzie' like it rhymes with 'snazzy.'"

"No. It's 'Nazi,' like 'putz,'" said Sheldon. It was imperfect but good.

"Snazzy putzes," said Lenny, going with it.

"They do have snazzy uniforms."

"What were you saying? What sounds nice?"

"All of it. There are hundreds of these resorts like you were saying before," Sheldon said, leafing through the guide. "They have a two-page spread here for Grossinger's and — Lenny — I got to be honest with you, there's no way they're gonna hire us for anything and I don't see anyone here letting you tell an evening of jokes. I mean . . . this place is serious. It's not like anything we've ever seen before."

"I don't need an evening. I need a solid ten minutes. I got that."

"About what?"

"Mostly Nazis."

"Doesn't sound funny."

"It's hilarious. You're gonna love it."

"Lenny," Sheldon said, as if his friend's name were a lament. "Look at the people listed here in their Golden Book on page seventy-two. Really famous people. Some of them are even on the radio. Eddie Cantor, Milton Berle, Louis Sobol, Barney Ross, John Garfield, Buddy Clark, Abe Lyman, Belle Baker, Leonard Lyons, Nick Kenny, the Ritz Brothers, and George White. If I added you, your name would be the only one on the list we wouldn't recognize."

"Belle Baker's a singer," Lenny said. "She's no threat to me."

"I don't think they're going to let you open for Milton Berle."

Lenny closed his notebook. This was serious business.

"I want us to get jobs at Grossinger's because it's where everyone goes. *Everybody*, Sheldon. There might be three hundred hotels or whatever, but this is it. This is the magical destination. This is Cinderella's ball. It's where you go to see and be seen. I don't expect to perform there. Obviously. I'll perform where I can. We'll get some bicycles so we can get around from place to place. I'll perform in those and we'll see where it all goes."

"I thought you wanted to start at the top and all that."

"We're going to start at the bottom of the top as bellhops and waiters and stuff. We'll make more money, we'll meet fancier people, and I suspect the food will be great. And there will be girls."

"There are girls everywhere."

"Rich girls angry at their fathers. That's the sweet spot."

"You'd better have a plan, Lenny," Sheldon said. "Or this is going to be a short trip."

Lenny did have a plan. And it was a doozy.

When the bus let them off in Liberty, Lenny took the vacation guide and flipped to the back to consult the Rand McNally map. Out on the street, he confidently pointed. "Thataway."

Vacationers and delivery trucks passed them on the thin road as they walked to the northeast, then turned north up an even narrower road that turned out to be the driveway to Grossinger's. When Sheldon saw it, he understood why it was called a resort.

"Lenny. It's a campus. There are like twenty buildings here. Maybe more."

"There's only one door we care about," said Lenny, sounding like Eliot Ness before a raid.

"I hope you mean the back door."

"No, my friend. I very much mean the front."

Sheldon and Lenny stood facing the fortress they were about to assault with nothing but Lenny's wit and Sheldon's guidebook. Lenny studied the lines of the faux Tudor facade and watched the bellhops pop out of the main door under the brown roof, grab the luggage of the guests, and zip back inside. Cars were lined up to approach the door. It was a frenzy of patterned effort that was as precise as a military parade.

Sheldon knew immediately that all hope was lost and that they should abandon this windmill-jousting nonsense, find a nice campsite for the night, and tomorrow they could take the bus back to Whately and skim rocks by the river. Because that was nice too.

"That one," Lenny whispered, choosing a victim. "Follow my lead and say nothing. If you have to say anything, you agree with everything I just said, and you don't make up anything. I got a system."

Sheldon nodded. He was fine with this. This wasn't his adventure. He was along for the ride. How bad could things get?

Lenny walked up to the main entrance as though he were the prodigal son of a sultan. He waved down a bellhop who was wearing black pants and a red double-breasted jacket that was at least two sizes too large. Sheldon trotted behind him.

"Hey," said Lenny, as though he were arriving for a party. "You one of the new guys?"

"What?" said the seventeen-year-old bellhop. He had a ruddy face that was turning redder in the sun, not brown the way Lenny and Sheldon were.

"Bus just got in. This is our first summer. Who are we supposed to report to?"

"You're bellhops?" the kid said.

"We will be once we're suited up. I can't remember the name of the guy. You gonna remind me or are you sworn to secrecy?"

"Oh. Yeah. Ben Adelman."

"No, not Ben. I know Ben. I meant the guy at the top. The fat cat in the office who never comes out."

"Oh. Mel Friedman. But he's not here this week."

"That's fine. Where's Ben?"

"I think he's in the concierge office."

"OK. Thanks. I'm Lenny and this is Sheldon. We'll see you around."

"Yeah," said the bellhop with no name or personality or interest. "OK."

Lenny marched into the reception and placed his hands on the counter-top as a pretty redhead approached him. Lenny ran his finger over the surface and examined it for dust. He then sucked his finger, and said, "Lemony. Nice touch."

This made the girl smile.

"I'm Lenny Bernstein and this is Sheldon Horowitz. We're the new bell-hops. Mel Friedman told us to come in today. Our bus was a little late and we're afraid that Ben Adelman's gonna fire us before he hires us. What's your name?"

"Miriam," she said, still smiling. She was a little older than Lenny and her red hair was braided in the back. Unleashed, it might have reached her waist and expanded to the hallway. Her eyes were hazel, and her look was patient. In it, Lenny saw love.

"We need your advice, Miriam. Maybe even some help. Would you help us?"

Miriam nodded a few times. There was a moment where things might have gone one of two ways. Either Lenny's ruse was working or Miriam was going to blow a whistle and a couple of linebackers were going to tackle them to the ground and then rustle them off as if they were calves at a rodeo.

But that wasn't what happened. Instead, Miriam pulled out two pieces of paper from a drawer on her side of the desk, placed them on the counter, and slapped down two pens. "Fill in these, bring them back to me, and I'll stamp them. You bring them to Ben and you just might survive."

"He's in the concierge office, right?" said Lenny, which Sheldon found unnecessary but smooth.

"Yes."

"We owe you one, Miriam."

"You owe me two."

"Is it too soon to tell you that I love you?"

"Probably."

"I'll save it, but you should know that every minute I'm not saying it it's because I'm building up the courage."

"OK," she said. "Bring the papers back once they're filled out." Then she shooed the boys away with the backs of her hands. Lenny might have been mistaken, but he was sure he saw rays of light dance out of her fingernails.

Ben Adelman was in his thirties and considered himself far too old for this kind of work because that was what his father, a successful owner of a meatpacking plant who'd once been a butcher, had said to him. "Men in their thirties should be doing something respectable and, frankly, better paid than managing ungrateful and masturbatory adolescents during tourist season."

In truth, Ben Adelman agreed. And if it wasn't for the women who came each season looking to avenge their husbands' indiscretions or were furious at being deposited here for the summer like so much compost, Ben might have found more dignified work. For now, he was content with the undignified work and the sex. To sustain this state of mind, he had a simple policy: Everything needs to go smoothly.

Ben was sipping a mug of hot coffee despite the heat when two unfamiliar teenagers walked in wearing rucksacks.

"No rucksacks in my office," he said, placing the mug on his desk.

"Right you are, Mr. Adelman," said the kid who was going to do the talking.

Lenny chucked them into the hallway and closed the door.

"Who are you two?" Ben asked.

"Your new bellhops, Mr. Adelman. I'm Lenny Bernstein and this is Sheldon Horowitz. Mel Friedman hired us. I think he was bullied by Dr. Green, but that's over my head so I'm not going to talk about it." Lenny stepped forward and handed Ben the papers with the blue-inked information and the red rubber stamp. Ben looked at the two knuckleheads and shook his head.

"Mel Friedman doesn't hire bellhops. Jennie and Harry Grossinger don't hire bellhops. I hire bellhops."

"I don't know about any of that. We work hard, do what we're told, and we stay out of trouble."

Sheldon figured that two out of three might possibly be true. Which two, however . . .

"Really?" said Ben, putting the papers on the desk and leaning back.

"That's our story and we're sticking to it, sir."

Ben looked at them. They looked like every other teenage bellhop he'd every hired. One of the kids had blue eyes, but aside from that, they were boilerplate.

Ben, resigned to the easy path, gave his spiel. "This is one of the premier hotels in the world. We have the best acts, the best patrons, the finest decor, and a gourmet menu that's kosher. Every week we order 300 standing ribs of beef for steaks and roast beef, 1,000 pounds of poultry, 27,000 eggs — all cracked by Rosie by hand — 1,000 pounds of potatoes, 500 pounds of Nova Scotia lox, 70 cases of fresh oranges for juice alone, and 700 pounds of coffee. Every single morning the bakery produces 4,600 rolls and another 4,600 mini pastries. We make 36 pounds of cookies with every meal and 800 portions of pie, and the guests have a choice of at least three kinds during lunch and dinner. Grossinger's covers almost 850 acres of land, and we're home to thousands of guests every week. We've got 60 chambermaids and 20 women in the laundry room washing 7,500 sheets and pillowcases and 20,000 bath towels every week."

Sheldon wanted to ask whether they also had a seven-ton steam engine like the armory did to power the place, but he kept his mouth shut. *Were all tours like this?*

"We are a machine of excellence and Grossinger's has everything. You two will be among the tiniest cogs in that enormous machine, but oddly enough, you'll be important ones because you will be the first and last people our guests see, and you don't get a second chance to make a good first impression."

"That's good," said Lenny. "That's a good line. I've never heard that."

"Don't interrupt. Do you two knuckleheads think you have what it takes not to fuck things up? Because that really is what this job is all about. Doing it is pretty easy. Doing it consistently and not fucking it up to the point where I notice it — that's the heavy lifting."

Sheldon thought this was an excellent question. In his heart of hearts, he had no idea what the answer was. Luckily, Lenny did.

"Absolutely!"

"Fine," said Ben, who in the deepest and darkest depths of his soul couldn't care less. "We're understaffed for the summer anyway. Ten dollars a week, you eat with the rest of the staff, you share a room. Normally, I'd put you in the attic but we're reshuffling so you two actually luck out and get a guest room we're not using. The toilet runs. Deal with it. I'll slot you into the schedules when I have time. Miriam will get you settled. To be clear: You steal, you're fired. You insult a guest, you're fired. I want to fire you because I want to, you're fired. Any questions?"

Neither Lenny nor Sheldon had any questions.

PIGEONS AGAIN

THEIR HOTEL ROOM was the greatest place on earth.

No question about it.

There were two separate beds—already made up with bedspreads—a dresser, a desk with a fancy lamp, two end tables, and a bathroom only for them.

It got better.

There was a window. That by itself wasn't miraculous. Their homes had windows too. This window, however, had a view. The boys would never know whether this was Miriam's doing or whether it was an act of God or a temptation from the Devil himself, but the fact remained that it looked out toward the lake. They couldn't see the lake. What they could see were hundreds of bouncing boobs and bare legs moving back and forth along the footpath on their way to either get wet or dry off.

Some of them were ugly. About half belonged to men. Many were not ugly and belonged to women. Some changed their understanding of what a woman was.

Lenny jumped on the bed in his socks out of sheer happiness while Sheldon sat on the yellow quilted bedspread reading the *New York Times* like an old man. If he was a smoker, he would have held a cigar between his teeth and never stopped shaking his head.

"I—can't—believe—all—those—tits—are—Jewish," said Lenny.

"Some of the girls are Cuban and Puerto Rican. They're with the bands."

"The more the merrier," said Lenny, still bouncing.

"They won't let us into the other hotels," Sheldon said. "No Jews. No

Negroes. No dogs. What you're looking at is an American-style fuck-you to everyone who told us to take our ball and go play somewhere else."

"I just love it here!"

"I got to hand it to you," Sheldon said, flopping down the paper. "You are one fast-talkin' Jew." He reached over for the ice tea he had ordered from room service.

The fittings for their new uniforms weren't until eight in the morning, after which they would have three hours of training, touring the grounds, and being told the rules. For now, it was vacation time. Sheldon wanted to go to the lake, but he couldn't entirely get Lenny's attention so he was stuck with the newspaper and the ice tea until the mastermind calmed down.

"I didn't come up with it on the spot, you know," Lenny said, bouncing. "I was thinking about this during every algebra class for a year. I even made various diagrams that depended on what the first bellhop said and whether or not we got the supervisor's name."

"You said you had a plan and you had a plan."

"We're going to be paid to be here!" Lenny said. "Everyone else is paying, and we're being paid! This is heaven. This is what it looks like when you're good. I realize that we lied our way in, so I have some theological thinking to do."

Sheldon didn't. He kicked back his ice tea like it was bourbon and slammed it down as though he were in a bar and someone was going to immediately slide another drink over. He had Bruno's confession. He knew the name of the Mob boss in Hartford the Krupinskis had screwed over. He knew about Lorenzo. He also had a job, his best friend by his side, some money in his pocket, and Mr. Henkler's .45 automatic.

Sheldon was a man ready to enter a casino and start pushing his luck.

He flipped up the paper again. Page fifteen caught his eye.

MESSAGE FOUND ON PIGEON IS BEING INVESTIGATED

NEW YORK, June 18 (AP)—Mac Gang heard a cooing sound on his garage roof shortly after midnight and thereupon found a wornout homing pigeon.

```
He turned it over to police, who found this penciled
note attached to one leg:
```

```
"12 car loads of munitions will arrive at usual place.
Watch out for Gover. Off 42264. Time is 12:15."
```

```
On the other side was:
```

```
"Deutschland Auber Alles."
```

```
Police are investigating.
```

Pigeons again.

"Sheldon!"

It was Lenny. He'd stopped bouncing, changed into a bathing suit, and was yelling Sheldon's name the way he usually yelled it after trying and failing to get his attention.

"What?"

"Swimming. Now. We're going swimming. Grossinger's has its own lake! Let's go."

"I think it's a pond."

"A distinction without a difference, as Miss Simmons would say. I'm leaving."

LIFE AND DEATH

L ENNY CHOSE TO COMMIT showbiz suicide during their third week at a nearby hotel called the Edgewood Social Hall. It was not exactly a high-priced or especially classy resort, but it was secluded in a tender valley of rolling green fields and mountain flowers bursting with orange pollen that attracted a symphony of bees. Lenny had convinced Sheldon to ride over there on their bicycles to scope it out during their lunch break. They surveyed it as though they were young generals preparing an assault.

"I see only death," said Sheldon.

"It's gonna be great," Lenny said.

"You're going to walk in there tonight and make jokes about Nazis and then come out smiling, that's what you think is going to happen?"

"I'm on a roll here, you have to admit it."

"Dice don't stay lucky."

They'd been working at Grossinger's for two weeks and two days. With nothing to buy other than ice cream and pizza at the local market, the pay and tips were turning them into millionaires as far as they were concerned. During every free moment they could find—when not ogling the girls or trying to figure out how to get lonely housewives interested in teenagers (they weren't)—they visited nearby hotels and tried to land Lenny a gig.

Tonight was going to be Lenny's opening act.

Tonight, he was going onstage at ten o'clock in front of an after-dinner crowd and under a spotlight. The act for that time slot had come down with a black eye, which apparently was a common ailment, and the guy didn't have the creative chops to work it into his act, so the manager, Whitaker, told him to piss off. Lenny—on his knees—begged Mr. Whitaker for the chance to fill in. Whitaker, with bigger problems than Lenny, agreed.

This was it. The beginning of it all. Lenny felt the weight of history on his shoulders. His first gig. The one that everyone was going to ask him about when he became a success later. "What was it like, Mr. Bernstein?" they'd ask. "It was a hot day and my buddy Sheldon and me went to check out the place before the big moment."

"You talking to yourself?" Sheldon asked, straddling his bicycle.

"I'm narrating my future autobiography, Sheldon."

"Should I be taking notes?"

"Tonight," Lenny said, looking off into the distance. He was speaking to the hotel, a whispered seduction to a lover. He gave himself the chills.

They'd been watching comedians almost every night for the past two weeks. Though they were both working the longest hours possible to bring in as much cash as they could, Lenny said that watching the other acts was the education he needed. Radio wasn't enough and newspapers were useless. He wanted to *see* the men walking back and forth across the stage like tigers in a cage. He wanted to see the way they removed the microphone and placed the stand to the side to show they meant business. He wanted to see how they warmed up a cold crowd, how getting personal with people in the front row got things moving—in one direction or another—and how to handle the hecklers. Lenny had ideas and plans, and made notes and notations to his notes, and Sheldon thought that if Napoleon had prepared this well at Waterloo the British would be French today.

The boys spoke to each other about comedy in military terms because war was in the air but also because it was the lingo used by the comedians themselves.

Comedy—for some reason neither one of them yet understood—was always talked about in terms of life and death. Comedians killed or they died onstage. They murdered their audience or were murdered by them. Some nights they brought the house down, and other times they bombed. It was a full-contact blood sport and it wasn't for the fainthearted.

Sheldon wasn't fainthearted but he didn't want to do it. Funny was good. Sheldon liked funny. But Sheldon would rather laugh at the world than have it laugh at him. It was more than personality, though. Sheldon sensed a relationship between making jokes and a threatening world, and he was coming to see that the first was somehow a response or even a reply to the second. When Sheldon asked Lenny about it, he was surprised to find that Lenny had actually thought about it too and had a pretty good answer.

"If they're laughing," Lenny said, still staring at the Edgewood, "how are they are going to bludgeon you over the head?"

It was a good answer. But no one was laughing in Europe now. Is that why everyone was laughing twice as hard over here?

Those were daytime thoughts. When the night finally came, questions were replaced by answers. Answers begot action. Action was the name of the game. And for Lenny, tonight, *tonight,* TONIGHT became *now.*

THE SPOTLIGHT HIT LENNY like a blinding slap so intense that it erased the audience of sixty men and women and undid the world that God had made and returned him to the moment of creation. Right here, right now, God created the heavens and the earth, and darkness was upon the face of the audience.

It was ten o'clock, and the audience was already sauced. The act before Lenny was a ten-minute argument between a mother and son. The mother gave her son hell for never calling, and at the end, they both realized that it was a wrong number.

It wasn't bad. But it wasn't BIG. It wasn't new. It was safe and straight and unadventurous. Lenny wasn't going to do that. He was going to break out of polite discussion and kill, kill, kill!

Sheldon was out there in the dark with orders to out-heckle any heckler, but beyond this thin lifeline, Lenny was on his own. Sheldon, for his part, had his head cradled in his palms at a table, and if anything was going through his head, it was "better him than me."

• • •

But Lenny didn't care. This was his moment. He was a hunter. He was a killer.

Right now. Right this very second. Right absolutely positively . . .

"Hello, everyone! I'm Lenny Bernstein," he said, when the manager gave him a bored two-finger cue to get on with things. "I can tell you already have a question about my age. The answer is, I'm forty-seven years old. I think I look pretty good for my age, but my wife, I think, is getting jealous and it's becoming an issue. I say to her, 'Honey, if you want people to think you look good for your age . . . tell them you're sixty!'"

A smattering of applause.

"I live in New York . . ."

A few claps.

"Oh, you've heard of it?"

A puff of laughter.

"It's not easy being married and . . . let's face it . . . this good-looking in a city as engaging as New York. Some of you, I can tell, are also from New York."

More applause.

"I'm not asking, though. I know a lot of guys come on stage and ask, 'Where you from?' I'm not gonna do that. I know what happens when you ask a New Yorker a question. I think we both know. They take over. You get one question with a New Yorker. That's it. This is why you can't interrogate a New Yorker. Could you imagine the Gestapo trying to interrogate a New Yorker?"

There was enough laughter from that one line—enough of an indicator to Lenny that all his intuitions were right, that he knew what no one else knew, and that this was going to *work*—that he plunged right into it.

"'Names, names! Ve want ze names!'" Lenny yelled out in a horrible Nazi accent that may have been Yiddish.

"'Names, names? You want names?'" Lenny answered as a loud, bold, self-confident New Yorker. "'Alan Moskowitz! That's a name! What a schmuck. He's lucky he's dead.'

"'No, vait. Dats not vat ve mean.'

"'And Alice Finkleman! There's another name. The mouth on that woman. A snake, I'm telling you. You tell her a secret, you've told everyone. I remember a time when —'

"'Um, no. I don't tink you understand ze qvestion.'

"'Don't interrupt me, I'm just getting started!'"

Lenny interrupted his imaginary dialogue. "This could go on for hours. There they are. Schmitt and Schultz of the Gestapo are outnumbered and surrounded by this one New Yorker. At some point, Schmitt loses it.

"'Enough! Stop! If you don't stop, ve vill MAKE you stop. We haff vays to make you stop talking!'

"At which point, Schmitt leans over to Schultz and says, 'Actually . . . ve don't.'

"'Vat do you mean, ve don't?'

"'Ve don't. Ve put everything ve had into ways to make dem talk so ve could say, VE HAVE VAYS OF MAKING YOU TALK! And den, you know, ze budget ran out.'

"'But za guy von't shut up.'

"'I know. Ve have a problem. Are you gonna tell ze commander? I know I'm not.'"

Lenny's New Yorker interjects. "'Excuse me. I can't help but notice that you are becoming somewhat frustrated.'

"'Ya. Zat's true.'

"'Perhaps I can help.'

"'Vould you mind?'

"'Not at all. If I understand you correctly, you want short and snappy answers to your questions. Perhaps if I ask *you* a few questions, you could give me some examples, maybe I'll get it, and then we swap things around again.'

"'Zat's not a bad idea.'

"'Let's say I was to ask you the name of your commanding officer. You would say . . . what?'

"'Colonel Augustus Humbolt.'

"'That's it? His name. Nothing else?'

"'Ya. Ideally, ya. Ve have a *lot* of qvestions to get through.'

"'Huh. OK, let's try another one. What does he want the information for?'

"'For ze invasion of Belgium.'

"'And when's that taking place?'

"'O-five hundred hours next Thursday.'

"'What are your force levels?'

"'Six panzer divisions coming from ze northeast.'

"'Any weaknesses in your defenses?'

"'Two of ze divisions don't have ammunition and we use some inflatable tanks to exaggerate our numbers. So, if you attack from ze south, you could vin.'

"'I have to admit, these are good answers. Punchy, informative, helpful.'

"'So, you start to get it?'

"'Let me throw you a curveball. If someone wanted to assassinate Hitler on Thursday, say, around ten, how would he go about it?'

"'Oh, zat's easy. Breakfast at ze Kaiserhof in Berlin, third table from ze back by ze window. Pull up in your car, shoot him with a rifle, drive off, bing-bang-boom, it all over.'

"'You guys are real professionals, I got to hand it to you.'"

The audience was hysterical. Lenny was prancing across the stage, his hands twitching around the microphone, his arms waving. Sometimes he crouched low like a predator and other times he hopped like a bunny. A man in the middle of the dining room started pounding the table with the flat of his palm in an effort to dislodge the cherry he'd accidentally swallowed. Everyone started pounding their tables too.

When the set was over, Lenny waved and walked offstage like Joe Louis after beating the crap out of James J. Braddock for the boxing heavyweight title back in 1937. But Sheldon knew that Lenny, like Joe Louis, still had something to prove. Joe Louis, as everyone knew, wanted a rematch with Max Schmeling, the German boxer. Sheldon was pretty sure that Lenny didn't know who or what he wanted to beat, but whatever it was, it was something powerful and impossible to see, a headwind of some kind. For the first time, Sheldon considered that maybe telling jokes wasn't the defensive move he had thought it was. Maybe it was a brave and new way to attack in a world gone mad.

Sheldon sat with a beer and watched the show. He'd never ordered a beer before or tasted one, but the freedom of the night demanded celebration. It turned out that he hated the taste. It had a nice color, though.

Lenny circled around and caught up to Sheldon when the set was over.

The boys hugged.

"You should call the cops," Lenny said. "I'm a murderer! I killed them. I slaughtered the whole place! It was a bloodbath! I'm ashamed of myself!" Lenny grabbed Sheldon's beer and took a swallow and then spit it all over the table.

"What is that? Is that beer?"

"It's beer."

"It's horrible."

Lenny ordered a Coke. He was parched. He was hoarse. And—according to Mr. Whitaker, who started shouting at the same time the Coke arrived—he was also fired.

Lenny's mouth opened, but Whitaker was fast with his finger. "Come with me," he said, index finger tall and commanding. "Not here."

Sheldon and Lenny—both of whom assumed Mr. Whitaker was making a joke—followed him past the tables and out past the bar to the front lobby. It was dark there and much quieter. From his pocket, Whitaker removed a five-dollar bill, handed it to Lenny, and said, "That's that. You had your fun. Got a few laughs. Now go home."

"Wait. You're serious?" Lenny held the fiver as though it were a dead rat.

"You can't do that act again," said Whitaker.

"Why not?"

"Why not? Why not? Germans and Nazis? Interrogations? Assassinating Hitler, that's why not. You can't talk about Nazis in front of a bunch of Jews."

"But you can talk about Jews in front of a bunch of Nazis?"

"That's not the point."

"It feels like it is."

"This isn't a news show! This is a comedy show. They don't want to hear about death! No one's here for commentary. You started with a joke about your wife. That was funny. A teenager pretending he's got a wife he's already sick of. You're aging better than she is. OK. You can probably make a bit out of that."

Lenny didn't understand. He was holding his head and shaking it back and forth like he used to do in class when the pieces of an idea didn't line up. God, he knew, had told the Jews that the world was a broken place and needed humanity's help to set it right. To a Jew, this implied that God wasn't pocketing a few of the pieces; the game wasn't supposed to be rigged. There is an answer, there is a solution, there is a pattern. You just need to apply yourself. Not just the Jews. Everyone. We're in this together. This is the faith. It also explains why we're exasperated all the time. But lose that faith in coherence and things go Kafka pretty fast.

Somehow this *had* to make sense.

"But . . ." said Lenny, "they were laughing their brains out, Mr. Whitaker. They came here to laugh and they laughed. How can you tell me they don't want to hear it when they already heard it and loved it, and I heard them hearing it and loving it?"

Whitaker wasn't used to explaining things to kids who thought life was geometry. The only reason he was hanging in there with Lenny was because of the pain on the kid's face, a pain that was altogether human and looked pleading. Lenny sincerely wanted to do right and didn't understand what the hell was going on.

It wasn't unreasonable.

"There are defamation laws," Whitaker explained. "There are obscenity laws. There are political considerations. I got people I got to do business with. I got people in the audience who might not be New Yorkers and might even come from German stock. You're sixteen. You don't know these things yet."

Lenny said nothing. Mr. Whitaker, looking at him, understood just how much the boy must be suffering to have actually shut up. It touched his heart.

"You got any other bits you're working on?"

Lenny opened his hands. "I got this thing where this grown-up realizes his parents have been lying to him his whole life so he finally confronts them, and they say, 'You started it.' And he says, 'How?' and it turns out that it's because they once asked him whether he pooed in his diaper and he said no, and from then on, it was war."

"You can't talk about poo."

"It's baby poo. It's not obscene. It's a parent and child bit. It's about, you know, life. Everyday life."

"You're giving me poo and Nazis, kid."

"Life and death, Mr. Whitaker! If I can't make jokes about life and death, you're not leaving me a lot of wiggle room. What am I supposed to do, make jokes about nothing?"

"Nothing would be good. There's a future in nothing."

"How do I tell jokes about nothing?"

"I don't know. I'm only saying there's a nut there to crack."

"Wouldn't something be better than nothing?"

"Not if it's polio."

Lenny was despondent.

Mr. Whitaker's shoulders dropped. This was like yelling at a puppy for being too happy. You can do it, it'll work, but no one comes out of it any better. Whitaker had been running comedians for a decade, and before that, he'd known vaudeville and before that, burlesque. Stamping out a tiny flame might be stamping out a forest fire. It also might be stamping out the stage lights that brighten up the whole world. It took the wisdom of Solomon to know how to handle a kid like this.

"Go think of something, come back, we'll try again. Stay clear of the Nazis," said Whitaker. "That's all-around good advice."

EVERYONE COMES TO GROSSINGER'S

BACK AT THE HOTEL, as they settled into the new routines, Sheldon learned the names of all the guests by studying the register whereas Lenny learned them by asking and taking them to heart. This produced the same results. Ben Adelman taught the boys how to check the arrival times of guests and then go outside to meet and greet them. They would tip their hats, load the luggage onto the red-carpeted and brass-edged four-poster trolley, and help the guests check in with Miriam or whomever was working the desk.

With access to all the keys, Sheldon and Lenny would proceed to the rooms, unlock them, and carry in the bags that they'd arrange on the folding suitcase stands at the foot of the beds. They never opened or unpacked them, but they made every other effort to help the guests feel immediately welcome and relaxed from the moment they stepped into their home away from home.

Sheldon and Lenny would demonstrate the lights, explain the features of the room, and detail the hours of the services and amusements. They explained how to call for assistance. Each gratefully if silently received tips, shared his name, and said that if there was anything he could do to make their stay more comfortable the guests should ask for him personally and the need would be met.

It wasn't a bad way to make a living.

Initially, Sheldon had been convinced they'd be discovered as frauds once Ben Adelman actually talked to Mel Friedman and found out that Lenny had fancy-talked his way into the job. But Mr. Friedman had come back in a very good mood from his trip because he'd been having sex with someone other than Mrs. Friedman, and when Ben Adelman saw Sheldon take his boss's luggage in without incident, any suspicions he might have had were dispelled.

It was a Friday morning in mid-July—the peak of the peak season—when Sheldon was surveying the incoming clientele and saw a name on the registry. He closed his eyes and opened them again to make sure he was seeing what he thought he was seeing.

"Miriam?" he said, calling her over so she could see it too.

It was 6:30 in the morning and quiet. Miriam had trimmed her hair into a series of waves and her hazel eyes smiled at him. Sheldon suspected that she had come to like him more than she did Lenny, perhaps because Sheldon was more taciturn and she believed that still waters ran deeper. Sheldon wasn't so sure about that—having stepped in his own fair share of still and shallow puddles—but he liked her attention more than he wanted to admit to himself because he didn't entirely know what to do with it. He didn't want to escalate matters with her, though, until Lenny found someone else to love, and so far, it hadn't been going well.

"Do we know them?" Sheldon asked, pointing at two names on the registry.

Miriam leaned over and put her cheek uncomfortably close to Sheldon's. He could smell the hotel shampoo in her hair and the Ivory soap she preferred over Palmolive. She pushed back her hair and placed it behind her ear so their faces were extremely close together.

"We know him," she said, giving Sheldon a smile and turning her head just slightly. "He comes up here every year with a different woman. He's quite the playboy."

"It says they're married. He has a new wife every year?"

Miriam chuckled. "You're so naive."

"I don't get it."

"We don't give rooms to mixed couples who aren't married. It wouldn't be kosher, so to speak. So, everyone looking for a romantic getaway says they're married and afterward, we don't pry. He comes up with a different Mrs. each summer. This time it's"—she checked the register—"Mrs. Mirabelle De Marco."

"Is that a popular name here? Mirabelle?"

"No. Sounds French. Very sophisticated."

"We're still pretending Europeans are sophisticated given current events?"

"They have croissants. And Paris."

"A year ago last month, the Nazis were goose-stepping under that big arch thing they have. I have to assume they were eating the croissants."

"What?"

"Never mind. What time do these lovebirds arrive? I want to greet them."

Mr. Alan De Marco emerged from the driver's side of a black Buick at ten minutes to ten with the air of a man who was here by invitation. He wore a panama hat and his complexion was healthy, even, and monied. He wore a white suit that shot the sun's light back to it with a wink; he drew a deep breath when he closed the door, knowing his ship had now dropped anchor and that there was still time before lunch to win over the natives.

The man snapped at Sheldon, who sprang to attention and opened the passenger door for the woman inside.

Aunt Lucy's yellow shoes pivoted into view, and the heels sank to the warm asphalt. Mirabelle emerged wearing a yellow sun hat that shielded her face from view, but the jig was up.

She didn't see him, didn't look at the bellhop. Instead, she held out her hand and Mr. De Marco, like one of Arthur's knights, came round to claim it. Nineteen years old, Mirabelle was the perfect model of French womanhood—as far as anyone there might know. Sheldon wouldn't have been surprised if she had the accent down pat.

Sheldon pushed the trolley ahead of him across the driveway and brought it to rest by the knight that Sheldon had already christened Sir Lies-a-Lot.

De Marco didn't bother to look at Sheldon as he signed a few papers for Miriam, who was at the front desk. Mirabelle still took no notice of her cousin. She was busy greeting an acquaintance who was as lavishly dressed as she was.

"Take the bags in," De Marco said to Sheldon. "We know the way."

"Yes, sir."

That was as long as Sheldon could be silent; patience was not his greatest virtue: "Is there anything I can help you with, Mrs. De Marco?"

Mirabelle turned to the bellhop, and when she saw Sheldon — sneering at her with knowingness, with sarcasm, with *power* — her eyed widened and she turned instantly from predator to prey.

"No," she said.

"Honeymoon?" Sheldon asked.

De Marco interrupted. "I beg your pardon?"

"It was noted in our register," Sheldon said, without taking his eyes off Mirabelle, "that you and *madam* are here for your honeymoon. If there was an error, I apologize."

"No, that's fine. Yes, it's our honeymoon. Isn't it, dear?"

"Yes," Mirabelle intoned in an unflattering and nasal B-flat.

"That's WONDERFUL," said Sheldon, with a shudder of glee. "You can't imagine how thrilled we are that you chose to spend it here with us at Grossinger's. Tickled, really."

"OK, kid," said Sir Lies-a-Lot. "Move the stuff in. We'll be having drinks by the lake in an hour."

"Of course, sir; yes, sir; right away, sir." Sheldon loaded the fine leather suitcases onto the brass trolley and bowed like a manservant as Mirabelle narrowed her eyes and tightened her lips.

$$\rightarrow$$

SHELDON HADN'T SPOKEN to Mirabelle since her graduation last summer in 1940. Their falling-out had happened around Christmas of 1939, a few months after the war had started in Europe and six months after Abe had disappeared from the graduation party. After that Christmas, they barely spoke, and when Mirabelle moved out after graduation, they didn't speak again. For the past year, Sheldon had been alone in that dreary house in Hartford with his few fair-weather friends and his library of books.

In the months after Abe disappeared, Sheldon took it hard but Mirabelle took it the hardest. It had never occurred to her that Abe would abandon her. She learned painfully that much of her strength and sarcasm, her wicked humor and irreverent attitude, had been made possible by the knowledge that she was safe and protected by her older brother. Her own mother, after all, had died in a terrible fire and her father was a distant man. It was Abe who was her bedrock. Without him, she became un-settled.

From the end of June until that Christmas, she and Sheldon grew much closer. They talked more. She stopped being sarcastic and superior, and opened up to him. She told him about the carrier pigeons and the biology class, and asked him whether he thought a girl could be a scientist. She talked about the music she liked, and she often confided her personal thoughts to him. The love that Sheldon had always had for her blossomed. Abe's absence was a hole in his life too, but Mirabelle filled it with a warmth he had not felt since his mother had died.

One night in December, when the trees outside their window were catching the first flurries of snow, she and Sheldon sat on the blue sofa listening to the radio while Nate was out. Kate Smith was singing a new song by Irving Berlin called "God Bless America." The Ku Klux Klan didn't like the song because it was written by a Jew, but that didn't stop it from being the third most popular song in the country. It was unabashedly patriotic, and people across the land were learning it by heart.

"Isn't it strange," Mirabelle had said in a far-off voice, "that this is the third most popular song on the pop charts, and the fourth one — just after it — is 'Strange Fruit' by Billie Holiday."

It was the kind of observation she had become more inclined to make since Abe left, observations about contradictions, about how the world doesn't fit together as one cohesive puzzle, and about how the results create strange mosaics that only the attentive can see.

It was a song about black bodies swinging from trees in the South. It was a song about the very worst of America.

"What do you think it means?" she asked Sheldon.

Barely thirteen then and still wanting more than anything to make her happy but not knowing how, he said, "The song's about murder."

"I know. And it's number four in the charts. And it's next to the most patriotic song ever written, which was written by a Jew who isn't wanted here either. One song is about the pain, and the other acts like the pain doesn't exist. And they're right next to each other as two of the most popular songs in the land. It must be a clue to something. Right?"

"Is there a mystery?"

"Sure. Who are we? What are we going to become? How are we going to get there? I think these are mysteries. I think the clues are in art. I think we know who we are from the art we make."

Sheldon knew the Billie Holiday song. He'd heard it many times. It sounded less like a song than a testimony, a lament. *A strange and bitter crop,* Holiday sang. He wondered what Abe would make of the song. Was that why he read the papers? Not only to be informed but to be a witness? But Abe wasn't a person to stand on the sidelines and witness something. Then again, how do you fight back on your own?

"Why do Jews write patriotic songs, Sheldon?" Mirabelle turned and brought a knee up onto the sofa. Her voice had become more present and directed. "Why do Jews write these patriotic songs, and make jokes, and sing and dance like your friend Lenny, when only thirty-nine percent of Americans think Jews should be treated like everyone else, fifty-three percent think we're different and should be restricted, and ten percent think we should all be deported?"

They had heard these numbers at synagogue. They were from a national survey taken in 1937. Some of the categories overlapped, making the numbers hard to follow. Still, the rabbi thought things were only getting worse because no one on the radio or TV or in Congress wanted to speak out against the Germans because it might bring America closer to war. So, Goebbels's propaganda was going unmet and unchecked all across the country and much of the world. Nazi propaganda was working.

"What do you think?" Sheldon asked, to buy himself time.

"I think we want people to like us, so we try to be likable. So we can blend in. So we can stop being different."

"I don't think that's it."

"What, then?"

"I think it's because we love America."

Mirabelle lay back on the sofa and considered his simple statement, and Sheldon didn't interrupt. He liked watching her think. It was a dramatic and expressive show that played across her face.

"That would make it an unrequited love," she finally said.

If the conversation had ended there, Sheldon and Mirabelle would still be talking to this day, bonded even closer. But Mirabelle shared a secret that shouldn't have been a secret and Sheldon couldn't forgive her. That was when they fell apart.

"I think that's why Uncle Joe signed up to fight in France," she said, laconic again. "And now Abe."

"What? Now Abe . . . what?"

They hadn't heard from Abe since he'd left in June. Or that was what Sheldon believed.

Mirabelle unfolded a letter from the right pocket of her skirt. It had purple and orange stamps in the corner and a large rectangular blue one that said BY AIR MAIL, PAR AVION. The return address was in Canada. The name at the top was Abraham Horowitz.

"What is that? Is that a letter? How long have you had that?" Sheldon asked.

"A few weeks."

"A few weeks!"

"Don't yell at me."

"Why the hell not? You've had that for a few weeks, and you didn't tell me? Why would you do that? What's wrong with you? Are you deranged?"

Sheldon never talked this way to Mirabelle. Never wanted to risk pushing her affections away, but this was a step way too far. There was no negotiating with betrayal.

"Nothing. I mean—"

"Where is he? When's he coming home? Does Uncle Nate know?"

Mirabelle didn't answer.

"I can't believe you're sitting here all moody wondering about song lyrics when you've got Abe's letter in your pocket!"

"OK, already!" she said, reaching her limit.

"Just . . . give it to me." He snatched the letter out of her hands.

"He's in Canada."

"Canada?" Sheldon had slid the letter out of the envelope but hadn't looked at it yet.

"He joined the RCAF."

"The what?"

"The Royal Canadian Air Force."

"The Royal Ca—are you fucking kidding me?"

"Calm down, Sheldon!" Mirabelle yelled back.

"No! You've known for weeks. I'm only hearing about it now." He looked down at the letter. It was handwritten on onionskin paper with a blue pen. "Is there more or is this it?"

"That's it."

The radio was still playing, but Sheldon had switched it off in his mind. He stood up from the sofa and walked to the dining-room table, where the overhead lamp cast a bowl of yellow light. Sheldon held out the letter and read as Mirabelle stayed seated behind him.

The letter began "Dear Mirabelle and Sheldon."

That did it. "It's addressed to me too! It wasn't even yours to hide!" Sheldon shouted.

"Oh, stop being such a . . ."

But Mirabelle ceased to exist. Why he'd tolerated her bullshit this long he had no idea. How close can you be to someone if all that was needed for them to slip away was for you to let go of the rope? He wasn't even sure she had genuine human emotions anymore. Honestly, to keep this from him?

"You're a monster," he whispered, as he started to read.

Abe's voice filled the space left behind by Mirabelle's absence, and Sheldon fell into his letter as though into Wonderland.

```
Dear Mirabelle and Sheldon,
     I'm sorry that I didn't write earlier. I didn't mean
to run away and leave you both behind, but if I stayed
in Hartford one more minute, I would have said things
I would never have been able to take back, and that
would have ruined everything for both of you who still
have to finish school.
     You know about the war, of course. What you might
not know is that Canada declared war on Germany a few
days after it started in September. I was in Buf-
```

falo at the time because my friend Alan has grandparents who live there, and he had a summer job lined up painting houses. I needed somewhere to go and it seemed as good as any and they let me stay in their basement for free and I got to work with my friend. Once the Germans attacked Poland and Britain went to war, though, I changed my mind.

Mr. Fowler was right about America not wanting to get into this. Maybe we never will. But I can't stand it and I can't stand watching it. I saw a photo in the newspaper of a girl in Austria wearing a dress like one of Mom's. They said she was a Jewess, which sounded like something foreign and dirty and mystical, but she was none of those things. She was pretty and young, and even though it was a foreign country, she was wearing the same clothes as everyone in Hartford, and she reminded me of Mirabelle. The Nazis were making her kneel on the pavement and scrub the street in Vienna with a wooden brush. Around her was a circle of laughing Austrians. I imagined Mirabelle on her bloody knees and it made me boil with hatred.

And then Kristallnacht came along and I thought —that could have been us. All those people there are exactly like us. The difference isn't them. It's where we live. It's the people around us.

Every time I read the papers, they talk about Jews being scared and terrorized and worried and weak and pathetic. The thing is, I don't feel those things. That's not me. That wasn't Uncle Joe. That isn't you two either. What I feel is a rage that's like the righteous hand of God calling out for vengeance from heaven.

God wiped out Sodom and Gomorrah for less than what's happening now. I can't imagine what's stopping

Him from erasing these people from the map. So, if He isn't going to do it, I will.

I took a bus up to Toronto and I joined the Royal Canadian Air Force. They said I might lose my American citizenship, and I said I would rather lose that than my honor.

The Canadians are great. The guys are all really friendly, and no one seems to have a chip on his shoulder. They put me in a training program for bomber recon over the Atlantic, but I don't know where I'm going to end up. Things are moving pretty fast now. I'll write more later. In the meantime, you can write me back at the return address that I put at the bottom. They'll forward things on.

I hope you aren't too mad to write back. I want to know you're both doing OK.

I'm sorry again for letting you both down. But I need to stand up for what's right and take the fight to them, and America's not willing to do that. And we think we're such heroes.

I love you guys. Tell Dad I'm not angry anymore. Not in the way I used to be. I know where to put my energy now.

Love, Abe

THE TRUTH

A T GROSSINGER'S, Sheldon was pushing De Marco's suitcases past reception when Miriam said something to him, but he was too preoccupied to hear it properly. His mind was filled with the sound of his own voice yelling at Mirabelle and calling her names that would have scandalized a sailor. The longer he chewed her out, the worse the insults became until he landed on the word "traitor." It arrived like a punctuation mark as he stopped at her door.

Room 112.

Sheldon opened the lock. It was the same as so many other rooms, yet it seemed like a den of sin and a torture chamber for his own heart. He was perfectly aware that he wouldn't be so angry at Mirabelle if he didn't love her, but knowing that changed nothing. If anything, it only made him angrier.

The idea that this man was going to have sex with her in here made him sick. How could the room be so bright and airy?

Joseph had once said that even in war some days are sunny and the birds sing.

Sheldon tried to think of some way to make his presence felt. Maybe short-sheeting the bed would work. That was a classic. Or clogging the toilet, or just waiting like Bogart to slap the guy around a little and call him a rapist. Sure, Alan was bigger, so Sheldon would lose the fight and get fired and Lenny would get angry, but . . .

He had no plan. He had to admit it. Usually, he was good at looking at a blank canvas and painting a solution, but he was dressed like a bellhop, he was furious, and he had no plan. It was a terrible feeling.

Grudgingly, he did his job and placed the suitcases on their respective stands and stared at them trying to think of what to do. Then he opened the suitcases and rummaged around in them. In hers, he found enough jewelry to fund a revolution.

This was not pawn shop loot. These were not gifts given to a beautiful girl. This was the kind of jewelry he'd seen in windows where the men inside the stores carried guns.

There must have been thousands of dollars' worth of diamonds and rubies and emeralds on necklaces, bracelets, and earrings. The jewelry was so exquisite that it couldn't even be worn in a place like this. Some of the people here had money, and some people here paid more than fifty dollars a week when they could be in Monticello paying twenty-two. But this suitcase contained Rockefeller jewelry. This was Queen of England booty.

This was stolen.

Sheldon replaced it and zipped up the bag a second before Mirabelle burst into the room and slammed the door behind her.

"What the hell are you doing here?" she asked him, hands on her hips, as though he'd been caught with the last cookie.

"You first!" he shouted.

"I'm doing whatever I want! I'm nineteen years old. I graduated, and I'm living it up! Now you."

"Oh yeah? Well, I'm . . . working!"

"Did you follow me? How did you know I was going to be here?"

"I was here first. How can I follow you if I was here first? Maybe you followed me."

"Keep your voice down. Sammy could hear us."

"Sammy?" said Sheldon, remembering the register and his conversation with Miriam. "Not Alan? What's his real name? Shlomo?"

"What the fuck is it with you, Sheldon, seriously?"

Sheldon plopped down on the bed to claim his spot. He crossed his legs. He took the stupid hat off his head—the one that made him look like an almost-fifteen-year-old Jewish bellhop—and then puffed up his chest, making him look like an almost-fifteen-year-old Jewish bellhop without a stupid hat.

"There are a lot of Jews here," he said. "I thought you were trying to get away from all this rather than deeper into it."

"You know what, Sheldon? Mr. Fowler was right. You're either moving your way up the mountain or you're not. And I am."

"Sleeping," he said. "Sleeping your way up the mountain."

"You're calling me a slut now?"

"Yes. You are a slut."

"Screw you, Sheldon. We're in an adult relationship. I'm an adult now. I'm in an adult relationship with a man with money, and you're still a kid and it kills you, but that's the way it is."

"Apologize," he said. He crossed his arms for effect.

"I beg your pardon?" Mirabelle said, shifting her weight even more aggressively to one leg.

"If you're not going to apologize for abandoning me and leaving me alone with Uncle Nate for a year, or leaving without a word, or changing your name, or pretending you're not related to me, or generally being a bitch on wheels, you WILL apologize for lying to me about Abe. At least for that."

"I didn't send him away. It wasn't my fault. You know how much I —"

"No, that wasn't your fault, but don't change the subject. You lied to me and the only reason you're angry with me is because you feel guilty, but you're too proud or self-absorbed or whatever to admit it. You think that if you do, you're weak. Well — it's not true. You dumped me and left me alone the way that Abe dumped us. But at least Abe apologized and knew he did something wrong. You're the weak one. And now you're with some gangster? Is he actually Mafia? You know what they did to our family."

"They didn't do anything, Sheldon."

"There was a black car outside our window in Hartford —"

"It wasn't the Mob."

"I saw the car with my own two eyes, Mirabelle. So did Abe. I know exactly what that guy looks like. And if you don't like that example, how about Lorenzo? The guy who drove me and my father off the road? And you're sleeping with one of them?"

Mirabelle knew what the man in the car looked like too. "The man in Hartford was handsome but a bit pudgy. No facial hair. A hat he wears slightly tilted back. Blue eyes that are actually quite soft and sad. I know what he looks like, Sheldon. Better than you. I saw him up close, and he was not the Mob. I know because I walked out to the car one night, tapped on the window, and demanded to know who he was."

She explained.

It was two nights after Mr. Henkler was killed when the story had hit the paper. The roads were still littered with the debris from the storm, and Mirabelle was shaking with the possibility of what Abe might have done. When her father was out and Abe was in the bathroom and Sheldon upstairs, Mirabelle wrapped her blue overcoat around her and marched out barefoot into the street and rapped on the window of the Chevy.

The man was reading a newspaper by the light of the streetlamp and tried to look casual when Mirabelle knocked on the window.

Arms crossed over her chest, she demanded, "Enough. Who are you?"

"Young lady—"

"I have a gun in the house. I will come back outside, and I will shoot you in the face, I swear to God as my witness. So, you answer me or you'd better be prepared to kill me because I can't take it anymore."

The man put down the paper. He introduced himself. He was an assistant manager at G. Fox & Co. and worked in the women's clothing section. He was a specialist in leather goods and gloves. He met a woman named Lila Horowitz who used to shop there. He had been training some of the salesgirls when Lila appeared, and he explained the merchandise and talked to her for a while. A month later, Lila came back and he approached her. It was innocent at first. It grew into more. The man explained that sometime around September or October of 1937 Lila disappeared. For a few months he had tried to accept this, but the more he thought about their relationship, the less sense it made. So, he started coming by this house in the winter. He knew Lila didn't live here, but he'd met her sister-in-law Lucy before and he figured that Lila must visit from time to time. He couldn't call or knock on the door without explaining himself, though, so he waited and watched and hoped, but Lila never returned.

"She'd dead," Mirabelle said. "My mother too. They died in the fire at the theater last year." She told him the name of the cemetery, and said, "Now you know."

After that, the car never returned.

Sheldon sat listening to the story. His whole world was coming unraveled again and this time he had no reserves. He couldn't walk back home through the rain again. He couldn't sleep on his own doorstep and burn the world down a second time. He couldn't.

"You're a liar," he whispered.

"I'm a bitch, Sheldon. I am not a liar," Mirabelle said.

"My mother was not having an affair. She was not cheating on my father. Why would you say something like that? You really are a monster, Mirabelle. I thought it was all a show but—"

"She was, Sheldon. I loved Uncle Joe too. He was wonderful, but he had dust on his boots and dirt under his fingernails, and he was a loner living in the woods who was shell-shocked from the war. He was one of the kindest and best people I've ever known, but your mom was—like—Vivien Leigh or Hedy Lamarr or something. She wanted to wear gowns and high heels, and dine at the top of skyscrapers. She wanted more. We all want more. I want more! You can't expect women to be perfect servants of your needs. We're people and we're trying to weave our way through obstacles you can't even see. You think being Jewish is tough? Being a Jewish woman is tougher."

Sheldon didn't say anything.

"It doesn't mean she was bad or didn't love you. It doesn't mean she didn't love your dad either. It just means she had an affair. More than that, we have no idea. You have to forgive her. Maybe even me," Mirabelle said much more softly now.

"Did Abe know?"

Sheldon had started receiving letters from Abe in Canada in the spring of 1940. Abe talked about his training and his goals, his buddies and his ambitions. Never once did he mention Sheldon's mother or an affair.

"No. I never told him."

Sheldon drew some deep breaths before asking, "Who is this guy, this De Marco? He looks like a two-bit crook, and he's up here every year with a new girl. You know that, right? You're throwing away your family, your history, your pride, your dignity—"

"Were you not listening? There are reasons I'm doing what I'm doing, Donny."

Sheldon was listening but he didn't understand. He wanted things the way he wanted them. He was tired of compromising.

Mirabelle lost her patience. "You're fifteen years old, Sheldon! Have some respect!"

"Aunt Lucy would be ashamed of you."

Mirabelle had had enough. She waved her arms around the room as though she were ordering the staff at the Waldorf around.

"Prepare the room. Do your job, and if you even hint that you know me, I will ruin your life."

"I don't know why I ever loved you," Sheldon whispered.

Mirabelle's arms fell to her side. Those words, more than anything Sheldon had said so far, sank into Mirabelle's heart. In many ways, Sheldon was all she had left too. Her father was no longer interested in her, and Abe was gone — bombing German U-boats from a base in Iceland. Sheldon may have been only a little kid, but knowing she had his undying affection had always given her a sense of self-worth and a grounding. She knew she could change her own future with her actions, but she had never really known that a person could call all of history into question with only a few words. It was a bitter lesson.

Hurt, Mirabelle turned and walked out of the room without a sound. She closed the door gently behind her. Sheldon was left alone in the room with thousands of dollars' worth of gems and jewelry.

And he knew exactly what to do with them.

NEVERSINK

SHELDON WALKED.

With a king's ransom of jewels wrapped in a cloth and tied to a mop that he carried over his shoulder like a hobo, Sheldon walked.

Dressed in the unbreathable wool garb of a bellhop, he walked under the full weight of a New York summer sun past Grossinger's Lake and through the pines of the heavy forest beyond—wild lilacs and aromatic white flowers that Sheldon didn't recognize now in bloom—until he reached Neversink Road, which ran gently downhill like an invitation to Hades.

After the Krupinski truck had turned over in the rain, Sheldon had walked for six or eight hours. Though only twelve years old then, he had learned that time is shredded by events and that distance is not measured in miles but in thoughts and memories. This time, on a tree-lined path that reminded him of home, he walked with purpose. He was going to find a river he had been told was there.

According to the fly-fishing brochure he'd taken from the Grossinger's lobby on his way out, the Neversink River was only five or six miles away as the crow flies. The Neversink River, said the brochure, got its name from an Indian tribe who called it the Ne-wa-sink, which meant "continually flowing." It didn't say what language the tribe spoke, and it didn't say which tribe.

It might have been bullshit. There was a lot of bullshit in the brochures. All rivers continually flow. Wasn't that what made them rivers?

The sweat on his face reminded him of real work and proper summers, of humping a rucksack through the woods with his father to bring their kills back to the house for storage. He didn't like seeing animals in pain, and the trapping sometimes made him wince, but Sheldon's father would dispatch the animals without fuss and as humanely as possible. He took no pleasure in it either. Together they'd lay the entrails at discreet stations in the forest where other animals would eat them and the bugs would thrive and the plants would grow. This way, everything was used and something was returned.

On their walks, Joseph would usually let Sheldon lead. Sometimes they would enjoy the silence of the forest, but it was a silence that was more than the absence of talk because the forest was never silent. It was a time for listening. Everything is music, his mother once said to his father, and they agreed. Where there is life, there is song. Hearing it requires only the capacity for appreciation.

Neversink Road started dropping more precipitously, and at one turn toward the north, the valley opened in front of him—a vista of tranquility and perfection. The hills were layered shades of green, and the trees were so densely packed that they seemed to form a single mass. So close to Grossinger's and the town of Liberty, this was nevertheless a lifetime away. Nothing about the place suggested the presence—so close by—of opulence and evening gowns, rainbows dancing across the polished floors from lit chandeliers, and the laughter of a thousand guests before a night of horns and music.

This place was home. It was a valley indistinguishable from the Berkshires or Hampshire or Worcester. Sheldon felt as if he were a boy in a Twain story, and the road he was on left Hartford and New York and the life of gangsters far behind.

The valley basin reached out to him like a clarion call. Soon he arrived at a tiny village called Neversink with a main street, a two-room schoolhouse, and a covered bridge. This was the New England of Whately. That it was on the New York side of the invisible border meant nothing to the trees or waters or the winds. It looked like it meant nothing to the way of life either.

On the porch of the general store, a man sat on a bench smoking a pipe. The shade looked welcoming and Sheldon was very thirsty. The man nodded as Sheldon stepped into the cool of the shop and bought himself a cold Coke from a humming refrigerator.

Outside, he took a pull on the bottle and the bubbles burned his throat with a nameless pleasure that was sweet and as cold as a quarry.

The man with the pipe laughed approvingly. "That's what they made it for. A boy like you on a day like this. You drink it all down."

"It's good," Sheldon agreed.

"You must be hot in that getup." The man's tobacco was aromatic and hung in the air around him.

Sheldon had forgotten how stupid he must look. He nodded sheepishly.

"No trains here and you're too clean for a hobo," the man said. "Should I keep guessing?"

Sheldon sat beside the man.

"I'm a bellhop at the hotel," Sheldon said, feeling like an escaped convict.

"The fancy Jewish one?"

Sheldon had never heard the words "fancy" and "Jewish" used together before, but he said yes.

"Those places started popping up twenty-five years ago. All that time, you're the first one to ever take a step in Neversink."

"This feels more like home to me than the hotel." Sheldon told the man he was from the Berkshires. Whately was actually in Franklin County, but his dad had always called it the Berkshires and that was good enough for Sheldon.

"Never been out that way myself. Heard they had some of the same problems we're having now, though. They lost that fight just like we're gonna."

Sheldon removed his coat. A breeze hit his sweat and he felt cooler.

"Problems?" Sheldon asked.

"That's not why you're here? Take a last look? If I was a boy, I'd want to see a doomed place."

Sheldon didn't know what he was talking about.

The street was empty and as dry as a fistful of ash. Everything glowed with the yellow haze of the sun that was sinking lower. Nothing was moving, not even the leaves. As plush and green as the valley was, the town could have been out West. If a cowboy had ridden through and tipped his hat, Sheldon wouldn't have been surprised.

"Where you from again?" the man asked.

"Whately."

"Never heard of it. What's it near that I might've?"

"Northampton's pretty big. We're a bit north."

"OK, yeah, OK, I can see it now. So, this story I'm gonna tell you would have happened in 1938. Your parents would have known about it. I'm surprised it didn't come up. Well, anyway, they called it the Valley of the Dammed. This was east of you a bit. Bunch of little towns no bigger than Neversink." He rattled them off on his fingers. "Dana. Prescott. Enfield. I forget the other one. Boston was growing, and it was getting thirsty, you see. And to get more water, they needed a new reservoir. So, in April of 1938 they disincorporated the villages, dug up seven thousand dead from the cemeteries for reinterment on higher ground, and workers from the city came in and destroyed those villages like demon hordes from the bowels of hell. The villagers were all run out, you see, and those hired ruffians smashed the houses and broke the windows and vandalized the churches and set fire to the woods; thirty square miles of forests burned for months. Thirty square miles. It's too much to hold in the mind. You just have to repeat the words. You must have seen the smoke. You must have known about it."

Sheldon said he did remember the smoke and the dark sunsets. It was seven months after his mother had died, and everything seemed darker that year, the sunsets more vivid. He had thought it was his imagination.

"No," said the man. "That was the Valley of the Dammed filling the skies with its own ghosts. They spelled 'damned' with two *m*s, you see, and everyone got the joke but no one laughed. That's our fate soon. They're going to start filling in this whole valley for drinking water. We got the word. We're marked here. I thought you came down to see. I know I woulda done."

He puffed on his pipe. The smoke only made the day hotter.

They were silent, and Sheldon had sat on enough benches like this to know the conversation wasn't over. He fiddled with the mop handle across his leg and idly wondered whether the shape of the gemstones against the cloth of the towel was obvious or not. The man wasn't looking anywhere near the jewels, though. He was looking into the past across the border.

"A town called Neversink is going to be 175 feet under the water, and a river that continually flows is going to come to a rest on top of it. How about that?"

Sheldon said nothing. There was nothing to say. It seemed important to listen, though. Looking around, he saw no children. He wondered if maybe he was the youngest person to know about this. That would make him, in time, the last person to remember.

"Sometimes," the man said, "when I'm staring into the sun too long, I wonder if some bureaucrat saw our name on a map, took it as a provocation, and thought it would be hilarious to drown us. We live in strange times. These days, even the dead are on the move."

Sheldon left the man behind when they were done talking. Less than a mile up the road, the sweetness of the Coke still on his lips, he found the gentle river that would someday quench the thirst of a million souls in New York after Neversink was obliterated from the map.

Without ceremony or doubt, Sheldon opened the towel at the end of his mop handle, grabbed the jewelry he'd stolen from Mirabelle's suitcase that she'd been smuggling for De Marco; and he threw the pieces into the river one by one.

When he was done, Sheldon walked into the water with his clothes on and submerged himself—if only for a moment—in the cool and silence of oblivion.

THE GUEST

I T WAS LATE AFTERNOON when Sheldon returned to his room. His clothes were stiff from his dip in the river. To clean them, he stepped directly into the shower, allowing the cool water and shampoo to rinse off the sweat and smell of his ten-mile walk. Cleaned and renewed, he dressed himself in a pair of blue jeans and a white T-shirt. Lenny was out. Sheldon sat on his own bed, crossed his legs, and picked up the house phone with one hand as he placed a copy of *The Thin Man* on his chest. He wasn't so interested in the plot, but he liked reading Nick and Nora's banter with each other. It was fun the way they were equals. Dashiell Hammett made it clear that they were Greek, but they were sharp-witted and fast in their dialogue and that made them sound Jewish to Sheldon. On the other hand, he'd never met anyone Greek.

Asta was a weird name for a dog, though. He didn't know anyone or anything else on earth named Asta.

Miriam was working the front desk and answered. He said he was sick. Real sick. *Green* sick.

"Oh, no, Sheldon! Did you eat something?" she asked, as he tried to find his place in the story. He forgot to add a bookmark or dog-ear the page, so he had to skim.

"Oh, please, don't mention food." He moaned.

"So, talking about things like spaghetti and meatballs or lasagna or clam chowder is probably a bad idea, huh?"

Sheldon smiled and moaned again. "I didn't realize you hated me so much."

"I don't. I just wish you were a little older."

"Lenny's older. I think he's forty-seven or something."

"Yeah, I heard about that. He's married, though."

"Things are shaky," said Sheldon.

"So, you think I have a chance with him?"

"With Lenny? I think if you asked him the time, he'd build you a clock."

"What about you?"

"Time doesn't move at all when I'm with you, Miriam."

"See," said Miriam, audibly moving the phone to her other ear and speaking in a lower voice. "Other boys don't say things like that to me. You're different from other people. You know that, right? Your brain doesn't work the same way."

"My dad used to say it would get me into trouble."

"Trouble's what I'm trying to get you into, but you keep resisting."

"You're almost eighteen. I'm basically fifteen. What's going to happen?"

"You ever kiss a beautiful redhead before?"

"No."

"That explains why you're asking."

Sheldon knew she was only flirting with him, but he knew she liked him too, and there were certainly moments — moments when he was alone — that he thought of her too. Mirabelle was older than Miriam was, and so he'd been in a kind of love with an older woman before. This felt more . . . real. Possible, somehow.

"Ben's going to come looking for me," Sheldon said. "Possibly with an axe. Can you cover for me? Say I told you earlier that I was sick? That I didn't know the rules about telling him directly?"

"Are you sick?"

"I'm . . . under the weather. In a way. There's a lot going on these days, you know?"

"Yeah. Summers."

"I guess."

All the talk about food had made him hungry. Sheldon called up room service and asked for a plate of the dinner special and told them to charge it to his room. If he went down to the cafeteria, his cover story would be blown, and he liked that his room was dark and the sheets clean.

He needed the rest. This morning he had suffered the shock of seeing and then fighting with Mirabelle. After that, she had destroyed the memory of his mother and the assumptions of his childhood, and then he had walked ten miles on one Coke, which wasn't enough fuel.

In his own way, he was sick and tired.

Twenty minutes later, Sheldon was dozing when someone started banging on the door. It was a fast and furious thump and not at all the knock of housekeeping or room service. Sheldon's heart pounded as he remembered that he'd stolen a pirate's chest of jewelry and it probably wasn't a mystery who stole it.

Opening his night table, he removed the .45 automatic. He checked to see if the round was chambered, and assured that it was, he disengaged the safety while keeping his finger on the outside of the guard as his father had taught him.

The door had a fish-eye peephole. Sheldon took a breath and looked.

It was Mirabelle and her expression looked especially grotesque.

He reengaged the safety and put the gun back in the drawer before returning to the door and letting her in.

Mirabelle burst inside and closed the door behind her. She locked it and slid the pathetic brass chain into place.

She didn't yell. This was new. Was it fear? Was Mirabelle actually afraid of something?

"What have you done? Give it back now or we're dead. Do you understand me?"

Sheldon's natural impulse — an impulse nurtured and cherished from his days in Miss Simmons's classroom — was to put on an innocent face and deny knowing anything. But in this case, it seemed pointless.

"The asshole you're dating is an asshole," said Sheldon, not finding this redundant.

"That's not your call," Mirabelle said.

She was dressed in the same clothes — the same yellow heels — but she didn't look like a princess anymore, didn't move like a movie star. She was a nineteen-year-old girl playing dress-up who was about to be sent to the principal's office, and she needed to talk her way out of it fast; otherwise her father was going to bring his hand down.

This was better, Sheldon thought. This was the equalizer he'd wanted.

"How did you meet him, anyway?"

Mirabelle crossed Sheldon's room and sat on the edge of Lenny's bed. The curtains were drawn, but they could hear the distant sound of children yelling, "Marco! Polo!" out by the lake. Mirabelle kicked off her shoes as if they were restraints and sat there looking for words.

"After we knocked over the pawn shop," she said calmly, "I had some jewelry that was worth something. Something more than the watches and your snow globe. I wanted to sell them, but I didn't know anyone I could sell them to. I needed to meet someone who could do that sort of thing. I went to the armory one day, and I met with Mr. Cluff. The old guy."

Sheldon remembered Mr. Cluff. Uncle Nate had introduced him when Sheldon had toured the factory that first time. There had been a banner hung across one of the halls that congratulated him for sixty-four years with the Colt Armory. Almost eighty-four, he'd started working there when he was nineteen fitting shell ejectors into revolvers. It was said that his fingers had become so sensitive that he could tell from touch whether the ejector fit properly into the countersink of the cylinder—an accuracy to a minute fraction of an inch. It was also said that he knew everything about the place.

Everything.

"I told him we wanted to sell some of my mother's jewelry, but the pawn shop had recently been robbed and I was scared to go there. I said my father didn't know either, but he was too embarrassed to ask. So, did he have any ideas?"

"That wasn't bad," Sheldon said. "I might have said they were pieces she gave you and that they made you cry and you wanted to get rid of them but couldn't tell your father because he'd object but . . . nice, all the same."

"Yeah. So, he told me where to go and I went. I met Sammy there."

"Not Shlomo?"

She waved that off. "He's a fence. Like a broker. He moves high-end jewelry from a seller to a buyer for a cut. He's discreet, doesn't ask questions; and he gets paid well. As a jewel thief myself, I don't have that much of a problem with it. He's not stealing milk from babies. Everyone's got an angle, and this is his."

"Not everyone," said Sheldon.

"Really? How did you get this job?"

Sheldon didn't answer.

"Right. So that's why we're here at the hotel, to sell hot items to some guy named Thaleman for cash. While we're here, we'll make a vacation out of it while Thaleman is having some fun with his foreign mistress. Sammy's not evil, Sheldon. He's not even Mafia. Not really. He just does the same thing as a pawn broker only without an office. He's rich, he's fun, he's good-looking, and he's nice to me. Yes, he's a bullshit artist. And a bit of a womanizer, but so what? You think Rockefeller and Ford and Carnegie weren't all full of shit? They were all thieves. They were just so good at it that they became respectable by creating a web of influence. Why shouldn't we do the same? Abe was right. We can be the hunters or the hunted. I like it better on this side of the gun. Now give me back the shiny rocks."

"They're gone, Mirabelle."

"Nothing's ever gone, Sheldon!"

Sheldon said nothing.

Mirabelle took his meaning and it enraged her because it had been her mother too. "The jewelry didn't burn to ash in a fire, you little asshole. They're rocks. Give me the rocks!" She stuck out her hand.

"I threw them in a river called . . . forget it. They sank. They're gone. I wanted you two to split up, and I wanted him in trouble, and I wanted you to come to your senses. You'll be better off in the long run. You'll thank me."

Mirabelle shifted on the bed. He wasn't sure if he was punishing her or testing her or both. She looked incredulous.

"Sammy called his people in Hartford hours ago to say their jewels are missing. They're coming up here to talk to him. Thaleman is waiting and doesn't know this yet. He's here with a suitcase of money to buy them. You think we were in a pinch between Mr. Henkler and the Mafia? Well, this time it's real. These are not good people, Sheldon."

"Who did he call?"

"Who? You know the names of the Hartford Mafia?"

"More than you'd think."

"Eric something."

"Ernie, maybe?"

"Maybe. Why?"

"Ernie Caruso?"

"I guess. I wasn't paying attention."

"If you're gonna play this game, Mirabelle, you need to pay attention to the details."

Sheldon sat on the bed beside her. He hadn't thought this far ahead, and it was immediately clear to him—in retrospect—that he was in trouble. Real trouble, and not from Mirabelle.

"Ernie Caruso is the guy the Krupinskis were doing business with. Lorenzo is his muscle. He's the guy who drove me and my dad off the road because he thought that Dad was Old Krupinski. If Sammy called Ernie, and Ernie's suspicious, he might send Lorenzo up here. If he does come up here and finds that Sammy can't produce the jewels—which he can't—he's going to assume that Sammy stole them. Lorenzo is a hit man. He will kill us. And by us, I mean Sammy and anyone standing near Sammy. I have to hope he hasn't been chatting about you by name. Not a lot of Mirabelles floating around here. You got to get out of here. Now."

Mirabelle was looking at the carpet, her eyes flicking back and forth as though she'd dropped the back of an earring, but Sheldon knew she was looking for a trapdoor, a way out of this.

"We're a four- or five-hour drive from Hartford," Sheldon added. "When did Sammy call Ernie?"

"Maybe . . . an hour after we fought. We came back to the room and started unpacking, and he saw that the jewels were gone and he went looney. I thought he was going to blame me, but he turned on you first. I covered and said that I saw them when I came back to the room to get my makeup after you were gone. So, he said someone must have come in afterward and that's when he called Caruso." Mirabelle looked at Sheldon. "He said they'd send someone. Someone to help."

Sammy had called Caruso a long time ago. A very long time ago. Long enough to . . .

Sheldon picked up the phone and called Miriam, who answered with her usual "Front desk, Miriam speaking, how may I help you?"

"Miriam, it's Sheldon. Look. This is a weird question but let me ask it straight out. Has anyone obviously not Jewish checked in during the last few hours?"

"Now that you mention it, yeah. There was a guy with a mustache who came in with no luggage and no sense of humor, and said that he didn't want dinner."

"Yeah. That's him," Sheldon said, mostly to himself.

"Not even cake."

"Yeah, I understand. What's his room number?"

Miriam had checked him into 218, which was on the other side of the building one floor up.

"Who is he?" Miriam asked.

"No luggage at all?" Sheldon asked.

"Just one of those doctor's bags. You know the ones? That open from the top?"

"Miriam," he said, trying not to sound worried. "Are there any security guards or cops or anything here?"

"There's Steve at the entrance. And there are police in Liberty, I guess. It's never come up. You're kinda scaring me, Sheldon. Are you making a joke? It's not funny."

"No, it's nothing to worry about. I just need to think. You on duty for a while?"

"Until nine tonight."

"Is Ben around too?"

"Yeah."

"OK. I got to put some pieces together. Thanks."

He hung up without saying goodbye because his mind was already past that.

Mirabelle crossed her legs beneath her on the bed like she did when they were kids back in Hartford. She opened her arms as if to catch a giant falling beach ball. "What are we going to do?"

"OK," Sheldon said, starting to pace around the room. "OK. It's possible

I really screwed up. Not as badly as you or De Marco did. I mean, really, Mirabelle. Calling your own assassin? And then you've got this Thaleman guy who's looking to score. Is he a psycho also?"

"I don't know. Sammy never talks about the buyers or sellers. He just said he's kind of a playboy and that he has an exotic girlfriend. Can you connect the dots for me, please?"

"Yes. OK. Here's what I think happened. My dad did business with the Krupinskis. He sold them pelts from the hunting and trapping. The Krupinskis sold the pelts to the Mob in Hartford. The Krupinskis screwed over the Mob, and the Mob came looking for them. We borrowed the truck, a man with a mustache drove us off the road thinking we were the Krupinskis, and they got their revenge. I always planned to look for the killer, but I never knew where to start. It was Abe who found out the name of the driver from Mr. Henkler, but that didn't help me. When I was back in Whately, I confronted Old Krupinski and it went better than I expected. I learned about Ernie Caruso from him. How he fits in doesn't matter now. I'm assuming, and it's not a stretch, that Lorenzo works for Caruso, and now Lorenzo is here at Grossinger's to torture your friend, because they don't believe for one second that he was robbed. They'll think he's pulling a fast one so he can keep the jewels and maybe sell them himself and keep the whole score. My hunch is that the doctor's bag is filled with stuff to clip people's fingers off. You following me so far?"

Mirabelle hadn't blinked or been sarcastic, so Sheldon figured he had her undivided attention.

"What are we going to do?" she asked.

"We're going to run. Or fight. Or think our way out of this."

"Run?"

"Or fight or think our way—"

"I heard you!"

The sun was shining directly onto the drawn yellow curtains, illuminating their room. Marco Polo had ended. The kids had moved on.

"Why did you do that, Sheldon? Why did you steal the jewelry?"

"Because he's a thief and he stole you! He doesn't get you and the jewels, OK?"

Mirabelle touched his hand. "Oh, Donny."

"Don't call me that!"

"You didn't think this through. That's not like you. You're our little thinker. You need to stay on the ball, kid."

"I did. I was just wrong. Probably won't be the last time."

"We have to run." Mirabelle was willing to drop her playboy and the entire angle. She was young. There were other solutions to a better—and longer—life out there.

"You can run," Sheldon said, Mirabelle's hand still on his. "But Lorenzo doesn't walk out of here. I've been looking for this guy for more than three years. Now he's here but doesn't know I am. No way he walks out of here a free man on two legs. No way."

"What are you talking about? The guy's an assassin, Sheldon. You're gonna do . . . what? You're a fourteen-year-old kid."

Sheldon pulled his hand away. "I know what I'm not gonna do. I'm not gonna keep putting myself to sleep every night with dreams about killing this guy. In the last three years, I've shot him, strangled him, drowned him, stabbed him, and burned him alive with a flamethrower. I've killed this guy so many times that I'm more shocked that he's *alive* than here at the hotel. I'm not gonna keep doing that. Not when there's another way. I just need to think of what to do. I need a plan."

"He's a grown man, Sheldon. You can't walk in there and start smacking him around. He'll kill you. Easily. I'm not even sure Abe could do it."

"Abe left me Mr. Henkler's .45 automatic. It's here in the drawer."

"You have a gun?"

"The one Mr. Henkler's wife said he left in the drawer at his desk. Abe took it and now it's here in my drawer. He gave it to me to kill Lorenzo."

"You could really do this?"

It was a good question.

All the room keys were hanging up in reception and there were a couple of master ones too. One way or another, Sheldon could open the lock, walk into Lorenzo's room, and shoot him twice in the chest and once in the head, and then walk out. People would hear the shots, but as soon as he stepped out of the room in his bellhop uniform, he'd be a free man. Who'd notice a bellhop in a hallway? No one.

"I've read a lot of mysteries and never once—not with Sherlock Holmes, or Philip Marlowe, or Nero Wolfe—has a story ended where the Jewish bellhop did it. Nothing connects me to him or me to you, for that matter. They might suspect your boyfriend, but he'll be long gone by then, and they might suspect Thaleman, and my feeling is—great."

"I don't think killing someone's so easy. I think it's hard. And I don't want you to be a killer, Sheldon. I don't think your parents would have either."

"You've never loved anyone as much as I loved my father—as much as I loved them both. You'll never feel what I feel. You don't know how hard this is." Sheldon stood up. "Go. Tell your boyfriend he's a marked man and that you both need to run. There's a bus stop on the road to Neversink. No one from the hotel goes that way. You two can wait there for the bus or taxi and then—you're gone. Forget the car. Trust me, they know what he drives. After that, I'll work something out."

Mirabelle worked quickly. She called down to her room, found Sammy there, and quickly explained their predicament, using the story of her uncle Joseph to paint the picture and focusing her boyfriend's attention on the consequences of his phone call to Ernie. Sammy was waiting for her at the designated staff exit in less than twenty minutes.

Sheldon asked Miriam to have a taxi meet them at the bus stop in thirty minutes, and during that window, he walked with them a mile down the road he'd traveled twice already today toward Neversink.

The bus stop was shaded and few cars passed. The three of them sat like refugees in dejected silence. Mirabelle had told Sammy that the bellhop was no one, a kid she paid ten bucks to make arrangements and ask no questions.

Sir Lies-a-Lot checked his gold watch every few seconds to see how soon the day might be over. The watch did not have the answer.

The cicadas made a racket in the sun-scorched field behind them, and the early evening felt so dry that the grass might have spontaneously burst into flame.

A 1933 Plymouth pulled up to their bench, and a man without curiosity loaded their bags into the car, ending for Mirabelle what had to be the shortest and most expensive vacation of all time. Sammy sat in the back seat like a defeated aristocrat on his way to exile. His eyes were vacant and lost. And although Sheldon felt bad for upsetting Mirabelle as much as he had, he couldn't help but feel a little triumph. After all, Sheldon had first laid eyes on Sir-Lies-a-Lot at ten o'clock this morning and had ruined him before sunset without drawing a drop of blood.

This was clearly a skill.

Sammy was long gone in his own thoughts as Mirabelle lingered outside the running car. She turned to Sheldon and said quietly enough for only the two of them to hear, "I should have been nicer to you."

"You were when it counted."

She leaned over and kissed him on the cheek. "I love you too," Mirabelle whispered, and then she stepped into the car, closed the door, and they were off.

HUNTER AND TRAPPER

BACK IN HIS ROOM, Sheldon washed his face and hands, and looked at the idiot in the mirror to see if he had any bright ideas, because this was far from over. Lorenzo was in the building—somewhere—and if he was doing anything, he was looking for someone called De Marco.

Grossinger's was not exactly Fort Knox with its information, and Sheldon suspected that Miriam had unwittingly given him Mirabelle and Sammy's room number by this point. Maybe Lorenzo would get in and maybe not, because she wouldn't have given him the key. If he did sneak in, he wouldn't find them, though. What he would find was some of their clothing because Sheldon had told Mirabelle to leave some behind; otherwise it would be obvious that they'd left. "You want this guy to think you're still there, but that he can't find you. It'll buy you time. And that's what you need."

Sheldon had recommended that Sammy leave the white suit. "It would be very convincing," he said, with as straight a face as possible.

Mirabelle's boyfriend had paid for the entire week up front, so the front desk didn't know—or frankly care—where they were so long as the room was empty at checkout.

Lorenzo was on the ground, Abe was in the air, and Mirabelle upriver.

"What do you think?" Sheldon asked the idiot in the mirror. "Shoot Lorenzo and join Abe in Canada? I could leave a note for Lenny saying I had to run."

"You'll never feel Miriam's breasts in your palms if you do" came the reply.

Strictly speaking, this should not have been a consideration. He shouldn't be weighing vengeance for his father's death against the chance to feel up Miriam in a broom closet.

Still: Once you get an idea like that in your head it's hard to shake.

He toweled off his face and stared deeply into his own blue eyes. He tried to imagine himself a Canadian. An airman. Looking down through a sight and dropping bombs over the deep blue sea to bust open some tin cans under the surface where German U-boats were hiding and hunting down cargo and passenger ships and the British navy.

The idea of it was fine, but it didn't feel right. Not at all. It felt like someone else's daydream.

His father hadn't fought for Canada. He'd fought for America, for an America where Sheldon could grow up and know for an absolute fact that he belonged — belonged as much as anyone whose first breath of life drew in American air.

Also, the air force felt wrong — Canadian or otherwise. If the spirit world was made of earth, wind, fire, and water, Sheldon's was a life of earth. A life in the army felt more appropriate. Or the marines, in a pinch; at least they fought on land too.

"I put on my bellhop uniform," he said to his reflection. "I open his door and walk in. I say, 'Excuse me, sir, I didn't realize you were here,' and then I kill him. Bang, bang, bang. There's no defense against that."

The Sheldon in the mirror didn't reply. He did, however, look skeptical, which surprised the Sheldon not in the mirror.

"What?"

His face knew if his mind didn't. So close to it; to the actual thing. And it felt wrong.

Sheldon straightened up and looked at himself for a hint about what he should do.

He tried to imagine himself older and looking back on his life. It was hard to do. Lenny thought that Sheldon had been living a magical and wild life, but Sheldon didn't see it that way. He felt like he was stumbling from one problem to another and using his wits to muddle through. What all of this was leading to, or might look like on reflection, was anyone's guess. It wasn't even really his question. What he wanted to know was how his father would feel about all this, and the answer was so obvious that he was ashamed for even asking it.

Take care of yourself would have been his father's answer. *Take care of yourself because your mother and I love you.*

This had very little to do with shooting a man in cold blood.

"Well . . . shit," he said aloud.

"Even if I don't shoot him," Sheldon said to the mirror—he was back in charge now, and he had a lecture to give—"there's no way this guy walks out of Grossinger's a free man. I'm going to pull a Krupinski maneuver on him and we're going to ruin that bastard. If I can take the Krupinski brothers out and this Sir-Lies-a-Lot guy, I don't see why I can't do it again when the stakes are up."

"How?" said the magic mirror.

"I don't know."

"Maybe you should figure it out," said the mirror.

"How about a little help?"

✈

LENNY WAS ONSTAGE again that night, and while he had taken Mr. Whitaker's advice and stayed clear of Nazis—for now—Lenny wasn't going to back off on the baby poo jokes without a fight. Every man has his limits, and there was still a bit there. And a real comedian doesn't back away from such rich veins of material.

That's the coward's way.

Sheldon hadn't understood why this was a battle worth fighting in a world—as he called it—"of barbed wire and mass murder" but the boys didn't pry too deeply into each other's business.

If there was one thing the Catskills didn't lack, it was a stage to perform on. The same guys were working the same circuit, and they ran from place to place making the same jokes. Some, Lenny would learn, told the same twenty minutes of jokes their entire lives. It was a scary idea but informative. If you haven't got the brains, you'd better have the legs. One way or another, you have to keep it all moving along.

Tonight, a slot had opened for him at the Hotel Cloister three miles up the road from Liberty in Parksville. Sheldon had invited Miriam on the logic that he needed a fresh perspective on his problems, and Lenny had told him that he needed all the support he could get. Lenny and Sheldon had both wondered how Mirabelle at nineteen was seeing a man in his thirties whereas Miriam was only a little younger and was happy to accompany Sheldon who wasn't even fifteen yet, but both concluded that the answer was in the box marked WOMEN ARE COMPLICATED; the same box that was slapped with a warning label reading, DANGER: CONTENTS UNDER PRESSURE.

Lenny sat at the bar, too young to drink, and watched one of the comedians tell a story about visiting a farm for the first time. He wasn't going to be a hard act to follow, but it was the sort of droning, middle-of-the-road storytelling that had these guys working day after day, a harmless background to the dinner people were eating. A chance to smile weakly and giggle from time to time all while appreciating that this was a vacation. Did you get to the top of this game by being special or by fitting in? How did it all work?

When was Sheldon going to get here?

Sheldon and Miriam met in reception. On his way, he had assumed it would be a night like any other, with the occasional family or couple passing the front desk or arriving late; the front doors opening only on occasion as the hotel's guests were already involved in one event or another. Unexpectedly, though, the lobby was full of extremely well-dressed people milling around as though they were waiting to enter a Broadway show.

The women were wearing long evening gowns and the men were in tuxedos. Others were wearing black or gray suits with thin ties; their hair was slicked down and their patent leather shoes reflected the chandelier lights with the same intensity as the jewels adorning the women's necks and wrists and ears did.

There must have been fifty people or more greeting one another and slowly working their way toward the Grand Hall.

Off to the side of all this, like a schoolgirl spectator, stood Miriam. She was in a long floral skirt and a blue cotton blouse that made her hair appear even redder under the blaze of the lobby's lights. Her shoes were sensibly low heeled for the bike ride they were about to take, and Sheldon wore a collared short-sleeved shirt and brown trousers. He was clean and fresh, and didn't look like a boy who was splitting his time between trying to figure out how to cage a dragon and considering how he could steal a kiss. As a couple, they could have been classmates or family. Only they knew—if Sheldon understood the evening correctly—that it was a date.

It was a date with a girl who wasn't Mirabelle.

It was the best way to deal with the situation.

He was sure of it.

He was not sure of it. The mirror might have been sure of it when it suggested this, but the mirror wasn't here right now, and it was known to like a practical joke on occasion.

Miriam smiled at him when he arrived. Her hands were behind her back, and a small purse crossed her chest so it wouldn't slip off on their ride.

"Ready?" she asked.

"What's going on?"

"Some big political fundraiser. A senator or something. I don't know the details."

"They're all very . . . sparkly," Sheldon observed.

"Power likes shiny," said Miriam. Sheldon nodded. There was something to that. The Egyptians, the Aztecs, and the conquistadores all liked shiny things.

A woman with a necklace of sapphires and diamonds passed Sheldon. She looked like a queen and walked like one too. Miriam saw him stare.

"Mrs. Ullman. A very rich widow. She comes to these things every year. Pulls out all the stops."

Shiny things and sparkly people and jewels reminded Sheldon that there was something he was supposed to be thinking about. The Krupinski maneuver he needed to play on Lorenzo had something to do with all this. He couldn't think of what it was, though. The jewels were gone. Very, very gone.

"What are you thinking about?" Miriam asked him.

"About how smart you are."

"You're a little weird," she said to him, rising slightly on the balls of her feet, making herself even taller than she was already.

"You don't know the half of it," Sheldon said.

The night was balmy. The inland hills grew cool; the temperature began to drop to sweater weather. But the land was holding on tightly to the last heat of the day. The fireflies were coming out in the field and twinkling a call to the stars. The wind was warm against their arms, and the trees rustled with the feeling of life. It was the perfect night for a ride.

Sheldon and Miriam collected their bicycles from a rack between two evergreens that almost reached the fourth-floor windows of the hotel. Miriam's was a girl's bike without a crossbar so she could step into it rather than throw a leg over it. Back in Massachusetts, none of the girls had such bikes because they always shared whatever they had with their brothers or accepted hand-me-downs, but the Catskills were a classy place.

Miriam knew the way. Grossinger's was on a slight hill so they caught their first breeze as they coasted down to the intersection and made the hard left that took them eastward away from Liberty.

They rode side by side on the quiet road lit by a bright moon that almost masked a universe of stars. Traffic was very light, and the loudest sounds around them were their own tires and the bullfrogs that croaked from the ponds behind the trees.

At first, they rode without talking. Miriam sat bolt upright in her seat, and her strong swimmer's lungs kept her from becoming breathless. Sheldon tried to hide his admiration for her when they turned into the parking lot of the Hotel Cloister twenty minutes later, and he worried that Lenny's voice was soon going to ruin this romantic mood.

Sheldon winced when his brakes squeaked as they pulled to a stop by a tree close to the entrance.

"We don't actually have to do this, you know," he said.

"It'll be fun."

"What if it's awful? It could be awful."

"I heard his Nazi skit was hilarious."

"I'm not comfortable with that sentence."

"Come on. It'll probably be OK."

Her arm through his, Miriam and Sheldon walked into the brightly lit hotel lobby toward Lenny's world.

Sheldon kept one eye on the exit.

Lenny was shadowboxing offstage. He wasn't just charged up and pumped. He was also angry. Out there, right now, under a hot spotlight, was a third-rate punk comedian getting laughs from one-liners he'd cobbled together by attending everyone else's routines at every other hotel. As best Lenny could tell, lice didn't travel in a schoolyard as fast as these jokes were stolen and circulated. Who even made these jokes? Where do most jokes come from? They have to start somewhere. His did. He'd written them. Hadn't he? He'd heard so many now that he wasn't even sure.

It was dark offstage, and there was a stool he'd been told to sit on, but he couldn't sit on the stool because it prevented him from pacing back and forth, and his legs needed to be working. They needed to be *moving;* he needed to go and go and go because his mouth was going to have to *fly;* it was going to have to articulate and enunciate and all those other fancy words Miss Simmons used about public speaking that seemed to mean the same thing—speak up!

"One minute," said some nameless lump next to him.

One minute? One minute was a lifetime. It was ten percent of the act. It was enough time to get or lose an audience. Race car drivers had more time to maneuver than a comedian did.

"Thirty seconds, kid. Look sharp."

"I'm thinking."

"You think too much."

"That's the least Jewish phrase on earth."

"Ladies and gentlemen!" said the theater manager. "Next up we got . . . a kid. That's all I know. He's a kid. I'm told he's funny, but only you will know. Let's welcome Lenny Bernstein from Massachusetts, of all places. Lenny, come on out."

• • •

Sheldon and Miriam sat together. She held his hand and he couldn't remember ever feeling this happy. He *had* been this happy before. He knew that. But his brain couldn't think of anything but Miriam's soft hand in his at the moment.

Lenny appeared onstage. Sheldon wondered what an appropriate prayer might be.

"Hello and good evening, ladies and gentlemen . . . of the jury. I'm here to tell you that a crime's been committed. It's true. Right here in front of our noses. They do that, you know. They steal material. I heard one comedian the other day tell the exact same joke as the comedian he heard the night before. He said, 'This hotel is so swank that a guy dropped a quarter, and when I gave it back to him, he tipped me a dollar.' I'm not stealing that joke, I'm just telling you a story about a guy who stole that joke. You see the difference.

"Here's another joke I heard a guy steal, but it's longer. A Mexican comes across the border on a bicycle with a giant rucksack. The guard says, 'What's in the bag?' The Mexican says, 'Sand.' The border guys look. It's sand. This happens every other day for six months. Rides up with a bag of sand. Nothing there. They let him in. A year later, the border guard meets the Mexican at a café. Says, 'Look, you were driving us crazy. We know you were smuggling something, but we couldn't figure out what it was. I won't arrest you. You got to tell me. What were you smuggling?' The Mexican says . . . 'Bicycles.'

"My point here," Lenny said, as the audience laughed, "is that the longer the story, the harder it is to steal. I did the math. Stories are too long to steal, and I don't want people using my stuff! So that's what I want to do tonight. I want to tell you a story so long that no one can steal it. I encourage you to get comfortable because it starts like this. Once upon a time . . . I was a child."

The audience giggled and Lenny pointed to a man in the front row.

"You too? You were a child?"

The man nodded. Lenny started to pick out other people in the audience.

"Child? You too. You were a child? Child. Child. Also a child?"

He used his hand like a visor to see deeper into the darkness of the theater. He found a guy way in the back. Lenny squinted. "You were . . . you were two children? [Beat] You were not two children. [Beat] You *have* two children. Where . . . in the trunk of your car? [Beat] No. Not in the trunk of your car. They're your children. I see. You have receipts. You got a good price? OK. That's nice."

Sheldon and Miriam were sitting at a tiny round table in the upper half of the audience area. People were smoking and drinking and laughing, and Sheldon had to hand it to Lenny. Whatever he was doing up there wasn't what Henny Youngman or Milton Berle did. He was doing his own thing and people liked it. How it was working, why it was working, Sheldon didn't understand. That, however, was not the thing on Sheldon's mind. All this talk of spotlights gave him an idea.

"Those fancy people we saw back at the hotel . . . ," Sheldon said, trying to get Miriam's attention. She was smiling up at Lenny in a way Sheldon didn't like. As though he made her happy. As though he might make her happy forever.

"Miriam!"

"What? He's funny!"

"Yeah, OK. Listen, those people back at Grossinger's for the event. Are they staying over? Did they book rooms and stuff?"

"Most of them, yeah. They get loaded and stick around. They don't want to drive all the way back to the city, and the train stops running after midnight. Why?"

There was something about this fact that needled Sheldon. There was a plan in there someplace. "You ever feel like the pieces are all lying around you, but you just can't figure out how they fit together?"

"No," she said.

Why would she? Miriam didn't have problems like Sheldon did.

"Well, anyway, it's coming together but it's not there yet."

"What's not?"

"The solution."

"To what?"

"The problem."

"That's a bit general, Sheldon."

"What's Lenny going on about now?" asked Sheldon, not wanting to share anything specific. It was, after all, a first date.

"Parents. He said he used to have parents too, which was funny, then he did this . . . listen, we're missing it."

Lenny was pointing to a beautiful girl in the third row. "Can we have the light on her? Thank you," he said, as the spotlight shined down. "You, on the other hand, did not have parents. You emerged from a shell out of the Mediterranean Sea fully grown with that long black hair flowing down your torso, your right hand covering your left—ba-boo-bage.

"Listen," Lenny said, sitting down on the edge of the stage, his feet dangling like a schoolboy's from a bridge. "I have to ask you," he said, addressing the young woman and getting personal with the microphone close to his mouth. "Have you considered, for even a moment, the possibility of leaving that guy and spending the rest of your life with me?"

The girl laughed and shook her head furiously.

"You haven't?" Lenny said, as though absolutely shocked but also delighted. "Oh boy! Do I envy you the daydreams you're about to have!" Lenny spoke with his entire body. "The two of us walking in Central Park during springtime draped in the latest fashions, the hem of your long summer dress tickling the instep above your sandals as you sip champagne and watch the sun track across the sky—the warm glow of Hollywood glamor accompanying your every glance and gesture. That's how it would be every waking second. Does that guy make you feel that way? He doesn't, does he? I know he doesn't. You know how I know? Because he takes you to places like this. I wouldn't come here in my free time. I certainly wouldn't brag about it to a date."

Lenny stood up again and the spotlight followed him. The audience was having a wonderful time and showing their appreciation. They thought he was hilarious. The guy in the corner of the stage was tapping his watch, but Lenny wasn't having any of that. Whoever was scheduled for the next slot might as well drop dead as far as Lenny was concerned. He was on a roll.

"When I was a child, these parents I was introducing you to a moment ago, they lied. I don't mean on one occasion. They lied to me about everything. Topics large and small. Do we have any more cookies? No. But we *did*. What are we having for dinner? Chicken. But it wasn't, it was *fish*. It was like this every day. One day, when I reached the age of sixteen, I found the courage to confront them. I said, 'I know you've been lying. I want to know why. Why have you treated me this way?' And my mother, without missing a beat, says, 'You started it!'

"I was taken aback. What had I done? Had all this been set in motion by . . . me? What if this was all my fault?

"'How?' I asked.

"My mother is not a dramatic woman. But this time she answers by putting on a Broadway show. The cast is her and a tiny little me. I'm two and a toddler, and she's playing both parts.

"Hands on her hips, she turns to Little Me, and asks, 'Did you poo?'

"Little Me is aghast. How did he get pulled into such a conversation? I know this because he has turned his head and placed his hand on his chest and looked up at his inquisitor. Little Me is befuddled. Be-baffled. Even slightly offended.

"'No,' says Little Me.

"'You didn't poo?'

"'Nope.'

"'So . . . it's me then. I pooed,' says my mother to Little Me.

"Little Me is starting to get anxious. He is only two but already understands that just because a proposition isn't true doesn't mean the inverse is automatically true. Little Me already learned this lesson when he asked for a cookie last week. He learned that just because *he* couldn't have a cookie, it didn't automatically mean that *she* could. Every time Little Me asked for a cookie and the answer was no, she didn't automatically stick one in her *own* mouth. Sometimes *no one* gets a cookie. Damned if he knew *why*, but my point is this: Maybe, in this case, no one had pooed. That made perfect sense.

"'Or maybe you're suggesting,' she said, leaning into it, 'that I'm having a stroke.'

"Stroke? A stroke?" Lenny yelled, walking around onstage with the microphone in his hand, "What's a stroke? I'm two. I don't know what a stroke is. I've been splitting my conscious time between learning the fundamental building blocks of human reason and trying to figure out whether I can push my belly button deep enough into my body to touch my own spine! And she's talking about strokes."

Lenny stood up very straight, put a hand on his hip, and took a long, long beat.

"Not here," he said to everyone in the audience, breaking from his story and shaking his head at everyone. "Wait until you get home."

The audience was barely able to breathe. Sheldon thought Lenny was rather funny, but none of this was that far from conversations they'd actually had. Maybe putting it onstage under a spotlight had a magical power he didn't understand.

When the audience stopped laughing to inhale, Lenny pressed on.

"'So, you're saying,' this is sixteen-year-old me again, my mother is done performing, and I'm trying to understand this, 'that I lied to you about having pooed and now, when you tell me I'm adopted and really Irish, that it's just your way of getting back at me for the hardship you suffered for being the parent *you* chose to be.'

"'That's exactly right!' she said!

"I look to my father. The patriarch. This son of David. I wait for him to rescue me from the crazy that I now know goes all the way down. But he doesn't. My hero is chewing his cud in the corner of the living room and nodding at whatever my mother says.

"Despondent, I go to visit my grandparents at the nursing home to try to understand the source of this. At the nursing home is my grandmother. The woman who raised my mother. The woman who walked out of Russia with a sack on her back so we could thrive in the United States and have the freedom and safety that she and her family never experienced. The moment I walk into the room, every serious question is wiped from my mind and a new one pops in that I have to ask. 'Grandma . . . did you poo?'

"And she looks at me the way I looked at my mother, and the tumblers fall into place. She says . . . 'No. Did you?'

"Thank you, everyone. I'm so glad to be here with you here in the

Catskills and not in Germany with a bunch of Nazis and all their many, many friends! Good night!"

Lenny got fired much faster this time.

As the audience clapped and cheered and Miriam wiped her eyes with a napkin, Sheldon excused himself and joined Lenny offstage in the dark, where Mr. Feynman—tall, skinny, red-faced even in the dark, and with a thick Brooklyn accent that made it sound like he was yelling no matter what he said—was shaking a bony finger at Lenny like he was conducting a demonic orchestra.

"And what's more, you'll never work this circuit up here again! I'll tell everyone!"

Lenny looked as dumbstruck as his two-year-old little self. "Why?"

"Aside from your going on for more than twenty minutes when you were allotted ten?"

"Yes," Lenny said defiantly. "I know the guy scheduled after me. I did you a favor. Leibowitz could bore the dead."

Mr. Feynman counted off on his freakishly long fingers the reasons he was firing Lenny. "You talked about baby poo. You hit on an actual woman from the actual audience. You talked about her left . . . what the hell did you call it?"

"Ba-boo-bage."

"You can't talk about a woman's ba-boo-bages!"

"How about *breasticles?*"

"You called this place a dump," Feynman yelled. "You insulted a guy in the audience—a guy who could have been a cop or a thug . . . I've heard of men's throats being slit for less than this. You're making advances on his girl in front of everyone! You insulted Mexicans and the Irish. The Irish, who are all cops, by the way. You compared my audience with a bunch of Nazis!"

"Favorably!"

"That's not the point!"

"Why does everyone keep saying that to me?"

"You're never gonna work in this town again. What's your name again?"

Lenny looked at Sheldon and Sheldon shrugged.

"Bruno Krupinski," Lenny answered.

Lenny always seemed to have an extra round in the chamber.

"Krupinski, you're out of here. You're blacklisted, you hear me!"

"This isn't the last you've heard from Bruno Krupinski!" shouted Lenny, though clearly it was.

Feynman was gone in two enormous strides.

Alone at the edge of the stage, Lenny lost interest in Feynman and looked at Sheldon with a pleading eye. "Did you like it?"

"It was funny. I liked it."

"You weren't laughing much. It was making me nervous."

"I knew the bicycle joke because we both heard it last week. I thought the bit about stealing the jokes while complaining about people stealing jokes was funny."

"What about the other stuff?"

"Well . . . you know. We both knew this about your parents. The stroke thing was new. I like the bit about the belly button."

Lenny nodded. It explained why Sheldon hadn't laughed much. He needed strangers, and the stranger the better. He vowed right there never to tell jokes in his hometown.

"I'm starting to understand why everyone changes their names in show business," Sheldon said, as they started to walk back toward Miriam. "You try, you die onstage, you come back as someone else and try again. There's a lot of death and reincarnation. You'd think the Hindus would dominate in this profession rather than us."

"Can I be you for a while?" Lenny asked. "I got a spot tomorrow night at the same time. I think the name Sheldon Horowitz could be a good name. I don't want to be Lenny Bernstein until I'm accepted, and we already killed off Bruno Krupinski."

"Sure, whatever. You're gonna need some new material, though."

"Maybe I'll steal some like everyone else does."

"Is it OK to steal?"

"Everyone steals. Knowing *who* to steal from is the real art."

That was it. That was the piece Sheldon was missing. *Knowing who to steal from.*

Mirabelle's boyfriend had come to Grossinger's to sell the jewels to someone who was still at the hotel, this Thaleman guy. Did Thaleman know him or was this an arranged thing? Sheldon didn't know. What he did know was that Thaleman must have a suitcase of cash and was waiting for the jewels to show up and so far they hadn't; the cash he must have in his room, a room that Sheldon had a key for. If he played this right, Sheldon could frame Lorenzo and get rich at the same time. The problem with his plan was that he needed some jewels and he'd just thrown his in the river. Miriam's guests, however, had given him an idea.

"Lenny, what time are you going on as me tomorrow night?"

"About nine."

"That'll work. I can't be there."

"Is that a joke?"

"No. I'm serious."

"That's too bad. Why not?"

"I've got to be in two places at once."

"You mean that you can't be in two places at once."

"No, I meant the first thing."

Miriam wasn't listening to either of them. She was watching some fifteen-year-old punk named Jerry Lewis fall around on stage. Sheldon wasn't sure whether all that clowning around was funny, but Miriam was in stitches and Sheldon immediately didn't like the guy.

MRS. ULLMAN

I N THEIR ROOM, Lenny slept as Sheldon stared at the ceiling. In his chest, he could feel the light thrumming of the very distant dance music that would end at one o'clock. He was wrecked from a long day, but he wanted to visualize his plan over and over the way Lenny memorized his comedy routines.

Sheldon tried to picture his plan, but his mind kept returning to their bicycle ride home. He, Miriam, and Lenny rode back at 11:30. Lenny swerved over the street to test the grip of his rubber wheels, and Miriam stood in her pedals as she glided down a long hill, raising one hand over her head and catching the wind in the folds of her skirt that flapped behind her.

The temperature had finally dropped, and the ride warmed their muscles as the air cooled their faces. The mosquitos weren't as bad as they'd expected, and the little gnats that usually swarmed around them on forested walks couldn't keep up with the speed of their bikes.

They'd felt good.

On this day, Sheldon had seen Mirabelle and lost her. He'd visited a town that would soon vanish from the face of the earth. He'd thrown a fortune in jewels into a river, and someday all of New York would drink the water that hid those sparkling gems. He'd heard his best friend fill a room with laughter and joy and be punished for it; and he'd seen how beautiful a girl can be when she feels happy.

It was exhausting. He fell asleep imagining Mirabelle on that bicycle instead of Miriam, her yellow dress leaving a trail of blinding light behind her.

•   •   •

Sheldon woke in a panic. He sat up in his bed and spun so his feet touched the ground. Every possible error he might have made came into his mind.

What if Lorenzo had broken into Mirabelle's room in the middle of the night and not found them? The guy was a murderous gangster, after all. He could probably break into a room. Would he have realized they were gone and returned immediately to New Haven or Hartford? That was possible. And what about the buyer, Thaleman? How long was he going to wait around for the seller to show up? Did Lorenzo know Thaleman? Probably not, because the whole point of Mirabelle's boyfriend's line of work was to fence hot jewels from a seller like Ernie Caruso to a buyer like Thaleman. Why use a middleman at all if they all knew each other?

Sheldon needed to get to the register to find Thaleman's room number. After that, he would need to work fast.

Showering and dressing as fast as a marine on maneuvers, Sheldon left Lenny snoozing as he made his way down the carpeted hallway toward the main lobby at 6:30. His own shift didn't start until ten so he had some time he wanted to use. He wore his full bellhop uniform to blend into the landscape.

A woman named Dorothy Reiser worked the night shift at reception. She was a widow who had lost her husband to cancer fifteen years ago and worked at Grossinger's during the summers because it reminded her of happier times. For the rest of the year, she was a teacher.

"Good morning," she said. "You're up bright and early."

"I like getting an early start," Sheldon lied.

"That's not common with teenagers."

"I walk to the beat of my own drummer, Mrs. Reiser."

"Your name's Sheldon, right?"

"Yes, ma'am."

"There's not much for you to do yet. The boys on the shift are still here, and they won't want you taking their tips from people coming in now."

"I understand, ma'am. I'm going to check the registry to see if anyone's coming in that I know."

"Whom I know. Not that I know. They are people, not objects."

Sheldon opened the heavy red guest book and ran his finger down the pages. Mrs. Reiser had other things to do than talk with one of the dozen teenage bellhops. So she didn't notice that Sheldon was flipping the pages backward, searching for the time Mr. Thaleman checked in and where his room was located.

Room 236.

That was in the same hallway as Lorenzo in 218. They'd probably walked right past each other and not known. Which was how Sir-Lies-a-Lot made money, Sheldon figured.

But still.

Mrs. Ullman — the woman with the sapphire and diamond necklace he saw in the lobby last night — was in room 122.

It was a pity that his plan had to involve her, but he couldn't think of another way. The tricky part was going to be getting inside Mrs. Ullman's room at a time when she wasn't there. If she'd been at the party all night, she might be sleeping in.

All of these problems were caused by Mirabelle — or at least they had started with her. But his solution had come from her as well. Mirabelle's old story about that war pigeon had given Sheldon the idea of using messages to move the players around on his chessboard at his command.

The third drawer down on the left side of the telephone contained all kinds of stationery. Some of it was for the guests who wanted to write letters, and some of it was for the staff who needed to fill out forms. The fourth slot down was used for messages between guests. Staff would often jot these down, place them into a fine envelope, and deliver them or else leave them beside the room keys that hung at reception. When the guests returned for their keys, the notes would be handed over.

Sheldon turned to look at the wall of keys. Ullman's key to room 122 was hanging there. That meant she was out of the room and possibly at an early breakfast, and that surprised him even though old people do tend to sleep less. Thaleman's key to 236 and Lorenzo's key to 218 were both off their hooks, so the men were still in their rooms.

"Mrs. Reiser?" Sheldon said. "Do guests have more than one key to their room?"

"Why do you ask?"

"I found one by the lake the other day," Sheldon lied, "and returned it to the slot here, but I wasn't sure whether the guest might still have been able to get in the room. I was just curious. It's my first season here."

"No. There's only one guest key per room. When they leave the room, they give the key to us for safekeeping. I'm sure the guest in question came right back here to inquire, so I'm sure all was well."

"Right. Of course. Sorry."

"No need to apologize," she said, without looking up from her paperwork. "It's good that you're curious. Most bellhops don't ask enough questions. If you keep at it, you could graduate to reception one of these summers."

When Mrs. Reiser left reception to attend to a back-office matter, Sheldon snagged both Ullman's room key and the key to the vacant room across the hall from hers, and left.

Mornings could be lazy times. The bars were open late, and many guests played cards and drank and socialized long after the bands had packed it in. The only person Sheldon passed in the hall was a woman walking dutifully after her two sons who were dressed for the lake. It was quite cool outside, and the sun had barely begun to work on the dew. Walking through the grass at this hour would soak their feet.

He tipped his hat.

"Ma'am," he said, without looking at her.

When they had passed, he opened a linen closet and removed an armful of towels that helped cover his face. Proceeding slowly to room 122, Sheldon calmed himself by remembering that—at this exact moment—he was only a bellhop carrying towels. He was not yet a person who had committed a felony.

He arrived at Mrs. Ullman's door and knocked, cover story ready in case she was there.

The longer he waited, the more chance that he'd have of being seen. He didn't like the waiting.

Without knocking a second time, Sheldon used the room key to let himself in.

The bed was unmade and the room unoccupied. Her exquisite gown from the fundraiser was arranged with care on the wingback chair; her shoes were side by side in front of it.

Sheldon closed the door behind him, placed the towels on the dresser, and after double-checking that the bathroom was empty, he started to work fast.

Ben Adelman's office contained a black vault with a polished silver wheel and a large handle. Inside, he kept cash and items that the guests wanted temporarily stored. Ben had shown it to Sheldon, Lenny, and the other freshman class of bellhops and busboys as part of their induction tour. Ben had used it as a prop to deliver a message: "There has been no crime at Grossinger's in more than fifteen years, and we only had to reset the clock because of some pickpockets." Ben told them not to be too proud. "There are thieves, assholes, and liars in the Jewish community just like in every other but" — he raised a finger — "they do not vacation at Grossinger's."

He then made a joke of naming the hotels where those people *do* vacation and everyone laughed.

The rooms, Sheldon learned, did not have personal safes. So, unless Mrs. Ullman was wearing her sapphire and diamond necklace to breakfast or had given it to Ben for safekeeping — which was very unlikely given that she had worn it all last night — it was here in this room. He simply needed to find it.

Where would an old woman hide her most valuable items on the presumption that no thief would ever — under any circumstances — look there?

Sheldon opened the drawer containing her underwear, closed his eyes and held his breath, shoved his hand underneath, and pulled out a fistful of bracelets, mismatched earrings, and the sapphire and diamond necklace.

A hole in one.

Sheldon opened the slit in his hat for the cardboard insert that gave it shape and slid the jewels in there, then he put the very heavy cap back on his head. He surveyed the room quickly for anything incriminating and then snatched up the towels. With a deep breath, he decided that a confident exit would be easier to defend than a sneaky one in case he was observed, so he swung open the door and strode with mock confidence into the hallway like a man on a mission.

Unseen and very relieved — though his heart was pumping enough to blur his vision — Sheldon stepped over to the vacant room across the hall and opened it.

The bed was stripped and the pillows fluffed and ready for the maid. The curtains were drawn to keep the room cool, and there was a hint of lemon and mothballs from the disinfectant used on the carpet.

Sheldon closed the door behind him. Using the bed as a sorting table, he removed his bellhop's cap and poured the contents onto the white quilted surface of the mattress. For a mesmerizing moment, he allowed himself to be taken in by their radiance and drama and depth.

They made Sheldon think of his mother's necklace. The aventurine. He remembered her promise that someday he would see the Far East and the wonders of Asia. What an impossible idea.

He heard sounds outside in the hall.

They passed.

Lifting everything and being sure to leave nothing behind, not even the backing of a single earring, Sheldon walked into the bathroom, removed the top of the toilet reservoir, and — with Neversink in his memory — plopped the gems into the water before replacing the top and turning off the lights.

Being a criminal mastermind was hungry work. Sheldon indulged in a hearty breakfast from the staff buffet and reported to his job at ten o'clock on the dot, where he found Lenny looking disheveled despite a long night's sleep. With a wave of his hand, Ben sent the boys outside to stand by the front door and — when arrivals and departures were slow — open and close the doors for the guests.

Sheldon and Lenny had this synchronized by now, so they functioned as mechanically as an elevator.

"Why are you so tired?" Sheldon asked him.

"I think it was last night."

"You talked bullshit for twenty minutes and rode a bicycle three miles. This knocked you out?"

"Somehow . . . yeah. I think being creative can knock you out."

"Huh."

By this time, the sun was high, the temperature was starting to rise around them, and the direct sunlight was scorching their faces that were already dark and healthy. It was going to be a hot one, a river day as they used to say in Whately. A lake day here. Lenny left to help an old bickering couple with their luggage, leaving Sheldon alone to hear the voice of Mrs. Ullman shout invectives at Ben Adelman, who stood with his hands raised defensively in front of him by the reception desk.

Mrs. Ullman had opened with a public display of outrage and demand for justice. Although Ben Adelman tried to urge her toward his out-of-earshot office, Mrs. Ullman was having none of it. She wasn't unaware that she was causing a stir.

A small crowd gathered at a safe distance, mostly on Sheldon's side of the glass. A woman had been burgled at Grossinger's. Heads were going to roll and the state police and FBI were going to be summoned; did Mr. Adelman understand the implications of what was happening? The world as he knew it was *over*.

To Sheldon's astonishment, Mel Friedman came down the stairs to the main lobby—Mel Friedman, a man rumored to have never seen the light of actual day or been submerged in a body of natural water.

Mel Friedman was a pale mountain of a man. He wore a black suit and suspenders with a thin black tie that was anything but a racing stripe. His feet threatened to burst out of his bluchers, and the tiny glasses on his eyes made him look menacing. Nero Wolfe would have been awed by this man.

Friedman spoke with a voice so deep and granular that he must have started smoking at five years old.

"Mrs. Ullman," he said, his labored breath expended after two words.

The timbre of his voice—a low rumble threatening a storm or an earthquake—was enough to capture the attention of the lobby. The glass between the speakers and the onlookers clipped some of Mrs. Ullman's higher notes, but it vanished as a barrier when Friedman spoke.

He wasn't a loud man because he didn't need to be. The effort he was making to speak was enough to hypnotize, but his staccato breathing made compound sentences impossible.

"The police have been summoned. The staff notified. We are mortified by this outrage. We will work"—he inhaled again—"diligently to resolve the matter. How may I serve you until then?"

Mrs. Ullman, realizing that she was in the company of a gentleman and a servant, calmed herself and spoke softly enough that neither Sheldon nor anyone else could hear any more through the closed doors.

Lenny appeared behind him. "What happened?"

Sheldon couldn't risk anyone overhearing the truth, so he told Lenny what he'd witnessed without further comment. "I saw her last night before Miriam and I came to see you. She was decked out in jewels. I think someone nicked them."

"That would be a drama."

"I'll say."

Two police cars arrived minutes later. The town of Liberty was a mile off, and despite all the summer tourists, the town cops were not especially busy. Sheldon assumed Mr. Friedman had told them to be discreet, which would explain why they arrived without flashing lights and blaring sirens.

Lenny and Sheldon opened the glass doors for the four policemen, who entered with revolvers hanging low on their utility belts. In that instant, Sheldon sensed the enormity of what he was trying to do: be the kid who outsmarted a man who killed other people for a living.

Sheldon considered that maybe — just this once — he had actually gone too far.

But Sheldon still had time to walk away from all of it. Last night's bicycles were on a rack a hundred yards away. He could collect his pay, pack what little he owned into his rucksack, and ride a bike down to the bus. If he got lucky on the timing, he could be twenty miles and a lifetime away in less than an hour. Lenny might be angry about it at first, and Sheldon would be reluctant to leave Miriam behind with thoughts of what might have been, but there was nothing actually pegging him to *this story,* to *this moment,* to *these acts* — acts that his father had never asked of him and probably wouldn't tolerate. And his mother? She'd be ashamed he was wasting his God-given imagination on something so petty as crime or revenge.

The trouble was that none of this felt petty or criminal. It felt like justice and a restoration of a piece of the world, the only piece that Sheldon knew how to fix.

Inside by reception, the four policemen finally convinced Mrs. Ullman to end the show and take her concerns into the back office with Mr. Friedman and themselves. When the door closed, life returned to normal; the audience dispersed to gossip, and the stage was cleared.

The boys ate lunch. Lenny's energy was back up, which made him more talkative. He had one more idea for a new act. He was about to explain it when Ben Adelman pulled them both aside and asked them to come into the dairy kitchen. Lenny looked at Sheldon, who shrugged unconvincingly enough to worry Lenny. Neither one of them had been into either of the two glatt kosher kitchens before. As Lenny and Sheldon stepped into that stainless-steel world of heavy scents and steam, they found about twenty of their colleagues already inside—which settled Sheldon's nerves immensely.

"I'll get right to it," Ben said to everyone. "There has been a crime. We're searching rooms for missing jewelry—including all of yours. One of our guests—a very rich and influential guest—has been burgled. No one has been burgled at Grossinger's since . . . actually, I have no idea. It's never come up. A missing wristwatch, a lost wallet, a bracelet slipping off at the lake. That's been the most of it over the years. This, however, is felony-and-prison material. As we search your rooms, we are going to find things. Because I can absolutely promise you that we know every possible hiding place in your rooms. We know what's under the mattress and inside the mattress. We know how to remove the fan in the ceiling in the bathroom. We know how to take off the backs of the radios. We know how to fish around in the toilets. We built this hotel. We know what's in the walls and why every floorboard squeaks. We know what rooms you're in, and you are not allowed to go back to them until we've been through them first. We have guards and trusted senior staff to ensure that. It's checkmate. So, I'm giving you all one and only one way out, one time only. I'm going into my office. If anyone wants to tell me what we're going to find before we find it, I suggest you come and tell me right now. If what's been stolen is returned, I will tell our guest that it was returned anonymously. The thief will be fired, of course, but not handed over to the police. You've played Monopoly? This is the Get Out of Jail Free card. There's only one in the deck. Meanwhile, go back to your stations. Do your jobs. The police will be watching the exits and the driveways and the bus stations and the train stations. We have counted the bicycles. We have instructed people not to pick up hitchhikers. If you did it, you cannot get away. You've got one hour to get those jewels into my hands. Any questions?"

No one had any questions.

There wasn't a sound in the kitchen.

"Dismissed," Ben announced.

The boys shuffled out of the kitchen, and it was Lenny who looked ashen. Sheldon couldn't think of why, because Lenny hadn't done anything. When they were in the lobby, Lenny pulled Sheldon into the men's bathroom and —after checking that they were alone—whispered to Sheldon, "I know about your gun. They're going to find your gun."

"Don't worry about it," Sheldon said.

"How can I not worry about it? It's a loaded .45. They're going to find it, and once the police find a gun in your room, we're fired. Maybe worse but definitely fired. Probably worse."

"They're not going to find it."

"Sheldon, you heard what Ben said. They know every spot to search and I believe him."

"I believe him too, but they're not going to find it because it's not there."

"Where is it?"

"It's down my pants."

THE MASTER PLAN

T HE HOUR PASSED WITHOUT a confession. Sheldon knew this because he hadn't confessed.

For the duration of their shift, they manned the doors and carried luggage down halls, their heavy trolleys occasionally clipping the uncollected newspapers in front of the guests' doors. As Ben had threatened, the police and senior staff were searching rooms. So far, though, no one was looking in the unoccupied rooms. Maybe that would come later—he wasn't sure. As Lenny once said, people's actions only look inevitable in retrospect.

When their four o'clock break finally arrived, they were both hot and desperate to jump in the lake if only for a minute. When Mrs. Reiser—still on duty—nodded them off, they sprinted down the empty halls, and restraining themselves when guests appeared, they barged into their room, stripped, donned bathing suits as though they were competing with each other in a swim meet, and hauled ass to the lake knowing that, as sticky and buggy and heated as they'd become on their run, the lake would solve it all the moment they dove in.

And it did.

Sheldon burst past the young sunbathers and the old people who had waded into the water up to their knees to kibitz. Losing both sight and interest in Lenny, he dove deep into the water and was rewarded with a tempest of tiny bubbles that sparkled green and brown all around him.

In that moment, if only for a moment, he was free, free the way people speak of freedom but don't really understand it. Under the surface with the world shimmering high above, he was free from time and responsibility, the past and the future, cause and effect. Free of light and dark, of want and fear.

It couldn't last. We can hold our breath for only so long.

Sheldon burst to the surface like a German U-boat breaching the Atlantic. His muscles were taut, and the hot sunlight hit his skin and burned off the delicious chill. He stood in water to his waist, the lake tickling the elastic of his bathing suit.

With a dramatic flick of his head, Sheldon swept back his hair and scanned the beach for a girl to look at in the hopes she was looking at him. Instead, Sheldon saw him: the man with the mustache.

Without a care, and with time to kill, the man was sitting on a folding beach chair under an umbrella. His shirtsleeves were rolled up, and he wore cotton pants that were also rolled up at the cuffs. He was barefoot and in one hand was a cigar; in the other, a glass of lemonade. Sheldon stared at him and the man took no notice.

A splash crashed into Sheldon's face when Lenny surfaced next to him. It did not break his focus. There, in front of his eyes, was the man himself. Not a memory. This was the actual monster who had killed his father, the monster with the cold eyes Sheldon saw that night in the rain on that quiet road south of Whately, a road that was part of home and should therefore have been safe.

The same mustache, the same angular chin, the same small black eyes.

What was he doing, the monster? Drinking lemonade, smoking, looking at girls, and basking in the sun like he was on holiday, and waiting for Mirabelle's boyfriend to come back to his room so he could kill him—or worse.

He stood, a statue by the lake from a lost civilization, the young and living all around him frolicking without a care.

If Sheldon could break his paralysis, he could recover the .45 from under his towel on the grass and walk over.

"You remember me?" he'd ask.

"Who the fuck are you?" the monster would reply because . . . what else?

"Look more closely," Sheldon would say without emotion—a guide. "Try to remember. The night. The rain. The car. We looked at each other before you turned the wheel. You knew there was a child in the car. You might even have seen my father and realized he looked nothing like Old

Krupinski or his two sons. You turned the wheel anyway. Try to remember."

"Yeah. I remember. So what? How the fuck did you surv—"

And then Sheldon would pump him full of lead. The Colt's magazine held seven rounds and could store one in the chamber. At four feet away, Sheldon won't even need to aim. The bullets would shred the towel, and the cotton would fill the air like down from a chick. Blood—glorious blood —would arc from his chest, his neck, and his eyeballs. The dead meat of him would twitch on the chair, and the lemonade would fall into his crotch as a final humiliation.

"The question isn't how I survived but why," Sheldon would say to the corpse. "I survived so I could do this."

Sheldon would toss the gun onto the body, wipe his hands on the remaining scraps of towel, and maybe even take a dip as a kind of baptism. Everyone would have run off screaming by then and he'd have the lake to himself.

Wouldn't even look back at Lorenzo. Nothing left to see.

After that, of course, he'd be arrested and sent to prison and maybe get life or the death penalty, but standing there in the water with Lenny backstroking beside him, Sheldon knew there was a bigger play here. More than revenge and murder. A way to win. Sheldon was going to lock away his enemy for years, get rich, and be a local hero.

"Bang," Sheldon whispered.

Mirabelle's early infatuation with carrier pigeons had stimulated in Sheldon an image of messages being able to fly through the air, messages that could evade missiles and navigate through fog and smoke and noise. Messages that sought out their own homes and would travel through hell to reach their own beds.

It had been an odd thing to imagine, a momentary fancy, like watching a balloon lost to a breeze. And yet, the story of the Lost Battalion was vivid and alarming and tragic and curious for him the way it had been for Mirabelle.

"How did they know the message really came from Major Whittlesey?"

Sheldon had asked her. "Maybe the Germans had got hold of Cher Ami and sent the message back telling them to stop the bombardment because it was working. Maybe it was a ruse."

"A ruse?" Mirabelle had asked. She liked his choice of words sometimes.

"A ruse."

"We know because Major Whittlesey survived and told the story. So, we know exactly what happened," Mirabelle had explained.

"Right, yeah, OK, after the fact. But in the middle of the shelling? How could the Americans know the message came from the other Americans and not from the Germans?"

"Well, how would they know Major Whittlesey was in command? Maybe Lieutenant Bob Billingham or someone else might have been in charge. The Germans wouldn't have known the name of the commanding officer."

Sheldon had nodded, but this hadn't felt like a complete answer.

"And besides," she said, on a roll. "Where would they have gotten the stationery?"

In November of 1938, soon after Mirabelle had learned the story of Cher Ami from Mr. Knightly, Hitler passed a law forbidding Jews from owning carrier pigeons.

Sheldon walked out of the lake and left the man with the mustache in peace with his lemonade. Mr. Knightly and Major Whittlesey, Mirabelle and Hitler, Cher Ami and Miriam at the reception desk had crashed into one another to give Sheldon his idea.

He now had pigeons to free and messages to send.

Back in his room, he removed the stolen Grossinger's stationery from his pocket. He had no typewriter like Abe had had, so handwriting would have to do. He wrote two letters. The first was to Lorenzo from Thaleman. The other was from Thaleman to Lorenzo. They weren't supposed to know each other, and both of them were waiting on Sir-Lies-a-Lot to serve as the broker — the middleman. On the other hand, they were both resourceful, and it wasn't impossible that they could find each other. So, if they got letters from each other, it would be strange but not impossible. Lorenzo would know the jewels were missing and Thaleman — if he was still in the hotel — would know that Miriam's boyfriend hadn't shown up yet.

Lorenzo to Thaleman: "Meet me at the Lansman's Hotel and Country Club at nine p.m. A kid named Sheldon Horowitz will be onstage doing a comedy thing. De Marco's missing and the stuff is too. We need to talk. We know you didn't take it. I have a mustache and a ring. Find me at the bar."

Thaleman to Lorenzo, sent at the same time: "I'm the buyer. De Marco hasn't shown up. My people don't like problems. Meet me at the Lansman's Hotel and Country Club at nine p.m. A kid named Sheldon Horowitz will be onstage doing a comedy thing. Go to the bar. I know who you are; I'll explain how later. I'll find you."

Sheldon put the two fake messages into Grossinger's envelopes, sealed them, and placed them inside the jacket pocket of his bellhop uniform with his gun — just in case. He'd swing by the buffet for a bite and a glass of water, and then resume his station at reception as he was supposed to. He already knew the room numbers of his two marks. When he could be the most inconspicuous, Sheldon would slip the envelopes into their respective mail slots; the men would collect them during the day or else another bellhop would deliver them by hand. At that point, the men would become stool pigeons — decoys to get them out of their rooms so Sheldon could carry out the material segment of his master plan.

SHELDON HOROWITZ: LIVE

I T WAS TUESDAY, JULY 8, of 1941 and almost 8:30 at night. Lenny was long gone for his gig at Lansman's, and Sheldon was sitting near reception. He wanted to see Lorenzo leave for Lansman's and he did. He even tipped his hat and wished him a good evening to see whether Lorenzo might recognize him, but there was no indication of it.

Sheldon didn't know what Thaleman looked like. Until Thaleman left, however, there was nothing Sheldon could do. He wanted it all done in one smooth gesture. The letter in the pigeonhole was gone so Sheldon surmised that he, like Lorenzo, had the invitation to the club. Until Thaleman showed up, though, Sheldon had nothing to do.

Miriam had the night off, and since no one was checking in at 8:30 on a Tuesday, it was a slow evening. Sheldon snagged a newspaper to keep himself company. The only one he could find in the lobby was the two-cent *Daily News.* It had the largest headline Sheldon had ever seen: U.S. OCCU-PIES ICELAND; MARINES LAND. The photo below showed British troops in Bren gun carriers carrying out maneuvers in the shadow of Iceland's snow-capped mountains. Iceland was a possible roost for Hitler's bombers, and a week earlier, the secretary of the navy, William Franklin Knox, had said that "the time to use the navy to clear the Atlantic of the German menace is now." Congress hadn't agreed to deploying troops outside the Western Hemisphere so Roosevelt did it anyway, claiming Iceland was part of the Western Hemisphere because it was west of the prime meridian. He broke the news to Congress after the fact and announced that marines had landed in Iceland a full 2,488 air miles away from New York in order to gradually replace the Commonwealth troops—mostly Canadian—who had occupied Iceland when Germany had invaded Denmark and Norway in April of 1940.

Roosevelt argued that a Nazi seizure of Iceland, which was now inside the German blockade zone, would be a threat to America's national security. Sheldon read the president's announcement to Congress: "As Commander-in-Chief, I have consequently issued orders to the Navy that all necessary steps be taken to insure the safety of communications and approaches between Iceland and the United States, as well as on the seas between the United States and all other strategic outposts."

Congress was furious. The isolationists in both parties said that since Roosevelt couldn't secure a declaration of war from Congress he was therefore "trying back-door methods" and trying to "trick people into war."

Sheldon read that there were fifty to sixty thousand Canadian and British troops on Iceland.

Abe was one of them.

Sheldon couldn't picture Iceland. The only land Sheldon could imagine without trees was a desert and he knew that Iceland wasn't a desert. He imagined blondes on camels crossing snow in the presence of volcanos. He'd never seen any pictures in the newspapers, and since he didn't go to the movies, he'd never seen any newsreels. From looking at maps, he knew it was small, and Abe had written once saying that Iceland was rugged and beautiful and strange like the moon. "A place with a midnight sun in the summer and no trees anywhere."

The Germans were moving west. Abe was moving east to meet them.

Abe's last letter to Sheldon, back in March of 1941, had said that he was going to Iceland because it was closer to the action and that he and his buddy Louis Bouchard were prepared for it, because up until then, it had been boring as hell in Halifax.

Abe had met Louis Bouchard during their air force training in Halifax, Nova Scotia, in late 1939 — soon after he had left Hartford behind, unable to contain himself and what he had done any longer. Louis was a Québécois from Montreal and was the calmest, quietest, most relaxed individual Abe had ever met. Nothing rattled him, annoyed him, angered him, or otherwise made him scream out of frustration or fear. Twenty-two at the time, he was six foot two and broad but not massive. Louis's physical ability to look over the entire world seemed to Abe like a metaphor for his disposition. During their intensive period of air training, Abe gravitated to Louis's demeanor the way a swimmer reaches for a raft.

Abe struggled with basic training. The problems were not physical. Abe was fit, fast, aggressive, and determined. He was the only Jew he knew who was preparing for combat, and while no one else there knew or — if they did — cared, this felt significant to Abe; he needed to be living proof that everything Goebbels said about Jews being weak and soft and evolutionarily inferior was a lie.

Because it *was* a lie. But truth wasn't enough. Truth needed to be demonstrated.

The problem for Abe with basic training was obeying orders and being respectful of authority. This is where Louis's calm demeanor and temperate attitude were a godsend to Abe.

Their first day of training was on a blustery Canadian November day that was as gray as the skies in the newsreels. It was damp and cold too, a damp that settled on Abe's face like a mask and seemed to be willing itself into his wool sweater and thin jacket.

There were twenty young men on the tarmac of the airfield. The officer who stood in front of them was barely older than Abe and looked younger on account of his fair skin and slender shoulders. He was effete in the way that enlisted men always thought officers were. Unlike them, he stood in a thick bomber jacket with a fleece collar. His legs were apart in a vain attempt to project authority. To his right was a giant of a man, a towering oaf who cast a shadow with his brow. They learned that the giant's name was Gallagher. He was a staff sergeant with dead eyes and black hair who wore the same outfit as the recruits. The differences between them were the chevrons on his arm and the fifteen years spent earning them.

"This is Sergeant Gallagher," said the lieutenant, whose last name turned out to be Clive. "Sergeant Gallagher has served in the RCAF for fourteen years starting in 1927. He has flown over the Arctic, the Atlantic, and survived not one but two crashes — one of them at sea off Labrador, where he was in near-freezing water for more than four hours, during which time he kept warm enough to stay alive by using wreckage from the craft and techniques we will be teaching you. His search-and-rescue flight teams have saved twenty-seven American, Canadian, and British sailors and aviators. He is our rock.

"I, on the other hand, was commissioned as a second lieutenant three weeks ago. I have never been stationed anywhere but here, and I have a total of six hours of flight training. I have never seen combat. I have never rescued anyone, killed anyone, or been wet for a sustained period of time. I will soon be coordinating troop arrangements with Britain's Royal Air Force Coastal Command, which means it is unlikely I will ever save or rescue or kill anyone. I am also short and weak. I have nothing on Sergeant Gallagher except rank, youth, and beauty. Sergeant," he said, turning to the expressionless mass on his right, "drop and give me twenty."

The old aviator dropped to the ground and counted off twenty push-ups.

Sheldon read how Abe stared at Gallagher's hands that dug into the pebbles on the asphalt, all of that upper body mass now being used against him as he had to fight gravity and the sharp edges of stones. Drizzle collected on the thick strands of his black hair as he shouted out the reps. When he was done, he rose, breathing only slightly harder, and said nothing.

"Rank outranks experience," said Lieutenant Clive. "We follow the chain of command. No one knows this better than men with experience. We do it because people above us know the big picture. Not because they're smarter or better than we are, although they might be. We all play our parts to make the machine work, and if we don't, it isn't a machine. Sergeant Gallagher will now lead you on a ten-kilometer run after which you will be assigned to paint the latrines. Fall out."

Abe found the honesty of all this clarifying. It also worked on his brain in a way he could understand. If Gallagher could take it, so could Abe. If Gallagher could run it, climb it, suffer it, so could Abe. He might never be as big and strong but that wasn't the point. The point was acting the man.

That night and every night after—with Louis always on hand to listen to a confidential complaint or a rant about military logic—Abe collapsed into an exhausted heap and caught moments of sleep throughout the day when it was possible. He shot a few guns, parachuted from a few planes, and spent a surprising amount of time wet given that this was supposed to be the air force. If this was what it took to be able to fight, though, he was prepared to do it.

When basic was over, they trained on aircraft. That was when everyone specialized. That was also when Abe's struggle ended and the fun began.

The sorties that the Canadians flew out of Halifax weren't finding or sinking many German ships or U-boats. It happened periodically, but so far it hadn't happened to his crew, and Abe was itching to drop bombs. "The Nazi swastika *really* makes the perfect bull's-eye, don't you think?" Abe had asked Louis. "And they helpfully put it everywhere!"

If Abe was in Iceland and American forces were going to replace him, Sheldon wondered where Abe might go next. Was it too late for him to come home and join the U.S. military? Sheldon didn't know how all that worked. He liked the idea, though, that Abe was the first American there —that he was leading the charge.

Sheldon sat at Grossinger's and thought again of joining Abe, perhaps after killing Lorenzo or getting him locked up.

But he couldn't because America was still not in the war.

Six children ran out of the dining room and started playing tag in the lobby. It was a good space for this but probably not an appropriate one. Sheldon looked around and noticed he was the only one who might pass for an adult and decided to ignore them.

He checked the watch Mirabelle had given him. It was 8:43. Thaleman's key still wasn't there and that worried Sheldon. It was true that guests often forgot and kept their keys in their bags when they left, but they were discouraged from doing so, and they were told there was a significant fine for losing them. In this case, though, it occurred to him that Thaleman might not want to leave his key at the desk on account of having the wads of cash in his room that he was going to use to buy the stolen jewels. He'd know the hotel staff would be able to get in there, but why would the staff go in there at night? Grossinger's didn't offer a turndown service, and if he put the DO NOT DISTURB sign on the handle, his room was about as safe as it could be.

Ben Adelman walked into the lobby and waved the children out. He sat down on a tall stool beside Sheldon.

"Quiet night?" he asked.

Sheldon was sure Ben or his team had already searched his room. The question was whether Ben had searched the empty room across the hallway from Mrs. Ullman's room too. If he had, Sheldon's plan wasn't going to work out so well.

"Except for the kids," Sheldon said.

"Where's your friend Lenny?"

"He has the night off. He wants to be the next Jack Benny or George Burns or whatever."

"Where's he performing?" Ben asked.

"I forget the name," Sheldon lied.

"Not you? You don't want to tickle everyone's funny bones?"

Sheldon wasn't sure if Ben was only toying with him or not. He glanced at the doors to see if any police were rolling up.

"I don't think the world's very funny right now," Sheldon said.

"No," Ben said, slightly taken aback. "You a reader?"

"You mean the papers?"

"Yeah."

"I guess I am, yeah. I got an older cousin in the Royal Canadian Air Force. He writes me letters. I like to keep up."

"Good for him."

"Do you think we should fight the Nazis? Most people don't."

"Of course we should."

"Why don't we say so?"

"Who?"

"Jews."

"Ah."

The annoying children came back. They were chasing a barefoot eight-year-old in a blue sundress with thin straps at the shoulders. She ran flat-out through the hallway faster than the speed of sound if Ben's efforts to yell after her were any measure. Four seconds later, the entire posse blurred past them. Ben didn't bother this time.

Sheldon continued to look at him for an answer.

242   DEREK B. MILLER

"If the Jews spoke up, what would we ask for? A resolution? A law? A strongly worded letter to Hitler? Of course not. We'd ask for war. There's no half measure with those people. If we asked for war, it would look like the Jews were trying to push America into an unpopular war, which is exactly what the Nazis are saying and it isn't true. It could be made to look like we're trying to do it for other Jews, that we're putting Jews before America."

"But it's the right thing to do, and it's the right thing for America too. And we're Americans. Why are we the only Americans not allowed to have an opinion?"

"It won't sound like we're Americans with opinions. It might sound like Jews plan to make money from the war, or else we're closer to the people in Europe than our neighbors. Or else it'll reinforce what Hitler's saying, that all of this was a Jewish plot, or . . . whatever. I don't know. I'm not Goebbels. If we speak, though, he'll say something and it'll look bad."

"So . . . Jews are getting murdered by the tens or hundreds of thousands and our best move is to shut up?"

Ben didn't have an answer for that.

"This Goebbels guy. He's smarter than all of us?"

"He's got a better seat at the table. I was studying to be a lawyer once . . ." He faded off and then changed the subject. "How old are you?"

"Almost fifteen."

"Why are you thinking about this so much?"

"I walk around here and my only thought is, Why isn't *everyone* talking about it? It's all comedy, music, food, and sex. It's weird."

"It is weird," Ben admitted.

Sheldon let out a long exhale. "How's it going with the investigation?"

"I can't tell you."

"Me in particular or—anyone?"

"Is there a reason I wouldn't tell you in particular?"

That had been a bad, bad question. Why had he asked that question? Because he wanted to know the answer, that's why. But that is *not* a good enough reason to ask a question.

"I'm just kidding," Ben said with a chuckle, to Sheldon's eternal relief. "But really, I can't tell you."

"That's fine," Sheldon said, no longer interested.

It was one minute to nine and no one had returned Thaleman's key. Which was going to be an issue. There was a master in the reception desk, but Sheldon couldn't keep it long in case someone came looking for it.

"So," said Ben, standing up. "I'm off. Nice talking to ya, Sheldon Horowitz."

"Good night, Mr. Adelman."

When Adelman left the building, it was four minutes past nine o'clock at night. Sheldon slipped behind the desk, grabbed the master key, and ran down the hall to the empty guest room where he'd stashed Mrs. Ullman's jewels.

The hallway to Mrs. Ullman's room was busy. Guests were walking back and forth on their way to a show, back from an event, on their way to their own rooms for a rest, or on their way to someone else's room. Sheldon was hesitant to make his move so visibly, but the clock was ticking. There was no other time in the foreseeable future when both Lorenzo and Thaleman would be out of their rooms.

In retrospect, Sheldon thought that he should have probably sent them to completely different places or else sent them both to see Lenny — who was performing as Sheldon Horowitz tonight — but not introduced them.

Why *had* he introduced them? Why didn't he write a letter that said, "I'm the short fat man in the fine suit and polished black shoes at the bar drinking Jack straight up. Strike up a conversation. Pretend you don't know me. If I trust you, I'll tell you." That would have kept them going for ages.

Why was he thinking about this? That option was a train that had left the station. He was set on a track now and he needed to speed up!

"Fine," he said aloud.

Not a single person looked at him. He was the only person in the hall who thought a bellhop walking down a hall looked strange. Once he took this fact to heart, he walked to the empty room, knocked twice just to be sure it wasn't occupied now, and then entered.

The room was dark and unchanged from when he had hidden Mrs. Ullman's jewels in the reservoir of the toilet. Sheldon flicked on the overhead lamp. Nothing—as best he could tell—had changed. The room was still not made up for guests, and he couldn't see anything to prove the place had been turned upside down in a search.

Sheldon looked at the window and saw himself staring back.

"Turn off the light, idiot," said his reflection.

It was a good idea and he did.

In the dark, he hoped no one was watching the room. It would have been a good idea for catching the thief. The police could have found the jewelry and cunningly left it to see who would come to collect it. They could be watching him right now. Maybe they drilled a tiny hole in the wall so they could look through it.

He was letting it get to him, the pressure of it. It was a strange combination of traits a person needed to have to be a top criminal: enough imagination to set it all up but not enough to become lost in it. The creativity to outthink everyone but yourself. Not a natural balance.

Your imagination is going to get you into trouble, his father had said to him. Had he known? What had he known?

He'd known his son. Nothing more and nothing less.

"Mrs. Ullman will get her stuff back, Dad," Sheldon whispered to the room. "I just needed to borrow it. Stop watching me, this is hard enough." Sheldon stepped into the bathroom, which was black and had no window. "And don't tell Mom."

The top of the toilet reservoir was easy to remove, and though he worried that Eliot Ness and the Untouchables were going to burst in the minute he stuck his hand in the proverbial cookie jar, he did it anyway.

The sunken treasure was still there.

Sheldon pulled everything out and toweled the pieces off before placing them in his jacket pockets; he wasn't going far.

Taking a breath, he calmed himself though he felt his heart pounding. When he had stormed into Bruno Krupinski's house, he hadn't been scared. He had walked in there with the wind of justice at his back. Why wasn't that happening now? Why was he so afraid now?

It doesn't matter, said his father's voice. *Do the job.*

. . .

Lenny Bernstein, aka Sheldon Horowitz by Night, might have finally found the one topic that wouldn't get him fired. He was going to tell jokes to a Jewish crowd about a topic they knew and understood, something straightforward and obvious but still original because no one had put it into words yet. Not *these* words. Not *Lenny's* words. It was a dark topic he was ready to shed light on through the vehicle of comedy the way Abraham stood on that dusty hill overlooking Sodom and Gomorrah — just before God razed them to dust — and raised his hand, and asked, "Forgive me for asking but . . . are you sure about this?"

That's comedy, right? Standing up to the obvious and demanding that it explain itself?

Lenny was still working on the details. But this. *This.* This he had down. He'd spent more than two entire hours working on this. Which really ought to do it.

In a few brief minutes, Lenny was going to explain the entire history and evolution and phenomenon of the persecution of the Jews.

And he had it down to four words. Four words that explained it all, that no one had ever heard before, but they'd get it and accept it the minute they heard it.

And it wasn't about Jesus. It never was. It was about what Christians really cared about, what united them as a people.

Lenny tapped the microphone.

He inhaled audibly. He exhaled.

"The Jews killed Santa," he announced.

Silence.

He had them. They wanted to know. To understand. And why? Because deep in their hearts they already knew he was right. They just wanted to hear it. That's all anyone wants, to be affirmed. Recognized. Heard.

Perhaps amused in the process.

He continued.

"The Jews killed Santa! This is what's got the gentiles all worked up. OK, we didn't stab the guy with a knife — we're not Italian — but we passed on the knowledge that effectively killed him in the minds of every Christian child.

"Please, think back to when you were a little kid waiting for Santa to spread cheer and toys on Hanukkah like every other Jewish child in America. And then, on cue, some prick walks up to you on the playground and says, 'My daddy says Santa Claus isn't coming to YOUR house because you're a JEW.'

"You started to cry. I know, I cried too. I went home to my father. There he was on a cold Massachusetts night in his slippers sitting in his chair with his pipe going and the newspaper across his face like a wall — like we wouldn't be able to find him back there — and I said, 'Daddy, little Tommy Goyim says Santa Claus isn't coming to our house because we're Jewish.'

"Perhaps," Lenny said, feigning anguish, "he heard the pain in my trembling voice. The pain of two thousand years fully delivered into the heart of a child in one jab. Here it was. The Christian resentment at its parent religion. Unwilling to accept the rejection. The lashing out as a response. The oppression. The sadness. So, my father put down the paper and looked at me. I could see on his face that he had an answer. This . . . *this* was what fathers were for. I'd always known there had to be something and this was going to be it! 'It's true,' he said, 'that Santa isn't coming to our house. BUT,' he added quickly, with a rabbinical finger thrust to heaven to halt my pain, 'it isn't because we're Jewish. The fact is, he isn't coming to Tommy's house either. And it isn't because Tommy's an asshole. Let me tell you why.'"

Lenny shook off the pain and weight onstage as though it were water from the back of a duck.

"The next day, I skipped to school enlightened. I flew on the wings of eagles back to that playground because I knew something Tommy didn't know. I approached Tommy, and I said, 'Tommy . . . you were right. Santa isn't coming to my house. But I also learned that he isn't coming to your house either. And it's because —'

"And I paused. Because I wanted to relish his pain. I wanted to say that Santa never existed. That gentiles made him up so kids could get used to absolute faith in the patently absurd. But I didn't have the heart, so I said, 'Tommy, he's not coming to our houses because the Nazis recently shot him down with antiaircraft guns somewhere over Poland and they're now eating the remains of the reindeer while handing your presents out to the Hitler Youth. Meanwhile . . . happy Hanukkah!'

"Thank you, I'm Sheldon Horowitz, and I will never be complete without your love!"

Sheldon was not there to hear Lenny's explosive bit because he was standing face-to-face with Miriam at 9:20 p.m. a few doors down from Lorenzo's.

She was dressed in a blue evening gown, looking as if she had stepped out of a Technicolor scene in a movie. In front of such a vision, Sheldon had never felt so small and so inadequate. If he hadn't been late and the sharp edges of Mrs. Ullman's treasured jewelry in his pockets hadn't been there to remind him of his purpose and intent at that moment, he would have collapsed into a puddle of water.

Miriam's neck was the most graceful curve Sheldon had ever seen, and her shoulders were as soft as a dove's feather. The thin fabric of her dress stretched across her breasts and wrapped itself tightly around their perfect sides before tapering down to her hips, where everything became expansive once again. In her high heels, she stood an inch taller than he was and Sheldon had to look slightly upward into her misty eyes. He felt a conflicted desire to both flee and remain there, transfixed, forever. Sheldon wanted her to break the spell for him so he could move, and speak, and even breathe again, but he wanted her to do it later; as later as possible.

She smiled at him and he failed to close his mouth or blink.

"You OK?" she asked him.

He heard the question and had no idea that he hadn't answered her.

"Sheldon?"

"Uh-huh."

"Aren't you coming to the dance?"

Dance.

Dance?

"What dance?" he asked.

"The dance. The big dance. With the musicians. And people. And me. You're not wearing that to the dance, are you?"

The dance.

There was a dance tonight. Sheldon had forgotten all about the dance. How had he forgotten about the dance?

He had forgotten about the dance because he was busy. He had a Mafia assassin to frame, a thief to rob, and vengeance to be delivered. These were all-encompassing activities.

"When does it start?" he asked.

"Now. Nine-thirty."

"It's nine-thirty already?"

"Almost. I don't have a watch."

Was she more beautiful than Mirabelle? He had never thought anyone could be more beautiful than Mirabelle. Was he only attracted to older girls whose names started with the letter *M*? He'd have to think about that.

He was gripping the gems so hard that his fingers threatened to bleed.

Lenny's bit was supposed to be ten minutes long. He'd run over, of course, but did that even matter? An assassin and a thief were meeting at a bar, and this was not the start of a joke. Sheldon had to hurry. He had to move.

Joy in life may be hypnotic but fear of death is a motivator.

To move, though, he'd have to stop looking at the way Miriam's red hair perfectly complemented the cobalt blue of her dress. And that was impossible.

"I thought you wanted to dance with me," she said, more confused than hurt.

"I did. I do. I want almost nothing more."

"Almost?"

Technically, yes. But Sheldon couldn't explain why.

"Do you want me to wait for you?" Miriam asked.

Did he? Did he want her to wait? Of course he did, but the timelines weren't accommodating. He had other things to do. His senses were returning. The sweat in his eyes helped focus his mind.

"I'll see you there," he said, refusing to compromise with reality.

"You sure?"

"I've never been more certain of anything in my life."

Lenny was riding his bicycle back to the hotel when a car started following him. The night air was a warm breeze scented with pine, and the fireflies lit up the fields around him to the sound of bullfrogs in the distant bogs. He was sorry that the real Sheldon had missed the show tonight. Lenny was getting much, *much* closer to not being fired and he was sure that this was a good sign. Shorter would be better. He still had a lot of work to do whittling away the extra words to make sure the story was funny all the way through, not only at the end.

Maybe the long stories weren't such a good thing, he thought. He'd have to think about it. He didn't know anyone else out there telling these long stories. Most comedians told jokes as if they were shooting bullets from a tommy gun.

The car behind Lenny wasn't passing him. The yellow headlights cast a shadow of him on the road ahead, stretching out his head so that it looked long and black and smeared across the asphalt. He waved the car ahead, but it didn't go.

Lenny measured the width of the road at a glance and found it plenty wide for a car to pass if it wanted to. He edged the bicycle closer to the dirt and scree at the edge of the road and tried to wave the car on again but it still followed him.

Starting to panic, Lenny tried to think of who might be in the car. He had offended everyone but no one in particular. He had no debts and no fights, no enemies and no girlfriends or ex-girlfriends who would want to scare him.

He had no friends with cars. No friends who lacked a sense of humor deep enough for this.

Lenny became afraid and thought of Sheldon and his father being run off the road. He pedaled faster, hoping to find a turnoff or a path.

The car sped up.

The bicycle rattled beneath him. The chain threatened to pop off the teeth if he rode any faster. The car engine revved. Lenny saw the edges of his own shadow grow sharper; the shapes of his legs became crisper as the headlights got closer.

There was no escaping off the road to the right; it rose gently but it would have slowed him just enough to be crushed under the wheels of the car. To the left, it fell downward into a valley, through grass so high and wild, it could have been hiding anything beneath—rocks or streams, crevasses or outcrops.

With the car only feet behind him and nothing ahead but the black sweep of lonely road, Lenny took a deep breath and—with the courage of a paratrooper on his first jump, blind with fear—he leaned hard to the left and jumped the edge of the road into the night.

The bicycle flew into the bottomless black of the field beyond; the yellow headlights turning hard after him.

THE CATSKILL SHUFFLE

THE HEART INSIDE SHELDON'S chest seemed to beat as fast as his wrist-watch. He clutched the edge of the porcelain reservoir with his left hand and plopped the incriminating jewels in with his right.

The top scrapped with a sound like sandpaper when he fit the heavy lid back into place.

Taking a deep breath, that part of the job now done, he dried his hand on Lorenzo's towel and left it damp.

Every moment that passed afforded Lorenzo a chance to return, walk into this room, and kill him.

Why had he sent those messages for them to meet? It was stupid. *Stupid.* He'd based his plans on pigeons. Who does that? He wasn't good enough at this. He wasn't a criminal mastermind. When he, Abe, and Mirabelle broke into the pawn shop, the owner actually shot at Abe on the way out.

Call that planning?

He pictured it all differently now. The two men meet at the hotel. They hear that Sheldon Horowitz is telling jokes. Sure, it means that Sheldon Horowitz can't be setting them up back at Grossinger's, but what if Lorenzo recognizes the name? It's unlikely, but after all these years, what if he learned the real identity of the person he had killed? Maybe Lenny—dark haired and the right shape and age—might look enough like Sheldon for Lorenzo to put things together the wrong way.

One way or another—for one reason or another—they'd realize they were set up. Once they did, they'd rush back here, Sheldon thought. Not on bicycles but in enormous ninety-horsepower cars with pistons pumping, dust on their tails, guns loaded, maybe as a team or maybe as competitors, and maybe afterward, one pops off the other. Lorenzo might have had the same thought as Sheldon. If Thaleman showed up, it means he'd come to do business. So, the cash was still lying around. From Lorenzo's perspective, all he'd need to do was kill Thaleman and take the money. The money was the real goal. Sending those messages might have started a bloodbath.

Jesus, Sheldon thought. What the hell was he doing?

And what about Thaleman? If he got wise to the setup and survived, he'd be rushing back here for his money.

In any case, Sheldon had to get that money first.

Inside the darkness of Lorenzo's suite, the fear of action was overtaken by the fear of inaction, and Sheldon—his wits gathered once again—threw open the door to the hallway and confidently stepped out.

A middle-aged couple was standing two doors away and turned to look at him.

"Yes, ma'am," Sheldon immediately said to the empty room behind him. "I'll have someone bring it right away." He then tipped his hat to the invisible matron, closed the door, turned to the couple, tipped his hat again, and walked on—empty-handed and empty-pocketed.

The couple smiled and then forgot he existed.

9:37 p.m.

Even if Lenny's bit ran long, it wouldn't take up more than twenty minutes. It was impressive enough that he could keep coming up with new material every few days, but a full twenty minutes of new blather seemed unlikely. And who was to say Lorenzo and Thaleman would sit there listening to him?

There was no knowing how much time Sheldon had left. All he knew for a fact was that he had *less*.

Less by the second.

Sheldon knocked on Thaleman's room. Hearing nothing, he walked in as though he'd been invited.

• • •

This room was completely different and so was the task. He wasn't planting evidence and then running. That was a quick job: in and out. But he had to find something now, and that was going to harder.

Fine men's clothes were scattered on the bed: a blue suit and a brown one, a green silk tie and a red one. A pair of expensive shoes were placed below the blue suit as though he'd been mixing and matching tonight. Whatever he'd chosen to wear must have been in the same vein. Why did he get dolled up to meet Lorenzo?

The dance.

It wasn't a staff dance. It was for everyone. A Latin guy called Machito was going to play. Miriam had said that it was Afro-Cuban music. Sheldon had never heard of this, but he knew it would give him a right to touch Miriam's waist, which already made it his favorite kind of music ever.

"Focus," he said to himself.

On the armchair across the room was a red dress.

Sheldon couldn't think of a reason why a red dress would be in this room. But he didn't have time to care because he needed to find the money and he convinced himself the best way to do this was to stop thinking so much and look.

What had Ben Adelman said in the kitchen? He had made an excellent list of where people might hide things.

- Under the bed
- Under the cushion of the armchair
- In the drawers
- Under the mattress
- Inside the mattress
- In the little vent on the ceiling in the bathroom
- In the toilet
- Whatever the hell else he'd said . . .

And then Sheldon thought: the closet?

Why not?

The closet had white louvered bifold doors. He pulled the doors open using their white knobs.

There, on an upper shelf above the hanging clothes, was a green duffel bag. He pulled it down, unzipped it, and saw thousands of dollars and a .38 revolver. So now Sheldon had two guns.

Sheldon heard a key slot into the hotel room door.

He stepped into the closet and closed it behind him.

As quietly as he could, Sheldon stepped farther behind the hanging clothes.

They smelled like women's perfume.

Why would they . . . ?

Oh, right, the dress.

Through the slits in the door, Sheldon saw a woman enter the room, and the second he saw her, he closed his eyes in disgust at his second massive blunder.

Mirabelle had said that Thaleman was here to have "some fun with his foreign mistress." Of course, she's the one who owned the red dress.

Inside she came. He watched her. She was in her late twenties or perhaps a bit older, but Sheldon was no judge of age. She was very slender and had thick black hair like many women here. She had a better tan, though. Her face was long and narrow, and while she wasn't traditionally pretty, she was very attractive with massive brown eyes, angular cheeks, and lovely curves Her dress was long and violet; something worn to a serious party.

There was a tall slit up the side.

She was nothing like Mirabelle or Miriam. There was an adultness that exuded from her in a way that Sheldon had not encountered before. Well, from his mother, yes. She was beautiful too. But this was a woman who wasn't family.

She started talking to herself—loudly—in Spanish.

Sheldon did not speak Spanish and didn't personally know anyone who did. He could distinguish it from French, German, and Yiddish; French was the singsongy one, German the scary one, Yiddish the German-but-not-scary one, and Spanish . . . the fast one.

He didn't know what she was saying, but he knew what she was feeling because she expressed it. She was fuming mad, and though he couldn't make out a single word, her anger was clearly directed at Thaleman—the no-show.

Angry, pacing, and muttering to herself (though gesticulating more than Sheldon's mother used to), she flicked off her shoes and they landed, very impressively, on the armchair. Sheldon suspected that this was not her first time performing the trick. She was using the tone of voice that people use to lecture someone who is supposed to be there but isn't, which is apparently the same in every language.

None of that was, strictly speaking, Sheldon's problem. His problem was finding a way out of the room before Thaleman came back and the two of them got into an actual face-to-face argument. She was already annoyed, and of course, he'd come back in a bad mood too. If Thaleman opened the closet to find him, Sheldon would have to shoot him with his own .38.

Which he didn't want to do. Lorenzo, maybe, but this guy was just a thief with a pretty girlfriend; one who'd been stood up and was peeved.

Option one was to walk out right now with the bag and make a run for it. If Sheldon did that, he was certain she'd start screaming as soon as he came out of the closet. And what if she could reach her shoes? She could probably plant one between his eyes and knock him out before he said a word.

The next option was standing there and hoping that the woman didn't open the closet. She was dressed to the nines like she was planning to go to the dance—but she wasn't, which would explain why she was so animated. If Thaleman had been so picky about his clothing, perhaps he too was dressed up. If he was a fancy-talker (and he'd have to be to get a woman this pretty to go with him), maybe he would apologize to her. Then no one would have to open the closet or get shot!

The woman was now waggling a finger at an invisible person and scolding him, and it struck Sheldon that if this performance had been in English he would have thought the woman was absolutely crazy. Strangely, in Spanish, it didn't sound crazy at all. Why a different language changed everything he couldn't begin to guess, but it made him think that maybe being foreign might make her react differently to a man in her closet.

How differently, however, was unclear.

It would be better if he walked out than if she walked into the closet, though. If she threw open the door and saw him—and he waved—Sheldon was pretty sure she'd scream and then beat the stuffing out of him.

She might be from another country, but she wasn't from another *planet*.

As he contemplated his options—with time slipping away and Thaleman getting closer every second—the woman placed her thumbs under the straps of her dress, pulled them away from her, and like in a magic act, the whole getup slipped down to her wide hips and collected there for a brief moment before she shoved her thumbs into the crumpled fabric and wriggled it down until friction surrendered to gravity.

She stood there in wine-colored panties and a lace bra.

Sheldon's mother had never worn red underwear.

None of the photos Sheldon had ever seen of women in their underwear had been in color.

This was new.

Would she know about the money? No, Sheldon thought—surprising himself by being able to think at all. This woman was not Thaleman's partner in crime. She was his lover.

Lucky son of a bitch.

That sealed it. There was only one way out of the room and only one time to do it.

Sheldon Horowitz burst out of the closet wearing Thaleman's jacket and —with a hat over his face in one hand and the filled-up gym bag and his bellhop hat in the other—he started walking.

On the move, he shouted fast and loud in an accent that might have been Latvian or Bulgarian if he'd ever heard either before. "You are very beautiful, and he is a big asshole! You deserve better. I am leaving now. You should leave too. Go to the dance. I am sure it needs you."

Sheldon crab-walked to the door, the gun dangling from his hand like an unneeded screwdriver. "You're very pretty. And that burgundy color is very flattering! Bye!"

The woman was slack-jawed and stunned into silence. Her head was slightly cocked to the side as though she was trying to gain purchase on the moment and failing.

Like a long jumper, Sheldon sprung out the door, slammed it closed,

leapt across the hall to the closest room he knew was unoccupied and then
— using the master key — burst in and whipped that door closed too.

Inside, he placed his back against the flat surface and slid slowly to the
floor. Knees up and butt down, Sheldon placed his head between his hands
and the pommel of the .38 against his temple, and he learned instantly that
the entirety of the world could sound like nothing more than the beat of his
own heart and the telltale sound of a ticking watch.

KILLER

I N THE VACANT HOTEL ROOM, with the beat of the party rumbling up from the floorboards, Sheldon recovered his wits. Standing up, he shed Thaleman's jacket and hat and stuffed them into the duffel bag, stripped a sheet from the bed, and wrapped the bag inside it. Twisting the top, he tossed the bundle casually over his shoulder so it looked like he was hauling laundry.

Sheldon marched directly to the front lobby, almost slipping on an uncollected newspaper on the floor, and found Mrs. Abigail Finegold at the desk.

Mrs. Finegold had been working at Grossinger's since it opened. As far as Sheldon knew, she had been installed there along with the lamps and carpeting and woodwork.

Mrs. Finegold had seen hundreds of boys like Sheldon come and go over the years, and her mode was to stick to protocol and systems and methods like a librarian at a military base. Sheldon believed that she would have been the world's perfect spy.

"Mrs. Finegold."

"Good evening, Sheldon. I would have expected you'd be at the dance. You're missing quite an event."

"Mrs. Finegold," repeated Sheldon—drawing a heavy breath to seal the evening and bring the final act into play. "I know where Mrs. Ullman's jewelry is."

Mrs. Finegold raised an eyebrow.

"I got called to fix a toilet—"

"You're not a plumber."

"No. But it's late and guests often ask for the people they know. Whenever we leave a room, we always say, 'If there's anything—'"

"I take your point. Go on."

"I went into room 218 after knocking because the toilet was running and annoying the people next door. I figured I could jiggle it a little, you know? Not fix it, really. For that I'd have to—"

"Get to it."

"Jiggling didn't help so I opened the reservoir at the top and looked in, and there they were at the bottom. Like pirate treasure or something. Room 218. At the bottom of the toilet's tank. You can't tell anyone it was me who found it. The guy in there? He has a gun."

"A gun?"

"Bullets and stuff in the nightstand. I'd call the police, Mrs. Finegold. Have them break down the door or something."

"We don't need to break down the door, Sheldon. We have the key. In fact, you have the key. Give it here."

"Right you are, Mrs. Finegold. Listen, I got to go."

"I think you should probably stay because—"

"Oh, no. They'll trust you. They'll listen to you. But a bellhop? Please leave me out of it. And don't go in there yourself, Mrs. Finegold. I think he's dangerous."

Without waiting for her to say another word, Sheldon flipped his sack over his shoulder, strode to the front doors, and pushed them open as if to let in the fresh air of a new day at a beach. Out into the night he stepped, with thousands of dollars in cash, two guns, and a friend to find in the dark.

✈

SHELDON RODE WEST toward Lansman's Hotel on a borrowed bicycle he intended to return.

There were no streetlamps and the road was black and unmarked. As he headed out to intercept Lenny and protect him if need be, Sheldon couldn't leave the feeling behind that he'd closed the cover on an ongoing story. Oh, to have been there when Ben found the jewels, when Ben called the police, when the police arrived and ambushed Lorenzo, when they wrestled him to the ground or maybe shot him full of holes like in a James Cagney movie.

Not that Sheldon had ever seen one, but he'd read the reviews.

He pressed hard on the pedals, building up speed until he was going so fast that he could barely control the bicycle. All that pent-up adrenaline inside his body was coursing through him, and he flew across the earth like God's face over the waters.

The wind cooled the sweat forming on his head and a chill trickled down his spine. He stood up on the pedals and glided through starlight and the shadows of trees cast by the moon.

Up ahead, he saw headlights in a field illuminating the spinning wheel of a bicycle.

The car was stuck in a ditch forty feet off the road into the high grass; the engine running fast. It was bulbous and black, and its roof looked like the carapace of a giant beetle. The headlights cast otherworldly rays into the wild flowers that swayed in the night breeze, into the chrome spokes that glinted and spun, twisted and wrecked.

Sheldon pulled off the road a hundred feet from the accident and dropped the bike. He hurled the green bag of money to the ground and drew Henkler's .45 from his belt, chambering a round and flicking off the safety as he ran. He knew — he absolutely knew — that it was Lenny's bicycle. Whether it was Lorenzo or Thaleman in the car, he couldn't tell, and he didn't care. All he cared about was his friend.

"Lenny!" Sheldon yelled.

This was all his fault. All his fault, he thought, as he stumbled over uneven ground, as he fought through overgrown grass and brushed the gnats from his face that were swarming to the sweat on his head.

"Lenny!" he yelled, hands locked outward, the barrel pointing at the car —a target as big as a barn that was willing him to plug it with lead.

He was close enough now. If he crouched and took aim, he could punch through the paper-thin sheet metal of the car's door. He'd miss at first, but he had seven rounds to get it right, and those bullets would eviscerate anything in that car.

"Lenny!" he yelled again.

"I'm here," said a pained voice from the grass close to the bicycle.

Nothing from the car. No movement, but now Sheldon was only thirty feet away and he could see a figure in the car. The silhouette of a slouched man.

He could shoot him from here. Even in the dark. He'd hunted by night.

Who even cared if it was Lorenzo or Thaleman? One down and one to go. That would be fine with him.

But Sheldon didn't fire.

Closer and closer he approached, step by step, ready to blast out the windows, blast through the door, pepper the beast, and blow the guy's head off.

Why wasn't he shooting? Was it fear?

No. He was angry.

He still wasn't shooting, though.

As he stopped twenty feet away from the car and placed that black shape in his sights—a perfect shot and he wouldn't even have to see the blood, the head would drop fast—he had to wonder what he was doing, and it dawned on him with a gentle simplicity: He couldn't see his target, and if he pulled the trigger without being able to see his target, his father would have been angry at him and he didn't want to make his father angry. He had never wanted that. Because he loved him.

"Lenny!" Sheldon yelled again. Lenny appeared in the yellow beams of the headlights, his face bloody and one hand on his head. He stood shakily. Seeing that Lenny was all in one piece, Sheldon—like an FBI agent on the hunt for the Mafia—now sprinted up to the car and pointed the gun right through the window at the man inside.

With the engine running, the dashboard lights were lit. Though they were faint, Sheldon could now see the face of the unconscious man. It took him only a glance to realize that he had never seen this man before, so it wasn't Lorenzo, and from the way he was dressed, it wasn't Thaleman either.

"What are you doing here?" Lenny asked him, hobbling across the ground toward the car.

"What?" said Sheldon, walking around the back of the car and circling toward the driver's side to get a better look at the man he didn't shoot.

"What are you doing here? It's the middle of night. You should be in bed."

"You're loopy," said Sheldon. "You hit your head."

The door was broken and partly open. The engine continued to spew out a thick oily exhaust that choked the air around them. Sheldon pointed the gun at the man. Whoever the hell he was, he'd still run Lenny off the road, and Sheldon was prepared to adopt a new motivation for shooting someone: He wasn't picky.

The driver was blond and young, maybe a few years older than Abe at most. He wore one of those new Aloha shirts from Hawaii that Sheldon had seen in a magazine. How it got to the Catskills from the Pacific he had no idea, but there was *no way* that the beautiful woman at the hotel would have gone to a dance with a guy who was dressed like this.

"Lenny, what the hell happened?" Sheldon asked.

They heard police sirens in the distance.

"He was following me. He was swerving around behind me. I got scared and went off the road, and he followed me into the field."

Sheldon could smell the stink of bourbon and vomit emanating from the car. It was revolting.

"This guy is pissed drunk. He was probably trying to get past you."

"Why did he follow me off the road?" Lenny asked, starting to regain his wits.

"I don't know. Maybe he was just following whatever was moving."

"I guess."

"You hurt?" Sheldon asked him.

"My head kind of hurts. And my arm."

"Nothing broken?"

"Doesn't feel like it."

Police cars were coming up the road and traveling in the direction of

Grossinger's. Sheldon wasn't sure whether these were the cops Mrs. Finegold had called or whether they were on their way here. If they were coming here, they'd be arriving at quite a scene. The car, the drunk, Lenny's head, the bike, the gun, and the cash. He gave himself a few seconds to concoct a story and came up with nothing.

"I think we should go."

"Yeah, OK. What about him?"

"Him?"

"Yeah. Him."

"He's lucky to be alive," Sheldon said.

Sheldon put Lenny's arm around his neck as if his friend were a wounded soldier and walked him out of the headlights into the darkness of the deep fields about a shadowed mile toward the lake. There, the boys could pick up the path that led them back to their bedroom. Inside and safe, they could sleep the sleep of comrades in arms; assuming, that is, that Lorenzo was gone.

The police cars drove right past them, which gave Sheldon new hope for a good night.

The night's quiet returned when they were far enough away from the wrecked car. By the time Sheldon collected the bag of cash, the first crickets started to sing again. Lenny started walking taller and on his own.

Sheldon asked, "Did you get fired again?"

"Not exactly," Lenny said. "I pushed it deliberately too far tonight. Wanted to see what would happen if I did it on purpose."

"They laugh?"

"They laughed."

"But the manager didn't like it?"

Lenny shook his head. "Too Jewish."

"What the hell does that mean?"

"I don't know. But whatever it means, it means a lot."

✈

THERE WERE NO BELLHOPS on duty after midnight. The trains stopped running, and no one checked in that late. If they did, there was someone at reception who could take care of it and a janitor who could be called in to carry suitcases if needed. There were, therefore, no bellhops in the lobby after Sheldon dropped Lenny off in their room and proceeded through the halls to the reception desk and lucked upon Lorenzo being handcuffed in the midst of three armed cops.

The enormous Mel Friedman was there and dabbing the top of his head with a handkerchief. He was talking with Ben Adelman and Mrs. Finegold, who was standing behind the front desk as though she were manning a machine-gun nest.

The sound of Latin music filled the lobby with vibrant rhythms. A trumpet of precision and virtuosity rang in joyful obliviousness to the somber mood of the management.

Mrs. Finegold snapped her fingers at Sheldon and tried to shoo him out of the lobby, but Sheldon was having none of that. This was the end of a story, and there was no way he was going to miss handing Lorenzo his hat.

Ben, also defying Mrs. Finegold, called Sheldon over.

"You did this," Ben said, shaking his hand. "Well done."

"Thank you. It wasn't easy."

"I was a little worried at first, I have to admit. I thought maybe you did it and planted the jewels to cover it all up, but the police here say they know this guy and the people he's connected to, and for them, it's open and shut."

"Why would you think I did it?" Sheldon asked, unable to leave well enough alone.

"You got a way about you," Ben said.

"What way?"

"Like your brain's always at work and there's more going on with you than seems to be going on. Like you have this . . . I don't know . . . rich inner life."

"Isn't that a good thing?"

"I honestly don't know."

"Yeah. Me either."

The cops shoved Lorenzo, signaling that it was time to go, so Sheldon —a doorman, a bellhop, a criminal mastermind, and the right hand of God—jogged out the front door to open it and let them all out. After they passed through, he ran to the police cruiser and opened the back door as though Lorenzo were the Prince of Wales.

"We got it, kid," said a large cop with a fat belly and a big gun.

"It's my job, sir," Sheldon said. "And we aim to please around here."

The cop didn't argue. There was no point. It was late and it was just a door. Lorenzo was shoved toward the back seat.

Before ducking his head, though, he stopped hard and looked Sheldon dead in the eye. "I'm going to find you," he said—his eyes full of recognition and understanding now. He'd put it together. The face from the car.

"If we meet again, Lorenzo," Sheldon whispered back, "you're gonna die."

The police car, with Lorenzo in it, drove away without the lights flashing or the sirens blaring. For Sheldon, the scene felt like Whately when he and the sheriff sent away the Krupinski brothers. When the taillights disappeared down the hill, all that was left was the sense of an ending.

Alone outside, Sheldon turned back to the hotel with plans to go see Lenny. That was when he saw Miriam pass through the lobby. She was holding the arm of a handsome young man, who was perhaps twenty years old. He wore a suit and tie, and had the posture of a man headed to Harvard. Passing reception, he stopped to shake someone's hand, and Miriam stood by him as though she were a senator's wife.

In that moment, she turned to look outside and saw Sheldon. He raised his hand, but she turned her head away.

PART III

THIS L

TAMING OF THE SHREW

L ETTER WRITING HAD BEEN a relaxing and satisfying way to stay connected to Mirabelle and Sheldon when Abe first arrived at ground
school in January of 1940. He'd felt bad about leaving them behind that
autumn, but by the new year, he'd been ready to reengage with the life he'd
left behind. Maybe because the path ahead was finally clear.

Some of the guys thought it was a bad omen to write letters before missions because it put everyone in a morose frame of mind rather than pumping them up like hunters before a kill, but Abe wasn't superstitious, and
unlike his Canadian friends, he was never afraid that he'd lose his anger.
That photo from Austria never left his mind.

Those quiet days of training coincided with quiet seas and not much
pressure on the air defenses off the Canadian coast. Until April of 1940,
the Germans didn't have an Atlantic base. The newspapers explained the
reasons for this better than the officers did. Nazi efforts to disrupt the provi-
sions being sent to Britain would have required them braving the treacher-
ous waters of the North Sea—and the British navy—or else they would
have to slip out through the English Channel, which was impossible to do
in numbers. All that changed in April of 1940 when Quisling helped the
Nazis take over Norway and France fell soon after. From then on, the Germans had free rein in the Atlantic.

The RAF Coastal Command dithered. All the best equipment and all the
political backing in London was going to the Bomber Command because
Churchill wanted to bring the fight to the Nazis and level Germany. That
choice left the Atlantic's merchant navy—and the four million tons of matériel it shipped every month—largely unprotected.

Abe took Churchill's decision personally because it meant he couldn't drop bombs on Nazis. It did, however, help him find his specialty.

He could have chosen anything he wanted. He was in the upper half of his class in general physical fitness, was the third fastest runner, and was the best distance runner on account of his slender physique and long legs and willful determination. Unlike some of the men, he had a high school diploma in hand, and having graduated with top marks, he was qualified for pilot training. His math skills were excellent. Even his eyesight checked out.

But Abe didn't want to be a pilot. To him, being a pilot was like being a caddy on a golf course. Pilots bring the tools to the field; it's the *bombardier* who actually uses them.

Louis, ever the gentleman, chose to be a pilot. Abe wanted to drop the bombs.

Being a bombardier meant training on particular aircraft (the Vickers Wellington and later the B-24) and — more important — on the top secret Norden bombsight, a piece of extremely expensive kit with internal gyroscopes and stabilizers that made it possible for the bombardier to lock in a vertical line to compensate for the pitching and rolling of the aircraft, and in turn gave him control over the range angle and, ultimately, where the bombs fell.

Or so went the theory. In any case, Abe wasn't allowed to include any mention of it in his letters home.

The geometry and practical exercises in the classroom gave structure to his creative desire to wreak havoc on German warships. Abe loved how each type of bomb trailed the plane on release at a different rate — the trail speed — and how the trail speed had to be matched to the airspeed and altitude when calculating the range angle for impact.

He relished the imagination involved in trying to visualize how wind was a factor in pushing the plane off course on a bombing run, requiring him to measure the drift angle and match it to the bomb trail. Beyond his high school math, he learned to calculate the more complex cross trail, which he calculated as the trail multiplied by the sine of the drift angle. He could visualize it, calculate it, and use the Norden to clutch-in the stabilizers that could take things from there.

The more complicated it was, the better, because it proved to Abe that the war effort needed him.

What Abe loved most was how the cold calculation of the mind produced devastating results. He felt like he was delivering back to the Germans the same recipe they were dishing out and that every time he got an equation right he was besting them at their own game.

Superior race, you say?

Can you catch this in your teeth?

Bombing U-boats was better than vengeance. It was the chance to be living proof that the German claims of racial superiority were false. Abe wanted to be a living counterfactual to everyone who thought Jews were degenerates and evolutionarily inferior. He wanted to *be* the truth. This was a motivation beyond vengeance. For Abe, excellence was a holy war and a battle for the truth about who and what he was.

Unfortunately, as Abe and everyone else soon learned, the Norden was a best-condition device that wasn't capable of learning or automatically adjusting when the situation became variable. And war, they learned, was a variable enterprise. The Norden couldn't account for changes in wind, battlefield smoke, aircrew stress, aircraft damage, bombsight obstruction from clouds or weather or glare, or any other real-life problem that was often faced. All of this added to the Norden's circular error probable, which was the tightest circle that could be expected from a bombardier even in ideal conditions, which no aircrew ever faced. This meant — though no one wanted to say it aloud — that bombing was more art than science.

Abe cared about none of this. Not the casualty rates from training accidents or the risks of being shot down or simply falling out of the sky due to mechanical or pilot error. He didn't care about the cold at altitude nor — once they were transferred — the cold of Iceland. Short of shooting Ger-

272 DEREK B. MILLER

mans through the scope on a rifle, the Norden was as close as he could get to putting Nazis in his crosshairs. These crosshairs were far above the target and he would never see the whites of their eyes like the Minutemen did with the British at the Battle of Bunker Hill, but it still beat sitting around in America waiting for Congress to remove their thumbs from their asses and join the damn fight.

In their remaining time in Halifax, the men smoked, played cards, and talked about the war they wanted to be in. What separated Abe from the Canadians most—to his surprise—was that he was essentially alone in wanting to talk about the Nazis. He had thought that this would be the obvious topic: who they were, what they did, and why they deserved death delivered in the form of aerial bombardment.

Even his best friends, like Louis, didn't want to talk about this. Their approach to it all was less emotional, less personal. If they did bother to discuss the wider canvas at all, they talked about the "British war effort" and the pathetic state of the RAF's Coastal Command and what they called the Black Pit. The Atlantic Gap that couldn't be reached by land-based bombers in Canada or the UK because of their limited range. Once a convoy crossed into the Black Pit after April of 1940, there was no land-based antisubmarine air cover, and the merchant marine was forced to rely on naval escorts that were seldom a match for the U-boats—at least early on.

"Don't you guys ever get angry?" Abe asked one day after folding his cards in disgust at their failure to line up correctly.

"About what?" asked Louis.

Abe took his question as an answer and let it go. What was he going to explain? The constant degrading humiliation of being Jewish? The relentlessness of being pronounced weak and incapable of honorable self-defense only to have the Axis machine demonstrate this by hurling its full mechanical weight at the throats of children as though that were proof? There was no explaining this to these guys. These were his friends and his comrades, but they weren't his people. For Abe, this was OK. They didn't need to feel what he was feeling in order to transport him and his bombs to the target.

• • •

For the better part of 1940, they patrolled the waters off Newfoundland and —like bad fishermen—caught nothing or had to turn back from possible encounters with the U-boats because their fuel ran out before they could try to halt the strangulation of Britain's flow of matériel.

In the autumn of 1940, they were transferred to Iceland. It wasn't until the summer of 1941—the summer that Sheldon outsmarted the New England Mob, locked up his nemesis, and became rich all in one night—that things got interesting for Abe too.

It started with Alvin Cobbler. Alvin always had news, and while no one believed him at first, everything he said later came true. Alvin was from a town called Medicine Hat in Alberta, almost two hundred miles to the southeast of Calgary, which to Abe placed it nowhere and near nothing. Alvin was filled with fascinating information that was either perfectly true or complete bullshit, and it was rare that Alvin knew the difference. He was thin and short with unruly blond hair. As best as Abe could tell, Alvin never stopped talking unless he was ordered to, threatened, or was unconscious.

"I'm telling you," Alvin said one Saturday in April of 1941. The temperature in Iceland was hovering near freezing and a frosting of snow filled the windowsills of their barracks. The sorties they had been flying off the coast until then—like their sorties from Halifax—had achieved nothing other than freezing them at altitude. Abe hadn't dropped a single bomb or spotted a single German U-boat. Which wasn't surprising. Their range sucked. The planes couldn't fly far enough into the Atlantic to find their targets. The Germans were mean, but they weren't stupid.

"The Americans are shipping some B-24s over to RAF Nutts Corner in Northern Ireland this coming summer," Alvin said. "My cousin in San Diego works at one of the factories building the things and he saw the paperwork. And I have it from a source who knows a guy who knows for sure—"

"Oh, fuck me, Alvin," said Abe.

"I'm telling you, some of the Liberators are going to RAF Coastal Command's 120 Squadron, and we're teamed up with them and that means we're going to fly them. We're going to get a long-range bomber. Don't you understand? We're going to be the first team to fly into the Black Pit. We're going to close the Atlantic Gap. Let the games begin, and all that."

Iceland, for the past seven months, had been blacked-out dark and witch-tit cold, but it hadn't been that bad because Iceland had something that no other place could boast about: Icelandic girls. Abe and his friends were the first foreigners to arrive in Iceland en masse since the Vikings, and every Canadian (plus Abe) was convinced that the girls must be sick of Icelandic boys and the profound lack of variety. The entire island was the size of a gumball so everyone had known one another since they were kids. And that is neither romantic nor sexy.

Enter Canada.

The Canadians liked to imagine themselves as exotic; and it was pretty rare for Canadians to be considered exotic. This moment—a fact they knew down to the man—was their one and only chance to capitalize on it.

Abe had been among the first group who had achieved measurable success. He'd met a girl named Ingunn in a local tavern. She was very blonde, full-figured, a few years older than Abe, and very excited about his being American. She'd seen the movies, learned the language (sort of), and wanted to go to Hollywood, which—quite by coincidence—was where Abe claimed he had grown up.

"You'd love it," he insisted.

By June of 1941, it turned out that Alvin—inexplicably, impossibly—had been right: A shiny new B-24 Liberator had been delivered to their windswept tarmac.

Their new commanding officer was a stocky, short, mustached, and uninteresting Albertan named Bachmann. Occasionally, and uninvited, Bachmann joined Abe and Louis and the rest of the crew for cards, but his conversation topics usually brought joy to a halt. He did, however, often share information at these games so his presence was tolerated.

Bachmann was not a bad guy. He wasn't evil and no one hated him, but if he vanished painlessly in a puff of smoke, the natural reaction would be to open a window and let it out. His thick mustache was borderline comical, and no matter how much PT he did, he never seemed to lose weight. But he was a reasonable midcareer officer and—he explained—he had a British cousin named Esther who worked for the new air officer commanding-in-chief of the Coastal Command, Phillip Joubert de la Ferté. As their base in Iceland was a new RAF Coastal Command site—and since Joubert sat on the Atlantic committee with the Bomber Command and Winston Churchill himself—Esther was feeding Bachmann privileged news.

Both Abe and Louis realized immediately that this was the kind of news that would have gotten them shot as spies if anyone had noticed, but somehow no one did. This meant that Abe and Louis and the rest of the crew knew things about the strategic air wing that no one outside of Churchill's inner circle knew. All this made playing cards interesting.

"We've been getting the shittiest planes," Bachmann announced one day, "because Bomber Command wants all the long-range ones for pounding Germany. Churchill likes pounding Germany because he's angry about the Blitz. He also wants to make a show to the Russians that we're doing something valuable on the western front. As we don't have a foothold on the Continent anymore, dropping bombs is about all we can do. That means that Coastal Command and the Atlantic battle are being largely ignored, which is why the U-boats are going to continue to sink all the merchant ships because we have no air wing that can stop them. However"—Bachmann paused to collect his winnings, which everyone had assumed would make him stop talking because that's how extortion worked—"you're getting a B-24 Liberator. The only one in Iceland. And it's equipped," he said to Abe, "with the Norden."

As Alvin had earlier insisted, this particular plane had been headed for RAF Nutts Corner but was later meant to be flown *back* to Reykjavík in the autumn. So, one particularly annoyed administrator figured they might as well just leave it here when it stopped for refueling and he'd fudge the paperwork.

"Want to see it?" Bachmann asked them when the card game was over.

They did. They really did.

It was past midnight, and because they were stationed at sixty-four degrees north latitude, the sun was barely below the horizon and the world was cast in a treeless twilight of pinks, purples, and indigos. The plane was alone on the airstrip and its fuselage was awash in a beatific lavender glow.

The nose art (straight from San Diego) read, *The Shrew.*

"It's a reference," Bachmann explained, "to a headstrong woman with a sharp wit from a Shakespeare play." This fact made the crew happy because they liked sharp-witted and classy women, especially when they were pictorially represented by stunning brunettes in black swimsuits, which was exactly what was painted above the name of the plane.

"She looks like my aunt Lucy," Abe whispered to Louis.

"I think that's Hedy Lamarr as a Vargas Girl."

"Whoever she is, she looks like my aunt."

"Your aunt must be a looker," Louis said.

"She was. She died in a fire with my mother in '37."

Louis frowned. It was a sad story, and it explained some of Abe's personality, but it also sounded like a bad omen.

"I'd keep that to yourself," Louis said.

They flew the B-24 on three missions over the next week that resulted in still more nothing. It was the night before their fourth scheduled flight, which everyone knew was canceled because of the oncoming storm, that Bachmann burst in on them two hours before mission time. "Up! You all have to go up now. Take the B-24. Up you go. Now, now, now, boys."

They all looked at him like he was crazy. It was very late, there was a storm coming, and it was American Independence Day. To the crew, these reasons overruled anything the Germans might be up to.

Abe was writing a letter to Sheldon, who was at some hotel in the Catskills where he and his buddy Lenny were working over the summer. Abe was trying to describe what July Fourth felt like in Iceland among a bunch of Canadians. He didn't have time to finish, though; Bachmann was quite animated.

"Get in the air!" Bachmann yelled.

"OK," Louis said, not moving.

"The Americans are coming!"

They all laughed. It was a joke. Bachmann had made a joke. Not even a bad one. They hadn't known it was possible. They ribbed Abe and congratulated Bachmann on his fine show.

"No, no," he said, standing with his hands on his hips. "The Americans are coming to take over the defense of Iceland, and all of us are going to Britain for the air war over Germany. That part you knew. Here's the new part. The 1st Provisional Marine Brigade is coming over from Newfoundland now. *Right now.* And they have a problem. A German problem. And you need to help them. Now."

"Argentia?" Louis asked, referring to the base there.

"Yeah. Right," Bachmann said more calmly, perhaps because he realized that no one would listen to him while he was hysterical. "Task Force 19. They're coming. An Avro of ours spotted a U-boat on an intercept with their convoy. But they're out in the Pit, and the Newfoundland planes can't reach that far. *The Shrew* is the only plane with the range to engage the U-boat. You're going west and you're going hunting and you're going *now* because you might not make it even if you fly flat-out. There are more than a thousand marines on those ships, and if you don't bomb the U-boat, they're going to die. Any questions?"

Louis had one. "What about the storm?"

"Yeah. It's going to be windy."

"How windy?" Abe asked.

Bachmann said nothing, which told Abe how windy it was going to be.

Abe thought about this: When you drop depth charges or bombs at altitude, the Norden's supposed to compensate for the cross trail in a wind, but a storm was more than wind. A storm is made of high- and low-pressure fronts colliding. They push the wind all over the place. You don't compensate for something like that. You avoid it. Especially in a plane.

Abe remembered throwing a ball with Sheldon in the hurricane of '38. Only twenty feet away from each other, they never caught a single one. Depth charges were no different from baseballs. Wind over the ocean was unobstructed and terrifying. Abe wouldn't be able to pattern the drops. They weren't going to hit a goddamned thing and he knew it.

A storm also meant terrible turbulence, and the B-24 was well-known to be a bitch at altitude; it would shake them all around like they were dice in a cup.

Abe checked to see how much everyone had been drinking. They were all going to be barfing it up. So, there was going to be that smell too.

Morris Campbell, the waist gunner, knew something about storms too, having grown up on a wheat farm in Saskatchewan north of Regina. Morris didn't need to know more about bombs than he already did to state the obvious. "U-boats are twenty feet wide. We won't hit a wheat field from altitude in a storm."

No one replied.

"We will miss. We will not hit the target."

"We'll hit something," Abe said.

Morris didn't laugh. No one laughed. A thousand marines were coming this way, a U-boat was going in the other direction, and a storm was wrapping the whole affair in a withering embrace.

"You don't need to hit them," Bachmann said. "You just need to be there. The Americans need to see that we're trying, and the Germans need to know they're at risk."

"We're going to die for show?" Abe asked.

"No," said Bachmann. "Show matters, but the sortie is real. The Germans run on diesel on the surface. Up top, the boats are fast enough to catch the convoy—assuming the intelligence from the Avro is right. But submerged, they have to run on batteries and they are very slow and the Yanks will be able to outrun them. And the Germans can't stay down forever; they have to surface to run those engines again and recharge the batteries. If *The Shrew* is up above, the U-boat will be forced to dive and slow down unless the captain is nuts. Also, if there's a wolfpack, they won't be able to coordinate an attack while submerged whether you're dropping charges or not. So, the charges don't need to be that accurate. You know all this!"

"Why not?" Morris asked.

"Why not what?" Bachmann said.

"Why won't they be able to coordinate an attack while submerged?"

"The only way they can coordinate is by radio," said Bachmann, checking his watch and wanting to hurry this along. "They can only use the radios on the surface because the cables from the aerial have to run down through the hatch. Their engineers couldn't think of any other way to design the things. Once they close the hatch, each U-boat is on its own."

Morris said nothing. Everyone looked at Bachmann, who said, "The plane. Get on the fucking plane!"

They rushed through the preflight check, and after that, they were up.

✈

THE HIGHER THEY FLEW, the less fuel they used, so they flew higher. The higher they flew, the colder it was, and they wished they weren't flying so high. At 20,000 feet, it was extremely cold.

After two hours in the air, Alvin called roll to see who hated their new airplane and everyone raised a hand. Despite its being much larger than the Wellington, the heaters were weaker. Moving around inside the fuselage was also awkward. Both waist gunners had to sit on the floor and wrap themselves in wool blankets.

Louis called down to Abe, who was scrunched up in the nose cone below. "You planning to see that girl when you get back?"

"Yeah, I think so. I hope so."

"What's her name again?"

"Ingunn."

"Jewish?" Louis asked, deadpan.

The entire crew laughed.

Louis looked out into the dark. Normally, U-boats surfaced and recharged their batteries at night, especially during the first four moonless hours. That was also when they hunted. With the sun already in the sky at two in the morning, they were easier to spot.

The Atlantic, though, was very big.

Louis checked the airspeed. This was as fast as they could go. Even in the long-range Liberator, they were facing a range problem if getting back was part of the plan. If they had to linger over the convoy, that would also cost fuel.

Louis steered them southwest into the face of the Gulf Stream. They were above the clouds. When they occasionally glimpsed the water, it was a pallid iron gray. The prospect of seeing a submarine seemed bleak.

It wasn't impossible, though, if they used geometry.

They knew the U-boat was on an intercept course with the convoy, so even if they didn't know exactly where it was—which they didn't—they knew where it had been spotted, they knew where it was going, and they knew that the paths of the convoy and U-boat would eventually converge. The closer those lines became, the greater likelihood that the U-boat could use its torpedoes against the Americans.

The navigator called in the time to Louis. "Seven minutes to convoy intercept."

"I'll take us down."

The four propeller engines slowed. *The Shrew* descended into the gray floor of clouds below.

The airplane shook more violently the lower they flew, and the visibility was terrible.

It was cold and dull in the nose cone. Abe looked down at the vastness of the ocean through breaks in the low storm clouds. The men were too cold for banter and the clock was ticking down to intercept. It was during that time that Abe came up with an idea. "Let's circle the convoy and make wider and wider circles while periodically dropping charges until we either force the Germans under or destroy them."

"You mean get shot at," Morris said.

"No, it'll be fun," Abe replied.

Louis could see his own breath when he exhaled. He was thinking about what Abe had suggested. The wind was now rattling them, and the windshield wipers were outclassed by the intensity of the rain pelting them.

"What do you think?" Morris asked.

"I think I see them."

"Who?" asked everyone at the same time.

"The Americans."

The only straight lines at sea are those made by men—or women, in the case of ship hulls, because it was the women back home who had built them. Even while looking for those lines, it had been hard to make out the ships. There were more of them out there out of sight; they were not distinct objects but part of the ocean.

Like the U-boat.

Aircraft can be tough to spot against darkened skies, and the clouds help to mask them. But the sound they made always gave them away. Louis didn't love Abe's idea. The problem with circling the convoy was that it showed the enemy where the convoy was; it was like drawing a giant circle in the sky.

Shots from a German antiaircraft gun punctured their fuselage.

None of the aircrew knew what had happened at first. They had never engaged the Germans before, and the sound of bullets puncturing the skin of the plane didn't seem as loud or dramatic as the crew might have expected. It had been loud in the plane to start with, but after the bullets passed through, it instantly became much louder. An annoying whistle came through the fuselage that sounded like a kid blowing across the top of a Coke bottle. It was Morris, the waist gunner, who noticed that the holes were round and plentiful.

"We've been hit!" he yelled. "And we're gonna get hit again!" he added.

"Do you see anything?" Louis yelled. Morris had opened the door. His harness kept him from flying out. He was looking for something to shoot at.

It was Alvin, though, who spotted the target first and announced it with his deafening .50-caliber machine gun. The tracer bullets fell slowly like flares to the far ocean below, each one directing Alvin's aim toward the surfaced U-boat that he was now locked in mutual combat with. The spent shells clanked to the floor all over the aircraft, rattling around and bunching up in the corners as puddles of brass.

Morris—whose own gun was pointing at the clouds as Louis banked the plane—had nothing to do other than freeze as the wind and rain soaked his leather jacket so he removed a shovel from the wall and started hauling out the hundreds of spent shells on the floor.

Louis called down to Abe. "Low and slow?"

It was what they had both been thinking about back in the hanger when they heard about the storm. Drop altitude from a long way off. Come in over the surface of the ocean nice and low, line up with the U-boat, and then unload the bombs and blast it to hell. Assuming, that is, that the U-boat's 20mm flak gun didn't shoot Louis through the windscreen first.

"There's a second one!" Alvin yelled. Louis pulled up on the stick, gaining them some distance and shaking off the oncoming fire.

Abe was trying to reason his way through their predicament too. The Norden was utterly useless in these conditions. He'd trained as though he were in a plane 20,000 feet in the air over a German forest with a building in the middle during a calm day with a moderate breeze. What the plane was doing now was banking at thirty degrees in the middle of a hurricane over a sheet of gray paper with a doodle of a U-boat on it.

"Can you do it?" Louis yelled to Abe.

With a tailwind and only a few hundred feet of drop, there wouldn't be much trail on the antisubmarine bombs and Abe already knew the terminal velocity of those. If Louis could fix airspeed and altitude, Abe could do the math. Sort of. Or at least he could eyeball it with a certain level of expertise. But, realistically . . .

"I'll miss," Abe yelled.

"It'll force them under."

"Yeah, but it's dangerous. I mean . . . if the point is to make them submerge rather than sink them, why go lower when we can go higher?" Abe tried to explain himself, but the incessant explosions of the .50-caliber gun were driving him nuts and his own nose was starting to run, which was an irritant in his mask.

Louis seemed to understand, though. He started to spiral upward in the general area of the U-boats so Abe could drop the depth charges as if they were land mines falling from the sky. Maybe they hit, maybe they were close enough, and maybe they didn't, but the U-boat captains would have to be nuts not to submerge and ride it out.

More antiaircraft rounds hit *The Shrew*. Louis took them up. Something near Alvin had caught fire inside the plane. Smoke was everywhere, and Morris dropped his shovel and reached for the fire extinguisher. As he worked on the fire, he called out, "You'll never hit anything if you don't aim."

"We're going to let the randomness of it all scare the shit out of them," Abe yelled.

Morris was strangely quiet while Alvin continued to pepper the Atlantic with lead.

"I thought you wanted to kill Germans."

Abe—staring down at the Atlantic—took Morris's question seriously.

He had wanted to kill Germans. In this moment, though, and in sight of the convoy less than a nautical mile away, Abe wanted something else even more. It was an extraordinary feeling; a burden was lifted from him when he realized there was more to all this than his own anger.

"I think I'd rather win the war," Abe said.

"Now!" Louis yelled, as he banked the plane.

Abe started the stopwatch.

If the U-boats did submerge, Abe and Louis would need the watch to time their turns and match them to the compass to know that they were bombing in the right spot despite where the wind took them next.

The harder they banked, the more Alvin was able to fire straight down into the water and the more the rain came in through Morris's side of the plane and smacked him in the face.

The rain smothered the remains of the fire, and the smell of smoke shook Abe for a moment, making him think of his mother. He shook it off. He didn't want to think about his mother, or Aunt Lila, or Mirabelle, or Sheldon, or even his father. He wanted to save the convoy.

When the second hand reached the twelve o'clock position on his black-faced Elgin watch, Abe shouted the words he'd been waiting to yell for almost a year.

"Bombs away!"

✈

THE SHREW RETURNED to the airfield to a hero's welcome. They had no casualties and less than an hour's worth of fuel in reserve when the wheels touched down in Iceland. The gambit had paid off and the U-boats had submerged, giving the convoy the time it needed to outpace the wolfpack. There was no evidence that they'd hit anything, but that wasn't why they'd been airborne. By the time Alvin called it and said they had to return to base, the convoys were safe.

Everyone was freezing cold, starving, and tired. They were all ordered to take hot baths, and Bachmann told them they had three days off for excellent work "starting now."

Abe slipped into his civilian clothes and immediately grabbed an empty supply truck and headed off for Reykjavík with something on his mind that he desperately wanted to share.

It was morning when he arrived at Ingunn's little red house in the city that was little more than a village. The arctic sun was high in the sky as though it were close to noon rather than early morning. The small city of Reykjavík glowed in tranquility and looked magical and foreign, a treeless community as isolated as an Amazonian tribe and peopled by blonds who seemed preternaturally attracted to brunettes. Walking up to Ingunn's door, Abe was sure that this was a place where humans were never supposed to live. A respite on a long voyage, maybe, but not a destination.

It was too cold here. Too bright. Too dark. Too isolated. No wonder Ingunn wanted some fresh blood, a foreign boy to cuddle. Maybe a ticket out of here. Who knows?

He didn't tell her. Or hadn't told her. But Ingunn had been his first. They'd done it three times now, and other stuff a bunch more. He hadn't really opened himself up to getting to know her — she was still imaginary somehow, still illusive, a girl you meet on vacation. He didn't love her — he didn't think so, anyway — but the intimacy was so intense and the warmth and gentleness and kisses so enveloping that saying it *wasn't* love might have been unfair or even wrong. It didn't feel eternal and inevitable. It simply felt . . . good.

Abe rang the bell and waited on the steps like a schoolboy. He desperately wanted to see Ingunn. He needed a hug more than anything else. A smile from a girl. They have no idea, he thought, what power they have.

He was smiling and hopeful when the door opened. It was not Ingunn who stood there, however, but a large man whose eyes were full of hate. A brother? A boyfriend? Abe didn't know. He didn't have time to wonder. The man's fist blasted out of the doorway and smashed into Abe's nose, severing an artery in his brain and killing him instantly.

FUNERAL

BRAHAM HOROWITZ OF HARTFORD, Connecticut, was to be buried beside his mother, Lucy, and his aunt Lila on the return of his remains to the United States courtesy of the Canadian government. Nate left a message with Mrs. Finegold at the front desk of Grossinger's, who saw fit not to write it on a piece of stationery but found Sheldon and sat him down.

The next day he left Lenny behind at Grossinger's and returned by bus with the green duffel bag full of cash, the two guns, and four days' worth of clean clothes. Nate met him at the door and said nothing to him. Sheldon climbed the stairs to his and Abe's bedroom and closed the door behind him.

Nate had already thrown away all the newspapers on Abe's dresser and had placed his clothes in canvas sacks to be donated to a charity. Unlike with Lucy's clothing, there had been no one to stop him this time, and now Sheldon had to look at Abe's remaining personal effects as he sat on his old bed. This — it was impossible not to think — is what people leave behind. That must have been why Joseph reached out to Sheldon in the car. To hand over everything we're not supposed to take with us.

That night — late enough that Sheldon wasn't even sure whether he'd been sleeping or not — there was a knock on his door and Mirabelle opened it.

When Mirabelle had pulled away in the taxi only days earlier, Sheldon had not expected to see her again. That they had been called back into each other's lives so soon was one of life's refusals to conform to expectations.

"May I come in?" she whispered.

Sheldon didn't have to answer. He moved over on the bed and made room for her. She walked to him and lay down next to him and put an arm around his shoulders.

Unprompted, she recounted what had happened after the taxi pulled away.

De Marco had broken up with Mirabelle in the taxi after they drove off from Neversink.

"You're blaming me for this?" she'd asked him, one leg crossed over the other as they pulled away from Grossinger's.

"Yes," he said.

"And . . . why?"

"I don't know. A hunch. We're done."

"Fine," she'd said. They had sat beside each other like estranged aristocrats for the remainder of the ride.

After arriving in Hartford, he had disappeared and no one she knew had any idea where he'd gone. It was just as well. To Mirabelle, his life had seemed glamorous, and in some significant ways, it was—the dinners, the nightclubs, the introductions, the money, the clothes, the champagne, and the discussions about exotic locations and the people whose gossip sold papers—but she had learned that it was all theater. The man was no doctor or lawyer. He wasn't a scholar or writer. There was nothing under his feet to hold him up. It was more like he was dangling from a rope instead, always trying to get higher but everything was always precarious. At some point, you either reach the top or fall off. And if there is no top . . .

"And then Dad called me and told me that Abe died," she whispered to Sheldon.

"I don't want to go back to that fucking cemetery a third time," Sheldon said to her.

"Me either."

Sheldon, Mirabelle, and Nate woke early, dressed appropriately, and sat in silence at the breakfast table. Nate was hunched at the shoulders and his face looked ten years older. Whatever spirit had remained in him was clearly gone. Sheldon and Mirabelle avoided looking at him. Comfort and love may have been what was needed, but Nate's grief was too powerful — too contagious — for them to confront.

The synagogue was sweltering hot as they listened to English and Hebrew words that fell on them like so much ash from a burning world. Neither Sheldon nor Mirabelle engaged with the sounds they heard, and both of them turned so far inward that they might have been standing on far-off beaches watching the waves break at their feet and concentrating on the shells glistening next to their toes.

Louis Bouchard had arrived with Abe's casket. A handsome man with sad eyes and a gentle way about him, Louis towered over everyone. He wore a yarmulke out of respect without knowing what it was. For all Louis's bulk, Mirabelle sensed that he was willing himself to be smaller, less conspicuous, more harmonious with those around him.

When the service concluded, Sheldon was a pallbearer along with his uncle, Louis, and three of Abe's schoolfriends, and they carried the pine casket out to the cemetery, where it was lowered into position. The weight of Abe's body inside the coffin dug into Sheldon's shoulder, the only physical sensation he would remember from the funeral.

Nate was not so lucky. It was when the rabbi and dozens of friends and family and congregants began to say the mourner's kaddish that Nate fell to his knees in the damp soil and let out a sound like the heavens giving way to hell.

Sheldon watched his uncle, and he knew that if Nate could have followed Abe to wherever he was going he would be gone as quickly as a prayer. He watched, with his own throat swelling, as the supporting wall that Nate had built for them all — so carefully, so meticulously — crumbled into nothing when faced with the destruction of the universe that had been his beloved son.

Sheldon turned away, unable to be the family he knew he should be.

· · ·

When it was over and the crowd began to break, Louis Bouchard approached Nate and took his hand.

When Mirabelle and Sheldon joined them, Louis spoke. He told them everything he knew: about Halifax, Abe's bombardier training, their boredom in Nova Scotia, their deployment to Iceland. He described the mission that saved the convoy. He explained Abe's relationship to Ingunn and how the man who turned out to be her older brother had only meant to punch Abe because that's what protective brothers do and how the man was now distraught and penitent.

"After it happened," Louis said, "Ingunn came to the base. She knew that Abe and I were friends. She cried and said it was her fault. I said it wasn't."

His storytelling was spare. And yet, the words he left out spoke to what he couldn't say.

Louis handed Nate Abe's letter. The one he was writing before *The Shrew* took to the air to defend the convoy.

Nate reflexively held out his right hand to take the letter. He looked at it—white, reflecting the sun's light, perfect and unbroken—and didn't move. It was Mirabelle who reached out and gently took it from him.

"I'll read it," she said.

"He addressed it to Sheldon," Louis said quietly. "He obviously didn't think this would be his last letter. I wouldn't read too much into it. He wrote before every flight. He was different that way."

"It's OK," Mirabelle said.

```
Dear Sheldon,
    I've been trying to imagine your life at the hotel.
I've never seen a hotel like that before. In Hartford
we only had those city hotels where cabs pulled up
and dropped off rich people, and then in Canada there
were sort of boardinghouses where travelers stopped
on long trips. Nothing that had grounds. A lake and
a golf course? That must be something. And all those
people not having to hide, or pretend they're some-
thing else, or spend all that energy trying to fit in
```

and make people like them. You can just be yourself
and be in your own culture and stuff. Sounds great.
It really does. I'd like to hear all those comedians.
I like laughing, but sometimes I think I've forgotten
how to do it. I think too much. These guys, though.
They help a lot. I feel like I'm with the right people
doing the right thing. I've never really felt that
before. I'm at war, but I guess you could say I'm at
peace with it. Does that make sense?

The thing about Iceland is that it's smack between America and Europe. Or close enough, anyway. It
doesn't look it or feel it, but when I'm in the air, I
see the expanse of ocean on either side and get a real
sense of how different life is on the shores to the
east and west. I know Europe and what's going on there
feels far away when you're surrounded by pretty girls
in some resort town. But it's not. It's really not.
We could hear those Nazis yelling from our bedroom in
Hartford. They came through the radio. They came in
print in the papers. I can feel them slinking around
underneath the Atlantic. I like looking for them. Like
roaches and I'm the boot.

I think I told you about most of the guys in the
last letter. The only thing really new is the plane.
They painted a Vargas Girl on the side for luck, but
she looks like your mom and it kind of rattles me a bit
because I always liked your mom and I don't like seeing her with her boobs busting out against her bathing
suit like that.

I haven't written to Mirabelle directly in a while
because I think she's even more pissed at me than you
are, but I need you to work on her a bit for me. It's
not right to fight. People are blowing up, Sheldon.
Bombs are falling. Nazis are gunning down families.

```
We can't squabble with each other. Not when people
would give their eyeteeth to be with the ones they
love again.
    And tell my dad too. I don't agree with him. We
can't assimilate ourselves out of existence to try and
please people who think we're inferior, but I get the
impulse and I know he wanted the best for us. We'll
work it out in the end.
    Shit, I got to go. This new guy, Bachmann, is all
worked up about something. I'll finish this later.
```

The letter wasn't signed because it wasn't finished.

When Mirabelle finished reading, it was Louis she looked at first.

✈

WITH LOUIS IN TOW, the family gathered at the town house to sit shiva, but by sundown, Mirabelle couldn't take it anymore. To avoid a scandal — only because her father couldn't take another one — she placed her favorite green dress and party shoes in a paper bag and marched out. She told Louis to follow her and, like a manservant trailing a maharaja, he did.

They retired to a bar in town — a brown place with pale people despite the summer sun. She changed in the bathroom and came out looking as though she should be on a yacht. She ordered a Bellini and he ordered a sidecar.

He was still wearing his yarmulke but Mirabelle said nothing. She wasn't sure whether that was because she was enjoying a private joke or because, somewhere in her soul, it comforted her to see him that way.

Mirabelle removed a cigarette from a silver case and Louis lit it for her. She leaned back in her chair and crossed her legs.

"I hate funerals," she said.

"Me too."

"Been to many?"

"Four," said Louis. "My uncle's when I was eleven, and two grandparents. Now Abe."

"Was he happy?" she asked, blowing out smoke.

"He was focused and determined," Louis said, sitting back slightly when the drinks arrived. "I don't know if he was happy, but he never doubted that he was in the right place and doing the right thing. I think he was . . ." Louis paused to consider his next words. Mirabelle smiled and he lost his train of thought.

"What?" he asked. Her smile confused him.

"No one pauses for words around here. To pause is to surrender. It shows you don't know what you're trying to say or that you can't keep up the tempo."

"I want to be sure I'm describing it correctly."

"I know," she said, sipping her drink. She licked the taste of prosecco and peach from her lips.

"It's true, though. I probably can't keep up."

"I know that too," she said, bringing the cigarette to her lips again, lipstick staining the paper filter.

"I'm good at other things," Louis said.

"We'll see," Mirabelle said, with a cracked smile.

"You're intimidating."

"You fly bombers through hurricanes over the Atlantic to attack submarines."

"That makes me a good judge of these things."

Mirabelle blew out her smoke and looked at him for a moment. She liked being called intimidating, but she didn't like the idea of a wall between them. Sammy had never been someone she could talk to. Most of her boyfriends weren't. Louis seemed different. He seemed like someone who might listen.

"There's this vaudeville comedian," Mirabelle said. "Seamus Cole. Sheldon and I were listening to him on the radio once. He was talking to George Burns, another comedian. They were talking about making people laugh and whether or not it mattered in a world falling apart at the seams. Cole said something like 'Life is a series of games played within games and nothing is real until a heart is broken or healed.' I remember thinking how profound that was. Until he said that, I was starting to feel like it was all games and more games and that nothing mattered at all. So, when he said that, I started crying all of a sudden because I realized it was true."

Louis nodded. She couldn't tell whether he understood or was being polite. Taking a cue from him, she decided not to interrupt his thoughts. She wanted to know what he'd come up with. Sitting there, cigarette in hand, Abe in a box, she realized that she was testing him.

"Content," he said.

"What?"

"Abe was content. He had found a way to be content with himself. I think he was haunted by more than he ever talked about. In the service and in the air, all that went away. I think he was content."

Mirabelle looked at this man in a yarmulke drinking from a martini glass. She scratched the top of her head, and this acted like a charm. Louis reached up, felt the almost weightless fabric, and smiled.

"How do I look?"

"Content."

She spoke about her mother. He talked about Canada. They talked about Nazis. About food. About the Catskills — the parts she wanted to, anyway. She talked about Sheldon.

Louis asked her about her work at Underwood.

She said that typewriters were uninteresting to her but that writers were, and sometimes famous people would show up to buy one or have their own serviced. Journalists and novelists mostly. "Margaret Bourke-White came by last month. That was amazing."

Louis didn't know who she was, and Mirabelle explained that she was the first female photojournalist hired by *Life* magazine. She was the one who had taken those famous photographs of the Soviet Union.

Louis still didn't know.

"What about the one of all the black people standing in a line under the giant poster of the white people in the car that read, WORLD'S HIGHEST STANDARD OF LIVING and THERE'S NO WAY LIKE THE AMERICAN WAY?"

"Never saw it."

"It was on the cover of *Life* in 1937. They were flood victims."

Louis shook his head.

"That was the year my mother died. We had the magazine in the bathroom. Maybe it wasn't as famous for everyone else as it was for me."

Louis said that he wanted to see her again. He said he had five more months to serve and that he'd be out by Christmas.

Mirabelle moved home from the apartment she'd been sharing with Sharon Miles, a girl from her graduating class. Nate stopped going to work for the next three months and sat in the parlor on the blue-velvet sofa day after day saying nothing. Mirabelle would tune the radio to different programs and announce to him what was on. Sometimes she would sit with him and sip coffee or a glass of wine. She often read to him as though he were an invalid.

As the days grew colder into autumn, she would wrap a blanket around him. At night he would retire from his silence and drift into unconsciousness. He ate whatever he was served and communicated mainly with gestures.

Sheldon turned fifteen in September of 1941 and doubled up on all his classes like Abe had done. Sitting where Abe used to sit in their room, he would do complex math problems and read the newspapers from front to back every day and stack the ones he'd read in their spot on top of the dresser.

Still unwilling to attend movies, Sheldon spent most of his time alone, reading, pining for new affections, burning for a love to replace what was lost, hungry for passions he could only imagine. This loneliness was a new weight.

Sometimes, when he reached a point in a story that seemed unrealistic or contrived, he would pull the green duffel bag out from under his bed and look at the stacks of money he'd stolen from Thaleman. It occurred to him that if he hadn't been such a hothead, he could have walked out with the stolen jewels too. Then again, if he'd lied to Mirabelle about throwing the jewels in the river and kept them instead, all of this would have felt different. Worse, somehow.

There can be a cost to contentment, and he was starting to see the range of ways that fate can demand payment.

With no real plans beyond graduation—a year early at this rate—he haunted the house more like a ghost than a boy.

On December 8 of 1941, everything changed.

PEARL

NATE WAS SITTING ON the sofa by the bookshelf and staring into the fire with a glass of whiskey as the condensation on the outside of the glass slid down toward the polished wood of the end table. He often sat with a drink without touching it. Sheldon realized, in time, that the presence of Nate's drink gave the formlessness of sitting there a name.

It was a Monday. Mirabelle had left the radio on before she left for work as she usually did. Sheldon had decided to stay home on account of a cold. He was so far ahead in his classes that he hardly thought it mattered, and no one much cared what he did anymore. At 12:30 in the afternoon, Roosevelt was addressing a joint session of Congress. Sheldon wasn't listening and was instead reading *Evil Under the Sun,* a new book by Agatha Christie. Since almost killing that drunk who ran Lenny off the road near Grossinger's, Sheldon's taste for crime novels had changed. They never matched the emotional intensity of the reality, and their distance from lived experience made him edgy. He preferred mysteries now to violence or revenge. Painless puzzles were interesting.

Sheldon looked up from Hercule Poirot when he heard the slow, anguished voice of the president coming on.

Yesterday, December 7, 1941—a date which will live in infamy—the United States of America was suddenly and deliberately attacked by naval and air forces of the Empire of Japan.

The United States was at peace with that nation and,

at the solicitation of Japan, was still in conversation with its government and its emperor looking toward the maintenance of peace in the Pacific. Indeed,
one hour after Japanese air squadrons had commenced
bombing in the American Island of Oahu, the Japanese
ambassador to the United States and his colleague delivered to our secretary of state a formal reply to a
recent American message. And while this reply stated
that it seemed useless to continue the existing dip-
lomatic negotiations, it contained no threat or hint
of war or of armed attack.

Sheldon didn't hear the rest of the speech because Uncle Nate spoke.

At first, Sheldon couldn't place the sound. When he looked at Nate, he saw that his uncle was looking at him.

"Uncle Nate?"

Nate was not an invalid. He cleaned himself and dressed. He shaved and wore a tie even though he hadn't gone to work since Abe's death. To Sheldon, he was a ghost, a soul that drifted through the world without touching it or being touched by it. His son's death was all-encompassing to him. There was no need for, or room for, anything else.

Sheldon understood—well enough, anyway. He remembered his own solitary walk from the car wreck that killed his father. That too had been a wordless time. Now, however, Nate was breaking his silence and speaking.

But it was only one word

"Springfield."

"Springfield? The city? In Massachusetts?" Sheldon asked.

"Your father said that if there was ever another war and he wasn't alive to see it, you were to go to Springfield. You have to go to Springfield. In Massachusetts. There's a bus."

"Me?"

"The recruitment office in Springfield. You need to enlist in Springfield. He was very clear about this in case America ever went to war again."

"Why?"

There were new messages from his father? His father had preferences and plans for him even now?

"What else?" Sheldon said. "Uncle Nate. What else? What else does my father want?"

There was nothing else.

"Springfield?" Sheldon asked again.

His father hated war, but he had said that it anchored the family deeper into America. He never said that he regretted going. He only said that it was awful. Would he have wanted Sheldon to fight?

Take it, Sheldon. Take it all.

"Uncle Nate," Sheldon pleaded. "Why did my father tell me to go to Springfield? Did he want me to sign up? To fight?"

"He said that if there's a war you should enlist in Springfield. That's all I know."

The story of the Japanese attack appeared in the papers accompanied by terrible images. The destruction was beyond Sheldon's comprehension. The entire Pacific fleet had been sunk or close enough. He had heard a reporter from KGU in Honolulu call NBC in New York during the bombing. The reporter there had witnessed the destruction from a nearby building. It had been going on for three hours by then. The reporter's voice made Sheldon see the fires on the ships and smell them burning.

At school, the implications were discussed all week. Congress declared war on Japan immediately, and everyone was gearing up for some kind of engagement. Some of the older boys enlisted while others wondered when the draft would start.

"You signing up, Sheldon?" asked a boy named Tommy, whose father played xylophone in a big band that toured the state. Tommy was excited; he wanted to fight.

"I don't know. It's the Germans I'm after."

Tommy shrugged. He didn't care about any of that. He wanted to march and wear uniforms and feel grown up. Sheldon didn't want to do any of those things.

Germany declared war on the United States four days later on the eleventh. That was when Sheldon stopped wondering what to do and bought a bus ticket for Springfield.

He had had other plans. Simpler plans for the future.

"I think I'm going to build a little cottage," Sheldon had said to Lenny at the end of the summer on the beach at Grossinger's Lake at dawn. The sky had been a pastel pink and the water was as smooth as glass. Lenny found a skimming stone but chose not to use it. He rolled it around in his hand as they avoided the topic of Abe's death and tried to think of the future.

"What do you mean?"

"You know. Put up a little house where the other one used to be. I guess when I'm eighteen the land's mine, you know? I figure I can probably have a small house put up for about two thousand dollars."

"You want to go back after school? 'Cuz I think we should go to New York."

"I think I want it to be there whether I'm there or not." Sheldon had plucked three tall blades of grass that were growing in the sand. He braided them together as he used to do with Mirabelle's hair when they listened to the radio—before they both grew up. "But, yeah, I think maybe I'll come with you."

"To New York?"

"Yeah."

"And do what?"

"Work. You know. Like the way people do."

"You want to be my manager?"

"No. I really don't."

"Not much to manage yet anyway. Think we can come back to the Catskills next summer?"

"We might have to pick another hotel."

• • •

Sheldon was born in Springfield in 1926, some thirty miles due south of Whately. Joseph and Lila hadn't been living there, and they didn't have any friends who did, but the hospital had been the best in the area, and so it was where Sheldon had first drawn breath. As he rode the bus north from Hartford, he couldn't think of any other reason his father would want him to go to Springfield.

The bus arrived in the snow and hissed to a stop. The door opened and the cold came in before the first person went out, a breath of life. Sheldon's boots splashed into a black puddle and above him the sky was slate gray. A few snowflakes fell or were blown from the rooftops of the buildings. With a rucksack on his shoulders and Abe's old wool coat for warmth, Sheldon trekked two miles to the recruiting station.

It was December 15, 1941, a Monday morning. He was skipping school for this, but he needed to know how it all worked so he could plan it out. He'd be done with high school in June of 1943 and that's when he wanted to lie about his age and join up.

The flag outside the recruitment center was flying at half-mast. A bell rang as Sheldon stepped inside, as though he were entering a greengrocer's. He had expected a queue of a thousand men standing outside, like in those photos of the Depression—or like the queue that had formed during the hurricane when they had built the levees to hold back the Connecticut River. That wasn't the case, though.

A man in a sharp blue uniform who was sitting behind a desk said, "Good morning. How can I help you?"

The man was middle-aged. He wore glasses, and Sheldon saw a medical insignia on his lapel.

"I want to sign up after I finish high school next summer," said Sheldon, unsure whether to stamp the remaining snow from his shoes. "So, I just . . . I don't know . . . I want to know how it all works."

The man looked Sheldon over. He nodded a few times. "Good for you."

Sheldon said nothing.

"Want to fight the Japs?"

"No. The other ones."

The man frowned. "You're not here because of Pearl Harbor? Everyone wants to join the navy now."

"I want to be a marine. And I want to go to Germany. I want to go to Berlin."

The man was impassive. He was still looking at Sheldon and nothing obvious on his face had changed, but Sheldon felt as though he was now looking at him in a new way.

"Why?"

"My father was in the army in World War I," Sheldon said. "The Yankee Division, 26th Infantry. He was in Apremont in France near Saint-Mihiel. I used to hunt with my dad. And track. I know my way around the woods. Marines get there first, right?"

"Yes."

"Well. That's it, then. No point in waiting around."

"What's your name?"

"Sheldon Horowitz."

"Where you from?"

"Whately."

"I'm going to check some records, and then we can do a physical."

"I want to finish high school. My parents wanted me educated."

"You're only shy a year and a semester, right?"

"Yes, sir."

"We can make a diploma happen. Stay there, I'll be right back."

Sheldon removed his rucksack and sat on a plastic chair. An American flag was curled around a pole in the corner of the room across from a rack with the officer's wool coat on it. A photograph of President Roosevelt was framed in mahogany beside a picture of a man in a military uniform Sheldon didn't recognize, a general of some kind.

On the table in front of him was today's *Boston Daily Globe* and a copy of *Stars and Stripes*. Picking up the military newspaper would have been embarrassing somehow, as though it would prove to the officer (if he ever came back into the room) that Sheldon was a romantic with big dreams of heroism. He thought it would make him look immature and he already felt short and insufficiently muscular.

RETREAT FROM MOSCOW

MOSCOW, Monday, Dec. 15 (AP)—Rampant Red armies declared today they had the Germans on the run in a
retreat approaching the scale of Napoleon's cold and
dismal retirement from Moscow and had overtaken the
backtracking Hitler legions with a headlong campaign
of extermination.

To the right was local news.

FIREWOMEN OF BAY STATE LEAD NATION

NEEDHAM, Dec. 14—American's first women's fire-fighting
auxiliary class was graduated here today when 60 vol-
unteers of the Massachusetts Women's Defense Corps
staged a demonstration and received diplomas at Central Fire Station.

   Jumping into nets from second-story windows, carrying hose lines up fire ladders and smothering "bomb"
fires, the women demonstrated what they had learned in
the six weeks' course in all forms of fire-fighting.

The officer returned from the back room holding a manila folder. He sat
at his desk and spoke to Sheldon.

"Sheldon Horowitz. Whately. Born September 7, 1926, in Springfield,
Massachusetts. Your father is Joseph and your mother is Lila. That's you?"

Sheldon didn't like that his birthday was mentioned. The officer looked
capable of both addition and subtraction, and he'd put together his age soon
enough.

"I said is that you?"

"Yes."

"Where are your parents? They know you're here?"

"They're dead. And yes."

The man didn't understand but continued. "It's laudable that you want to join. But we don't need you yet."

"Maybe you do."

"Maybe you're right. Maybe we do. But that's not your call. You've got the paper there, right? Front page, below the fold on the left. You see it?"

Sheldon did see it. The first paragraph said it all.

```
MEN OUTSIDE 21-35 AGE MAY NOT BE DRAFTED

Washington, Dec. 14 (AP)—War Department officials
made clear today that it would be a long time—
perhaps never—before any men outside the 21-35 age
group are drafted for the Army despite the proposal
to require all aged 18 to 64, inclusive, to register.
```

"You turned fifteen a few months ago. You're three years shy of having to register, and the War Department's not even interested in you for another three years *after* you turn eighteen." The man then mumbled something that sounded to Sheldon like "notwithstanding the medical issues," but he was certain that he didn't hear it correctly because he had no medical issues. "Until you're eighteen in September of 1944, this is isn't even a discussion, and I hope the war will be over by then. Meanwhile . . . go be a kid. We're fighting for you. You don't need to fight for us. You can pick up the baton later. That's how it all works."

The man closed the file. Before Sheldon could stop himself, he looked the man dead in the eye and said in a quiet voice, "I'm no coward."

The officer's face drooped.

"I'm going home tonight to see my wife, and when I do, I'm going to tell her that a fifteen-year-old orphan came to my office today wanting to sign up and fight the Nazis as a marine so he could be the first boots on the ground during the liberation of Europe. No, Sheldon Horowitz, you are no coward. And I'm sure your father knew that from the moment you took your first steps. What I'm telling you is that your job, right now, is to go live. My personal advice? Go make something. Build something. Fix something. The whole world's breaking. We need all the help we can putting things together."

He then told Sheldon to have a good trip home and that he heard the weather was supposed to break later. It'll be a cold but pretty one.

Sheldon wandered out of the austere building into a future that continued to change and change and change again no matter how often he thought he knew what he was supposed to do and no matter how often he set about trying to pick a direction and go there. He thought of when the hurricane uprooted trees and the river overflowed its banks, and it was obvious then that everything he'd thought was permanent could be overturned and washed away, but it hadn't crossed his mind until now that perhaps all of this might never settle down. The whole thing. All of life, always. Maybe this wasn't a "phase" as his mother used to call it. Maybe this was how it worked.

He told Lenny he wanted to put up a cabin. And he would. But standing there in the melting snow on a December day, all he could think of was his father's clock and how he really did need to get that fixed and—once he did—how he'd need a wall to hang it on.

FRENCH

Afterreturning to iceland following Abe's funeral, Louis had thought he was going to be out of the military by Christmas, but then Pearl Harbor happened, and shortly after that, Germany declared war on the United States. Unwilling to let Louis's expertise go to waste, the RCAF sent him to an airbase in Britain until the spring of 1943. During their time apart, he and Mirabelle wrote letters to each other faithfully.

Mirabelle didn't fall into another failed romance, nor did she make the mistake of looking on this new chance too lightly. It was because of Abe, and she knew that. It was because of Abe that she had met Louis, of course, but it was also because of Abe's death that her wanderlust and rebelliousness had been tempered. Her misadventure at Grossinger's may also have played a part.

When she buried her brother, she also buried her need to be an adult, because she became one on that day.

As they corresponded—and unbeknownst to Mirabelle—Louis was flying antisubmarine patrols over the Bay of Biscay near Lorient between Brest and Nantes. Louis and his crew were pulled out of *The Shrew* and placed back into a Vickers Wellington, this one fitted with a new Leigh Light that could spot U-boats at night. On one challenging run, they met flak from a land-based antiaircraft gun, and one bullet struck the cockpit window, shattering off a piece of glass that severed a nerve in Louis's right arm. He brought the plane home to England safely, but on recovery, he had a twitch in his hand that wouldn't go away. By the autumn, it was clear that his recovery would never be complete, and—while no longer in pain and otherwise well—he no longer had the reflexes or dexterity to be a pilot. He was discharged. The war, for him, was over.

Sheldon graduated in June of 1943. Mirabelle watched him from the bleachers. The day was cloudless and perfect. She wore a red dress with white polka dots and a wide-brimmed hat to keep off the sun. She was joined by three of her friends, one of whom had a sister graduating.

Louis Bouchard had driven down from Canada in his father's Plymouth.

Their meeting was chaste. He kissed Mirabelle on the cheek while holding one of her hands in both of his.

Sheldon's graduating class threw their caps high into the air where they soared; half the class fetched them after they landed, and the other half forgot they had existed. Sheldon didn't care. He was the youngest to graduate, he had a plan, and he was on his way.

He thanked Mirabelle and Louis for coming, kissed his cousin on the cheek, and then promptly vanished. He joined some classmates rather than his family for a meal that night and attended a party where he kissed a girl named Molly, who pushed him into a guest room, inexplicably shoved him into a closet, and then closed her eyes and slid her right hand down his pants.

The next day Sheldon was up and packed. Uncle Nate was back at work, but his ambition and social climbing days were over. Only forty years old by the calendar, Nate was already deep into middle age. His wife and son had died. His daughter would soon be gone, and he had no capacity to remarry; though eligible, he lacked any reserves for generous love.

Nate was drinking coffee and reading the papers.

"So," Sheldon said, trying to get his uncle's attention, his green duffel bag full of money sitting beside a sack of clothing and a jacket.

"Good morning," said Nate. His voice was flat. He had not been to the graduation ceremony, had not seen Mirabelle with Louis, and had not watched Sheldon receive his diploma with high marks. "Well done yesterday."

Sheldon didn't take his uncle's absence from the graduation personally. He knew it would have revived memories his uncle couldn't bear.

Sheldon drew a deep breath and said, without preamble, "Thank you, Uncle Nate."

"For what?" Nate said, not looking up.

"For taking me in when Dad died. For giving me a home. Thank you."

"Oh." Nate lowered his paper. He looked away, as though remembering a distant conversation about a once-important topic. "Yes. You're welcome."

"I'm going back now," Sheldon said. "Unless you need me and want me to stay."

"To Whately? There's no house there anymore."

"Yeah. I'm going to rebuild. Not the same house. More of a small cottage, I think. I'm going to stay with Lenny and the Bernsteins while it gets built. They said it's OK. Lenny's got one more year, and then we're going to head down to New York. I figure I can maybe use the cottage later."

"You have money for this?"

Sheldon had forgotten that he didn't officially have money for this. Luckily, Nate wasn't thinking critically these days.

"You can use your insurance money," Nate said.

"What?"

"The insurance money. From the fire. It's been in escrow. I was going to give it to you when you turned eighteen, but I see no reason why you shouldn't have it now."

"I don't understand, Uncle Nate."

"Your parents' house in Whately was insured against fire and arson. The insurance company paid out when those brothers were arrested and convicted. It's a touch under three thousand dollars. Twenty-seven hundred, as I recall. It should be more than enough these days." Nate seemed more engaged now with a less emotional matter to address. "Maybe instead of using the money to pay for the building costs, we could talk to a bank and arrange a loan. You could take out a mortgage at two percent or so—I could cosign it because you're a minor and my credit is excellent. We could invest the remaining capital in war bonds. If you can make the payments to the bank with either your work earnings or the dividends from the investments, you should be in good shape. With some equity in the land and the cottage, you could come out of this in a strong position ten years from now when you're a young man and ready to marry. Whately may not be a big draw, but Northampton is a college town, and after the war ends someday, people will want to live nearby. Europe will be weak after the war, and we'll be strong. The economy will surge." Nate seemed to come to a conclusion for both of them. "Yes. This is a good idea. A respectable investment with ties to your heritage. Let's do that."

Sheldon looked at his uncle. He had no idea his father had insured the house. The depths of his connection to the past never seemed to end.

What the conversation made Sheldon think about was the seven thousand dollars in cash he'd stolen from Thaleman. Perhaps, he thought, he ought to be thinking bigger. Maybe when he turned eighteen, he could repeat his uncle's model but maybe with a place in New York City. Move in with Lenny. Find a job while Lenny told jokes. It was a good idea. He felt a sense of possibility.

Of course, when he was eighteen, he'd have to enlist. But when he got back . . . New York City.

"The bus leaves for Massachusetts in an hour, Uncle Nate. I'll come back to visit in a month or so. We can do all those things you talked about. I really appreciate it."

"Yes." Nate paused. "Goodbye, Sheldon. Good luck."

✈

LOUIS BOUCHARD'S GRANDMOTHER had handed him the ring and begged him to find a "nice girl" and settle down and find happiness in small things. She spoke to him in Québécois; a language in which the vowels were more rounded, the slang unique, and the enunciation more distinct than the language of their French cousins.

"What if she isn't so nice? What if she's fabulous and dangerous?" he had asked her.

"It'll either be much better or much worse," his grandmother had correctly concluded.

A good marriage proposal, he knew, was daunting. In the Royal Canadian Air Force, "getting it right" had been easy to define. There was a right way to prepare a plane for flight, to fix an engine, to prepare for takeoff, to fly in formation, and to approach a bombing target. There did not seem to be a right way to propose marriage, though. In the military, things were the right way precisely because they led to predictable and anticipated results. It was harder to do things the right way with people, since the same acts can lead to different outcomes.

Mon dieu.

Louis wanted to propose someplace pretty, someplace memorable, someplace that would later invite a romantic retelling so all the girls would swoon when Mirabelle recounted the moment. Louis hoped that their grandchildren would listen to the story and believe that they could lead lives as beautiful and rich and loving as their grandparents had.

There were practicalities, though. He also needed a place that worked in his favor in case she was uncertain; he didn't want to spook her. It needed to be serene and not too intimidating.

The place he chose was Mystic, Connecticut, and the occasion was the opening to the public of the last of America's wooden whaling ships, the *Charles W. Morgan.*

Louis had been reading the American newspapers since arriving in Hartford. As Sheldon and the other graduates had been milling around on the field before the series of interminable speeches that always accompanied these events, Louis sat reading the *Hartford Courant*, which contained an article about the ship.

Mystic, to Louis, was the kind of place he was looking for. The name was idyllic and the black-and-white photographs suggested a quiet coastal village typical of New England. The ship was the last survivor of the once great American whaling fleet that had numbered more than 2,700 ships once upon a time. The *Charles W. Morgan,* he learned, was built in 1841 and had traversed the entire globe. The ship had survived the hurricane of 1938 when it was moored in South Dartmouth, Massachusetts, and she had sailed to Mystic a month before Pearl Harbor. To Louis, the *Charles W. Morgan* was a beast born to hunt, but in her maturity, she had become a symbol of resilience that was put to rest in a place of beauty.

This sounded like Mirabelle. Strangely enough, it sounded like Abe too. And the more Louis considered this, it sounded a little like Sheldon as well.

A strange thought.

He put down the paper and looked at Mirabelle as the mortarboards were hurled into the air, and she turned to him and smiled.

Louis and Mirabelle were engaged in Mystic in July of 1943. Mirabelle watched Louis kneel on a stone by the harbor and offer her the ring. Mirabelle looked at it and marveled at how the exchange of such a small rock could alter fate, a tiny stone in the flow of time that changed the course of an entire river. She looked down at him and knew that there was a kind of happiness waiting for her, the kind she had been longing for since her mother had died. It was also the kind that took her away from everything that might bind her to an identity she didn't choose but was born into. A circumstance. A condition. A fate.

Abe had embraced it and had become victim to it and died. Sheldon was grappling with it even now. Mirabelle, however, thought she might have found a way out of a bad dream.

She looked at the ring and Louis looked at her.

When she was little, Mirabelle would hold things in her dreams. A leaf, a stone, a teddy bear. The things seemed absolutely real in her dreams and they were something she wanted. She would hold on to them so tightly that she was certain beyond certainty that they were in her possession. When she woke, though, she always found them gone. It never felt like they hadn't existed. It felt like they had been stolen or ripped away at the last minute. The idea that they had never been there at all, that they had only been figments of her imagination, was too outrageous to believe.

One day a new thought came to her: Why would she have held on to them so tightly if she didn't already know they were illusions?

There, in Louis's outstretched hand, was such an object. A small and glittering stone. This time, however, she was not gripping it and trying to drag it across to another universe. This time it was being offered to her, as though the world were asking for her hopes to be true.

"Yes," Mirabelle said.

Part of her was very certain, the more childish part that wanted to prove the world wrong. The other part, the adult in her—the part of her that knew everything was temporary and that only death was real—wasn't so sure.

"Yes," she said again. "I will marry you."

They debated marrying at a church or synagogue, in America or Canada. They chose to marry on a beach in Massachusetts in September. Mirabelle wanted a chuppah to cover them, the Jewish symbol of a new home being created. Sheldon and Nate, barefoot on the beach, would hold two of the four poles that supported the canopy.

They found a pastor (the fourth they asked) willing to perform an interfaith and strangely liberal marriage. Louis's parents were stoic through the process, holding their tongues because their son had survived the war and Nate Corbin's son had not. They were hesitant about the marriage but were wise enough to see that Mirabelle was a vision of grace and femininity and sexual power and against that—as mere parents—they were nothing.

It was a doomed marriage, they believed. A doomed promise in a world at war.

But what of it? What isn't?

After the ceremony, Sheldon approached Mirabelle and hugged her.

"Mirabelle Bouchard," he said. "You're finally French."

1944

O N JUNE 6, 1944, the Allies invaded northern France and regained a
foothold on the Continent. In September of that year, when Sheldon
finally turned eighteen and was planning to enlist, the tide of the war
had irrevocably turned. The Allies had already liberated Florence and Paris,
and the war didn't need him anymore.

This was exactly what the same officer said to Sheldon at the recruiting
station in Springfield after he had recovered from the shock of seeing Sheldon again.

"You might be the only guy in America who has tried to enlist for this
war twice," the officer said, adjusting his glasses and shaking his head.

"I read about the death camps," Sheldon said. "I can shoot a bobcat at
four hundred yards in a storm at dusk. Germans are bigger."

"The war's going to be won. It's going to be over soon."

Sheldon, at eighteen, was taller, stronger, and had even less respect for
authority than he'd had a few years ago, but like Abe, he thought he could
tolerate it if there was something worthwhile on the other side of obedience.

"Why are you always in my way?" Sheldon asked.

"That's not polite or fair," said the man, though his tone lacked convic-
tion.

"It's a serious question. We're at war. It's not over. I'm eighteen and I want
to fight. Let's fill out some paperwork," Sheldon said, tapping the table.

"You're 4-F, Mr. Horowitz. I didn't tell you that last time because I didn't
want to break your spirit. I needn't have worried, obviously, but there it is.
We don't need you. And more to the point, we don't want you."

Sheldon had no idea what that meant and said so.

"It means you're medically unfit."

Sheldon looked down at his stomach. He didn't feel unfit. A little shorter than some of the monsters he'd seen in the recruitment posters, but he was hardly unfit.

"That's not the kind of fit I mean. I've got your file. You have medical issues that disqualify you. You know that."

Sheldon stood like a statue and was completely confused. "What the hell are you talking about?"

"You are clubfooted, for crying out loud. It says so right here in your file. Both feet. Born that way. You can walk, but you can't run and never will. Your father submitted the paperwork to the senior medical officer here in Springfield"—he checked another page—"in April of 1928. You weren't even two years old yet. My hunch is your father understood war and mortality better than most, and wanted to get things on record early in case anything came up. Now it has. It's highly unusual, but people with shell shock have been known to be jumpy about the prospect of future wars and . . . so there it is."

Sheldon disappeared from the officer's view for a moment and the very next moment Sheldon's right foot was up on the desk.

They both examined his perfectly normal right foot.

"The other one," said Sheldon, "is exactly the same as this one except for being completely different."

"Huh," said the man.

"Huh is right," said Sheldon. "I can chase you around the parking lot if you need more proof."

The man looked back down at the papers. They had every signature and every stamp imaginable. He looked at the medical officer's name again and then looked up.

"Why did you come here?"

"What do you mean?" Sheldon asked.

"To Springfield."

"I live in Whately. I've been there for more than a year."

"Now you do. The last time you were here you lived in Hartford. Why did you leave Connecticut to come up here in 1941 and try to enlist in Massachusetts? There's a recruiting station in Hartford. You could have walked there."

"My uncle told me to."

"He did, did he."

"Yeah. Why?"

"You didn't find that odd?"

"I found the Japanese bombing us odd. And Hitler declaring war on us odd. To be honest, Springfield didn't make the cut."

That was all he needed. The recruiting officer was ready to solve the puzzle for them both.

"Your father called in a favor when you were born. He must have known a military doctor here who was willing to build up a file on you and make sure it was found if you ever tried to enlist. Why he thought you might enlist I have no idea."

"That doesn't make any sense," Sheldon said. "I was born in 1926. The war was over for seven years by then and we didn't get into a new one until 1941. Why would my father have pulled strings for me when I wasn't even two years old yet?"

"Were you close?" he asked Sheldon.

"Yes."

"Always?"

Sheldon's shoulders grew slack. "Yes," he said.

"I didn't know your dad," he said. "But I know that a man sees a war and doesn't want his son to see it. That makes perfect sense to me. Someday you might have a son and you'll be torn between serving your country or saving him. Your father made sure you would never see enemy fire. That should make you feel—"

"Don't tell me how that should make me feel!" Sheldon said, slipping his foot back into his sock and shoe. "My father didn't know the Nazis were going to exterminate every last man, woman, and child who was born exactly like us! He didn't know I'd grow up to be one of the able men standing between them and death. He was a hunter and a trapper, and I grew up hunting and trapping. He loved me, I get that. More than you will ever know. But there's a job to do, evil is on the march, and my feet are fine! Change the paperwork, please."

The man shook his head. "No."

"What do mean, 'No'? What kind of recruitment office is this?"

"I mean no. I mean doing that means getting a medical examiner down here. And if I do that, he's going to see this file—"

"Throw it away. Start fresh."

"That's a felony, and I could be court-martialed. In fact, whoever doctored these papers could be court-martialed too. The man who signed off on these papers—and, no, I will not give you his name—must have owed your father a favor, and I'm guessing it's because your dad saved his life or something equally serious. We don't talk about it, but military men keep a ledger in their heads. The idea is to come out even by the time we cross the finish line one way or another. If there is any honor in war, that's it. It's often the best we can do, and it's the only thing within our control. Now as it happens, I don't owe you a damn thing. So, I'm not risking my career to send you to the front in a war that's almost won. It's too late to liberate Paris and get laid. I suppose there's still Berlin, but trust me, it won't be the same."

Sheldon stood there, and for the first time in his life, he couldn't find an angle. The Krupinskis, Grossinger's, Lorenzo, Thaleman—there was always a play. Now? When it actually mattered?

"So the new doctor finds the file and sees it's wrong. Big deal. So, he fixes it, right?"

"No. Because he'd be obligated to report the error, and now you'd be repaying the guy who repaid your father by getting him in a heap of trouble. Honor is a *system*, Sheldon. That's why they call it the honor system."

"What if I ignore you and drive to Ohio and sign up there? Or Rhode Island? Or Mississippi? You can't stop me. It's not like that file's everywhere. Or maybe I jump across this desk and wrestle you for it."

"You'd be in jail before you got to basic training."

"This bites." Sheldon backed off the desk and flopped down in a chair.

The man let Sheldon stew for a minute before he walked around his desk and sat beside him. He offered Sheldon a cigarette, which he took and even lit, but he only toyed with it because he didn't like smoking.

"Remember what I said last time you were here?" the man asked.

"'Go fix something,' you said."

"It was good advice. The world's even more broken now."

"*Tikkun olam,*" Sheldon mumbled.

"What does that mean?"

"It's a Jewish thing."

The officer didn't like standing between a father's obligation to his son and a son's obligation to his father. It felt like the wrong place for the government to be. There he was, though.

He had also come down hard on the father's side. Why? Because he was a father too. And despite Sheldon's sour puss, he felt no guilt whatsoever.

"What does that mean, a Jewish thing?" he asked, mainly to kill time.

"It's Hebrew. It basically means any activity that improves the world."

This was bar mitzvah stuff. Lenny stuff. The fact that it was coming up at an army recruiting station in Springfield struck him as two parts ridiculous and one part inevitable, like everything else on this planet.

Sheldon explained it with a flat and uninterested voice, as though he were talking to someone while changing a tire. "Jews believe the world is inherently good because God said it was good seven times while making it. But we also believe he made it imperfect and that we were all placed in the Garden of Eden to work it and protect it. *Tikkun* means 'repair' and *olam* means 'for all of time' or else 'the world.'"

"Jews are supposed to do this?" the man said, leaning forward. "The chosen people? That sort of thing?"

"No. Everyone is," said Sheldon. "God chose us to receive the law and share it, not fulfill it by ourselves. We're God's carrier pigeons. Maybe that's why everyone keeps shooting at us."

"So, is there anything you want to fix?"

Anything? Sheldon thought. Sure. Movie theaters and fire prevention, the rate at which film burns, the safety of cars, our ability to make God account for Himself. All kinds of things.

"My dad's clock is broken. I want to fix that," Sheldon muttered.

"Perfect. You can go repair time like that Hebrew thing said you should." The man smiled. He was an engineer. He'd solved a puzzle. This was success. This was happiness to him.

"A clock," Sheldon repeated.

"Listen, kid. Maybe someday you'll save someone else's life because I just saved your life, and maybe I did it because your father saved someone else's life, and all of us are keeping our ledgers balanced. My suggestion is, do what your father told you to do, go fix his clock, and wait for your moment. You never know. Someone might need you someday and—just maybe— today is what makes that possible."

"I doubt it."

"Don't be so sure. You're still in the morning of your life."

The cottage that Sheldon built in Whately was a traditional Cape house with a center door and a window on either side of it, a second-floor attic with windows on the sides, and a porch in the back facing the woods. Sheldon had presented the builder with a budget, and the builder gave him three choices on how to spend it. Sheldon chose the one that looked the most familiar.

When it was done, he'd bought furniture from estate sales and filled it up with as little as necessary. Hudson Bay blankets like the ones he had as a child. Double beds in the third bedroom, a queen for the spare, and a king for the master. A desk in the corner. A country-style pine dining set and hutch. A sofa and rug in the living room. His books from Hartford and some more he'd bought at a church fundraiser.

He placed the broken clock on the wall and hung some landscape paintings he had found at the yard sale as if he were preparing a stage for new actors who might never arrive.

When it was done, Sheldon had a ghostly feeling that the house was not his. Nothing from the fire remained—everything there was new to him. The family he was preparing it for didn't seem to be his own future. He had thought that the house would anchor him anew in Massachusetts, but once it was finished and the door painted a lovely teal—bursting out, modern and vibrant, against the traditional grays of the shingles—he didn't feel connected to what he'd created. He was glad he had built it, but it wasn't until he returned from Springfield after trying to enlist again that he understood the problem. The house had no soul.

It wasn't the house's fault. He was simply restless and it didn't feel like

home. Somehow and someday, Sheldon knew the house would find a purpose. He just wasn't sure what it was.

When Sheldon returned from Springfield, rejected and resigned to having missed the war despite its not being over, Lenny asked him if he was
ready for New York.

They were sitting on the grass in front of Sheldon's new house. The door
was open behind them and the leaves of early autumn were starting to turn.
The calendar and the earth saw this as a time of endings, but for former
schoolboys, it still felt like the start of a new year and a new beginning.
Lenny wanted to get on the road.

"You really want me to come?" Sheldon asked.

"It's time," Lenny said sagely.

Lenny was right. Sheldon had been living frugally and working odd jobs
and even trapping and hunting. Nate, to his credit, had arranged the paperwork as he'd promised. The house was built, and with Thaleman's cash,
Sheldon had money to burn but very little of it coming in. It was time to
step out as an adult.

He didn't have a plan, but Lenny—as usual—did.

"New York?"

"Bingo."

"What am I going to do there?" Sheldon asked. "My only skills are hunting, trapping, stealing, and revenge. Is there a club there for people like
me?"

"I know what you're not gonna do. You're not gonna sit on the grass for
another year and wish you were killing Nazis."

"I should be standing?"

"You should be wishing something else. Remember when you were little
and your dad worked as a cobbler during the winters when the hunting
season was over?"

"What about it?"

"And he let you add up the costs of things and put them into that big
book with all the complicated lines in it?"

"Again, Lenny—"

"You always seemed calm when you were doing that. I thought maybe you could be an accountant."

Sheldon threw a clump of grass at Lenny, and it struck him on the shoulder, leaving a patch of dirt that Lenny didn't wipe off.

"Or a cobbler?"

"I don't want to make shoes. He didn't either. It was money in the off season. I liked sitting with him in the quiet, that was all."

"My great-aunt lives in a neighborhood called Gramercy in Manhattan. There's a fancy park nearby. The place is on . . . I don't remember . . . Seventeenth and Third or somewhere near that."

"This means nothing to me," said Sheldon, trying to pluck enough grass from elsewhere to fill in the hole he had made hurling dirt at Lenny.

"Doesn't matter. What matters is, she owns a town house, and there's a separate entrance to a basement where you can build a workshop or start a store or . . . whatever. She's more than seventy, she's put it on the market, and what I'm saying is, you need to buy it."

"You want me to buy a town house in Manhattan with a basement workshop?"

"Yes, I do. And I'll live in it for free, obviously, as I break into show biz, and you'll set up a repair shop or whatever in the basement, which has an entrance for the customers from the street."

"I see why you like this plan."

"I don't know the details, but my dad was talking about the sale of the town house. You can buy the whole building for less than you have in that green bag and the leftover from the insurance. You'd still have some cash on the side. And if I get to live there, my aunt will definitely sell it to you. We get hard up, we take in a tenant. But eventually we'll have some money and then . . . you know . . . a life."

"We're talking what, seven thousand or more for a town house?"

"You can take out a loan like you did with this place. I think the town house is a good investment. I don't think New York's at the top of the market yet. Meanwhile—you can rent this place out."

"We're in the middle of nowhere. Who'd want it?" Sheldon muttered.

"You're kidding, right?"

The answer was so obvious that Sheldon had somehow missed it but Lenny's expression triggered his brain. "You mean Mirabelle and Louis."

"You told me that Louis was offered a teaching position at Smith College in Northampton. Engineering or physics or something. It's a short ride down the road from here. You should rent the house to them for whatever they can afford and help them get on their feet. Give 'em a break. Keep the place in the family, you know."

Sheldon nodded, as much to himself as to Lenny. This was the obvious thing to do.

Lenny stood. He brushed himself off, including the dirt on his shoulder, and without humor or doubt in his voice, he said, "It's time to move on."

LENNY'S PRAYER

BILL HARMON WAS a ruddy Irishman from New York who walked into Sheldon's basement workshop one afternoon in early August 1945—a few months after Sheldon closed on the town house and a few days before Emperor Hirohito announced the Japanese surrender—and confessed that he owed Sheldon money and told him not to worry because he would have it in a few days.

Sheldon had no idea who the guy was.

"Bill?" the man prompted him. "Bill Harmon?"

Sheldon thought that the man looked familiar in the way that everyone on his block had started to look familiar. But since he and Lenny had moved in, they'd been so busy that they'd barely looked up. The basement had been the biggest nightmare, with a half century of junk piled in there, mostly waterlogged newspapers, magazines, 78 records that had warped or cracked, clothing that had been eaten away by moths and mildew, and furniture that someone was probably supposed to have repaired but was either too half-assed to do it or died too soon.

Or just in time.

It was a tough call.

Cleaning out the three upper floors had been a hassle too as neither Sheldon nor Lenny was especially strong. They were wiry and had spirit, but neither one wanted to be the low man on the sofa when they had to spin it around the corner of the staircase.

"You're doing *great*, Sheldon!" Lenny had yelled from up above.

After the basement had been cleaned out and disinfected and turned into a clean sheet of paper for a new purpose, the two of them had stored the nicest antiques down there until Sheldon looked at the furniture and lamps and shelves and mirrors — all styles the boys couldn't stand keeping in the house itself — and said, "Huh."

"Huh, what?"

"Huh, let's hang out a shingle and sell the stuff."

"We're using this place as a closet until we can figure out what to do with it all," Lenny said.

"Let's say we're done. Let's say we're an antique store and that all this is for sale. Rather than hire a bunch of goons to take it away, let's get people to pay *us* to take it away. It's what Tom Sawyer would have done."

The timing turned out to be auspicious because when the war had ended, everyone in Europe had come home and they needed furniture. And lamps. And irons for those shirts they needed to wear when they interviewed for jobs or got one.

They also needed clocks, and that was something Sheldon had only one of, and that one wasn't for sale.

One boring Thursday, while he was babysitting the furniture and Lenny was out doing Lenny things for Lenny reasons that Sheldon didn't want to know about, Sheldon unpacked his father's clock and placed it on his workbench to assess the damage.

The Krupinski brothers hadn't been nice to it. They hadn't deliberately harmed it, but they clearly had had no sense of how delicate the thing was inside and how gently you're supposed to handle it.

He'd had it stored up in Whately, and now that he was in New York there was a good chance he could get it repaired. Or a reasonable chance, anyway. The clock still looked OK. The face was a sheet-metal bronze with roman numerals, the hands were thin and elegant, and the case was wooden with some garish flourishes. Inside were two weights that dropped slowly after being wound to the top, thereby uncoiling the balance spring and granting the machine life. When it functioned, as Sheldon vaguely remembered now, it struck once on the half hour and then chimed the hours accordingly. Now it did nothing.

As Sheldon knew nothing about clocks, what he was really assessing was whether it looked repairable. Was the glass intact? It was. Were the pieces all there? They seemed to be but who knew? Was the case beyond repair? It was a bit scratched up, but it was structurally sound. As Sheldon was spinning gears around trying to get a sense of the whole, a man rapped on the window of his door and Sheldon opened it.

"Fix clocks?" the man asked. He wore a three-piece suit and a tie. Everything about him screamed money. He looked busy and was the kind who wanted straight answers even if they were wrong. Sheldon had his number immediately. "Yup," he said as convincingly as possible.

"I'll drop it off tomorrow," said the guy as he turned and left.

The next day the man came back with a clock smaller than Sheldon's but far more elaborate and obviously very expensive.

"What's wrong with it?" Sheldon asked.

"It's broken."

"I'll give you an estimate in a few days. Leave your number and I'll call, or else you can drop by. You agree to it, I'll fix it. If not, take it home, no charge. If you don't come back for three months without collecting it—broken or fixed—it's mine. We good?"

They were good. The guy left and Sheldon practically followed him out the door to find someone who knew how to fix clocks.

Three blocks away, Sheldon found a general fix-it shop run by a guy named David Cho. Cho was Asian, in his forties, and had relocated from San Francisco after a nasty divorce he didn't want to talk about but talked about anyway. He knew everything there was to know about clocks.

Though Cho's shop was on the ground level, it was twice as dark and uninviting as Sheldon's workshop. Nothing inside looked fixed or for sale. Sheldon couldn't figure out the business model. Maybe everything behind Cho was spare parts.

Cho didn't strike Sheldon as someone highly motivated or on the move.

Cho looked at Sheldon's client's clock and spotted the problem right away. He explained it in gibberish and Sheldon nodded because nodding kept Cho talking.

"So . . . you'll fix it?" Sheldon asked when Cho paused.

Cho lit a cigarette.

"Eight bucks, three days."

"OK." It seemed steep but what did he know? "I got another one. You like to work on these things? You sticking around for a while?"

"She took the kids," Cho said by way of an answer.

Sheldon called his client when he returned to the shop.

"Fifteen bucks, four days," Sheldon said.

People started showing up for repair services, not just furniture and lamps. Sheldon built a network of shops specializing in everything from watches to phonographs and brokered the transactions for a cut. Everything was going swimmingly until Bill Harmon walked in.

"Who are you?" Sheldon asked, trying not to sound unkind.

"Bill Harmon," the guy said, taking off his jacket and hanging it on the rack beside the door like he owned the place. "Jesus, you've really turned this place around. Your back must be broken."

Bill Harmon was in his midtwenties, a bit older than Sheldon, but he carried himself like he was in his forties. There was a sure-footedness to the way he strolled around, and he wore his clothes as if a suit felt natural on him and he might know how to talk to women, the police, and other scary people. The guy was making himself very comfortable in the shop, and for no reason he could put his finger on, Sheldon liked him.

"You've been here before?" Sheldon asked, taking off the cobbler's bib that he liked to wear while fiddling with things. He rolled up his sleeves.

"I came over one time when I was chasing a mouse. Little bastard slipped through a hole in the wall that led over here, and I thought, Not this time, pal, so I popped by and the old lady let me in. As soon as I saw what this place looked like, I knew the mouse had won. I mean . . . my God, the things she had packed in here. Then again, you take an immigrant, put her through the Great War, the Depression, widowhood, and then another war, and you got to cut her some slack, you know? Hold on to stuff! That's what my parents always said to me. So, I did. Now I got a pawn shop. Or it's got me. I don't know."

"You're telling me," Sheldon said. "Oh, so that's you. With the trumpet in the window?"

"You want it? I'll give you a good price."

"I don't play."

"Never too late to learn."

"Too late to get good."

"Yeah, that's true." Bill plopped himself into a wooden chair a few yards away from Sheldon and crossed his legs. He removed a pipe from his pocket and raised his eyebrows at Sheldon, who waved him on, so he lit up. "You should come in. My place is the mirror image of your place. We're neighbors, after all."

Sheldon glanced outside because the light had changed. A man's legs had stopped outside his window. The trousers were gray wool and the shoes were black leather. They were a decade out of style and badly scuffed. Sheldon couldn't see his face and waited for him to come down the steps, but he didn't. He just stood there.

"You were saying before . . . ," Sheldon said, fading off deliberately.

"Oh, yeah. Right. So, I owe you three months' back rent," said Bill, ignoring the shadow cast by the man's legs. "I know that, and I wanted to let you know that I know that and that I'm not a deadbeat. I'll pay you for one month on Friday, and if you don't mind, I can pay you the remaining two months two weeks from Friday because I got this jackass over a barrel and he's going to pay up for what he bought, and then I'm more than good."

"How's that?" Sheldon asked. He was trying to understand why Bill owed him money at all, but Bill heard the question differently

"Get this, he's got a woman on the side, right? Comes to me and buys a whole apartment's worth of furniture so he can set her up nice in her own place and then . . . boom . . . doesn't pay up. So, what do I do? I find his wife! I threaten the guy. I say, 'Look, you pay me, and you keep the good life. You don't and it's all over with the girls, plus you end up with two apartments full of furniture that you're going to have to sell to me, assuming I'm willing to bail you out. By the way, what you owe me just increased by ten percent.' Do you love it or what?"

"That's not a bad one. But I'm still back at you owing me money."

"I realize you don't know me from Adam, but — my word of honor — I'm good for it."

"No, it's not that. I don't get why you owe me anything at all."

"You're my landlord."

"How do you figure?"

"You ever wonder why the basement's not as wide as the town house?"

"I have wondered that."

"They split it in two. I've been running my place for two years. I was a little older than you when I started. I paid the old lady. Now I pay you."

"No kidding," said Sheldon, genuinely surprised that he owned not one store but two.

"You've got to read the fine print. Not every building comes with its own Irishman."

The legs in the windows moved off. There was something vaguely familiar about those shoes, but Sheldon couldn't place them.

"My buddy Lenny's performing a comedy thing at a supper club tonight. His first gig since his Catskill days. Food and booze and a few laughs. None of it's good, but they cancel each other out. How about it?"

✈

LENNY BERNSTEIN'S MOVE to New York hadn't been as smooth as he'd expected. At first, it had been a dream come true, which quickly became a challenge. For years he had talked about the move and spent his time coaxing Sheldon while making big plans, swimming in the ethereal possibility of it all. Now, however, he had to commit, like a diver standing on a rocky ledge over blue water. There were no half measures here and no going back except in humiliation and ruin. And if he did, then what? He didn't have another dream.

This was the world's greatest stage. All it promised was an audience for the bold. This is partly what shook Lenny to his bones.

New York was not a complete mystery, though. Having visited and now having lived there for a few months, Lenny could identify the Chrysler Building, the Empire State Building, and Rockefeller Plaza. The streets ran in sequential numbers, which helped him navigate the city. None of this —not even the noise and energy—was the problem.

Landing a job. That was the problem.

It hadn't occurred to him at the time, but the Catskill resorts were all family owned and that meant that the Mob wasn't involved. New York City, however, was different. Back during Prohibition, the Mob ran the speakeasies and booze. When drinking became legal again, they turned the speakeasies into clubs and ran those. Since the Mob owned the clubs, the comedians had to work for the Mob. There was no way around it. Unfortunately, Lenny didn't have an in with the Mob. Sheldon, of course, knew all of them but not in a helpful way.

What Lenny learned in time was that the Mob might be in charge but they were still running businesses and—at least at the day-to-day level—those businesses operated more or less like all other businesses. The Mob needed people to do normal things like serve drinks and cook and clear tables and—as it happened—tell jokes. And so Lenny decided to give it a shot. He'd been going to the same nightclub every night to adjust to the comic sensibility of New York City and see how he might fit in. Eventually, he walked up to the proprietor and asked for a gig.

"You got experience?"

"Catskills. Three summers. Knocked 'em dead. I'm offended that you haven't heard of me."

"Uh-huh," said the guy who hadn't smiled at Lenny's joke, but maybe he had on the inside because he allowed Lenny to try a few lines and finally —tonight—gave him his first job.

Lenny waited on a stool beside the bar in a room that smelled like wood, steak, and lies. He was watching an act dragged over from vaudeville that involved a dog running between spinning plates as a guy played "Sing, Sing, Sing" on a kazoo. The guy must have spent years on this and here he was.

Success? Who knew?

New York had a comedic affinity with the Catskills—a shared timing, a shared dramatic tone—but it was also the Big City, and the audience wasn't already happy and on vacation and liquored up. Lenny noticed that they were more demanding and their standards were higher because they had plenty of choice. And some guys were back from the war. You could tell.

His heart beat a little faster when the plates stopped spinning, the dog came to a halt, and the song ended. It was fear more than stage fright. If there was one truth about this place—the kind of fundamental truth where the shovel hits bedrock and you know you're on solid ground—it was that New York didn't care if you lived or died.

Lenny's biggest problem, though, wasn't facing the dream, landing a job, or even adapting to the local color. It was carrying the weight of what he knew that he hadn't previously known.

Sheldon had never stopped stacking newspapers. He stacked them now in Gramercy the way he'd stacked them at Grossinger's, and in Whately, and in Hartford, and in his new house. Lenny knew the habit had started with Abe, but he'd been hoping that it would end. It didn't. If anything, it became worse as the news became worse, and the news became much worse as the war came to an end and the facts of Germany's conduct became known. And not only Germany's.

Lenny had been avoiding newspapers. In his commitment to stay away from topical matters—per the instructions of everyone who'd ever fired him and in line with the Motion Picture Production Code that deemed what was acceptable and unacceptable in American society—Lenny had been working diligently to make jokes about only the most everyday of human experiences. The newspapers, he reasoned, would only fog his mind and confuse him about what was important and what was not. It had not occurred to him that not reading the newspapers might do exactly the same thing.

What Lenny eventually learned was that the Russians had found the first of the camps in July of 1944. He learned this when he heard a well-dressed woman talk about it with her friend on the bus outside Whately. The woman was whispering as though the Jews should be ashamed, as though weakness of that magnitude must be hidden.

Lenny had asked Sheldon about it when he arrived home. Sheldon fished out a *Boston Daily Globe* article called HOW NAZIS MURDERED 2,000,000 that had the subheading of BABIES, WOMEN AMONG VICTIMS OF LUBLIN CAMP and handed it to Lenny by way of explanation.

Sheldon had known exactly where the article was.

The article was written by James Aldridge and Lenny had been shocked to see that it hadn't even been the day's headline; in fact, it was below the fold on the front page and placed directly next to another article called U.S. COMPUTES TAX ON NEW SIMPLIFIED RETURNS BEING PRINTED.

> LUBLIN, Poland. Wednesday, Aug. 30 (NANA) (By Wireless)—This is the Majdanak concentration camp of Lublin. It is the first German concentration camp seen by war correspondents in Europe, and this is one of the most notorious.
> Here more than 2,000,000 people were killed by the Germans and that figure becomes believable when you see the camp.

The article had explained how Aldridge had entered the camp through fields of vegetables that included cabbage; all of it rotting. Lenny remembered how odd it had seemed for the journalist to mention this seemingly insignificant detail until he learned the real reason later.

In the camp, Aldridge went to visit one of the gas chambers. He described looking through the small window that the executioner had used to regularly watch men, women, and children suffocate and die. There were holes in the ceiling and walls where the gas came in.

The dead were taken to the furnaces. Aldridge described seeing the condition of the bodies; how the arms and legs had been snapped at the joints so they could be folded up and thrown inside to be burned.

But even then the killing and dishonor and evil wasn't done.

> Then there is a siding where trucks took the ashes from the furnaces to the field. I saw the ashes in high piles, and mixed with manure and weeds to form a compost for fertilizing the cabbages. Looking at the quantity of ashes that one man was reduced to and looking at these piles and piles of ashes, it is easy to calculate that hundreds of thousands of human remains are scattered around these fields.

> On one field there is a pile of shoes—perhaps 500,000
> —and half of these, I noticed, were women's and chil-
> dren's and babies' shoes.

The story continued. But Lenny turned to another; the one that came flooding back to him now, moments before he was to go onstage with his act. There had been many other stories since then. But this had been the first he'd read, and so it haunted him.

On page four there had been an article by Daniel De Luce headlined, 4 GERMANS BLAME 'ORDERS FROM ABOVE' FOR LUBLIN MURDERS. Half-way down was the subheading WOMAN BURNED ALIVE. The article quoted N. A. Stalb, "a blond, six-foot German butcher, arrested in 1939 for selling meat in the black market." He had become a member of the barracks police detail while incarcerated at Majdanek.

> "I have seen a tractor haul as many as 400 corpses at
> one time from the 'bath and disinfection house' to
> the ovens on the hill," he said. "One day I saw the
> bodies of 157 Polish children who had been gassed.
> Another time I saw a group of Polish women marched
> up a hill to be shot to save the trouble of gassing
> them. They were ordered to disrobe. One refused, a
> girl of about 28 or 29. Two men tied her hands and
> legs, put her on a steel stretcher and thrust her
> alive into the white-hot oven.

Waiting for his turn in the spotlight, Lenny tried to imagine this girl, this real human being who was modest and shy, or maybe proud and strong and rebellious. Someone who refused to strip naked and be shot, and was instead burned alive. He thought about her and the kind of people who would do that and why they were willing or even happy to do it.

The article didn't mention when Stalb saw this. It could have been in 1944 but it could have been earlier. Could Lenny have been at Grossinger's with a thousand Jews who were laughing it up as millions—six million was the estimate now—were being murdered across the Atlantic?

But then again, they *had* known. Not the numbers, not the methods, not the details, but the accounts of murder, brutality, and marginalization had been in the papers since the late 1930s. He and Sheldon had put those papers in front of hotel room doors every morning. You had to step over the information to get to breakfast.

How had they kept laughing through it all?

Lenny needed to answer this question. He needed to understand how the world was laughing its greatest laughter while also crying its greatest tears. He felt as though the soul of man had been split in two and that the sound of the rupture had silenced all talk.

Laughter is a great defense. Had Jewish Americans been defending themselves?

Laughter, like love, makes us forget the rest if only for a moment. Were we pushing back the knowledge?

Comedy can create pleasure in others who might hate us. Were we trying to be loved in a world so full of rage?

Comedy forces us to look anew at what we consider normal and reassess it. Were we doing this every minute of every day with small things because we lacked the courage to face the big ones?

They wouldn't hire us or publish us or educate us at their universities or let us into the inner circles. Was comedy the only space for us to spread our wings?

Lenny asked his rabbi and his rabbi said, "The Greeks separated comedy and tragedy. We never did."

Was that an answer?

Or was all of this too generous? Lenny wondered. Were we simply oblivious? Were we too focused on survival or selfishness to hear those screams that weren't in English? Too proud of our own achievements in America to see others as ourselves? Too glad to have left that hellhole called Europe and too scornful of those who hadn't been courageous enough to have done the same?

Or were we too frightened to feel the pity that would have forced our self-reflection and prompted us to action?

At ten o'clock that night, Lenny stood in a corner of the restaurant and waited patiently for his turn onstage. He looked at Sheldon, who was sipping a whiskey and sitting beside a man Lenny didn't recognize.

Lenny didn't know the answers to the questions he had asked. He wasn't sure if the questions had answers, and if there were answers, whether they were the same for everyone. It seemed enough, though, to realize that all his thoughts directed him toward the same prayer that he now uttered under his breath to a God he hoped was listening.

"Dear God," said Lenny Bernstein, "give me the strength to be joyful."

✈

Sheldon, Lenny, and Bill left the supper club at 1:30 in the morning after having had a few drinks. Lenny was sleepy and wanted to go to bed, so Sheldon sent him ahead through the bright lights and flow of people on Third Avenue to their town house. Bill, true to his culture, true to his *commitments,* had taken it upon himself to teach Sheldon how to drink properly. Bill's left arm was flung over his new landlord's shoulder for both camaraderie and support as they finally arrived at Sheldon's diminutive stoop and walked down the few steps and entered while Sheldon listened with a grin to Bill explain how Irishmen drink (and how Sheldon can too if he applies himself). "It involves not only whiskey," Bill explained, "but its consumption. Just having the whiskey alone isn't enough. I hear people say, 'Oh, I had whiskey,' but . . . so does the grocery store! Grocery store's not drinking, though, is it? No. That's why it has so much whiskey, but it isn't drunk. Or happy. I've never met a happy grocery store. 'As happy as a grocery store.' No one ever says that. That's because a grocery store doesn't understand what it means to be Irish."

With plenty of booze still inside an old globe bar Sheldon had forgotten to empty, the two settled into fine furniture and tested their limits.

As the night progressed, Bill became—in turns—generous, funny, chatty, emotional, confessional, and finally a bit weepy. Once that settled in, it was time for singing songs that Sheldon didn't know, and that was the first time in the entire evening he felt as though he'd let Bill down. Which is part of the reason he had hauled Bill up and walked him out of the shop while he listened to how much Bill loved his own dad and how bad he felt for Sheldon for losing his own father, "who sounds like he was a helluva guy."

Sheldon smiled as he opened Bill's door for him (keyholes move and Sheldon had better aim) and he smiled a farewell smile as he tossed Bill onto the brown sofa in the back office, where Sheldon was pretty certain Bill had napped before.

"Do you want to stay for a drink?" Bill mumbled facedown into a pillow as Sheldon switched off the light. "There was something I was meaning to tell you and I forgot what it was. It's gonna come back to me. Mark my words."

In high spirits — in all the best ways — Sheldon walked out the door and took the trumpet with him.

Harry James's band was back on the charts with a new song called "I'm Beginning to See the Light," and while Sheldon couldn't play the trumpet, it was fun to sit back in his workshop in the black of a New York night and pretend to play it. He'd discovered that Kitty Kallen's singing on this track came through beautifully on the Zenith phonograph that a guy named Walters had dropped off to have fixed.

"You fix these, right?"

"Sure, sure," said Sheldon.

Did Sheldon fix these? Of course not. A guy named Frank Bromley on Eighth and Lex fixed them, and Sheldon transported them back and forth and collected a cut. And now that Walters's Zenith was working properly, Sheldon spun up some records.

He played the flip side first.

This city life did have something going for it, he thought, lighting a pipe. Everything was close by. Every sensation was intensified and existed, indiscriminately, beside every other one. As the James record spun, Sheldon thought again about Nate's talk of Yankee ingenuity and Hartford. If his uncle was here now, Sheldon would say to him, "Maybe, Uncle Nate, but that was then. New York has the ball now." Manhattan was a place without much greenery or trees, no animals roamed the woods behind him, and every movie theater was a haunted house that whispered to him like a graveyard as he walked by, but all the same, it was a place pulsing with life and vitality.

The 78 record played itself out, and pipe in mouth, Sheldon swung himself off the stool and went to flip it over. After he placed the needle down and the band struck up again, he turned to look out the window and saw the one thing that he knew was going to drive him nuts about living here: vagrants.

There were legs in the window again, and rather than facing away as though the person was waiting for a cab, they were facing his building, which suggested that a zipper was going to be opened and that it was going to be raining piss down Sheldon's steps.

Springing to action, Sheldon skidded to the front door, unchained the lock, and whipped the door open.

"Not here, not now, not ever!" he yelled.

He looked up hoping not to see a prick.

Standing there was Lorenzo.

He was wearing the same suit he'd been wearing at Grossinger's the night that Sheldon held the police car door open for him. The shoes were the same shoes, and Sheldon suspected that the dust on them was the same dust. Five years had passed, and Lorenzo stood there like a ghost sent up to earth from hell to avenge his own death.

From his angle at the bottom of four steps, Sheldon looked up into his face like a child watching a parent or else a patron eyeing a statue on a plinth. Lorenzo had lost weight. His face was gaunt and he seemed a decade older—his darkened eyes were set farther back in his skull, and he had a complexion that promised never to wash clean. What captured Sheldon's attention most was the thick scar that ran across Lorenzo's throat from ear to ear. How he'd survived having his neck cut open Sheldon couldn't imagine, but the man before him was a dead man; a man who had known himself dead because he had been killed and was supposed to be dead now but somehow wasn't—had somehow survived.

This was the infinite moment between seeing Lorenzo and the one in which Lorenzo reached for Sheldon to kill him.

In the cool of the summer night—miraculously pleasant given how hot the day had been—it made sense to Sheldon that the Mafia had sent someone to kill Lorenzo either in prison or when he got out. Maybe they paid off a judge to commute his sentence so they could kill him afterward. Maybe they tried to kill him inside prison and found, to their astonishment, that Lorenzo wouldn't rat out the man who had sliced his throat. Is anyone that tough? To have their throat slit open and still follow the code?

Lorenzo's were the stony eyes of a man who had lost all motivation but revenge. They were cold enough to be instructive.

The man who had killed Sheldon's father now towered over him; his hands—as though in slow motion—were reaching down to grasp Sheldon around the throat and squeeze the life out of him as painfully and as intimately as possible.

Sheldon was standing at a bad angle, an impossible angle. His right hand was on the doorknob and his face and chest were wide open to the night.

Lorenzo knew this. There was no murderous smile and no sound. No wink or provocation. Only a softening in his face as though he had received the present he had wanted and all that was left was the taking.

Sheldon lurched back and pulled the door closed with all his weight, but Lorenzo was too fast. He hooked his left elbow into the doorway and reached out to grab Sheldon with his right arm.

Sheldon released the door and slapped Lorenzo's hand away. Two steps inside the shop, Sheldon grabbed the back of his office chair and slammed it into Lorenzo's left knee, which arrested his momentum and gave Sheldon a second to turn and run.

Sheldon had hunted enough to know that animals freeze when threatened and how paralysis is the first line of defense as most predators' eyesight is attuned to detect motion. But there was no way he was making that mistake.

Lorenzo didn't go down. He grasped his knee and grimaced, but he didn't limp. Instead, he sprang after Sheldon, who'd run to the back of the long narrow shop looking for something to fight with. There had to be something here. Anything. Where were his guns? He still had guns. He had Henkler's .45 and Thaleman's .38. Where the fuck *were* they?

He'd been listening to Harry James when he had first seen Lorenzo, and as he whipped around a display case for smaller sale items—earrings, necklaces, war medals, and watches—a gentle jazz guitar set up the entry of Kitty Kallen's mellifluous voice singing, "I've never cared much for moonlit skies . . ."

It was obvious that Lorenzo's eyes were adjusting to the dark. He stood for a moment and surveyed the room. Sheldon had been the son of a hunter and a trapper and an occasional cobbler, and he knew a few tricks about killing, but Lorenzo had been a murderer.

Sheldon, inexperienced, was looking for a weapon but Lorenzo was looking for exits. Finding none other than the door he came in, he chose his line of attack, a line that took him straight toward the back wall.

Sheldon hopped behind a display case, planning to keep it between him and the killer just like he used to dash away from Lenny around his mom's kitchen table. He was pretty sure that if Lorenzo got his hands on him he would lose, and right now all Sheldon had going for him was youth, dexterity, and a will to live. This guy in front of him didn't seem to have any of those things and was being driven by pure hatred, anger, and vengeance.

Not that Sheldon hadn't been fueled by these things too, once upon a time, but he'd changed. He hadn't put himself to sleep with thoughts of murdering this man—not even once—since the police car's taillights had disappeared down the hill toward Liberty back in '41. Not even after he had visited his father's grave and the empty box beside it that belonged to his mother. When he'd laid his father to rest and saw their names side by side, Sheldon had wept. He'd wept at seeing his family together again, their names locked together in eternity, and he now understood—years on and at the edge of adulthood himself—that whatever his mother had done with another man—whatever decisions she had made—had been something private and distant and personal. Mirabelle had been right. It made her no less of a mother, or a wife, or a woman. Maybe that was the wisdom of the cemetery: It was a place to allow conclusions to be reached.

If Sheldon had grown and changed, Lorenzo clearly had not.

Lorenzo grabbed the edge of the display cabinet and overturned it. He pushed aside anything Sheldon might run around, anything that might protect him and keep him alive. A beast, Lorenzo was plowing a path to his prey as if he were darkness itself trying to push back the light.

Sheldon backed away. Behind him was the bathroom. It had a door but no window—only a fan in the ceiling and a vent only large enough for a gerbil. If he backed in there, there'd be no way out.

Kitty Kallen was almost done with the song.

Lorenzo wasn't advancing on Sheldon yet. For him, there was no rush. He pressed a cabinet to one wall and then overturned a display table by the other. He sent the lamps from an estate sale smashing to the floor and created one and only one path for Sheldon to the outside world.

Could Lenny hear this upstairs? What if he came down? Would he be killed too?

Sheldon looked around one last time for a weapon. This place had been filled with nothing but weapons before he cleaned everything up. Broom handles. Shard of glass he could have wrapped in cloth to make a shiv. Copper pipes. Broken chair legs. It had been endless.

All that was left now was the Louisville Slugger in the umbrella stand by the front door that was as far away as Las Vegas.

He continued backing away.

Sheldon didn't know how to fist-fight. He'd wrestled with buddies and he'd shot guns. He was five foot seven, 155 pounds, and twenty years old.

Lorenzo was in his forties and was a five-foot-ten-inch merchant of death who killed people for a living.

When Sheldon's right heel touched the wall behind him, it sent a signal to his brain that it translated as *attack.*

This was it. Fight or flight, and there was nowhere to run.

Like a sprinter at a starting gun, Sheldon let out a war cry and ran directly at Lorenzo and leapt. His right hand was balled into a mighty fist and the sheer inertia of him — the weight of a youth in flight — was going to crash down on the assassin and knock the daylights out of him, clearing his path to the door and the street and anyplace Sheldon wanted to go next because all the world is not only a stage but an enormous connected network of highways and byways, that could lead Sheldon to any place but here.

Lorenzo, though, had other ideas.

With the grace of a dancer, Lorenzo grabbed Sheldon out of the air and body-slammed him down onto the floor like a sack. The air was knocked from Sheldon's lungs, and as he tried to suck in the missing breath, Lorenzo reached down to strangle him to death.

Sheldon couldn't breathe. Lorenzo's arms were amazingly long. Leaning into it, Lorenzo arched his back to pull himself even farther away from Sheldon's flailing hands while increasing the pressure.

He tried to punch him, scratch him, kick him off. He'd seen a cat on its back before; an animal in a trap. It did anything and everything —

Sheldon made contact for a brief second with Lorenzo's groin, forcing him to let up for a moment; a moment just long enough for him to suck in a lungful of air and push back the cloud over his eyes.

But Lorenzo was quick to return; his tolerance for pain impossibly high. He was not a normal man. He was a man who had been left for dead with his throat slashed open. A kick in the nuts was not enough to stop him.

If there had been a way to flip over, to crawl out, Sheldon would have done it, but Lorenzo's powerful hands were around his throat again. A vision passed through Sheldon's head of a pistol in Lorenzo's belt, or maybe a knife. Did he really come here tonight planning to murder Sheldon with only his hands?

Sheldon frantically scratched at Lorenzo's jacket, trying to find purchase on anything hard, anything with a handle.

There was nothing.

This man had brought nothing but hate. He didn't want Sheldon dead. He wanted him to *die*. Slowly, deliberately, painfully, and at his own pleasure and leisure.

The pain was unbearable. Sheldon could feel his eyes opening wide and his mouth gaping open as he tried to pull in the slightest breath, and at the moment when Sheldon's entire body started to writhe in a death throe . . . there was a *CRACK* and Lorenzo disappeared.

Gone. Not even a puff of smoke. He simply vanished from sight as though snatched from this earth and banished directly to hell.

A sweet lungful of air inflated Sheldon's body and went straight to his mind. He had no other conscious thought other than *I am breathing*. When his mind made space for a second notion—after a time immeasurable—he saw in front of him a form, a shape. It looked at first like an angel; the archangel with his flaming sword, though now the flame was extinguished and slung over his shoulder like a batter at a warmup at Fenway Park in Boston where the Red Sox play.

Except they liked the Yankees here.

The Yankees were an awful group of people.

Maybe the figure above him wasn't an angel at all. Maybe it was God. Maybe Sheldon was looking up at the blurry face of God. The face one no one had ever seen.

Not until now. Not until Sheldon.

"You all right?" said a voice that might have been the One that had spoken to Abraham and Moses and Joshua . . . had it not had such a heavy Irish accent.

Sheldon wasn't sure he could talk at all.

"In your own time. It'll come back."

It wasn't Gabriel or God but Bill Harmon who, despite having kicked back more than half a bottle of Jameson and fallen asleep almost an hour ago, was now standing up straight and tall with Sheldon's Louisville Slugger over his shoulder and a hand extended for Sheldon to take.

Sheldon reached up and grabbed it. Bill brought him to his feet.

Bill looked him over. Putting down the bat, he took Sheldon's face in both of his large hands and turned it from side to side and surveyed the damage to his neck. He nodded a few times to himself, convinced that Sheldon would probably live.

"That's a boy, come on back," Bill said.

"Hey," Sheldon said.

Bill looked down at Lorenzo. His line drive through Lorenzo's skull had been so forceful that Lorenzo had disappeared from Sheldon's view faster than a baseball leaves a stadium. They both looked down at him. He wasn't moving.

"Do we know him?" Bill asked.

"Yeah," Sheldon said, his voice a whisper, then a rasp. "He killed my father back in 1938. I set him up to take a felony rap as revenge. I guess he got out."

"Came looking for you."

"Apparently so."

"How'd he find you?"

Without a word, they both looked at Sheldon's telephone.

"You're in the book, aren't you? You listed your number," Bill said disapprovingly.

"It's my first phone."

Bill shrugged. He'd done stupider things himself.

"He dead?" Sheldon asked.

Bill kicked Lorenzo. Then he bent over and checked his pulse. Finally, he turned him over and stared into his dead eyes.

"Yup."

"Well. Good for us. Bad for him."

"Should I feel bad about this?" Bill asked. He was still drunk but surprisingly high-functioning. If Sheldon had had a quarter of what Bill had consumed, he wouldn't have been able to find the door, let alone make a judgment and swing a bat.

"I feel like I should feel bad about it," Bill continued. "It's just that . . . what else could I have done? And it's been such a great night until now!"

Sheldon was thinking more practically. They couldn't just leave Lorenzo here.

"What do we do with him?" Sheldon asked.

"I suppose he's too big to flush down the toilet."

"In this shape, yeah," Sheldon said, still thinking.

"Don't worry about it."

Sheldon looked at his tipsy savior. "What's that supposed to mean?"

"I mean . . . I know all the cops in this town and the ones I don't know I'm probably related to. I'll explain it, they'll understand, they'll haul him away, problem solved. It's not like this was our idea."

"I hadn't thought of it that way."

They both stood there looking at Lorenzo. Dead or not, he had a presence.

This was the man Sheldon had first seen in a downpour, a confusion in a storm. This was the man with the mustache who had evaded Sheldon's detective work for years and was later summoned to the elegant glamor of Grossinger's resort to torture Mirabelle's boyfriend until gemstones fell from his eyes instead of tears. This was the man even the Mafia couldn't kill, and who was finally laid out — hard and permanently — by a drunk pawn broker with a mighty personality and a swing to match.

Sheldon crouched down for a final look. Staring into Lorenzo's open eyes, Sheldon didn't feel a damn thing. He had put this all to rest back in the Catskills. If he hadn't been sure, this was his proof.

Sheldon stood up and brushed himself off and then looked at Bill. As his mind cleared, the wider context of the night returned to Sheldon, and he asked, "What are you doing here? I left you facedown and mumbling a shanty or something."

"I remembered what I wanted to tell you."

"What was it?"

"I don't remember."

Now it was Sheldon's turn to look disapproving.

"A lot's happened since then!" Bill said in his own defense.

Sheldon's father's clock struck two o'clock in the morning. The sound was crisp and light.

"You really think it's all going to work out?" Sheldon asked, as Bill picked up the phone to call the precinct.

"Sure. After what the world's been through these past years, no one's gonna give any thought to these little twilight crimes."

AFTER: 1947

MABEL

MABEL ZIEGLER HELD the left hand of Sheldon Horowitz outside the ticket booth of the Rialto on a cold November day in 1947. The marquee was lit up with the title of a new movie, *Gentleman's Agreement,* which starred Gregory Peck, Dorothy McGuire, and Celeste Holm, and was directed by Elia Kazan. By next year at this time, it would be nominated for eight Academy Awards and would win for Best Picture, Best Supporting Actress, and Best Director. Sheldon was looking at the entrance to the movie theater with trepidation. It would be his first movie since his mother had died a decade earlier.

"Oh, come on," Mabel said, giving him a tug.

She was nineteen and he was twenty-one. She was slender, a little shorter than Sheldon, and had hair blacker than a Nordic night. Mabel's family had moved to Manhattan from Chicago eight months earlier. She'd met Sheldon three months ago when she and her father stopped into a Gramercy pawn shop to buy a box of tools they'd seen in the window. A rather affable man named Bill Harmon had insisted they meet his landlord next door and promptly introduced Mabel to Sheldon. Bill had backed out of the shop, giving Sheldon a double thumbs-up on the way and nodding like a fool.

Mabel returned to Sheldon's shop two weeks later on the pretense of wanting to buy a lamp, and Sheldon asked her out for a walk, which she accepted. The weather in late September had been unusually fine, and Sheldon spoke little, prompting her to tell him stories instead.

Mabel liked to talk. She was an avid tennis player and wasn't sure how she was going to keep that up here in Manhattan, but there had to be a way.

New York was very different from Chicago, but they were both big cities and she was used to that, and she was very committed to seeking out the city experiences she liked best—browsing in bookstores, hearing authors speak, eating in wonderful restaurants, shopping in fine stores, finding the best places to watch sunsets, and listening to beautiful music. Did Sheldon like music? She was mad for it. Mabel was certain that if there was a universal language it would have to be music. Didn't he agree? What else could it be? Music is math and vibration. Did he know about Albert Einstein? He said everything is vibration. She wasn't quite sure what that meant, but it seemed to suggest that everything was music—just vibrations and someone to appreciate them. That was a whole universe in itself. Isn't that interesting? How big and how small a universe can be at the same time?

Sheldon was enraptured by her mind, by her acuity, by her expansive curiosity, by the shape of her ass and the sway in her walk, by the look in her eyes when they fell on something worth seeing—a look so charismatic that it stole the show from whatever had inspired her.

They took many more walks, finding that the act of walking was a stimulant to conversation.

It was when Mabel suggested they attend a movie that a new domain of conversation began. She had been shocked to learn he hadn't attended one since 1936.

"You were ten years old," she said. They were at a coffee shop sitting in a booth, he with coffee and she with tea and lemon.

He said he'd gone with both his parents, a family event on a weekend. They saw Shirley Temple in *Captain January*. It was about an orphan girl who lives in a lighthouse with a kindly old sailor. In retrospect, it was an odd premise.

"And that was the last time?"

"Yes."

"That was a million years ago."

Sheldon explained why. He described the fire in Hartford. He explained his father's death, his moving in with Abe and Mirabelle and Uncle Nate. He explained the parts he wanted to and left out the rest.

Mabel listened. She knew many people who had lost loved ones because of the war and what had happened across the ocean. She didn't say she was sorry. She listened instead.

Sheldon explained that film was still made of nitrate and that it was as prone to burning as ever. Mabel had never thought about fires before. Now that she had, she still wasn't afraid of them. She also wasn't afraid of the dark or being trampled under fleeing people. Meanwhile, there was a specific film she wanted to see.

"It's time to go to the movies, Sheldon," she said gently.

There was a fine drizzle that night, like the mist from a waterfall. She and Sheldon stood in line wrapped in worsted wool. It was dark and the city lights reflected off the glimmering streets. The men wore hats and the women wore scarves. Sheldon's collar was up, and he looked to Mabel like a turtle in retreat. She told him so, and he didn't disagree.

Stoic and full of masculine pride, Sheldon proceeded to the front of the line. That pride failed him at the ticket booth. He wanted to leave. Mabel wasn't having it. She placed her gloved hands on the counter and leaned forward, and she spoke loudly enough for Sheldon to hear every word.

"How many exits does your theater have, please?"

"Ma'am?" asked the ticket woman with the cat-eye glasses.

"I experienced a fire in a movie theater once, and theaters scare me. But I want to see the movie. Can you tell me whether there's an emergency exit, please?"

Sheldon watched her lie for him and absorb his fears.

"Two entrances at the top of the stairs and two exits at the bottom on either side of the screen. We've never had a fire," the woman said, her tone flat.

Sheldon could feel the line growing restless behind them.

"It's fine," he said to her. "Let's get seats."

"Two on the aisle," Mabel said. "The left side, preferably. Toward the back and near the exit, please."

"You can sit where you like, ma'am. This ain't a communist country."

• • •

Mabel and Sheldon watched the movie.

Gregory Peck, as Phil "Skylar" Green, is tall, dark, and handsome. In the opening scene, the audience learns he is a widower with an only son, and Mabel held Sheldon's hand tighter. The father and son are in New York so Phil can write a long feature story on anti-Semitism, a topic suggested by the magazine's editor. Phil doesn't want to do it. The topic was dry and saturated with numbers and polls and statistics, and he doesn't like taking on an assignment that he can't grab and make his own. Phil isn't Jewish, but his best friend from childhood—Dave—is. Dave is a captain in the army and still overseas.

Phil explains his difficulties to his sick mother. In all the other stories he's written, he lived the experience. He'd been a part of it and had learned what to write. It was during his complaint to his mother that a light bulb goes off and he finds the right approach: He'll pretend to be Jewish and see what it feels like.

It turns out that it doesn't feel good.

Having fallen in love with Kathy, the editor's niece and a divorcee with no children, the two are fast on their way to a wedding, but her upper-class Christian family isn't comfortable with Phil's assumed Jewish identity. Kathy wants Phil to play it down with friends and family, and not mention it to her preferred wedding venue, the Flume Inn, which didn't accept Jewish patrons. It wasn't like Phil was *actually* Jewish, she says. He could surely drop the act from time to time so they could live like normal people. But Phil won't have it.

After his son is tormented at school for being a "dirty Jew," Kathy tried to comfort the boy by saying, "It's not true, you aren't a dirty Jew! You're no more Jewish than I am!" and Phil seethes. He turns his anger toward the Flume Inn, driving up there and demanding to know whether the hotel was indeed "restricted." The manager calmly asks whether Phil was inquiring to be sure that Jews weren't there or whether he was inquiring because he *was* a Jew. Phil shakes with anger and the manager—taking his silence as an answer—rings his bell. As Phil stands there helplessly, the bellhop removes Phil's bag from the lobby and places it out on the street without a word.

As Gregory Peck stands there, impotent and fuming, Sheldon saw Abe on the screen. He also saw the power of film. He saw his own story being told for the first time. And he was in awe.

When Phil returns broken by his experience at the inn, Kathy sees this and insists they talk. She is tired of being told she is wrong all the time and she needs him to stop this foolishness of pretending he is Jewish for a mere magazine story.

Phil, of course, is tired of her *being* wrong all the time.

Phil doesn't apologize, because he is angered by Kathy's easy complacency. After little Tommy was bullied, she had been wrong. Very wrong. "You only assured him that he's the most wonderful of all creatures, a white Christian American. You instantly gave him that lovely taste of superiority, the poison that millions of parents drop in the minds of children!"

Kathy fights back. She accuses Phil of thinking all along that she is an anti-Semite.

He insists that he doesn't. "It's just that I've come to see that the nice people who aren't, who despise it and detest it and deplore it and protest their own innocence, nevertheless help it along and wonder why it grows." That's the biggest discovery he's made, Phil tells her. About the nice people, the good people. The silent complicity.

When the film was over and the lights came back on, so too did the theater's colors. Mabel and Sheldon were holding hands. She smiled at him as they stood, and he helped her with her coat.

They left through the entrance and returned to a bracing cold night and a gusty breeze. The mist had turned into a light flurry of snow that blew across the streetlights like radical stars breaking free of convention and conformity.

It was only nine o'clock and Mabel wasn't expected home until eleven. They found an Italian restaurant nearby and ducked inside.

A waiter sat them at a table with a red cloth and lit the candle that was between them. He left them with menus and brought water after taking their drink order. Gregory Peck had made Sheldon long for a martini and Mabel joined him.

She wanted to know everything. What he thought. What he felt. Who he *was*.

He wasn't quick to answer.

"What did *you* think?" he asked.

"I think it was shocking," she said, crossing her legs. From Sheldon's angle, her thigh was visible as the bottom edge of the slit on her blue skirt fell away. No one could see but him. The experience was his alone.

"I had no idea that it was so bad that they had to make a movie about it," Mabel said. "I always knew we were on the outside looking in, but I never really thought this could change. It makes me wonder if we're the same as Europe."

"We're not," said Sheldon without a moment's hesitation.

Mabel. Her name was old-fashioned even in 1947. Mirabelle had been right about names. They conquer and control. A woman like Mabel was more like Mirabelle than some great-aunt. She needed a name with three syllables, a name to be announced on arrival. Maybe something Italian. Or Portuguese. Biblical, perhaps, but one that evoked a lingering taste of the sea. Exotic. Blue. Watery.

Leonora.

Maybe when they have a daughter . . .

The drinks came before Sheldon could finish his answer or his daydream. Mabel removed a cigarette from a silver case, and Sheldon lit it with his father's lighter.

Mabel looked at him with a wry smile. "You don't think so?"

"No," Sheldon said, recovering. "The movie made me feel great. After everything's that's happened, I feel like someone's noticing. Someone's saying we're not going to stand for this anymore. We know what this leads to. Someone's saying that we need to get better. America is telling us . . . that we belong . . . and maybe it isn't an unrequited love after all."

If we had heard this earlier, Sheldon thought, maybe Abe would still be alive. Maybe Mirabelle wouldn't have tried so hard to be anything but Jewish. Maybe Nate wouldn't have tried so hard to fit in that he disappeared as his own man. Maybe the dead would be alive and all the beauty they took with them would surround us all here and now.

Maybe.

Instead, Sheldon was living in this version of the world with a building in Gramercy, a buddy named Bill Harmon, and the woman he is going to marry sitting across from him. But not yet. Not too soon. He doesn't want to spook her.

"America is the greatest party going," Sheldon said, trying to sound suave. "And I think the night's still young."

ACKNOWLEDGMENTS AND DENIALS

Thank you to my wife, Camilla, for everything one might ever thank an-other person for. Thanks to my kids, Julian and Clara, for appreciating what I have to give and being understanding when it's not enough. Thanks to Rebecca Carter; PJ Mark; Bill Scott-Kerr; Lauren Wein; Jaime Levine; David Hough; Marianne Vincent; everyone at HMH and Transworld, the editors, copy editors, and cover designers; and the never-thanked *booksellers* who have, for a decade, wedged copies of my novels into readers' hands and made my life as a novelist possible. God bless you.

Meanwhile, no thanks go to all the scholars who blew me off and didn't respond to my letters of inquiry in the mistaken impression (I can only as-sume) that their peer-reviewed papers would have more of an impact than this novel would and who didn't recognize that art is one of the best vehicles for the movement of ideas into society. Let's consider any mistakes in this book theirs, shall we? Oh . . . *let's.*

The line "If they're laughing, how can they bludgeon you to death?" was stolen from Mel Brooks. Mel Brooks is also known to have said, "Knowing who to steal from is an art." Who he stole that from I have no idea, but I suspect foul play.

The idea that newspapers "don't tell us what to think, but tell us what to think about" was first noted by Bernard C. Cohen in his 1963 book, *The Press and Foreign Policy.*

The long quote from Mark Twain about the Colt Armory is taken, as claimed, from *A Connecticut Yankee in King Arthur's Court.*

The B-24 bomber wasn't delivered to Iceland until September of 1941. My June deployment is fictional but suited the story. I was willing to stretch the facts here because weirdness like this happens all the time in war. Need more? Try my second novel, *The Girl in Green.*

The statistics about Grossinger's were taken from Tania Grossinger's *Growing Up at Grossinger's* (2008, Skyhorse Publishing, New York). The numbers, according to Ms. Grossinger, reflect the mid-1940s, not the early 1940s, but I think they are close enough for rock and roll and I couldn't find better. I took some liberties with Grossinger's grounds and the locations of rooms at the hotel to suit the needs of the story. I visited the remains of the hotel in the summer of 2019. Everything had been destroyed and I was probably the last interested party—other than the workers—to see the debris being cleared away.

Although this is a work of fiction, the following all happened more or less as portrayed in the story—if not to my characters, at least to somebody: Hartford's industrial history; Joseph's World War I experiences; the New England hurricane of 1938; all facts and figures and dialogue about anti-Semitism or racism in America as well as the laws, policies, and genocide against the Jews in Europe; the general story of the Borscht Belt and the birth of modern comedy (which no scholars seem to link to the concurrent tragedy of the Holocaust, which the former scholar in me finds weird and is a research agenda begging for attention); the stories of Neversink and the Valley of the Dammed; Americans joining the RCAF, who were later called Gun Jumpers for "jumping the gun" and going to war; the RCAF's role in the Battle of the Atlantic (though I invented Abe's story); America's deep unwillingness (by both parties) to get involved in World War II until the Japanese bombed us and Hitler declared war on us; the fact that Jewish immigration was treated (outrageously and fatally) as a national security threat, much as Muslim immigration is treated like that today; and Laura Z. Hobson's novel-turned-movie that, in my opinion, laid the foundations for gonzo journalism (before Hunter S. Thompson) by having Phil Green *be* the story he was writing.

The story of the Lost Battalion and Cher Ami is also true. What Mr. Knightly did not mention to his class was that years later, after the war, Major Whittlesey committed suicide by jumping into the ocean from a ship traveling between New York and Havana. I don't know why.

Abe's thoughts on Judaism are strongly influenced by the writings of Rabbi Milton Steinberg and . . . well . . . my own thoughts, I suppose.

Lenny's reference to the Escapist is a nod to Michael Chabon's *The Amazing Adventures of Kavalier & Clay*. In a way that I don't entirely understand, I feel like this book is in conversation with that one.

Lenny's comedy routines were written by me and were "ahead of their time" in style but I wrote them a bit anachronistically to better fit the needs of this story, to suit contemporary tastes, and . . . because they made me chuckle.

Speaking of which, Jerry Seinfeld mastered the art of telling jokes about nothing. But I think Lenny has a point and there's still an argument for telling jokes about something.

The term "twilight crimes" and the definition provided at the beginning of the book are mine. For a long time, *Twilight Crimes* was the working title of this book. I hope the term and its meanings catch on.

This book is indebted to my first novel, *Norwegian by Night*, which tells the story of Sheldon's final adventure. It took me years to understand his early life. Now I do and I hope that the readers of *Norwegian by Night* have come to know him better. For those who have yet to read that novel . . . more Sheldon awaits you (you lucky devils).

And for the record, Santa is alive and well, and loves this book and thinks it would make an excellent Christmas present.

—*Derek B. Miller, Oslo, Norway*